The Surprising Life of Charlie Glass (Size 18 and a bit)

Angela Woolfe

arrow books

Published by Arrow Books 2013

2 4 6 8 10 9 7 5 3

First published in Great Britain in 2013 by
Arrow Books
Random House, 20 Vauxhall Bridge Road,
London SW1V 2SA

www.randomhouse.co.uk

Addresses for companies within The Random House Group Limited
can be found at:
www.randomhouse.co.uk/offices.htm

The Random House Group Limited Reg. No. 954009

A CIP catalogue record for this book
is available from the British Library

ISBN 978-0-099-56469-0

The Random House Group Limited supports the Forest Stewardship
Council® (FSC®), the leading international forest-certification organisation.
Our books carrying the FSC label are printed on FSC®-certified paper. FSC is
the only forest-certification scheme supported by the leading environmental
organisations, including Greenpeace. Our paper procurement policy can be
found at www.randomhouse.co.uk/environment

Typeset in Sabon by Palimpsest Book Production Ltd, Falkirk, Stirlingshire
Printed and bound by CPI Group (UK) Ltd, Croydon CR0 4YY

ACKNOWLEDGEMENTS

With very many thanks to Leslie Whittaker for sharing her shoe expertise, Ed Rumsey for sharing his car expertise, and Dr Linda Papadopoulos for sharing her invaluable expertise on perceptions of female beauty and body image.

Also huge thanks to Selina Walker and Gillian Holmes, and to Clare Alexander.

'Any girl can be glamorous. All you have to do is stand still and look stupid.' Hedy Lamarr

PART ONE

Chapter One

If Lucy could see me now she'd get all huffy and puffy about me behaving like a waitress.

'Gaby wants you to help with the *catering*?' Lucy screeched, when she called me last night, just as I'd begun the fiddly process of piping pistachio cream on to six dozen halves of pale-green macaroons. 'I thought she got everything catered! She gets her children's birthday parties catered. I bet she gets an average Tuesday morning breakfast bloody catered! Why does she want you to help with the catering for your own father's memorial service?'

'Because her usual caterer has let her down at the last minute, and there's nobody else available at short notice.' I paraphrased, slightly, what Gaby had actually said when she'd called earlier in the day, which was that there was nobody else 'decent' available at short notice. 'But really, Luce, it's not a big deal. It's a tea party after the service, so it's just a few crustless sandwiches and dainty cakes.'

'So? Why can't modom cut the crusts off a few sandwiches herself? Why can't she do a trolley-dash round Waitrose and get a few dozen boxes of mini bloody yum-yums? Not that I'm suggesting Waitrose makes stuff as delicious as yours, Charlie,' Lucy added, loyally. 'But that's not my point. What are you making, anyway? You're not going to go berserk, are you?'

'God, no, not at all,' I said, wondering – as I still am – if baking three dozen pistachio macaroons, the same number of miniature scones, five whole lemon drizzle loaves, three Victoria sponges and (my *pièce de résistance*) one perfect, glossy, gleaming Sachertorte *might* count as going berserk. 'Like I said, it's not a big deal. Just a few cakes. And if I have anything left over, I'll bring them round to you on my way home from Gaby's tomorrow.'

'*If* you have anything left over? All the guests work in fashion, Charlie. I don't know why Gaby's bothering to cater it at all. Honestly, couldn't she just stick a couple of lollo rosso leaves on a plate and see if anybody dared to take a nibble? Oh, and talking of mad anorexics, is Robyn gracing your dad's memorial with her presence, or is she having too hectic a schedule of detox wraps and sea-salt scrubs at Chiva-Som?'

Robyn is my other (half) sister, and Lucy's no more a fan of her than she is of Gaby. In fact, to say that Lucy isn't a fan of my sisters is rather like saying the French Revolution was a bad time to be a bit posh.

'That's not fair, Luce,' I'd told her last night, putting down my piping bag for a moment so that I could hurry and check the oven to make sure lemon drizzle loaf number four wasn't browning too much at the edges. 'Robyn really got herself into a bad way after Dad died. She needed to get away from it all. And,

4

yes, in answer to your question, she's back from Thailand and she is coming to the memorial.'

'And the Ice Queen? She Who Must Not Be Named? The High Priestess of Mordor?'

These three are all names that Lucy (and, OK, I too) have attributed, over the years, to just one person.

'Diana? No. She's not coming.'

'To her own late ex-husband's memorial service? But she looked so happy at the funeral, bless her coal-black heart. I'd have thought she'd be taking the opportunity to be right up there at the front of the church tomorrow, popping champagne corks and singing "Roll Out the Barrel".'

'Nope. Bunions. Well, to be more precise, surgery to remove her bunions. Won't be seen in public until she's back in her heels, apparently.'

'Good. I hope the surgery hurts. And then I hope she gets another great big bunion, right in the same place. In fact, I wish a plague of bunions upon her.'

Which tells you pretty much everything you need to know about the way Lucy feels about my step-mother. And the fact that I didn't object in any way tells you, I guess, pretty much everything you need to know about the way *I* feel about my stepmother too.

'Well, just promise me one thing about tomorrow, Charlie. Promise that even if you're making the food, you won't let Gaby turn you into a waitress for the afternoon. Or any other kind of dogsbody.'

'Lucy, making a few cakes isn't being a dogsbody! You know how much I love cooking. And don't you think it's nice that Gaby actually thinks I'm good at it? Good enough to serve her snooty fashionista friends? Gaby doesn't usually think anybody's good at anything! And anyway, I'm doing it for Dad, really, not for—'

'You're avoiding the question.'

'Fine,' I sighed. 'I promise, Lucy, that I won't let Gaby turn me into a waitress for the afternoon.'

'Or any other kind of dosgbody?'

'Or any other kind of dogsbody.'

Well, one broken promise out of two isn't so bad!

Anyway, it was unfair of Lucy to imply that I'm being turned into some kind of dogsbody, because Gaby's put a huge amount of effort into this afternoon, too. She's managed to transform this rather shabby, empty space – Dad's original flagship store, up the less posh end of the King's Road – into a perfectly pristine party venue, complete with freshly white-washed walls, newly polished floor, and big black-and-white photos of Dad hanging everywhere, with ELROY GLASS: DESIGNER, FATHER, LEGEND printed beneath. Which is a nice echo of the obituary in *The Times* the other week, where the writer called Dad 'the legendary bad-boy of British design whose subversive footwear has graced the feet of the glitterati since the seventies'. *And* Gaby stage-managed the entire memorial service, complete with eulogies and hymns and choirboys: she's been desperate to give full vent to her superb planning skills ever since she was (in her view) cheated out of organising a proper funeral,

thanks to Dad's suddenly coming over uncharacteris-
tically religious right at the end and asking to be
buried in the traditional Jewish manner, meaning
within twenty-four hours of his death, and therefore
without giving Gaby the time to do things 'properly'.

(Lucy also asked, in our phone call last night, why
on earth Gaby was holding the memorial service in
a Church of England church, when Dad was Jewish
by birth and atheist by conviction? I don't know the
answer to this question, but I think it probably has
its roots in the fact that Gaby's not all that keen
on . . . well, her roots. And in the fact that all the
synagogues are in dismal bits of north London while
St Anthony's church is picturesquely and glamorously
located on one of the smartest streets in Chelsea.)

'Charlie?'

This is Gaby now, waving me over to where she's
standing, by the far wall next to one of the black-
and-white framed photos of Dad. She's stepping away
from the crowd of very thin, very groomed, very
surprised-looking women she's been talking to, which
is just one of the many crowds of very thin, very
groomed, very surprised-looking women who have
been invited to the memorial. Today's illustrious guests
are mostly fashion editors and buyers, with a smat-
tering of VIP customers thrown in for good measure.
Not who I'd have invited, if I were the one actually
hosting Dad's memorial – I'd have asked, oh, I don't
know, his extended family, his oldest friends, and just
a few of the doctors and nurses who took such good

care of him these past nine and a half years – but then, Gaby *is* the PR director of Elroy Glass Limited, so she must know what she's doing.

'Oh, for crying out *loud*, Charlie,' Gaby hisses at me, now, when I manage to totter across the floor without fatal mishap. 'Couldn't you have worn something a bit more suitable on your feet?'

I shoot her a bit of a look. 'Well, the thing is, Gaby, when I got dressed this morning, I didn't know I was going to be doing quite so much walking about with a heavy tea tray.'

'A nice flat ballet pump would have been a much better choice.' She has missed – or ignored – my pointed remark. 'Where did you even dig those shoes out from anyway?'

'They were my mother's.' This silences her, but I carry on anyway. 'And I wanted to wear something Dad had made, and the ones he made specially for Mum are the only ones that fit me. Oh, which reminds me: did I tell you that there are at least two hundred old pairs of Dad's shoes in a load of boxes up in the storeroom?'

'*Fantastic*.' Gaby rolls her eyes. 'More crap to sort out.' She's looking stressed and tetchy – or, rather, even more stressed and tetchy than usual. It's a wonder, really, that she looks as immaculate as she does: head to toe in sharp black Armani, her dark bob practically blinding me as it reflects the light, her skin and nails buffed to perfection, and her eyebrows – of course – meticulously tweezed into enquiring arches. She's perfectly at home, here, amongst all the thin glossiness. It gives me an odd glow of pride in her: my sister Gaby, the thinnest, glossiest and most surprised-looking of them all. 'Look, I called you over because I need you to go and help with Robyn.'

'Help?' I cast my eyes about the room, looking for our other sister. There she is – chatting animatedly to a redhead in a black dress. But I can't see what Gaby is looking so worried about: Robyn doesn't *look* like she's about to howl, or burst into hysterical song, or produce a pair of kitchen scissors and start hacking off her own hair, all of which unexpected delights she blessed us with at the funeral three weeks ago. 'She seems OK.'

'She's high as a fucking kite,' Gaby whispers, furiously. 'And that girl she's talking to is a journalist for *Grazia*, and the last thing I need right now is to have to explain to Mummy why her darling daughter is being described as "confused" and "excitable" in an article on page four of Tuesday's magazine. Just go and get her away, will you? Becca can handle the tea on her own for a bit.' She waves a hand at the other girl who's been carrying around a tea tray – a mousy girl in Edna Everage glasses who I think is either Gaby's au pair or her cleaner – and mouths '*Come on, come on, keep it moving*' at her. 'Please, Charlie,' she adds, turning back to me. 'Robyn listens to you.'

Which is a pretty obvious attempt at desperate flattery, but if you knew how rarely Gaby utters the word *please*, you'd do what she asked you, too.

'No problem, Gab. I'll go and sort it out.'

'Good. And when you've done that, Charlie, pop up and bring down the rest of the cakes, would you? I thought it might be nice for me to say a few words about Daddy, and I could do it before I cut into that Sachertorte. It was his favourite, wasn't it?'

'Yes!' I try not to look too amazed that she recalled this. 'He loved it! I used to make it for all his birthdays, remember, and—'

'Good, good. I can use that.' She nods, thoughtfully, as if she's just been asked to deliver a eulogy about a near-stranger, and is carefully gathering together any little snippets of personal information she can find. 'OK, Charlie. Thanks for your time.'

Knowing when I'm dismissed, I set out decisively across the packed room, my mission to make it over to Robyn without slip or stumble. Or ankle-twist. Or, for that matter, an incident involving any of my vertebrae. Balance, I'm quickly working out, is the key to successful high-heel-wearing. Heels like these ones thrust your weight forward, throwing you off your usual centre of gravity. And with a bum like mine, believe me, that's a heck of a lot of usual gravity to throw off.

'. . . and I'm telling you, the hot-stone massages there were absolute heaven,' Robyn is saying, in a tone that's merely mildly manic, as I approach her and the journalist. 'I really felt like the stones were kind of *drawing* all my grief to the surface. Honestly, I'd recommend Chiva-Som to anyone who's just had a death in the family. You know, I've even been thinking a stay there should be made available on the NHS. Not two weeks, of course, but maybe just one week, or even a nice long weekend . . . Oh, hey, Charlie!' She greets me with a little wave. 'I've been telling Eloise here about what an awful state I've been in since Daddy died. I mean, the mess I was in at the funeral. Cutting off my beautiful hair, and everything!'

Of course, I should mention that even without her beautiful hair, even with the gamine crop her hairdresser has turned her self-inflicted damage into, my sister Robyn is still a total stunner. Sharp of cheekbone, long of eyelash and pouty of lip, she would have been a model, like her mother Diana, if she'd grown a critical couple of inches taller. She's skinny enough to be a model, thanks to a triple whammy combination of great genes, a fondness for eating disorders and an even greater fondness for cocaine. Today she's looking even more model-like than usual, in a thigh-high black minidress and her usual six-inch heels with – disloyally – a slash of Louboutin red on the sole. It's all a bit much for three o'clock on a Friday afternoon (let alone your own father's memorial service) but at least it makes me feel temporarily better about my own ill-advised choice of footwear.

'Honestly, without amazing people like Charlie to support and care for me, I don't know how I'd have survived my daddy dying at all!' Robyn goes on. Her pupils, now I'm up close, are a little bit dilated, and she's wearing a rigid smile. 'She was the one, weren't you, Cha-Cha darling, who sat me down after my daddy's funeral and said: "Book yourself a first-class flight right this very minute, Robyn. Take yourself off somewhere lovely and warm and sunny, where you'll have time to grieve, and heal, and pamper yourself."'

'Er – I suppose I *might* have said the thing about grieving and healing,' I begin, 'but I'm not sure I said—'

'Sorry – who is this exactly?' Eloise-from-*Grazia* asks Robyn. (She's another stunner, is Eloise: so young and so naturally beautiful, in fact, that I'm surprised Robyn has put her looks-related paranoia on hold for long enough to talk to her.)

'Charlie, you mean? She's my sister!'

'Your *sister*?' Eloise's lovely mouth falls open in amazement. 'But you . . . sorry . . . I mean, she just looks *nothing* like—'

'Half sister,' I interrupt, with a smile, to save any further embarrassment.

'Oh, but Gaby and I never think of her as a *half* – do we, Charlie darling? At least, *I* don't.' Robyn grabs a pistachio macaroon from a plate that's being whisked past by the frantic Becca, and makes all the 'ooohing' and 'aaahing' noises she always makes when confronted with food, to divert everyone's attention from the fact she's not actually eating any. 'Surely you know, Eloise, that my daddy was an absolutely awful womaniser? Mistresses in every port, illegitimate offspring everywhere?'

'That's not exactly true!' I say, as Eloise's green eyes

12

widen, to match her open mouth. 'In fact, that's not true at all. There's only Gaby and Robyn and me! And Dad was only married twice – to their mother and then to mine.'

'Oh, yes, I do recall something about that now.' Eloise-from-*Grazia* looks rather embarrassed. 'Didn't he . . . er . . . run off with the Irish cleaner, or something, while he was still married to Diana Forbes-Wilkinson?'

'Yes! The Irish cleaner was Charlie's mother!'

Before I can add any mitigating information to Robyn's pronouncement, we're interrupted by the *Tatler* photographer whom Gaby, in an impressive coup, has persuaded to cover the event. He asks us all to pose for him, then, after a swift glance at the image on his digital camera, asks me if I'd mind stepping to one side: 'So I can just get the other two on their own instead.'

Evidently I'm not *Tatler* material.

'My mother was the housekeeper,' I tell Eloise, as soon as the photographer has wandered off to take more shots of thin blonde people. I'm determined to give Mum her due, and to make one other very important fact clear. 'And Dad didn't *run off* with her.'

'That's true. Well, true-ish. I mean, it *was* the seventies, Eloise – Mummy was already cheating on Daddy with most of the neighbours before he took revenge and shagged the cleaner. God, *sorry*, Cha-Cha.' Robyn slings a bony arm around my shoulders. 'You *know* I don't mean anything horrible about your mum.

Especially not today, when the three of us should all just be thinking about poor Daddy.'

For the first time today – in fact, almost for the first time since Dad died, three weeks ago last Wednesday – I feel a stab of something painful, somewhere deep down inside. So I gather it up as quickly as I can, pop it into a mental box marked *To Deal With Later*, and carry on as if Robyn hasn't spoken.

'Anyway, Robyn, I came over here to tell you that somebody really wants to talk to you . . . er . . . over there.' I gesture, vaguely, towards the swirling vortex of blondes filling the room. 'That blonde woman in . . . um . . . the black dress.'

'*Fuck*, that's Jessica from *Vogue*. Sorry, El darling, but I have to go and talk to her, or she'll just get uppity and refuse to take my calls from now on.'

Robyn is already high-tailing it across the store, leaving me and Eloise-from-*Grazia* stuck with each other.

'Well, Robyn seems quite . . . high on life this afternoon,' she says, as soon as my sister's out of earshot.

'Oh, you know Robyn. Always high on something!' Which wasn't what I'd meant to say at all. Gaby is going to *kill* me. 'High in a . . . a metaphorical sense, I mean!'

'And you're the third Glass sister,' Eloise continues. She's gazing at me with curiosity in her beautiful green eyes. This may not be much, I grant you, but it's more interest than anyone else has shown in me this afternoon. 'The cleaner's daughter. Wow – your family is complicated.'

'Housekeeper. And what family *isn't*?'

'So do you work for Elroy Glass, too?'

'God, no. I mean, I don't work for Elroy Glass the company. I've been looking after Elroy Glass himself for the last nine plus years! Dad, that is,' I add, in case she hasn't understood me.

'Looking after him? As your *job*?'

'Um, yes. Absolutely,' I add, hoping to make this fact sound better than she's just done. I smile at her. 'Motor neurone disease is pretty life-altering, you know. Dad needed someone to help him do everything, from eating and washing to . . .' I stop myself, before I start to regale a total stranger with depressing details about the day-to-day indignities of living with a debilitating neurological condition. (Also, I worry that I shouldn't have added the smile. The smile, on top of the unnecessary personal details, could well be making me look like a member of a cult, or an escaped lunatic.) 'Anyway, yes, in answer to your question. Looking after Dad is . . . sorry, *was* . . . my full-time job.'

'Wow. That must have been hard.' But Eloise-from-*Grazia* is distracted already as a skinny blonde waves at her from across the room, mouthing, *Come and say hi, sweetie!* 'Oh, sorry . . . I really need to go and get round a few more people. But it was nice talking to you . . . er . . .'

'Charlie.'

'Charlie.' She hoicks her bag up further into the

15

crook of her arm, turning away as she does so. 'And my condolences, of course, about your father.'

It's the first time anyone has said this to me at Dad's memorial.

I fight back the prickly feeling that's crept up, quite suddenly, in my throat, and go and busy myself with another tray of teacups.

Chapter Two

I suppose I should be more upset by Eloise-from-*Grazia* forgetting my name and then swanning off to talk to someone more interesting. But it's hardly worth getting offended. I mean, fashion people aren't going to waste their time chewing the fat with someone who's so obviously not one of them.

I'm not one of them, in fact, in more ways than you'd think. Mostly because I'm the combined size of *three* of them. And I'm not Putting Myself Down when I say that, by the way (Putting Myself Down being another one of Lucy's pet peeves). I'm just stating an out-and-out fact. The average size of the women in this room has to be . . . a six. And if it is, then I am definitely three times that. At least in the bum department, seeing as my (roughly) planet-sized rear end is the reason I had to buy my new dress in a size eighteen rather than the sixteen which fitted OK everywhere else. It's a wrap dress, specially ordered from the euphemistically titled 'Curve' section on ASOS, so at least I've managed to fasten the tie-belt a bit tighter around my waist, and hopefully not *look* as though I'm (partially, at least) a size eighteen. I felt pretty good when I put it on, especially after teaming it with these shoes. They're peep-toed with four-inch heels, and they're made from soft, silver leather that's covered with tiny, glittering crystals. Impossible to walk in but magical to look at. Anyway, what with the new dress, the vintage shoes and my very best make-up, I was congratulating myself on scrubbing up well, until I got to the church earlier and realised that everyone else was kitted out in Armani Privé or new-season Stella McCartney.

Talking of Armani, Privé or otherwise, Gaby has caught my eye from across the room. She's mouthing *Sachertorte!!!* at me as if she's a drowning woman and the only thing that will save her is a life-raft made from traditional Viennese chocolate cake.

Fine – Sachertorte it is. I stop faffing with teacups and set off for the staircase at the back of the store to climb up to the first-floor storeroom where I've stashed the rest of my baked delights.

It's a yet more tortuous progress because the stairs here are shallow and uneven. This isn't exactly news to me, but navigating them in spindly heels is an entirely different ball game from running up and down them in sensible buckled Mary-Janes, the way I used to when I was a child. This, Dad's original flagship shoe store, was Lucy's and my favourite Saturday-morning hang-out when we were six and seven. Down on the shop floor, where the scary-eyebrowed fashionistas are now fiendishly networking, there was a thrilling air of decadence, with loud music, popping champagne corks, and a revolving door constantly admitting perfumed and glamorous customers, who all seemed to be half in love with Dad. But up in the stockrooms above, things were even more thrilling, at least for a couple of six year olds. In the first-floor stockrooms, you could play endless hours of 'shoe shop' with the pairs of shoes you secretly took down from the shelves; or, up in Dad's airy, light-filled studio on the second floor, you could pull up a couple of chairs to one of the many windows and spend whole afternoons 'spying' over the backyards of the neighbouring stores, which would occasionally – grippingly – feature the canoodling couple from behind the counter at the café next door, or some of the staff from the nearby health-food shop, gathering to smoke weird-smelling home-made cigarettes out the back.

Of course, this place hasn't housed an Elroy Glass store, much less a flagship one, ever since my stepmother Diana finally got her way four or five years ago and moved operations to a swanky new site on Bond Street instead. She is the CEO, and Dad had been so ill that he'd stopped even the pretence that he was still designing many months previously, so I suppose it was her prerogative. The old store has been let out to a succession of businesses ever since – most recently an antiquarian book dealership – but seeing as it's not really at the plum end of King's Road (really, it's more like the prune end of King's Road), it's never exactly regained its old atmosphere. In fact, after Gaby's swift and merciless makeover downstairs, to get the place suitable for today's party, it's more lacking in atmosphere than ever before. Which makes the quiet, still calm of the unchanged upper floors feel almost melancholy by comparison.

Still, melancholy or not, at least now that I'm up here on the second floor I can have a little sit-down for a couple of minutes, take the weight off my feet even if I can't get the shoes off them. Actually, it's not a case of *if* I can't get the shoes off. I really, really can't get the shoes off. I've spent so long on my feet today that they've pulled their usual trick of swelling up from all the exertion, and the shoes are practically welded on.

There aren't any actual chairs up here in Dad's old studio, just these big packing cases, filled with old pairs of his shoes, that at some point have been moved up here from the more convenient first-floor stockroom by one of the many intrepid but unsuccessful shopkeepers who have leased the place over the last few years. I've used one of the convenient packing cases to store my cakes on – the two remaining lemon drizzle cakes, and the rich, glossy Sachertorte that Gaby has sent me to fetch – but there's another packing case free, luckily, for me to perch on and rest my protesting feet.

'Oi! Charlie!'

The voice takes me by surprise. It's pretty muffled, and appears to be coming from outside. Though the windows up here are grubbier than they used to be in Dad's day, there are still enough of them that I can easily look out over the back of the store. Two buildings along, and almost at a right angle to the back of this building – the site of the old health-food store, actually, where the dodgy cigarettes were smoked – a man is waving at me from an open second-floor sash window.

It's Ferdy Wright, the love of my life.

Well, OK: *secret crush* is probably a more accurate description. You can't call someone the love of your life unless they're actually in love with you, too – can you? And Ferdy Wright isn't in love with me. We're just friends – and fairly new friends, at that. His dad, Martin, has been a kind of friend of the family for the best part of two decades, but I'd never met his son until Martin broke his ankle skiing two winters ago and I bumped into Ferdy during hospital visiting hours, when I was dropping by with an Ian Rankin and a box of praline seashells for his dad. We got to chatting by the coffee-vending machine and our friendship just kind of blossomed out of that.

I get up from my packing case, manhandle one of the windows open and lean out to greet him.

'Ferdy! What are you doing there?'

'Plumbing in the staff toilet!' he calls back. 'But don't get me wrong, Charlie. My life's not all glitz and glamour. The rest of my day has been spent with the Health and Safety people from the council, discussing how to block off access points for a variety of delightful rodents!'

I should explain: the reason Ferdy is two buildings along at all is because that's where he's setting up a new branch of his ice-cream parlour business.

It's called Chill, and he already has two branches – one in Soho and one just off Marylebone High Street. They're really gorgeous: proper old-fashioned Italian ice-cream parlours with retro fifties decor in appropriately ice-creamy shades of strawberry and pistachio, but with modern touches like slouchy leather sofas and free WiFi. And more gorgeous still are the ice creams themselves, all home-made and delicious, from traditional Italian flavours like dark-chocolate Tartufo and zabaglione, to Ferdy's trad-with-a-twist confections like blackberry ripple and lemon-meringue crunch.

And more gorgeous *still*, of course, is the owner himself. Even from this distance I can make out his wide, welcoming grin and the cheery gleam in his pebble-coloured eyes. His hair is messy and tufty and a kind of dusty-brown (dusty because that's its natural shade, I mean, not dusty because he doesn't bother to wash it; in fact, I've surreptitiously inhaled his hair on several occasions, and I'm thrilled to report that it smells very freshly washed indeed, with sparkling notes of citrus and peppermint). As for his build, he's not what you'd call *perfectly* in shape (actually, he has a distinct hint of ice-cream-induced tummy) but he's tall and broad and strong-looking, which is incredibly handy for this silly fantasy I sometimes have.

I won't give you all the embarrassing details, but there's this part where Fantasy Ferdy sweeps Fantasy Me into his arms, and lifts me up on to his Fantasy

Horse. And there's a rain-lashed moor in there, too, the bleak landscape of which Fantasy Me has been wandering for some unspecified reason, looking artfully dishevelled in a ragged bodice and a thread-bare cloak, until Fantasy Ferdy rides out of the mist and does his whole lifting-me-on-to-his-horse thing. Which is why, like I say, it's so handy that he's strong-looking, because despite the fact that my brain seems perfectly able to conjure up misty moors and whinnying horses and shabby chic mid-Victorian garments, it isn't able to conjure up a Fantasy Me who's thin. My Fantasy Complexion may be porcelain, my Fantasy Lips may be like rosebuds, and my Fantasy Hair may be glossy and swingy rather than mousy and curtain-like, but Fantasy Me is still a doughty size eighteen.

'I was thinking about you this morning, actually,' Real-life Ferdy calls out, now, from his window.

'You were?'

'Yes. I'm trying out a new mint *stracciatella* ice-cream recipe and I really need to get your opinion on it. There's an issue with the amount of chocolate chips. Honey – she's the interior designer for the new store – tasted it yesterday and she thinks there are too many. And I think there are too few. So I thought to myself, Who else is there who can give me proper advice about all-important chocolate quantities but my head of R and D? That's you, by the way, Charlie. It's an unpaid position, I should warn you, but one of great influence and honour. I

23

expect,' he adds, pushing up his sash window so that he can position himself more comfortably, sitting on the inside ledge rather than leaning out of it, 'you'll be getting calls from top headhunters quite soon, trying to poach you to go and work for rival ice-cream makers, people who promise six-figure salaries and exciting foreign travel. But don't forget that I was the one who discovered you, Charlie Glass. Don't bite the hand that feeds you unlimited ice cream, that's all I'll say.'

He's joking. Well, he's joking about the rival ice-cream companies. And it's an exaggeration that he's calling me his head of research and development. Because obviously I'm nothing of the sort. But then, this is kind of the basis on which our friendship has blossomed since we first met. I think he was only being kind at first, because we'd discussed my dream of working with food one day, but he started bringing round samples of his ice cream for me to taste and comment on. The first few times we tried them together, but after that Ferdy really seemed to start taking me seriously. He started bringing round so many that we couldn't taste them all at once, so I became more methodical about it, blind-tasting the different varieties after he'd left and writing up proper tasting notes to email him.

I couldn't help feeling that he was a bit taken aback the first time I emailed an entire page of (single-spaced) notes on his bitter-chocolate sorbet, but honestly, ever since, he seems to really value my opinion. For example, when I emailed to let him know that his blackberry ripple was *good and sharp, but might benefit from some crunch?* he emailed back within five minutes to ask *do you mean biscuity kind of crunch or honeycomb-y kind of crunch? And should I try similar ripple thing with rhubarb?*

'I'd love to try your . . .' I won't attempt to say the word; I've never been able to pronounce properly what I call Scratchy Umbrella ice cream '. . . new mint ice cream, Ferdy. Whenever you want.'

'There's no rush. You're busy. Anyway, what are you doing there?' he carries on, gesturing at my window. 'I thought you said you never went to your dad's old store.'

'I don't. Not usually. It was his memorial service this afternoon.'

'Oh, Charlie.' The limitations of holding a conversation across a fifty-foot space are becoming clear. Ferdy looks stricken but he's still having to shout. 'Oh, God, I'm so sorry. You should have said! You know I'd have come, if you'd mentioned it.'

'Don't worry, you weren't invited! I mean,' I add, hastily, when I see him look a bit put out, 'nobody was. Nobody normal, that is.' I'm just going to have to hope that none of Gaby's illustrious guests have stuck their heads out of the back window downstairs for a smoke. 'It's fashion people,' I clarify, 'and really, it's more of a business thing than a . . . Dad thing. My sister's the one in charge.'

'The bossy sister, or the loopy one?'

Now I *really* hope nobody's stuck their head out of the back window for a smoke.

'Gaby,' I say, wishing I hadn't told Ferdy quite so much about my family. 'But I guess she does need to do the client-schmoozing stuff. She is the Head of PR, after all.'

'Oh, right. Still, I wish you'd told me about today, Charlie. I'd have come and taken you for lunch.'

He would?

Like, as in lunch . . . out?

I know this sounds weird, given that we're friends and everything, but Ferdy and I have never been *out* together anywhere at all. Partly that's because until around three months ago he had a very pretty girlfriend called Davina, but also with Dad so ill these past few months, I couldn't even go down the road to Tesco without getting Lucy to come in and sit with him for twenty minutes. This, though, was the thing that transformed me and Ferdy from friend-*ly* to proper friends, because when he found out that I was so house-bound he immediately volunteered, without taking no for an answer, to come and sit with Dad whenever Lucy wasn't available and I needed to get something important done out of the house. Thanks to Ferdy, these past months, I've been able to get the shopping done, go to urgent dentist's appointments, and – once or twice – just have an hour or so walking by the river to clear my head.

It was also the thing, I have to admit, that turned Ferdy from a guy-I-had-a-bit-of-a-crush-on into the unrequited love of my life.

As for his motivation . . . well, I don't know. Lucy (of course) is convinced that these are the sort of kindnesses you'd only show someone if you were wildly in love with them. But I think these are the sort of kindnesses you show someone if you just happen to be a seriously good guy. Not to mention the fact that, thanks to his dad Martin, Ferdy knows I've not always had the easiest time of it, even before Dad got ill. I'm pretty sure that his generosity is nothing more than the result of his exceptionally sweet and gentle nature. After all, if he *were* (hah!) wildly in love with me, there are all kinds of other ways he could show it.

Like . . . like asking me out for lunch, for example?

The mere thought that this might – just might – mark the beginning of a new phase in our relationship is enough to make me wobble off my shoes slightly. I have to grab on to the windowsill for safety.

'Charlie? Christ – are you OK?'

'I'm fine, it's just these silly heels I'm wearing!'

'Good. Because I'd really rather you didn't plummet to your certain death from an open window today, if it's all the same to you.'

'Oh, I don't think it'd be certain death. I'd break an ankle, probably, or maybe a thigh-bone . . .'

'Either way,' Ferdy interrupts me, thankfully, before I can get started on fractured hips or shattered pelvises, 'I'd prefer it if there weren't any plummeting at all. I mean, I'd be *prepared* to come and eat sandwiches by your hospital bed, but if we're going to do this lunch at any point, I'd rather do it properly.'

This lunch? Now he's so determined to do it that he's calling it *this* lunch?

I ought to be able to handle a situation like this one. I mean, Ferdy's only suggesting a bloody *lunch*, not a torrid all-night sexathon in a five-star hotel. I should be able to string the words 'lovely', 'would', 'yes', 'lunch' and 'be' into a coherent sentence, then move on to the easy, practical matter of coordinating a suitable day, time and place. But I can't speak. So I decide to muster up one of those flirty swooshy-hair moves Robyn does when men are around, in the hope that Ferdy will take this as encouragement. And if it all goes wrong, I'm so far away from him that it'll probably just look like I'm avoiding a bluebottle or something.

So I risk it. I go for the hair-swoosh.

I shouldn't have. I've forgotten that my centre of gravity is already thrown off by the spindly four-inch heels.

I wobble for the second time in as many minutes, but this time it's a really serious wobble. As my head comes back to its usual, non-swooshy position, I try to grab the windowsill for support. But I misjudge the height of it. I try to grab something else for support. But there is only air. My remaining option is to flail wildly backwards until I come to a halt, in a sitting position and with a real thud, on top of the packing case behind me.

No. It's not a thud, sorry. It's more of a . . . squelch. Because I've come to a halt on top of the Sachertorte that was on the packing case behind me.

28

Ferdy may be fifty feet away, but I'm pretty sure he can still see my face above the windowsill, so it's imperative that my expression DOES NOT give him any indication, whatever that indication might be, that I've just sat down on a chocolate cake.

'Charlie?' Ferdy is looking a bit uncertain. 'Was that just you falling off your shoes again? Or is the idea of us having lunch so appalling to you?'

'No! It is the shoes, I mean. Lunch would be . . . brilliant.' I'm desperate to make him realise that I am, actually, keen, which is probably why the next thing I hear myself say is, 'Or dinner even!'

'Dinner?' He looks startled. 'Just . . . you and me?'

Shit. I've pushed things too far.

'I didn't mean . . . I'm having friends over tomorrow night, in fact!' It's a lie, but it's a get-out-of-jail card. After all, a pre-planned dinner with friends, to which I'm casually inviting him at the very last minute, couldn't be further away from the date that's so obviously spooking him right now, could it? 'So why not swing by?'

'I could . . . swing by.'

'Brilliant! Well, I'd better let you get back to your toilet.'

'What?'

'Your plumbing, I mean . . .' It's not ideal that, right at this moment, beneath my left buttock, the Sachertorte gives a squelch so loud I'm almost certain he can hear it fifty feet away. 'And I'd better get back to my memorial.'

'God, yes – look, I really hope it all goes OK, Charlie.'

'It's all fine! It's great, in fact. I'll see you tomorrow, Ferdy! Eight o'clock all right?'

'Yes, eight is all right.'

I get up, give him a wave, and close the window. I make very sure not to turn my back until he's given me a little wave of his own and disappeared through the window. Then, and only then, do I start trying to inspect the worst of the damage.

It's a toss-up between which is more destroyed: the chocolate cake or my new ASOS 'Curve' dress.

Nope – it's definitely the chocolate cake.

On the bright side: at least the sponge must have been lovely and light, because if it had been chewy and tough it might have done a better job of withstanding the backside blitzkrieg.

On the less bright side: I can hear sharp footsteps, and – barely a moment later – Gaby appears in the stockroom doorway.

'Oh, for Christ's sake, Charlie,' she says – astonishingly, for her, more in weariness than in anger. 'You've sat on the Sachertorte.'

There's really no point in trying to deny this. 'Yes.'

'*How?*'

'Well, it was the shoes . . . I wobbled . . .'

'For Christ's *sake*.'

'But, you know, Dad loved lemon drizzle cake, too! I don't think it'll ruin your little speech, if you still want to make it . . .'

30

'It doesn't matter what cake it is,' she says. 'I just wanted something ceremonial to cut after my speech, that's all. More to the point, you can't possibly wander around the party with what looks like . . . well, never mind what it looks like. And Becca can't manage all by herself, and Robyn is still acting like a liability every time she opens her silly great mouth . . . But I'm on my own. As *usual*.'

She sounds weary, rather than irritated, which makes me feel even worse.

'Look, Gab, I'm really sorry. Give me five minutes and I'll probably be able to scrape the worst of it off.'

'Don't be ridiculous. It looks awful.' She sighs. '*Honestly*, Charlie. You are *hopeless*. And I could really have done without this today, you know.'

Which is unfair, because it's not as if I regularly go around sitting on cakes. But Gaby's just said this as if sitting on cakes is my life's work. Whereas, to the very best of my recollection, I've never sat on a cake before. Though I do admit that today probably wasn't the best of times to start.

'You shouldn't have *worn* the shoes, Charlie, if you were going to be a liability in them. Still, I suppose we should be grateful for small mercies. At least you didn't fling a boiling hot teapot over Keira Knightley or anything!'

Which is even more unfair, because I never came close to flinging a teapot over anyone. And anyway, Keira Knightley isn't here. I know, because Gaby was

31

moaning, all morning, about Keira Knightley turning down the invitation.

But Gaby doesn't seem in the mood to care about being unfair.

'Look, I think it'd be better if you just headed home, Charlie, OK? You're no use to me now, all covered in chocolate cake. What if you got it on one of the guests, or something?'

It's not that I want to stay – in fact, it's not like I really wanted to be here in the first place – but I don't particularly want to be unceremoniously ejected from my own father's memorial either.

Mind you, as a not terribly grief-stricken shriek of fashionista laughter floats up to the second floor, I'm reminded that it isn't, really, Dad's memorial at all. It's a networking event. For people who, for the past few years, wouldn't have known Dad from a hole in the ground. And he would have felt just as out of place here as I do.

'Sure. I'll go home.'

'I mean, it's not exactly your kind of crowd, is it?' Gaby is obviously feeling a bit guilty, not quite looking me in the eye as she comes to pick up the tray holding the two remaining lemon drizzle cakes. 'But, you know, thanks for the cooking, and everything.'

'That's OK.'

'I . . . well, I appreciate it, Charlie.'

'No problem.'

I follow her out of the stockroom and down the rickety staircase. Halfway down, I hear a sudden clatter of heels, and Robyn appears at the bottom of the stairs.

'*There* you are,' she tells Gaby. 'I've been looking for you for *ages*. *Tatler* want a photograph of the two of us together . . . isn't that right?' she asks the *Tatler* photographer, who's lurking behind her, pretending that he isn't eyeing up her tiny, peachy little bottom.

'Yeah,' he says, 'I've been told we need a pic of the Glass sisters . . .'

'Then we *have* to have Charlie in the picture too!' Robyn declares, reaching around Gaby to practically pull me down the last few stairs. 'You can stand in between us, Charlie, and stop Gaby from digging her nails into my arm or stamping her heel into my foot.'

'*One time* I did that,' Gaby spits at her. 'And it was only because you kept trying to get in front of me in all my wedding photos.'

'Oh, I don't think I should be in the photo, really,' I say. I'm all too conscious of the fact that I was hardly the photographer's pick for Look of the Year *before* I got Sachertorte all over myself. 'Besides, I was just leaving . . .'

'Bollocks to that,' says Robyn, looping an arm through mine to prevent any attempt at escape. 'You're a Glass sister, aren't you?'

'*Is* she?' the photographer mutters, not that inaudibly.

'Anyway,' Robyn adds, as Gaby places herself on my other side and we all wait for the photographer to get his shot right, 'I'm looking really podgy in loads of my photos at the moment. If I stand next to you, Cha-Cha, I look teeny-tiny!'

Just as the camera flash goes off, Gaby obviously remembers that she's still holding the tray of lemon drizzle cakes. Quick-thinking as ever, she shoves it sideways into one of my hands, so that nobody could mistake her for the waitress amongst the three of us.

Then, as soon as this Kodak moment is over, Gaby grabs the tray from me again, and Robyn sees someone she simply has to talk to, and they both stalk back into the hub of the party, leaving me with the *Tatler* photographer.

'Would you mind,' I ask him, 'if I had a look at the picture?'

'Knock yourself out,' he says, handing me the camera so I can peer at the display window on the back.

It's not a great photo. It's not even a good photo. Gaby is looking slightly startled, so determined is she to divest herself of the domestic-looking tray before a solitary *Tatler* reader might spot her with it. Robyn looks her usual photogenic self – at first glance – but on a closer inspection is rather wild of eye and gurning of mouth, presumably thanks to whatever narcotic she's recently inhaled. And I . . . well, the less said about my (shiny, frizzy, overweight) appearance the better. The only positive function I'm fulfilling in this picture is that I do, indeed, make Robyn look teeny-tiny. And, I guess, that – if printed in *Tatler* – I might make most of the readers feel better about themselves, too.

But nevertheless, it's the three of us. It's the Glass sisters. Not united in a single picture since the occasion, over twenty years ago, when Dad took us all to Bethnal Green for the day, to visit his Uncle Mort. Dad kept that picture on his bedside table right up until the day he died: a seven-year-old me, standing in between a nine-year-old Robyn and a twelve-year-old Gaby. Gaby is frowning at the camera with the disapproving expression she wore throughout that entire day at Uncle Mort's, where she found the cousins too loud and the house too small and the food too Jewish. Robyn is pouting, as she did that entire day, because Dad had refused to drive via Knightsbridge, where she wanted to try on a new party dress they were keeping aside for her at Harrods. And I – thrilled by the exotic food, enjoying the noisy cousins but, most of all, loving every rare minute I got to spend with my sisters – am beaming wide enough to pull a muscle, and trying to put an arm around Gaby and Robyn to draw them both closer.

'Could I get a copy of this?' I ask the photographer, now, thinking that – unflattering a shot though it is – it might be nice to prop it up beside the old photo on Dad's bedside table for a while, until I've psyched myself up to clear out his room. I feel that Dad would like this, somehow. I feel that, amongst the ghastliness and fakeness of this memorial, the photo might stand in true memorial to him: that he may be gone, but he still has three daughters who – in their own ways – loved him.

'Sorry. Making copies is a load of hassle. Look in the magazine for the next couple of months, though. You never know – you might see it on the party pages.'

But I can tell from the photographer's tone of voice that the picture won't be on the party pages. That coverage of Dad's memorial will be limited to his pictures of the very thin, very groomed, very surprised-looking guests instead.

The photographer takes back his camera, slings it around his neck, and heads back into the party to carry on achieving this mission. And I slip out of the door on to King's Road, making sure I don't transfer a smear of chocolate icing from my dress on to Gaby's pristine white walls as I go.

Chapter Three

It's half-past seven on Saturday evening when the doorbell rings.

I know that this has to be Lucy, because I asked her to come early, rather than Ferdy whom I'm still expecting at eight.

She's standing on the doorstep with her phone pressed to her ear, looking a bit stressed. This means that the caller either has to be a customer, or her boyfriend Pal. He's meant to be coming to dinner tonight, too, but Lucy said he'd be coming straight from his circuit class at the gym, so he probably won't get here until around eight himself. Pal is Norwegian (I only mention this because otherwise it appears as though he's been named after a brand of dog food; actually you pronounce his name like *Paul*) and he's an accountant somewhere in the City. He and Lucy have been an item for almost six months.

'Customer,' Lucy mouths at me, nevertheless reaching over to give me a quick hug as she comes through the door.

She's a big one for hugs, Lucy. She's also really good at them, thanks to the fact that she's in the perfect zone between skinny and plump, and has – I hope this won't sound weird – quite the most marvellous chest you've ever seen: a proper, heaving, wandering-on-the-moors-in-rags-worthy *bosom*. This evening, her remarkable bosom is covered up in an unusually prim cashmere cardi, which she's teamed with a much less prim denim mini and knee boots. I've got the impression, recently, that Pal has expressed a preference for Lucy to wear more conservative clothing, because she's been swapping her customary Joan-from-*Mad-Men* sweaters and tight tops for Mrs Thatcher-style blouses and buttoned-up cardigans. It's a revolution that hasn't quite reached her bottom half yet, however; if anything, her hemlines are getting shorter and her heels higher, as if to cling on to her essential Lucy-ness in any way she knows how.

'Arrrrrr,' she's saying now, into her phone, 'that do be correct. It do be five of Her Majesty's finest pounds and ninety-nine of Her Majesty's finest pence for standard delivery. And that way, me pretty, you'll be getting your swag by Wednesday at the latest.'

I should point out that there's a perfectly good and work-related reason why she's talking into her phone in a gruff West Country accent. Though her proper, full-time job is working for a luxury adventure-travel company called The Bespoke Planet, Lucy has quite recently started up her very own small business: YoHoHo.co.uk, a pirate-themed party supplies website. She's always wanted to run her own business, and her plan is to make YoHoHo successful enough that she can stop pandering to demanding travel snobs at The Bespoke Planet and pander to demanding

38

party-organisers instead. The sooner this happens, the better, because she's already started to do well enough with YoHoHo that she has to take enquiry calls from customers in the middle of the day. Seeing as part of her (rather unusual) branding strategy is to conduct all customer-related business in a West Country-accented pirate voice (hence the *Arrrrr*, and also some *Shiver-me-timbers-ing*, not to mention the occasional chorus of *Sixteen men on a dead man's chest*) she spends quite a lot of time, when she's meant to be doing her proper job, dashing off to answer her phone in the loo.

'Arrrr, yes, me pretty, there do be parrots available on the website. Just be clicking on the Stuffed Birds and Other Accessories section and ye'll be finding three sizes to choose from . . . Thanking ye kindly, me pretty. Shiver me timbers! You don't happen to know,' she asks me, in her normal voice, as she ends the call and throws her phone back into her handbag, 'what might be a suitably pirate-ish way of saying *goodbye*? I tend to end calls with *shiver me timbers* or *walk the plank!* But neither of those feel quite right, somehow.'

'Have you thought of trying *fare thee well, me hearties*?'

'Fare thee well, me hearties.' She tries it out in her pirate voice again, and looks pleased. 'Oooh, actually, that could work. I'll give it a shot, next time. Wow, Charlie, you look *great*,' she goes on, standing back to look me over. 'I love what you've done with your hair.'

'Really?' I pat my head, uncertainly. I don't usually put my hair up like this, but I remembered that the divine Davina, in a photo I saw of her on Ferdy's phone, had her hair all piled up on top of her head, so I'm hoping it's a look that he likes. 'And is what I'm wearing OK?'

'For a pair of black trousers and a white shirt, it's OK. I still don't know why you don't wear more dresses, Charlie. Or that nice skirt you found at Westfield, the black-and-white vertical stripe one that makes you look all curvy.'

I don't tell Lucy that, seeing as I've put on a few pounds since our last shopping trip to Westfield, the black-and-white vertical stripe skirt won't go up over my hips any more. (Nor do I mention how much I love her for trying to claim, just like the good folks over at ASOS, that my figure isn't 'fat' but 'curvy'.)

'Because dresses involve high heels,' I say, 'and I don't intend to finish this evening with my oh-so-amusing party trick of squashing a Sachertorte. Anyway, I wanted to look, you know, casual.'

'So that Ferdy doesn't think you think it's a date?' She raises an eyebrow. 'I don't think there's too much chance of him thinking you think it's a date anyway, Charlie, seeing as you've invited another couple.'

'But that's even worse!' I stare at her in horror. 'Oh, God, he might think I think it's a *double* date!'

'Charlie, for the love of God.' Lucy starts to bustle me down the stairs, towards the kitchen in the base-ment. 'Stop stressing about what Ferdy thinks you might think. In fact, stop *thinking*, full stop. This is going to be a perfectly nice evening. You always said how difficult it was for you to have people over while your dad was so ill.'

She's right; I did. In fact, there were times – I feel guilty now – when I used to get properly whiny about it all. I'd see other people – young, old, middle-aged – pottering around the supermarket on a Friday afternoon, picking up packets of smoked salmon and sticks of crusty baguette that were obviously intended for sophisticated dinner parties with friends; or I'd see the same kind of people heading out for Earl's Court Tube on a Saturday night, with a bottle of wine under one arm and a box of posh chocs in the other, presumably off to the very same dinner parties the supermarket people were shopping for. And honestly it used to make my heart hurt, how much I wanted to be able to do the same. I'd try to make myself feel better (and I do know how pathetic this sounds) by dreaming up the precise menu I'd cook, if I were the one hosting. I'd even come up with seating plans. Because for me the Holy Grail of adulthood was always the sophisticated dinner party.

Mum and Dad used to host fabulous ones, right here in this very flat. Mum would get all dressed up in the beautiful printed-silk kimono-style dress that Dad bought for her in Paris, and those sparkly, spindly heels. Earlier in the day she'd have made a rich beef Stroganoff and allowed me to help her set the table with the best linen and Dad's mother's antique silver candlesticks. I can still remember the sound of the grown-ups' ringing laughter and the mingled scents of boozy beef and Mum's beloved Anaïs Anaïs, which I'd smell, through a haze of sleep, when she'd slip into my room to place a kiss on my forehead before rustling back out again in her silk dress, and closing the door gently behind her.

'So, please,' Lucy is saying, as we reach the kitchen, 'just relax and try to enjoy it. Anyway, I'm dying to meet this Ferdy you've been banging on about . . .'

'I've not been *banging on* about him.' I dart for the cooker, suddenly paranoid that the pecan pie I've got browning in there might be *over*-browning. It's not. It's fine. Paranoia still lingering, I open the lower oven door and have a sniff of my beef Stroganoff. It smells fine, too. In fact, it smells delicious. As well it might, seeing as it's precisely the same recipe that Mum used to cook, all those years ago. 'I've mentioned him a few times, that's all. Glass of wine?' I add, hoping – actually, knowing – that Lucy will be easily distracted from this line of discussion by the suggestion of alcohol. 'I've got some white nice and cold in the fridge.'

'Mmm, yes, brilliant.'

Lucy plonks herself down on the banquette beneath the skylight, which is our favourite place to sit with a glass of wine and chat. It's been our favourite place to sit with a glass of wine and chat for almost a decade, ever since I first came back here to live with Dad. And long before that, when we were children, it was our favourite place to sit with juice and biscuits and chat. But all that stopped when Dad disappeared to Morocco and I was sent to live with Gaby and Robyn and my stepmother Diana. Still, this place – this slightly shabby, split-level, ground-and-lower-ground-floor flat in a mansion block in Earl's Court – has always been Home to me.

'What's this?' Lucy's magpie eye has spotted something on the coffee table beside the banquette. 'Hey! What are you doing, eyeing up the competition?'

She's picked up, from the top of the pile of magazines I'm always meaning to tidy away, a brand-new travel magazine from Incredible Expeditions, who are indeed The Bespoke Planet's major competition.

'Oh, Luce, of course I'm not eyeing up the competition. They send the free magazine here, that's all, because Dad always used to travel with them.'

'You've *turned down corners on the pages*,' she says, in an accusatory tone, flicking the magazine open. 'Camel safari in Egypt? Rainforest camping in Costa Rica? Dog-mushing on the Iditarod Trail? *I* could organise all these trips for you, Charlie, if it's adventure travel you're after! And I'd get you a bloody great discount, too!'

'I'm not after adventure travel.' I pour us both glasses of wine – larger ones than I'd usually plump for myself, but I don't see any way I'm getting through this evening if I remain even slightly sober – and head over to sit down beside her. 'I was only looking, out of interest. Anyway, I definitely wasn't looking at . . . what did you call it? Dog-mangling?'

'Dog-mushing.' She brandishes the open magazine page at me. 'It's sledging with husky dogs. On the Iditarod Trail in Alaska. I sent a client off to do that only the other week. Though it sounds a bit full-on, to be honest, Charlie. I think you'd be better off with the camel thing.'

'Lucy, honestly, I wasn't thinking of dog-mincing. On an Alaskan trail or any other.'

'Then why have you turned the page down? God, Charlie, you weren't thinking of *this*, were you?' She holds the magazine out again, stabbing a finger at the other article on the dog-mushing page. 'New Body Boot Camp in the Scottish Highlands?'

'No! Well, not exactly.' I take a long drink from my wine glass. 'I mean, dawn yoga and three-times-daily hill-runs? Nothing but lettuce leaves for breakfast, lunch and dinner . . . Can you really see me doing that?'

'For someone who's not really thought about it, you seem to know an awful lot about it.'

This is probably because, secretly, I have thought about it. Thought about how amazing it would be to just . . . vanish for a while, then return to London in a triumphant glow of good health and thinness. Because there are times – like last night, for example, getting back from the memorial – when I can't help but wonder what that would be like. Getting thin, I mean. What it would be like if people's eyes didn't boggle, incredulously, if they notice me at all, on finding out I'm related to Gaby and Robyn.

Of course, I know in my heart of hearts I'm never actually going to *do* it. I'm not lying when I say that dawn yoga and a diet of lettuce leaves aren't my cup of tea. And anyway, now that Dad's gone, what I need more than anything else is a job, and I simply don't have the money to swan off, *à la* Robyn, for a nifty little detox somewhere warm and sunny.

Lucy sets the magazine down, somewhat disgustedly, as though it's creating a nasty pong that's pervading the kitchen.

'Seriously, Charlie, the Scottish Highlands? You'd come back blue with cold and brown with rust! Ooooh, you know, if you really want to get a bit healthier –' she tactfully avoids the words *lose weight* '– there are far more enjoyable places I could arrange for you to do a boot camp. Vietnam, or New Zealand . . . or there are some amazing-sounding places in California, for example, that Duncan's been on at me to go out and try.'

'Lucy, you should go!'

'Oh, well, Pal's really not keen on me going away as much as I used to, because he works such long hours, and it can sometimes be hard enough for him to find the time to see me . . . I mean, for us to find the time to see each other . . .' She takes a Lucy-sized slug from her own wine glass. 'But anyway, why don't I ask Duncan if you could check out a couple of these boot camps for him instead? I don't know if he'd be able to pay you, but you'd get a free holiday, and—'

'Thanks, Luce, but I'm really not seriously thinking about travel at the moment. There are more important things I need to be getting on with. Like finding a job, for starters.'

'You don't need to panic about that just yet, Charlie. Your dad arranged for the flat to be left to you, didn't he?'

'Yes, but that's all there was for me to be left! Dad was totally out of cash by the end, Luce.'

And I do mean totally: Dad was always rubbish with money, but being so ill for so long would have outfoxed even the most careful financial planner. On paper, he was a wealthy man when he died, but all his assets were tied up in this flat (which, Lucy is correct, Dad did arrange to leave me in his will) and – far more so – in Elroy Glass Limited, where he'd clung on doggedly his majority share holding, no matter how often anyone tried to buy him out. He did sell some of his shares a few years ago, when the boiler gave up and the car gave in, and we were *really* desperate for cash, but that took him dangerously close to losing his majority stake. Losing that would have meant ceding more control of the business to Diana, which was why Dad refused to countenance letting his share dip below fifty-one per cent.

Lucy pulls a face. 'I still don't see why old bossy-pants and lipgloss-for-brains are getting left half each of your dad's shares. Surely everything should be divided up evenly between the three of you.'

'I am getting an entire flat, Luce.'

'But that's only worth a fraction of the shares!'

'Well, I don't know.' Actually, I don't want to think about it too much, because then I start to get all prickly and chokey about the unfairness of it all. Which is unfair of *me*, because unlike bossy-pants and lipgloss-for-brains – sorry, unlike Gaby and Robyn – I don't, actually, have any moral right to Dad's shares in the business. I've never worked for Elroy Glass, like they both have (well, like Gaby has; I'm still not sure exactly what it is that Robyn does for the company, apart from falling out of nightclubs wearing Elroy Glass shoes and getting her picture in the gossip magazines. Maybe you could call it advertising?), and anyway Dad's company was something he started up with Diana, Gaby and Robyn's mother, long before he met *my* mother and fell in love with her. 'You know, Luce, I'm just not sure I have any—'

'If you say *moral right*, I'm going to chuck this glass of wine over you.' Lucy is shooting me one of her fiercest looks. 'What moral bloody rights do Gaby and Robyn have to a load of Elroy Glass shares landing in their laps? They're both bloody loaded to the eyeballs as it is . . .'

'Diana's got a lot of family money. That's not their fault.'

'. . . but what *is* their fault is that they're a pair of the laziest, most overly entitled cows the world has ever known! I mean, remind me, Charlie – how many times did they come to visit each week, while your dad was ill?'

'Lucy . . .'

'Sorry, I'll rephrase the question: how many times did they come to visit each *month*?'

I take a gulp (a Lucy-sized one, this time) from my wine glass and stay mutinously silent.

'Or should I make that, how many times did they come to visit each *year*?'

'Oh, now, that's really unfair. They came more than once a year, Lucy! They came . . . loads more than that.'

'All right then, how often did they offer to take your dad to a hospital appointment, or else to come and look after him for one night so that you could go out for a change?'

'If this is about me missing your birthday party . . .'

'Five! You missed five of my birthday parties, Charlie, because you couldn't leave your dad, and because neither of his other daughters fancied getting off their bony arse and pulling their non-existent weight. And anyway, my birthday parties didn't matter! I mean, yes, of course I wanted you there, but that's really not the point. I just wanted you to have a night off once in a while, Charlie. I just wanted . . . oh, I bet this'll be Pal.'

She breaks off, mid-berate, as her phone rings in her bag. 'Hi, babe,' she answers it. 'No, it's number one-*one*-seven . . . sorry, I thought I told you that . . . I'll come up and meet you, OK?' She gets to her feet, knocks back the rest of her wine and starts for the

48

door that leads to the stairs. 'Look, I don't want to quarrel, Charlie. Let's forget it. I just want you to enjoy yourself with Ferdy tonight.'

Shit – I've completely forgotten about Ferdy! This is the danger of sitting around on the banquette quaffing wine: you forget you actually have a dinner to host.

While Lucy goes upstairs to fetch Pal, I dart to the mirror above the telephone table in the hall and check that my up do hasn't started to become a down-do, and then I hurry to the range again to check on dinner. Stroganoff: still smelling good. Glazed carrots and potato gratin: both looking rich and delicious and keeping nicely toasty in the warming drawer of the ancient range cooker. Pecan pie: browning happily. I don't know why I'm bothering to worry about the food part of this evening at all. If there's one thing I can do, it's cook. Flirting with Ferdy, sneakily finding out whether he's at all interested in me or letting him know that I'm interested in him . . . these are the parts I'm bound to make a hash of. But dinner itself shouldn't concern me.

'. . . then it was my mistake, babe,' Lucy is saying, as she clatters down the stairs in her knee boots, leading Pal into the kitchen. 'I must have told you number one-*two*-seven. I'm really sorry.'

'Yeah.' Pal starts taking off his Puffa jacket and looking for somewhere to stow his gym bag. 'You definitely said one-two-seven.'

'I know. Sorry.'

Seeing as Lucy's been coming to this flat over a period of roughly twenty-five years, since we met on our first day in infants school, it's highly improbable that she told Pal the wrong number. No, let's be completely frank: it's absolutely impossible. What's much more likely is that he wasn't listening when she told him the right flat number, and that Pal – in this, as in everything – is unable to believe he's got something wrong. A fiction that Lucy is perpetuating by apologising to him.

'Pal, hello! How are you?' I graft a smile on to my face and head over to give him a kiss on the cheek, which he returns with his customary enthusiasm (i.e. not a lot). 'Let me put your bag over here. God – I'm so impressed that you're dedicated enough to go to the gym on a Saturday night!'

'I'm training for the marathon. It's not dedication, it's just good sense.'

'Well, yes, but even so!'

'Even so – what?'

Ten seconds into our first conversational salvo, and Pal has already left me flummoxed. This is a pattern with me and Pal. Actually, it's a pattern with Pal and pretty much everyone I've ever seen him talk to. You provide an opening pleasantry; Pal provides a chilly statement of fact; you come back with something foolish and meaningless, but obviously well meant; Pal behaves as if you've just turned up to a convention of Oxford philosophy professors who have gathered to discuss the meaning of life, and started burbling at them about your favourite sandwich fillings. He makes me feel like an idiot. He makes Lucy *act* like an idiot. While all the time being, himself, the actual idiot.

Admittedly, Lucy's form on the boyfriend front hasn't been exactly stellar in the past – over the last three years, she's been in relationships with Aaron (druggy), Rob (shouty), and Nathan (secretly married, with a wife and a toddler back home in Watford) – but Pal represents a new low. Admittedly he has a good job, his own flat, tall, blond good looks and the single-mindedness to train for the London marathon. But despite all this, I HATE HIM. Well, that may be unfair. I hate certain *things* about him. The way he treats everyone like an idiot, as I've already mentioned. The way he isn't bothering to hide his superior smile, now, as he surveys my slightly shabby kitchen. The dismissive way he treated the waiter when I met him and Lucy for brunch last weekend. The way he drones on about his job, as if it's the most interesting subject in the world (I mean, come on, he's an accountant, not a war reporter or a Hollywood movie star) and about Norway, as if it's the best country in the world. (I'm quite sure the fjords *are* beautiful, and the Social Security system *is* peerless, but once you've heard about one fjord or tax break for working mothers, you've honestly heard about them all.)

But, most of all, I hate the way he treats Lucy.

'Let me get you a drink,' she's saying now, conveying

him to a seat at the kitchen table and heading to the cupboard for a glass. 'Charlie and I have been drinking white wine, but I'm sure she's got some red, or a beer?'

'Lucy, you know I'm not drinking tonight. Does your friend have any coconut water?' Pal asks her, as though I'm not here.

'I don't know. Charlie, you don't happen to have any coconut water, do you?'

'Coconut *water*?' I blink at her. 'Er – I might have a tin of coconut *milk* somewhere at the back of a cupboard, if that's any use?'

'No, no, coconut water is different.' Lucy is looking a bit flustered. 'It's this thing Pal drinks when he's been training, to replace all the electrolytes you lose when you sweat.'

'Oh. Then, no, I'm afraid I don't have any of that. I try to avoid situations where I'm sweating, myself!' I add with a smile to Pal, who doesn't smile back. 'But, um, isn't Coke meant to be good for rehydration? I've got some Coke.'

Pal winces, as though I've just offered him a glass of bat's blood spiked with industrial solvent. 'Coke is full of sugar.'

'Diet Coke, then?'

He doesn't dignify this with a reply. 'Just some water, I suppose,' he says to Lucy. 'Sparkling, if she's got it.'

I'm sorely tempted to ask, Who's *she*? The cat's mother? – but for Lucy's sake, I do nothing of the

52

sort. Anyway, I couldn't say anything, even if I really wanted to, because the doorbell's just gone.

I gaze at Lucy, frozen in terror.

'That'll be Ferdy!'

'Excellent! This is going to be a great night for you, Charlie.' Despite the disapproving presence of Pal, Lucy is, temporarily at least, her usual self again.

'But I don't know what to do. I don't know what to say. You know how rubbish I am at flirting . . .'

'Don't flirt!' she says, in a tone of voice that suggests she's only just managed to leave off adding *for the love of God, woman, no*. 'Just be yourself, Charlie.'

'I was being myself yesterday,' I point out, 'when I sat on a chocolate cake.'

'Well, just don't be that part of yourself. Anyway, you're wearing flats tonight. Look, he obviously likes you, Charlie, or he wouldn't be coming to dinner at all. Isn't that right, Pal?'

'What?'

'A guy doesn't come to a girl's house for dinner unless he likes her.'

'That depends.' Pal shrugs. 'He might, if he didn't have anywhere better to go.'

Upstairs, the doorbell goes again.

'I promise you, Charlie,' Lucy says, casting the briefest of despairing glances in Pal's direction, 'Ferdy is coming to dinner because he likes you. He tried to ask you to lunch because he likes you. Let's just accept, as a starting point, that he likes you. And see where the evening goes from there.'

53

Heart racing, hands clammy, I head up the stairs to answer the front door.

When I open it, Ferdy is standing on the doorstep.

He's holding a large bouquet of multicoloured gerberas and wearing a very broad, slightly nervous smile.

'Hey,' he says.

'Hey!' I reply.

Then we both stand there, blinking at each other, until I realise that I'm supposed to be inviting him inside.

'Sorry, please come on in . . .'

I step back and hold the door open wider so that he can come through. The sleeve of his coat brushes my arm as he passes me. I shiver, ever so slightly, with the overwhelming desire to have more of him touch me.

'Yep, it's freezing out there,' he says, obviously mistaking my shiver for one of cold, and turning to shut the door behind him. Then he holds out the gerberas towards me. 'I think these poor things might be suffering from frostbite.'

'Oh, no, they look perfect!'

'Really? I didn't know if you liked them. I thought they were nice in the flower shop. But out here they just look a bit like big, brightly coloured daisies.'

'I love them.' I take the gerberas. 'Precisely *because* they look a bit like big, brightly coloured daisies.'

'Great.' His smile broadens even further, and the nervous edge comes off it. He starts to remove his coat and scarf, revealing jeans and a crisp white shirt beneath. It's the first time I've seen him in something so smart – usually he's wearing baggy khakis and a lumberjack shirt – and the white shirt makes him look so very much like the Fantasy Ferdy of my overactive imagination that it's all I can do not to fling the gerberas aside, leap across the hallway and throw myself into his arms. 'I did something right, then!'

'Oh, you do plenty right.'

'Sorry?'

'Nothing!' I grab his coat and scarf. 'So, you should come downstairs and let me get you a drink! And meet my friend Lucy. And her boyfriend.'

'Oh, the Norwegian guy you've told me about? The impossible one?'

I nod, and start to lead him down the stairs. 'But please, Ferdy,' I add, in a whisper, as we reach the bottom of the stairs, 'don't mention to him that I think he's impossible.'

'Don't worry, Charlie.' He grins, and puts a hand on my arm. 'It'll be our secret.'

I know it's only a hand on an arm. I know he's not sweeping me into a passionate embrace, or leading me masterfully towards the bedroom. But I don't think I'm imagining the little spark that just passed between us. And I certainly don't think I'm imagining the slight softening around his eyes as he smiles down at me.

'Wine,' I say.

'Sorry?'

'Wine. Glass of. Let me get you.'

Having inexplicably turned, it seems, into Yoda, I dart into the kitchen, put the gerberas on the dresser and head for the fridge before I can say anything else stupid.

'Oh, you must be Ferdy!' Lucy says, as he follows me into the kitchen. She heads towards him and extends a hand, while I shoot her a grateful look. 'Lovely to meet you. I'm Lucy, Charlie's best friend. And this is my boyfriend, Pal.'

'Great to meet you, too. I've heard loads about you!' Ferdy takes the glass of wine I've just handed him, and chinks it to the one I'm holding. 'Cheers,' he says, with another of those very particular smiles at me.

'Cheers,' I say back, with a smile of my own. I'm surprised to notice that I suddenly feel a bit more relaxed. This all feels very comfortable, now that Ferdy is standing in the kitchen, and we've all got a glass of wine, and Lucy is looking so approving, and Pal . . . well, the less said about Pal, the better. But even his I'd-rather-be-anywhere-else glower can't take the shine off this moment. I'm suddenly struck with a vision of how the evening is going to go: lots more wine and laughter around the table, Ferdy's arm gradually creeping around the back of my chair, Lucy giving me a knowing look and withdrawing as soon as we've drunk the coffee, me and Ferdy left alone in the kitchen, me suggesting we break open one of Dad's old brandies, Ferdy suggesting we take the brandy over to the banquette under the skylight . . .

'Something smells amazing,' Ferdy is saying, now, turning to look at the oven with genuine interest. 'I can't believe I've never actually eaten a meal cooked by you, Charlie!'

'Oh, you're in for a real treat,' Lucy says. 'Charlie's a fantastic cook, in fact . . .'

She breaks off, suddenly, as the doorbell rings once again.

This is odd, as I'm certainly not expecting anyone else.

'Hang on, I'll just see who it is and get rid of them,' I say, putting my wine glass down on the table as I head back up the stairs towards the front door.

A small, extraordinarily pretty blonde girl is standing outside. And she's crying.

At least, I think she's crying. There are no actual tears, and no sign of red or puffy eyes, but her shoulders are shuddering and her lips are trembling.

'I'm so sorry!' Her voice is tiny and breathy. 'But is Ferdy here?'

'Ferdy?'

'Yes, I was just with him two minutes ago. I was carrying on to get the Tube and he was coming to this block of flats for dinner with somebody called Charlie.'

'I'm Charlie.'

'Well, is he here?' she gulps.

'Er . . . yes . . .'

'Then could you get him for me?' she asks, her lips trembling so fast they become an actual blur. 'Please?'

'Right. I mean, sure.' I take a couple of steps

backwards, lean down the stairs and call out, 'Um, Ferdy? Could you pop upstairs for a second, do you think?'

He appears in the stairwell, glass of wine still in hand, and starts coming up.

'Everything OK up here?' he starts to ask, just as the blonde girl rushes past me towards him, throwing herself into his arms in exactly the way I wanted to only a few minutes ago.

'He's dead, Ferdy!' she sobs, into his chest. 'My mum just called, and he's dead!'

I stare at Ferdy, who's patting the girl's hair and making rather uncomfortable there-there noises.

'Jesus, Ferdy . . . what's happened? Is there anything I can do?'

'Don't worry.' He passes his wine glass towards me, obviously worried about spilling it. 'It's just her cat.'

'*Just* my cat?' The blonde girl gazes up at him. 'Ferdy, I've been telling you for ages how much I love Mittens, and how poorly he's been!'

'Yes, I know, but I was just reassuring Charlie that it wasn't a person who'd died, or anything.'

'Mittens was a person to me!'

'Sure, but . . .' Ferdy stops patting her hair and shoots me an embarrassed look. '*Sorry*,' he mouths, before continuing, 'Charlie, this is Honey, by the way.'

Oh . . . wasn't Honey the name of the interior designer he mentioned to me yesterday? The one who thought there were too many chocolate chips in the Scratchy Umbrella ice cream?

'I'm so sorry about this,' Honey says, dabbing her eyes and turning to me. Now that I'm getting a chance to look at her properly, I've never seen anyone so fluffy bunnyish in my life. Her hair is the colour of . . . actually, of honey, her eyes are big and pale blue, and she's wearing the cutest little skater skirt beneath an oversized parka with a fake-fur-trimmed hood. 'We had a late meeting at the store to discuss paint samples, and I was terribly upset because my mum had just called to say Mittens had taken a turn for the worse . . . and Ferdy was *so sweet* about it that when she called back just now to say Mittens had gone, the only thing I could think to do was come and find Ferdy where I'd left him.' She gulps. 'And I know you were supposed to be having a lovely dinner, and now I've turned up and ruined it all!'

'No, no, you haven't ruined it all!' I say, patting her on the arm. (Obviously she has, a bit, but I can't exactly tell her that, can I, with her beloved cat just dead and all that?) 'You shouldn't be alone at times like these.'

'Oh!' She shoots me an adorable, rather watery smile. 'Well, if you *do* have room for one more?'

'Honey,' Ferdy says, rather sharply, 'I don't think Charlie meant . . .'

'It's fine, honestly.' Because what else am I supposed to do: throw this fluffy bunny of a girl back out on to the street, still crying about the demise of Mittens? Besides, she's pretty much invited herself now. It's too embarrassing to tell her to go away again. No matter how much her presence is going to obliterate my cosy vision of midnight brandy on the banquette . . . 'There's plenty of food to go around. Besides, the more the merrier, right?'

'That's *so nice* of you, Charlie! I should have known you'd be nice, seeing as you're a friend of Ferdy's!' Honey takes off her parka, hangs it on the peg by the front door, and then starts to trip daintily down the stairs in the direction I point her.

'Charlie, you really don't have to do this,' Ferdy says, in a low voice, as he follows me down after Honey.

'Don't be silly. I know what it's like to lose someone you love.'

'Yeah, but people, Charlie. Not cats.'

But there isn't time for him to say any more, because we've reached the kitchen and now there's a lot of general greeting and merriment going on. I'm a little bit surprised, I admit, that someone who was in tears about their poor cat only three minutes ago is nevertheless now managing to introduce herself to Pal and Lucy with such enthusiasm. But I'm probably being mean-spirited, and Honey is just a bit of a trooper. After all, Lucy has gone on and on to me about how strange she finds it that I don't seem to have cried, yet, about Dad dying. And I of all people should know that some of us just prefer to keep our grief under shiny, happy wraps, in case it seeps out and overwhelms us.

And anyway, I can't deny that adding an extra

person is already making everything seem a bit more buzzy and party-like; a bit more like the atmosphere at Mum and Dad's dinner parties of yore. Pal's certainly perked up, for example, ever since Honey materialised. He's got up from the kitchen table and is chatting to her in the most animated way I've ever seen from him, only breaking off to ask Lucy if she could get him a beer.

'I thought he wasn't drinking tonight,' I hiss at her, as she passes me by the cooker on her way back from depositing cold beers with Pal and Ferdy. She's shoved a glass of white wine into Honey's tiny hand, and is now generously refilling her own wine glass.

'Well, he's obviously changed his mind,' she hisses back. 'Anyway, who the hell *is* she?'

'Interior designing new premises. Dead cat,' I mutter, which – and this is one of the many benefits of two and a half decades of friendship – Lucy understands without me needing to add any more info.

'Well, I don't like the way she's flirting with Pal.' Lucy seems oblivious to the fact that, from where I'm standing at least, Pal is doing sterling work of flirting right back. He's roundly ignoring Ferdy, who's still looking about as comfortable as a turkey the week before Christmas, and telling Honey all about his (profound, and long-standing, apparently) interest in interior design. She knocks back a good half of the wine in her glass. 'She's incredibly annoying.'

'She's incredibly pretty.'

'Charlie, you think everyone's incredibly pretty.'

'I do when they look like the girl from a Timotei advert.'

'Exactly. Annoying. And she's got her sights set on Ferdy, by the way. I can tell.'

'But you just said she was flirting with Pal!'

'Doesn't mean she's not after Ferdy. She's obviously one of Those.'

Those is Lucy's term for what other people might call a man's woman: what Lucy herself, with great scorn, once described more fully as a 'gosh-you're-such-a-big-strong-man-and-so-clever-too-whereas-I'm-so-weak-and-silly-I-can't-even-take-my-own-clothes-off-would-you-do-it-for-me? kind of woman'. Lucy's younger sister Kitty is one of Those (evidently quite a lot of it is in the name, if Kitty and Honey are anything to go by) and has wound Lucy up to breaking-point over the years by entrancing and delighting all the men in Lucy's life, from her crushes to her actual boyfriends, until eventually tripping daintily up the aisle with a rich and handsome businessman at the tender age of twenty-two. Lucy was twenty-five, and a scowling, lilac-clad bundle of fury in the back of the family photos, after enduring the consolation of kindly relatives throughout the reception. ('Chin up, Lucy, love, it'll be your turn next!') Pretty Kitty is now a mother of one angelic girl, with another on the way, and living in rambling Edwardian splendour with the rich and handsome businessman in Surrey.

I only mention all this because there's just a chance that Lucy is looking at Honey and seeing Kitty instead.

And that this could account for the fact she's just refilled her wine glass for the third time so far this evening.

'Why else would she have come chasing after him to cry about her dead cat?' Lucy asks, now. 'I bet he's told her all about you, and she's jealous . . .'

'Luce, for God's sake, can we ditch the wild conspiracy theories?' I crouch down to pull the pecan pie out of the oven, hoping the blast of heat might account for my cheeks turning pink. 'Can you just get everyone sitting down at the table?'

'Oooh, yes, and I'll sit next to Ferdy and talk you up!'

'Lucy . . .'

'Don't worry, Charlie. I'm on the case.'

And she is, as she manages to organise things so that it's herself and Ferdy opposite Honey and Pal, with a seat for me in between Ferdy and Pal at the head of the table. Ferdy shoots me a quick smile as I put the beef Stroganoff down.

'It looks as good as it smells, Charlie.'

'Thanks.' I raise a smile in return. Trouble is, I'm wishing it was still ten minutes ago, that Honey had never arrived, and that Ferdy was still giving me those special, could-be-something-between-us smiles instead of the rather nervous, excessively polite one he's giving me now. 'It's my mum's recipe.'

'Awww, that's so *nice*!' Honey – proving Lucy wrong – is clearly just as adorably perky in conversation with other women as she is with men. In fact, now I come to think of it, she seems to end every single sentence she utters with an exclamation mark. 'I love using my mum's recipes, but then all that happens is that Mum wants me to cook for her instead of the other way round! I hope your mum still cooks it for you, Charlie, sometimes?'

'I'm sure she *would*,' I say. 'If she could.'

'Too busy?'

'Too, um, dead.'

Which, as conversation killers go, is up there with the best of them. It even beats any conversation killer that Pal might have to offer.

'Oh, my *God*!' Honey gasps, clapping a hand to her mouth. 'I'm so *sorry*!'

'It's OK,' Pal tells her, reaching over to pat her on the other hand. 'It was a long time ago. Like, twenty years or something. Isn't that right, Lucy?'

Lucy shoots him the dirtiest look I've ever seen her shoot him. 'It *was* twenty years ago, but that doesn't make it OK.'

'But really, Honey, it's fine that you asked about her,' I say, hastily, sitting down in my seat in the hope that it might bring an end to this line of discussion. 'You weren't to know.'

'This is one of the things that I always think is so amazing about Charlie,' Lucy says, meaningfully, to Ferdy. 'The fact that she's so *kind*, and *generous-spirited*.'

'Er – yes,' says Ferdy. 'She's . . . very kind.'

'But Ferdy told me your dad has just died too,'

Honey says, her blue eyes gazing at me sorrowfully. I'm concerned that this talk of death is going to tip her into tears about Mittens the cat again, but so far she's staying strong. 'How did your mum's death even *happen*?'

'She was in an accident,' Ferdy tells her, in the kind of voice you use when you want to impart information swiftly and minimally, and bring an end to the conversation. He shoots me an embarrassed look.

'What kind of accident?'

'Hit-and-run,' I say, because I want to spare Ferdy the awkwardness of not knowing whether he's allowed to reveal this or not. (It's a subject he's incredibly sensitive about, partly because he's just a really nice guy, but partly, too, because his dad Martin – or DI Wright as I knew him back then – was the first senior officer at the scene of Mum's accident. And, poor man, the one who had to tell me and Dad that she hadn't survived it, when we arrived at the hospital. He took the whole thing quite badly to heart, evidenced by the fact that he stayed in touch with me over the years: with formal visits while I lived at Diana's, and then with casual drop-ins for tea and a chat, with increasing frequency after he retired, while I was taking care of Dad. That's why I think of DI Wright as an old family friend. It may be a pretty tragic way to have made somebody's acquaintance, but I'm no less fond of him for that.) 'Anyway!' I add, super-brightly, partly because I don't want my longed-for dinner party to descend into utter misery and mawkishness, and partly because – as I hope you'll understand – I tend to do my very best not to think about Mum dying at all. 'Who's for the first portion?'

'This is another thing that's so incredible about Charlie, don't you think?' I hear Lucy saying to Ferdy. 'How cheerful she is about awful things . . . like her mother's death. How brave she always was about it. And it was so awful, because it was only a month before her eighth birthday, and her mum was just on her way to collect her from my house when this car just—'

'Let me take your plate, Lucy!' I interrupt. Because I know she's trying to talk me up, but I suspect all she's actually doing is making Ferdy feel sorry for me. And I may not know much about men, but I suspect that *cheerfulness* and *bravery*, while fabulous attributes for a character in an Enid Blyton novel, aren't exactly high on most men's lists of qualities they look for in people they fancy. I mean, if that's all Ferdy wanted in a companion, he might just as well get himself a plucky Labrador. 'Small portion or a big one?'

'Small portion,' Pal answers for Lucy, before she can speak. 'Don't forget, babe, we're eating at my brother's tomorrow lunchtime. My sister-in-law's an incredible cook,' he adds to Honey. 'Just incredible.'

'Oh, I'm pretty sure Charlie's an incredible cook, too,' Ferdy says, with a pleasant smile in Pal's direction.

'My sister-in-law cooks *professionally*.' Pal's nose,

as ever, is put out of joint by someone daring to imply he's said something inaccurate. 'As a matter of fact, for the past two years, she's been a full-time cook for an *extremely* wealthy family in Holland Park. She does all their dinner parties and all their big events. She even goes away with them sometimes when they go to one of their other properties. They wanted to take her to New York with them for a month, but unfortunately she and my brother are moving home to Oslo in a few weeks' time, so she's had to give them notice.'

He sits back, doubly pleased with his perfectly idiomatic English – *give them notice* – and his relent-less quashing of Ferdy's suggestion that I might be in the same league, cooking-wise, as his sister-in-law.

'Well, she sounds amazing,' I say, quickly, before Ferdy (who's looking a bit pissed off) can say anything else, and before Lucy (who's started to look a bit despairing) feels the need to mop up Pal's aggression, the way she so often does. 'And what a brilliant job! I don't suppose it's still going, is it?'

'What do you mean?'

'Well, I'm looking for a job at the moment, and I've really been hoping to find something food-related.' I've only started up this line of chat to keep the peace, but actually, now I've said this, I realise I want to pursue the topic. 'I mean, I worked in a café in my gap year, and I had a part-time job in a bistro in Manchester in my first term at university, so I still have the proper hygiene certificates and stuff . . .'

'Oh, Charlie, come on.' Lucy is staring at me across the table. 'You don't want to work as a cook for a bunch of snooty rich people! It'd be like . . . like being a servant! You're so much more talented than that – don't *you* think she's more talented, Ferdy? I mean, she could do *anything*, couldn't she?'

'Er . . .'

'Actually, Luce, I couldn't do *anything*. I'm not qualified for all that much. Two terms of an Italian degree isn't exactly going to have headhunters beating a path to my door!'

Lucy looks simultaneously annoyed that I'm Putting Myself Down and thrilled that she's spotted yet another opportunity to Talk Me Up.

'Of course, she only dropped out of uni,' she says, turning to Ferdy, 'to come back down to London and look after her dad. Even though her dad didn't actually look after *her* for years, because he had this nervous breakdown after her mum died, and she had to go and live with her bitch of a stepmother . . .'

'Lucy!'

'. . . and she was a godsend to her horrible sisters, because neither of them took the slightest bit of interest in caring for Elroy. But that's the thing about Charlie, you see, Ferdy, she's incredibly selfless like that . . .'

Much as I love Lucy, right now I'd happily upend the entire pan of Stroganoff right over her head. I wish to God she wouldn't do this: make me out to be some kind of superior being, some kind of unimpeachable saint. I'm not a bloody saint. Dad was dreadfully disabled; he needed someone to take care of him; Gaby and Robyn were obviously never going to step up to the plate, so I did. It's not saintly. It's making the best of a shitty situation. Not to mention the fact that Ferdy isn't going to be any more wowed by my supposed sainthood than he is by my cheerfulness and bravery.

I shoot Lucy a look that must be pretty fierce, because she takes the hint and shuts up.

'Well, I think it sounds an *amazing* opportunity!' Honey says. 'I mean, being a cook isn't like being a *cleaner* or anything, is it?'

I don't embarrass the poor girl any further by saying that my (dead) mother was once a cleaner, and I shoot Lucy another of my astonishingly effective looks to prevent her from saying so either.

'You should definitely go for the job, Charlie!' Honey tilts her head, prettily, in Pal's direction. 'Why not give her your sister-in-law's number?'

Pal opens his mouth to say (I'm quite sure) that I'm woefully under-qualified and totally unsuitable, but his desire to be a hero in front of Honey trumps this at the last moment.

'Well, I suppose that couldn't hurt . . . I'd have to check with Marit first, of course.'

'That would be really kind of you, Pal,' I say – and, to my surprise, I mean it. 'Thank you ever so much. Now, you must let me give you some food! Can I give you some potato gratin, Pal, on the side of the Stroganoff?'

'Christ, no.' He pulls a face. 'All that butter and cream? I might as well give my marathon spot to somebody else right this minute, check into the cardiac unit and be done with it!'

'I expect there's probably a fair amount of butter and cream in the Stroganoff, too,' Ferdy says, looking at Pal with open dislike. 'Are you going to refuse to eat that as well?'

'Butter and cream in it?' Pal eyeballs Lucy across the table. 'Didn't you tell your friend I can't eat that kind of crap?'

'It's not crap,' I say, fighting the urge (for the second time this evening) to tip the pan over the head of one of my guests. My recent goodwill towards Pal has evaporated, as swiftly as it materialised. 'It has a bit of butter and cream, yes, but they're both organic, and the meat is organic, too . . .'

'Oh, dear, is there *meat* in it?' Honey interrupts.

'That is generally the way,' Lucy says, looking as if she'd like to do a bit of pan-tipping herself, 'with a beef Stroganoff.'

'What a shame! I don't eat meat! Those poor little cows and lambs and pigs . . . You don't happen to have any chicken in the fridge, do you?'

'Because your sympathy for slaughtered farm animals doesn't extend to chickens?' Lucy asks.

'I'll just have some carrots,' Pal says, holding his hand out for the empty plate I'm still holding, then peering dubiously down at the dish of glazed carrots. 'Though it looks like there's butter on these, too.'

'Then I'll have *loads*,' Ferdy says, leaning over to seize the dish of carrots and starting to heap them, pointedly, on to his own plate. 'Honey, even if you can't eat the stew, you'll have some carrots, won't you?'

'Oooh, no, I don't like carrots. Sorry, Charlie! Would you mind if I just called for some delivery sushi, or something?'

'Yeah, I'll get in on that,' says Pal.

'Pal!'

'Come on, Lucy, you know I can't skip a meal after training.'

'But Charlie's gone to so much trouble . . .'

'It's OK,' I say. I want to save Lucy's agony, and let's face it, this dinner party couldn't be more of a disaster if aliens were to land on the street outside, take us back to the mother ship, and spend the rest of the night sticking probes in all kinds of unpleasant places. In fact, as the evening has gone so far, alien kidnap and unpleasant probing might actually improve matters. 'I don't mind, honestly.'

'Well, I think it's pretty rude,' says Ferdy, obviously blaming Pal.

'Me too,' says Lucy, obviously blaming Honey.

'I'm telling you, it's *fine*. I just want everyone to have something to eat! And I'd bring out the dessert, but I don't think Pal is going to get along very well with pecan pie and clotted cream!'

'Oh, is that the pudding?' Honey pulls a regretful face. 'I'm allergic to nuts, Charlie! I'm so sorry!'

Upstairs, the doorbell rings, unexpectedly, for the fourth time this evening. It's a mercy, albeit an unexpected one, because it means that I can abandon all the nut-allergic, cream-phobic stress and tension for a few blissful moments. Mum and Dad's dinner parties weren't like this, were they? Everyone claiming food allergies and spurning the food in favour of delivery?

I open the door to find a pleasant-faced young man I vaguely recognise, wearing a grey suit and carrying a large briefcase.

'Charlotte Glass?'

'Yes . . . I know you, don't I?'

'Well remembered!' He sticks out a hand. 'I'm Oliver Winkleman. Your father's solicitor.'

'Oh, yes, Mr Winkleman!' I met him for all of three minutes, in this very hallway, when he came round for a meeting with Dad last October. It was when Dad was getting bad enough that he was insistent about what people always call, depressingly, *getting your affairs in order*, and so Mr Winkleman – actually, Mr Winkleman's boss, Dad's long-time solicitor Alan Kellaway – was summoned to come and help. 'You came with your boss, Mr Kellaway.'

'That's right. But your father and Mr Kellaway had . . . a bit of a difference of opinion that afternoon. So your father appointed me his executor instead.'

'Yes, I remember him telling me something about that.' Dad's falling out with Alan Kellaway was hardly a surprise – Dad could start a quarrel with a paper bag if he really put his mind to it. 'But why are you here now, Mr Winkleman?'

'Well, I do hope I'm not disturbing at all.' He glances, uncertainly, at my up-do (still resolutely not becoming a down-do; it's the most successful part of the evening so far). 'You look as if you're going out?'

'No, no, I'm staying in. I mean, I have . . . people here. For a dinner party. If you can still call it a dinner party when fifty per cent of your guests order take-out sushi, that is.'

'Ah. Your sister said you wouldn't be busy.'

'My sister?'

'Sorry, sorry – half sister!'

'No, I know that, I mean – which sister?'

'Mrs Porter.'

'Oh, *Gaby*.'

'Yes. She's asked me to . . . er, this is a bit awkward, actually. I mean, didn't she call ahead at all? To let you know?'

'To let me know what?'

'Well, obviously it's your father's will-reading this coming week, and I think Mrs Porter . . . well, I wouldn't usually be doing this on a Saturday night, but she's extremely keen for me to make a list of all his personal effects in advance.'

'His personal effects?'

'Yes.' He shifts his briefcase from the right hand to the left, looking so uncomfortable that I wonder, for a moment, if some probe-wielding aliens might have got to him before he showed up. 'Anything of value. She mentioned, for example, that he might have some bits of jewellery from his mother and his aunts, and perhaps some valuable candlesticks . . . ?'

I stare at him. 'And she wants an inventory? In case . . . what? I stuff them up the chimney-breast for now and flog them on eBay later?'

'No! Well, I mean, not *you*. I think . . . well, the reason she's so keen to get the inventory done so quickly is because she's a little bit worried that your other sister – Robyn, is it? – might pop round unannounced and start . . . laying claim to anything expensive-looking . . .'

I sigh. It might be the most depressing part of Gaby's nature that she feels the need to send round a solicitor to make an inventory of Dad's things like this, but then I suppose it's also the most depressing part of Robyn's nature that she might easily appear on the doorstep one day this week and try to squirrel away Grandma's antique candlesticks and Great-Auntie Rachel's pearl earrings.

'You'd better come in, then.'

'No, really, if you've people over for dinner, I'm sure I can find a better time . . .'

'It doesn't matter. Honestly. In fact, I've even got about half a ton of food going spare. If you eat meat and don't faint at the sight of pecans, that is.'

It turns out that both the above apply, and that Olly is, by his own admission, hungry.

'But really, Charlotte – sorry, *Charlie* – I won't

make a peep,' he says, as he steps into the flat and starts removing his suit jacket. 'I'll just take a plate of food and let you get on with your dinner. The last thing I want to do is ruin your evening!'

Chapter Four

I never thought I'd say this after the débâcle that was Saturday night, but there was *one* good thing that came out of the dinner party. And that one good thing is the reason I'm sitting here, three days later, on a lush leather sofa in the poshest house I've ever been in, waiting for my first job interview in almost ten years.

Honestly, you've never seen anything like this house. It occupies almost the square-footage of my entire mansion block, a huge, white-stuccoed, early Victorian edifice behind high iron gates on an eerily quiet road to the southern side of Holland Park Avenue. There's a huge, Bentley-filled driveway out the front, and out the back is the largest private garden I've ever seen in London (actually, pretty much the largest private garden I've ever seen *anywhere*), a gorgeous expanse of bucolic green that I can see out of the French windows. It has an indoor pool (I know this because Annabel, the leggy, efficient girl who showed me in, said she was going downstairs to see if she could find Mr Broderick in the pool), and it has a gym (I know this because when she couldn't find him in the pool she said she'd also looked in the gym), and it has a library (I know this because that's the room I'm waiting in now, surrounded by mahogany bookshelves and volumes and volumes of books, on this lush leather sofa by the French windows).

Oh, and it even has a *lift*, for Pete's sake. And I know this because Annabel has been striding around with her iPhone out in the hallway, badgering some poor lift-maintenance man about an appointment for which he was due at eleven but for which he (apparently) won't make it until noon.

Annabel isn't the very best advertisement for taking a job here, it must be said. But Marit, Pal's sister-in-law, who not only turned out to be surprisingly sweet and helpful but who also gave her former employers a call on my behalf, suggesting they see me for the cook's job, told me that the Broderick family themselves are delightful people. A Frank Broderick and a Susannah Broderick with a teenage son (Rob? Ron? I've forgotten what Marit told me, which isn't a great start) who still lives at home. The father – Frank – is in a wheelchair, though whether through age or infirmity I don't know. Still, I suppose this might explain the lift. Though it probably wouldn't explain why Annabel was trying to find Mr Broderick in the gym, of all places.

Anyway, she still hasn't come up trumps on the Mr Broderick front, so I'll have to find a way to while away the time until she does, and keep my nerves at bay.

I get up and go to have a little look at the fan of magazines and papers laid out on a gorgeous Art Deco coffee table, pick up a couple of my favourite travel magazines and head back to my chair for a bit of a flick through. Actually, one of them is the same issue of the *Incredible Expeditions* magazine that Lucy was accusing me of betraying her with the other night. I leaf my way to the page with the 'New Body Boot Camp' article, re-reading for the fifth (or is it the sixth?) time the writer's extolling of the solicitous ex-marine trainers, the delicious portions of salad, the daily Think Yourself Thinner meditation sessions. And it sounds absurd. I was being ridiculous to think that the best way to kick-start my new, post-Dad existence is through something as frivolous and silly as getting thin. There are other ways to start rebuilding my life – serious ways, and plenty of them. This job, for example. It's a great opportunity that's fallen into my lap – no matter that it's a slightly overweight lap. It's a great opportunity, and I intend to make the most of it.

'Charlene?' Annabel has popped her head around the doorway of the library again. She's phenomenally healthy-looking: clear-eyed and glowy-cheeked, though that may just be an excitable flush from spending the last ten minutes barking at the lift-maintenance man on the phone. I guess she's some kind of personal assistant or private secretary, because she's far too glamorous ever to be considered as anything so domestic as a housekeeper. I mean, Mum was a house-keeper, and Mum was beautiful, but Annabel looks like she could just have stalked off a catwalk in Paris or Milan.

'Actually, it's Charlotte.'

'What?'

'My name. Charlotte. Or you can just call me Charlie, because that's what my friends . . .'

But Annabel isn't interested, either in my friends or in getting my name right. 'I've just managed to get hold of Mr Broderick on his mobile. He should be here in five minutes. Can I get you anything in the meantime? Tea? Coffee? Biscuits?'

'No, thank you.' Tempted though I always am by the offer of a biscuit I've made a huge effort with my appearance this morning, and I don't want to go into this interview with crumbs all down my front. 'I'm perfectly OK just to wait.'

'Fine. Oh, and by the way, I should have said before – please keep your phone in your bag while you're inside the house.' She nods at my mobile, which I've been fiddling with to relieve the boredom, and which is still sitting in my lap. 'The family consider it a security risk.'

'A *security* risk?'

'Yes. People taking photos . . . those photos finding their way into newspapers . . . I'm sure you understand, with a family like the Brodericks, that privacy is at an absolute premium.'

'Er – yes. I understand.' I'm kicking myself now for not asking Marit more about exactly who these Brodericks *are*. What if they're people I'm meant to have heard of? The name doesn't ring any bells with me, but then I'm rubbish at general knowledge.

'Good.' Annabel gives a brisk nod. 'Well, I'll leave you to prepare, then.'

Which begs the question, doesn't it: prepare *what*?

I mean, after Marit called back yesterday to tell me she'd arranged an interview, I did spend several hours getting as prepared as I possibly could. But now Annabel has made me feel that there's more I could be doing. More I should have done. *Great.* Just what I needed, at the last minute, to boost my rickety confidence. And I can't even ask her what she meant, exactly, because she's disappeared into the hallway again.

When my mobile rings, I practically jump out of my skin trying to get to it before anyone hears it.

'Lucy?' I hiss into my phone when I finally locate it and see that it's her calling. 'Look, I can't talk . . .'

'I was just calling to wish you luck.'

'Thanks, but I really can't talk. I'm not meant to use a phone while I'm here. It's a security risk, apparently.'

'Security risk?'

'Yes. Do you know who these people are? I mean, did Pal's sister-in-law ever mention them to you?'

'No, all I know is that they're stonkingly rich. Though that's probably enough of a need for security in itself. Oh, and the son is a racing driver, of course.'

'A racing driver?' I'm filled with respect for the teenage Rob/Ron. 'Wow. That's pretty impressive, for a teenage boy.'

'What? Jay Broderick's not a teenager.'

'Jay? I thought he was called Rob. Or is it Ron?'

'He's not called either. He's called Jay. Charlie, surely you've seen him in the papers and stuff, when he won the Formula One World Championship a few years back? Tall, dark-haired, half-Japanese or something. Definitely not a teenager. At least,' she adds, with a rather filthy giggle, 'if he is a teenager, he's the most ridiculously hot teenager I've ever seen.'

'Oh, well, there must be more than one son, then . . . shit, Luce, I have to go!'

'You're not being stormed by SAS men, are you?'

'No, but I can hear voices in the hallway . . .'

I end the call and shove the phone back into my bag. Lucy may have been joking about the SAS men but I wouldn't like to cross Annabel in a hurry. I can hear her now, outside the library door, sounding rather more soft-edged and easy-going than she's done with me or with the lift-maintenance man.

'. . . great to see you, too! Sorry to have been hounding you, but this girl has come for an interview to replace Marit, and I knew you were already coming over to see your father this morning. And I know you don't like him to be bothered with staffing issues.'

'It's fine, Annabel.' This is a man's voice, laidback and confident. 'You know you can hound me whenever you like. And you're looking incredible after your holiday, by the way. The Maldives, was it?'

'That's right!' Annabel sounds as if she's simpering. 'We got back on Friday.'

'And did that boyfriend of yours finally get his arse into gear and pop the question?' There's a flirty smile in the man's voice now. 'Remind me of his name again? Boy, was it, or Man, or something?'

Annabel actually *giggles*. 'Guy! And, no, he didn't pop the question, Jay. We've only been going out six months.'

'Six months? Six days should have been enough for him to know you were the one!'

Annabel giggles again. 'Oh, Jay . . .'

'Right, so, where's this cooking girl you've got lined up for me to meet?'

'In the library.' Annabel sounds slightly put out, perhaps because she was hoping the flirtation would go on a bit longer. 'I assumed you'd conduct the interview in there? Unless you want to take her down and show her the kitchens?'

There are kitch*ens*? *Plural*? But before I can think any more about that, Annabel is peering round the door. 'Charlene? Mr Broderick is here for you now.'

'Great! I mean, it's Charlotte, actually . . . but thanks so much.' I get to my feet, hauling my briefcase-bag with me, and head her way. I can't help noticing that her top button has come undone: the crisp white shirt she was wearing buttoned all the way up when I arrived is now revealing a good deal of golden skin and even the smallest hint of lacy bra. 'Your top button's come undone, by the way,' I whisper, help-fully.

'It's fine.'

'No, it's really undone . . . in fact, it might even be the top two buttons—'

'It's *fine*!' she snaps, giving me a bit of a look.

So I say no more about it, and simply follow her meekly out into the marble-floored hallway, where a man is waiting, his hands thrust into his jeans pockets.

Sweet *Jesus*, he's good-looking.

He has to be the Jay that Lucy was going on about, because his almost absurdly handsome features are obviously part Asiatic. His eyes are sooty and almost black, his hair likewise and shiny as a brand-new conker, and he's blessed with that soft lips/strong jaw combo that gives the faintest of feminine touches to an otherwise relentlessly masculine face. But it's not just his face. If anything, his body is even better. He's over six foot and broad-shouldered, with the kind of lean upper torso that probably comes from many, many hours spent in the gym, but that somehow manages to look as if it comes from many, many hours doing much more attractive, manly things, like chopping wood, or tilling fields, or throwing some insanely lucky girl around a bedroom . . .

Because that's the final thing about his looks. He's not merely handsome, with a fabulous body. He's also *sexy*. His appeal isn't like Ferdy's, stemming from pleasant looks and a gentle demeanour. This is not the kind of man who makes your brain concoct silly romantic fantasies of misty moors and whinnying horses. This is the kind of man who makes you think of hotel rooms, and mussed-up sheets, and drinking champagne in a shared bath, with scented oils making your damp skin all slippery against each other, and . . .

'Hi, there.' He smiles and approaches me with one hand outstretched. 'I'm Jay Broderick. And you are . . . ?'

'Charlene,' Annabel answers for me, which is handy because I seem to have lost the power of speech. 'Like I said, Jay, she's here about the cooking job.'

'Hey, I tell you what, you wouldn't be able to whip me up a bit of breakfast, Charlene, would you?' He pats his stomach, flat and taut-looking beneath his blue-checked shirt. 'I haven't had breakfast, and I only had three hours' sleep, and if I don't eat something I'm going to get all cranky . . . and we wouldn't want that, would we?'

His smile turns rather devilish, as he directs this final remark in Annabel's direction. Who – it only now occurs to me – hasn't had an accident with her top two shirt buttons at all. She's deliberately undone them for Jay's benefit. Which I can hardly blame her for. If *I* was the kind of girl who had a chance with Jay Broderick, I'd be stripping to my undies, throwing myself at him and begging him to take me now, this very minute, on the marble floor . . .

'Charlene? How about it?' He's smiling at me again. It's a perfectly pleasant smile, but I'd kill for one of the devilish grins he just treated Annabel to. 'Just some bacon and eggs, nothing fancy.'

'Um . . . yes, I could do that . . . but actually, my name's—'

84

'Great! I can interview you while you cook. Come to think of it, the cooking can be *part of* your interview.'

'Oh, Jay, I don't know about that,' Annabel says. 'She won't have public liability insurance, and she isn't under any kind of contract—'

'Annabel, relax. How much damage can one person possibly do, cooking a plateful of bacon and eggs? You're not planning to slice off a couple of fingers when you cut bread for toast, are you, Char?'

'Not planning to, no.'

'Not planning to blind anyone with hot fat from the frying pan?'

'Oh, God, no!'

'Then I think we'll be all right. Excellent, here comes the lift,' he says, when there's a sudden creaking from the shiny brass double doors to the right of the hallway. He puts a friendly hand on the back of my shirt – which, like a teenage girl, I vow I'll never wash again – and steers me towards the lift. 'We can go down to the kitchens in this. If you get the job here, you'll have to get used to this thing. My father had it installed when he finally succumbed to a wheelchair a couple of years ago, but now he likes everyone to use it. Especially his cook – *I* swear you'd be faster climbing four flights of stairs up to his office but he was always moaning at Marit that his food was cold if she did that . . . Oh, Hamish mate!' he says, as the lift doors open to reveal someone standing in there. 'Were you here to see the old man?'

'Yeah.' Hamish is short and pink and shiny, rather

like a pig fashioned from a balloon by a clown at a children's party. He looks pleased to see Jay, shaking his hand and slapping his back as he gets into the lift, and completely ignores me as I follow. 'Fucking hell, Jay, it's been ages. In fact, we need a proper catch-up. I was just talking to your father about a couple of matters regarding the trust, and—'

'OK, then why not come and have a coffee with me now?' Jay suggests, pressing the button to close the lift doors. 'This lady here is interviewing for Marit's job, and she's about to cook me breakfast.'

'Marit?' Hamish's eyes goggle. 'The hot Swede?'

'I think she was Norwegian, actually, mate.'

'Swedish, Norwegian . . . who cares? She was hot. And she's *leaving*?'

'Yeah.'

'Well, then, you need to replace her with someone equally hot! Not . . .'

'Hamish!' Jay snaps.

I feel my face flood with colour.

'Hey, are you all right?'

Jay Broderick is looking at me with mild concern, probably because I've just turned the colour of boiled beetroot.

'I'm fine!' I say. 'Just . . . er . . . not a fan of lifts, that's all. A bit claustrophobic,' I add, hoping this is explanation enough for my bright red cheeks.

'Yeah, I said it was slow . . . mind you, it should have opened by now.' Jay reaches behind me to press the door-open button. 'That should do it.'

The lift doors do, indeed, open.

But then they stop opening, abruptly, when they're only halfway apart.

This might not be such a big deal if we'd actually reached the basement floor. But we haven't. We have, however, left behind the ground floor. And where we are right now is trapped, with half-open lift doors, somewhere between the two.

All three of us stare out at the blank expanse of brick wall ahead.

'Shit,' says Jay. 'This isn't good.'

He reaches behind me again and presses the LG button. We go nowhere. So he presses the G button. For a thrilling half-second we jolt upwards. And then we stop again. A foot-wide gap has appeared at the top of the wall.

Annabel's face appears, sideways, in this gap.

'Oh, my God, guys! Are you all right? OK, hang on,' she adds, before any of us can reply. 'Let me just press the button outside the doors.' She disappears again, so that all we can see are her legs.

'Well, I don't know about you, Jay, but I'm quite happy staying here for a bit longer, with a view like that.' Hamish takes a step forward. 'You know, if we get the angle right, we might even be able to see up her skirt . . .'

'Jesus Christ, Hamish.' Jay pushes him backwards. 'Annabel? Are you pressing the button?'

'Yes . . . and you're still stuck.' Annabel's head appears again. 'God, Jay, I'm so sorry about this.

We've been having problems for a while, but it's never got stuck with anyone in it before. But, look, I've already called the maintenance man this morning . . .'

'He won't get here 'til noon,' I hear myself say.

Annabel shoots me a look of dislike. 'And he won't get here 'til noon, that's right. But it's almost ten forty-five now, so . . .'

'Annabel sweetheart, we can't wait that long. Charlene's claustrophobic. Are you OK there, Charlene?'

It takes me a moment to realise that he's talking about me.

'Oh, honestly, I'm fine! And it's Charlotte, by the way.'

'What's Charlotte?'

'My . . . um . . . name?'

There's a bit of a silence.

'OK, CHARLENE, YOU JUST TRY TO STAY CALM,' Jay says, very loudly and clearly, and in exactly the tone of voice you'd use if you thought someone was losing it so badly that they've just forgotten their own name. 'I'VE GOT THIS UNDER CONTROL.'

He steps forward, takes a speculative hold of the shelf of marble flooring at the top of the wall, and places both hands on the horizontal surface just above his head. After a quick, 'Mind out of the way, Annabel!' he hauls himself upwards.

Well, if I wasn't feeling hot and bothered a moment ago, I certainly am now. I mean, *Jesus*, I can actually see his back muscles rippling under his shirt. They ripple some more as he twists his body sideways, squeezes through the narrow gap and pulls his legs up behind him.

A moment later his head appears in the foot-wide gap.

'Easy!' he says, with a grin.

Well, yes, it probably was easy, for a man with upper-body strength like that.

'COME ON THEN, SWEETHEART.' Jay reaches his arm further into the lift and snaps his fingers, a thrillingly masterful gesture. 'GIVE ME YOUR HAND.'

Even if I could ignore the thrilling masterfulness of this (and I can't), how can I possibly turn him down? He's telling me to hold hands with him! His intention is to keep me calm, presumably, until the maintenance man gets here. I mean, I'm not such an idiot as to think he wants to hold hands *romantically*, or anything. But if I get to hold hands with the sexiest man I've ever met, I'm not going to quibble about his motivation.

I take a step towards him and reach up. His grip is firm and his hands are pleasantly cool to the touch, and I'm looking right up into his inky eyes, and for a moment it's all just as wonderful as I thought it was going to be.

'Ready?' he asks.

'Ready?' I echo.

'Count of three?'

'Count of . . . sorry?'

'On the count of three,' he explains, patiently, 'you jump and I'll pull. OK?'

No, no, no, no, no! This is not OK!

He actually thinks he can pull me up?

I mean, we all know he's strong – God knows, we've just had (thrilling) evidence of that – but unless he happens to be made from reinforced steel girders and galvanised titanium, his plan is a total non-starter.

'You know, I think I'll just wait for the maintenance man, if it's all the same to you? I mean, it's perfectly comfortable in here – quite cosy, in fact – and . . .'

But Jay – still under the impression he's listening to the ramblings of a lunatic in the throes of a panic attack – ignores me.

'Hamish, for crying out loud,' he says. 'Help me out here. Give her a leg up, can't you?'

'You have to be kidding me.' Hamish hasn't bothered to lower his voice, perhaps because he, like Jay, thinks I've gone into some kind of semi-catatonic state, or (more likely) just because he's one of those men who thinks fat girls are better off ignored. 'A leg up? Who do you think I am, the Incredible Hulk?'

'Hamish, that's not funny.'

'It's a *bit* funny. Do you seriously think you can winch her out of here? And even if you could, how's she going to fit through that gap? I mean,' he adds, with a snigger, 'we all know you're an expert at getting something huge into a tight space! But I think in this case you might finally have met your match.'

'Oh, just shut the fuck up, Hamish! You can be a real dick, you know that?'

And then, if I weren't mortified enough by what

Hamish has just said, Jay gives the hand he's holding a well-meaning squeeze.

'OK, darling, looks like it's just you and me, then. So like I said, on the count of three . . .'

'I'm perfectly fine here!'

'One . . . two . . .'

'Honestly, I'd much rather . . .'

'. . . three . . . hup!'

I have no choice. On *hup*, he pulls and I jump.

Which is when there's a sudden, extremely nasty popping sound.

It's come from his shoulder.

Jay gives a sharp gasp of pain. Then he lets go of my hand as though it's scalding hot, rolls sideways, and disappears behind the lift doors.

But on the bright side (I seriously need to find a bright side here) the lift has suddenly taken it upon itself to stir back to life. It suddenly judders upwards by about three feet, not all the way back to the ground floor but certainly far enough that I can easily scramble up the three foot or so of remaining wall.

Jay has propped himself up against the nearby staircase, with Annabel leaning over him. (Leaning, I can't help noticing, with quite a lot of her bounteous cleavage spilling out from those undone top buttons.)

'Do you need me to call a doctor?' she's gasping. 'An ambulance?'

'No, I'm OK, honestly, it's an old injury. I just need to pop it back in . . .'

Which he does, with an even more ghastly sound than it made when it popped out.

'I'm so sorry,' I mumble. 'I'm so, so sorry.'

'*Fucking* hell, mate!' Clambering out of the lift behind me, Hamish looks, if anything, even more pale and sweaty than Jay does. 'I *told* you it was a bad idea to try hauling around a heifer like that!'

If you could dislocate your sense of self-worth, if your self-esteem could make a nasty popping sound, the way Jay's shoulder has just done, you'd have heard another of those ghastly noises coming from me. Not that I'm trying to underestimate the pain Jay must be feeling at the moment. But I can't help wondering if the agony of humiliation I'm feeling would give a dislocated shoulder a run for its money.

'It wasn't her fault,' Jay says (though he doesn't, I notice, actually dispute Hamish's claim that I'm a heifer). 'This shoulder's never been the same since I dislocated it on the Suzuka Circuit.'

'Is there anything I can do?' I croak. 'Anything at all?'

But Annabel and Hamish are too busy fussing over Jay to pay me any attention.

I'll be honest: for once in my life, I'm very glad that nobody seems to notice me.

I don't care any more about getting the cooking job. All I want is to get away from this place and never come back.

'Again, I'm really, really sorry,' I mumble, as I sidle towards the front door.

I may be, as Hamish so considerately put it, a heifer; I may have a bum the size of a small planet; I may weigh enough to dislocate a man's shoulder when he tries to lift me. But the supremely ironic thing is that all of this somehow combines to make me pretty much invisible. So invisible, in fact, that I can slip away from the scene of my crime without anyone even noticing.

The bigger you are, it seems, the less anybody sees you at all.

Chapter Five

I make the mistake of arriving before either Gaby or Robyn for the will-reading on Thursday. Gaby, according to her assistant, is on her way back to the office from a meeting with a fashion stylist at the Dorchester, and Robyn is . . . well, just on her way. It's not quite two o'clock in the afternoon yet, so she probably only got out of bed about an hour ago. Honestly, if she makes it any time before three, we should probably all consider ourselves grateful.

But the reason that my early arrival is a huge mistake is that, without Gaby or Robyn, without even Oliver Winkleman the solicitor, I'm alone, on her turf, with my stepmother.

That's right. The Ice Queen. She Who Must Not Be Named. The High Priestess of Mordor herself.

Diana.

She's looking at me now, from behind the colossal oak desk in her office. It's two floors above the shop, with large windows facing out over Bond Street, and it's decorated in Diana's usual style, which is to say that everything is over-sized, extremely expensive, incredibly ornate and entirely without charm. I've often felt as though Diana picks out furniture that's big and solid and overblown almost as if to exercise her iron will over everything, inanimate or otherwise. Her desk in this office is Gotham-esque, and the Chesterfields at her house are mammoth, and the swirly Venetian mirrors she likes to hang on every available bit of wall are roughly the size of the ones you see in stately homes and National Trust houses, but still Diana dominates her space. And, should there be any doubt, she also dominates everyone else in it.

Of course, she's an extremely striking woman. She was a successful society model before she met Dad in the early seventies, and those looks are still in evidence today: high cheekbones that are always, but *always*, emphasised by an ash-blonde chignon, and an angular frame that she sets off to dramatic effect in sharp tailoring and bold jewellery that would drown a smaller, softer woman. Today, for example, she's wearing head-to-toe navy (wide trousers and a kind of Japanese-style wrap shirt in extremely stiff cotton) accessorised with onyx earrings the size of quail's eggs and a heavy beaten-gold choker around her neck. Usually she'd be nudging six foot with the assistance of her customary four-inch heels, but today – thanks to her recent bunion surgery – she's slumming it in a mere kitten heel, the closest Diana will ever get to a flat shoe. Her handbag, within reach by the side of her desk, is her usual black quilted Chanel 2.55.

Although I did my best to put together my very smartest outfit for the will-reading, I felt shabby and creased the moment I walked in here. And that's without Diana even having pointed out that I look shabby and creased. Which she will, I guarantee you. For Diana, where I'm concerned, cruel and mocking jibes are de rigueur.

'So! Charlotte!' she says, with one of the smiles that Lucy calls *a Diana special*. (It's anorexically thin, Arctically cold, and never comes within a thousand miles of reaching her eyes.) 'How are you? I haven't seen you since Elroy's funeral.'

She says this as though, under normal circumstances, we see each other once every couple of weeks. We don't. Dad's funeral was, in fact, the first time I'd seen her in about four years. And I'd happily have gone another four without a further meeting, let me tell you.

'I'm fine. How are you? How's Michael?'

Michael is Diana's fourth husband. The fact that there have been four people in the world who were prepared to marry her is a total mystery to me. But then, there were people who were prepared to marry Stalin, weren't there? There are people who are prepared to marry convicted serial killers. On that basis, there really is no accounting for taste.

'Oh, he's fine. You know, you really must come and stay with us one weekend in the country, Charlotte, when Gaby and the children are down too.' This remark has been perfectly timed to coincide with the arrival of her assistant, bearing a tray of tea things and a plate of madeleines. Which is entirely consistent with Diana's age-old MO: delightful in public, diabolical in private. 'It would do you good,' she adds, as the assistant sets down the tray and leaves, shutting the door behind her, 'to get out of London for a weekend. Away from that grim little flat!'

I clear my throat. 'It's not grim.'

'Oh, darling, it's totally grim!' Another anorexic smile, accompanied by a little flurry of laughter. 'Admittedly I haven't seen the place for donkey's years, but if it was grim back then, I can't believe it's a palace now! Right on that corner where the buses thunder down Earl's Court Road, wasn't it? I'm sure you can practically reach out of your bedroom window and touch a passing number seventy-four. Oh – though it was a basement flat, wasn't it, if I remember correctly? So you probably can't reach out of any window at all!'

'It's ground floor and lower ground.'

'Really, Charlotte, there's no need to be so defensive.'

'I'm not being defensive, I was just—'

'It makes you sound terribly bitter. Though God only knows what you've got to feel bitter about.'

'But I was only—'

'And nobody likes a bitter woman, Charlotte. Men especially. Oh, that reminds me – did Robyn tell me you'd started dating someone?'

'No.'

'Well, maybe it was Gaby, then. I'm sure one of the girls mentioned it. I'd love to hear all about him!'

'There . . . is no him.'

'So you're *not* dating someone?'

'No.'

'Oh, dear. Poor old Charlotte. Still, never mind. I mean, you're only twenty-seven, aren't you?'

'Twenty-eight.'

'Ah. Well, even so. Plenty of time to track down some nice man who might be interested! I hear dating websites are very good, these days, for girls who find it hard to attract a man in the usual way. I mean, I don't even think you have to exchange photographs, or anything, until you've spent a bit of time emailing back and forth. And I suppose you could even get a friend to help you write the emails, if you were worried you were going to sound dull, or a bit thick, or something.'

I imagine you're probably wondering why I don't grab the tea tray and fling it, madeleines and all, into Diana's smiling face. Or pick up her Chanel 2.55 and beat her insensible with it. Or open the window and shove her out so she splats, shocking the Bond Street shoppers, on the pavement below.

Why I just sit here and say nothing to defend myself at all.

Lucy's explanation for what looks like my total and utter wimpishness is that the moment I step into Diana's orbit, I immediately regress to my childhood years in that big, cold house in Fulham where I grew up. I don't want to get all Dickensian about it, but it wasn't the happiest childhood. I'm sure there are some women who would be capable of being kindness itself to the small daughter of the tragically killed woman who was the catalyst for their husband leaving them . . . but Diana wasn't one of them. Diana's the kind of woman who preferred to bully, torment, and kill with a thousand tiny cuts. The kind of woman who'd arbitrarily refuse to let me eat at the dinner table because she'd suddenly take exception to 'seeing such an ugly face'. The kind of woman who'd decide I should be the one to get up every morning at six to walk Gaby and Robyn's Labrador – lovely golden-haired Heidi, my one source of comfort in that house – and who'd then suddenly announce, when I came home from school one day, that Heidi had been taken ill, seen by the vet, and put down. The kind of woman who wouldn't let me come down on Christmas morning to open presents with Gaby and Robyn by the tree, because that was a tradition reserved 'for family'.

Lucy's probably right, but I think it's a bit more specific than that. Because I date my own frozen, passive behaviour around Diana to one very particular moment. The first moment I ever met her, in fact, three days after Mum died. DI Wright and a social worker took me round to Diana's to spend a few nights. Dad was in such a state about the accident that he couldn't function – a state that lasted, as it turned out, for the best part of ten years – and there was nowhere else for me to go. I have this crystal-clear memory of Diana opening the front door to us, greeting DI Wright in a fixed, unsmiling manner, and not even bothering to look down and acknowledge me.

All I could think was that somehow, I didn't know how, I'd done her some terrible wrong, and that if I was very, very well behaved from now on, it might just fix it. When I finally began to cotton on that it was my very presence that was inflicting a terrible wrong on her, I stopped trying merely to behave well and started trying to behave, as far as I possibly could, as if I wasn't there at all.

So I stay quiet. I try not to let on that anything has upset me. It's self-preservation, pure and simple. Live with Diana for ten years, and you'd get pretty good at it, too.

'Oh, Gaby darling,' Diana suddenly says, as the door opens and Gaby strides into the room. 'How was the meeting with Poppy?'

'Waste of time. She's been cosying up to Tamara Mellon again.' Gaby shrugs off her trench coat and hangs it on the burnished-brass coat stand next to the office door. 'All her clients are going to be in Louboutins at the BAFTAS. I couldn't even get her to promise us a Downton daughter. Oh, hi, Charlie. Yeah, I'd love a cup of tea, thanks,' Gaby says, even though I haven't offered her one. 'Oh, and you never told me whether or not Oliver Winkleman came round to you at the weekend, to make the inventory like I asked him?'

'Yes, he came round. I had people over for a dinner party, but—'

'You know, I'm still fuming with Elroy that he stopped using Alan Kellaway at the last gasp and took up with this Winkleman instead,' Diana interrupts. 'I mean, I don't even *know* this Winkleman. He sounds about twelve years old on the phone. And honestly, I don't know why we have to go through this whole rigmarole with Elroy's will. We all know what the damn thing says. You and Robyn get his shares in the business, Charlotte gets the flat. Actually –' she turns to me with a smile so thin it's in danger of dying from starvation '– I'm not at all sure that it was worth your coming along today, Charlotte. Any queries that the girls or I have are going to be about Elroy's business interests, and nothing to do with his leaving the flat to you.'

'Mummy, don't be absurd.' Gaby doesn't look at Diana as she says this. 'Of course Charlie has to be here for Daddy's will-reading.'

'But, Gaby, it's a *family* affair.'

'Mummy . . .' It would be going too far to say there's a warning note in Gaby's voice, because even she, fearsome as she is with pretty much everyone else on the planet, is far from her usual steely self when it comes to dealing with her own mother. And it's not even reproachful, because nobody reproaches Diana. But it is a note of sorts. 'Charlie is . . .' She pauses, pressing her lips together, perhaps before the word *family* can escape them. 'Well, she's entitled to be here.'

'Oh, she's entitled all right!' Diana's smile is hardening, her eyes are becoming just a little too bright, and the atmosphere is changing from unwelcoming to downright hostile. This is the thing about Diana's tempers: they turn on a pinhead, and are so lightning-fast that – even after years of practice – you never see them coming. 'Just like her mother was when she felt *entitled* enough to steal my husband!'

'Mummy, don't,' Gaby says, in a low voice.

'Well, that's the only reason she's here today at all, isn't it? Swiping an entire flat from under our noses, a flat that Elroy only had to buy because he wanted to shack up with her mother! That money would be yours and Robyn's otherwise, Gaby! Do you still want to defend her, do you still want to be her very best buddy, when she's doing you out of part of your inheritance?'

'Mummy . . .'

But this is all Gaby can say, because there's a soft knock at the door then and Diana's assistant appears with Oliver Winkleman in tow.

'Mr Winkleman, how nice to meet you.' Diana gets up from behind her desk to go and greet him, turning on the full force of her considerable charm. You'd never think, to look at her, that less than ten seconds ago she was gearing up to spit venom all over us. 'I'd like to say I've heard a lot about you, but I'm afraid Alan has never mentioned your name to me!'

'Well, I don't see very much of Mr Kellaway.' He returns her handshake, managing not to turn to stone in the process. 'He's the senior partner, you know.'

'I *do* know. He's also a very dear friend.'

This is a bit of an understatement, seeing as Diana

has been conducting an on-again-off-again affair with Alan Kellaway for many years. I used to see him arriving at the front door late at night whenever her second husband Gordon was away on business, and one Saturday lunchtime, when Diana evidently believed she had the house to herself, I actually saw him in the kitchen preparing a champagne tray while wearing nothing but white Y-fronts and a pair of Argyle-pattern socks.

'Charlotte darling –' Diana glances in my direction '– would you get Mr Winkleman a cup of tea? And a couple of the madeleines, if you can bring yourself to? She has to be persuaded to let other people have a nibble of cake,' she adds, turning back to Oliver with a smile and a wink, 'otherwise I honestly think she'd just scoff the lot herself!'

And with this, her revenge on me – her revenge for Gaby trying to defend me – is wreaked, proving that there's never any point in anyone else trying to defend me, because her wrath will just descend on me anyway.

So I pour Oliver a cup of tea, and one more for Gaby, bung a madeleine on the side of each saucer, and take the cups over to the plum velvet-covered sofa, where he and Gaby have both taken seats. Diana has gone back to her desk, but she's not sitting behind it as before. She's perched on the front edge of it, like a friendly newsreader.

'That looks great, thanks so much, Charlie,' Oliver says, glancing up from the sheaf of papers he's getting out of his briefcase.

'You call her Charlie?' Diana asks, sharply. 'Well! Isn't that all nice and cosy and familiar?'

'We've met a couple of times now,' Oliver says, 'haven't we, Charlie?'

He's so unaware, poor soul, of the minefield that he's treading into that I'm tempted to take that madeleine and stuff it into his mouth like a silencer.

'Only briefly!' I say, desperate to stop him strolling into one of Diana's traps.

'Yes – just this past weekend when I went to do the inventory, and of course when I first went to meet Mr Glass last year.'

'Odd that you've met Charlotte, when *I* hadn't met you,' Diana observes, with one of her smiles.

'Ah – well, Charlie was the one taking care of Mr Glass, of course . . .'

'We *all* took care of him,' Gaby says, quickly. It's one of the traits she happens to share with Diana: her insistence on presenting a good face to outsiders. 'It was a family effort. Wasn't it, Charlie?'

I make a vague noise of assent, then go and take a seat on the smaller, leather sofa at the back of the office, as far away from Diana as possible. I've just sat down when the door is flung open – no knock this time – and Robyn flies in.

'God, I'm late, I'm late, I know!' she gasps, stalking through the doorway in a flurry of skin-tight denim, real fur, and Jo Malone Nectarine Blossom and Honey. Her hair has grown several miraculous inches since I last saw her at the memorial – divine intervention or a trip to the extensions salon, who can possibly say? – and is held back from her face by huge Tom Ford sunglasses. 'I've kept you all waiting *ages*, I'm so sorry!'

'Actually, we've not been waiting.' Gaby has spent many long years attempting to take the wind out of Robyn's sails, and she's not about to stop now. 'You're very nearly on time!'

Robyn completely blanks her. She trips across the office instead, to fling her arms around Diana.

'Ooooh, Mummy, you look fab! That necklace is just to *die* for. Oh, God, sorry!' She throws a hand to her mouth. 'Can you *say* that, at a *will-reading*?'

'It's perfectly fine,' Oliver says. Or rather, croaks. He's a man, after all. And men are reduced to croaking wrecks in Robyn's presence.

'Oh, hel-*looooooooo*,' Robyn purrs at him. She pulls off her sunglasses, does the swooshy thing with her hair that went so badly wrong for me when I tried it on Ferdy, and fixes Oliver with her huge violet-tinged eyes. 'You must be Daddy's lawyer. It's *so* nice to meet you. Especially as I'm, like, *totally* clueless about all this horrible last-will-and-testament stuff. Is it going to be just like one of those TV murder mysteries? Will all Daddy's dirty little secrets be revealed?'

'Robyn!' Diana says, but indulgently, which is the way she almost always talks towards her favourite daughter. 'Your father didn't have dirty secrets! Well,' she adds, with a glance in my direction, 'none we don't know about already.'

'Oh, Charlie darling, I didn't see you! What are you doing, hiding all the way back there? I'm going to come and be all cosy with you!' Robyn trips her way back towards my sofa and squeezes her teeny-tiny jeans-clad bottom in beside me, slipping one arm under mine. (I've never known whether Robyn simply has no problem showing me physical affection in front of Diana, or if it's just that she's never noticed how much her mother hates it.) 'This is so *fucking* exciting!' she declares.

She sounds – and looks, come to think of it – faintly manic, and I can't help wondering if the effects of last night's partying haven't worn off yet. In fact, from her inappropriate outfit, platform heels and sooty, dilated eyes, I wonder if she came here straight *from* last night's partying.

Gaby shoots a sour look across the office. 'Thank you, Robyn. But I'm sure Mr Winkleman would like to get started.'

'Well, yes.' Oliver taps his fingers on the sheaf of documents neatly stacked in a plastic wallet. 'I don't know how much your father told you about his intentions . . .'

'Don't worry, we know all about what Elroy wanted,' Diana says. 'Splitting his shares equally between Gaby and Robyn.'

'Ah,' Oliver says. He looks down at the papers. There's the faintest flush spreading across his cheeks. 'I . . . I wasn't aware that Elroy hadn't updated you.'

'Updated us on what?' Diana is still smiling, of

course, but her eyes have narrowed to slits, and they're fixed on Oliver like he's a tiny bug she'd very much like to crush beneath the heel of her shoe. 'What stunt has my ex-husband pulled now?'

'I'm not sure you can call it a stunt,' Oliver says. 'Plenty of people make changes to their wills, even at the very last minute. And Mr Glass's decision wasn't really a last-minute one. He made these changes back in October. And as of course you are aware, he died in February.'

'Look, Mr Winkleman . . .' Gaby begins.

'Oliver, please!'

'*Oliver* . . . could you just hurry up and explain all this?' Her bare legs are jiggling, slightly, beneath her crisp black shift dress. It's a nervous energy I remember from all the previous stressful occasions in Gaby's life, like the day she went to Oxford for her university interview (she asked me to take the train all the way there with her, to quiz her on the contents of her revision cards) or the morning she was waiting for her A-level results (she had to get me to open the envelope for her, to reveal an entirely unsurprising string of As). 'We're all agog.'

'Well, it's pretty straightforward, even if it isn't exactly what you've been expecting.' Oliver glances down at the papers he's holding and lifts the top one from the folder. 'Now, this is Mr Glass's last will and testament . . .'

'That doesn't look like his writing!' Diana says.

'No, it isn't in Mr Glass's writing. He dictated it.'

'Dictated it?' Gaby demands. 'Why on earth would he do that?'

'Because by that point, he hadn't been able to hold a pen for over six months,' I say, quietly.

'Charlie is right, of course. Mr Glass was having a lot of difficulty holding a pen. But he was able to sign here, at the bottom . . .'

'Ooooooh.' Robyn clutches my hand. 'It's like Daddy's speaking to us from behind the grave.'

'*Beyond*,' Gaby snaps. 'And this isn't a fucking seance, Robyn. Can we just get on with it, Oliver?'

'Ah, well, like I say, it's in his own words, so you'll forgive any . . . er . . . colloquialisms. This is direct from the horse's mouth, after all.'

'It's not a real horse,' I whisper to Robyn, who's just given a little yelp of excitement. 'It's just an expression.'

'So . . . *The last will and testament of Elroy David Glass*,' Oliver reads from the paper. '*I'm going to keep this simple. I don't have a lot of what they call assets, firstly because the business was the only asset that ever really mattered to me, and secondly because that bitch Diana walked away with all the money from the house when she finally divorced me.* I'm so sorry, Mrs Forbes-Wilkinson,' Oliver stutters, in Diana's direction. 'I'm only reading exactly what Mr Glass wanted me to write down . . . *So all I have to leave my girls, as they already know, is the following: a few random bits of family jewellery and silver –* they're the things I inventoried for you, Mrs Porter,

108

just this past weekend – *the flat in Earl's Court, and my remaining fifty-one per cent of the business. As regards the flat, I'm told it's worth a reasonable amount . . .* of course, we'll bring an estate agent in just as soon as you like, to get you a current market valuation,' Oliver adds, '*so I'm leaving it to be split, fifty-fifty, between my much-loved elder daughters Gabrielle Rosemary Glass and Robyn Lucinda Glass.*'

I feel like the leather sofa has just fallen away beneath me, taking the rest of the world with it.

Dad's given Gaby and Robyn the flat?

He's given them my home?

There's a horrible buzzing noise in my head. A thousand questions pile on top of each other.

Where am I going to live? Was Dad trying to punish me for something? Did he forget that Gaby and Robyn already have homes, not to mention handy trust funds, out of Diana's family money? Was it something to do with Mum? Has there been some kind of mistake? *Where am I going to live?*

'Oh, *well*.' Diana is rolling her eyes as she finally moves off the front of her desk and goes round to sit in her chair behind it. 'Is that *all*? Really, Mr Winkleman, you had us all worried there, for a moment!'

'*They can do what they like with the place,*' Oliver reads on, '*on the strict proviso that my youngest daughter Charlie is allowed to stay there rent-free for a full six months after my death, or until she's had time to find herself somewhere new to live.*'

'But it's still . . .' It's my turn to interrupt, though my throat is Sahara-dry. I swallow. It doesn't help. 'It's still my home. And I thought Dad was leaving it to me.'

'Goodness, have you ever heard anything so spoiled?' Diana stares around the room. She's incredulous and she wants an audience to witness it. 'Not everyone has a beautiful London flat fall into their lap, you know, Charlotte!' She doesn't seem to notice – or care – that only fifteen minutes ago she was describing the very same flat as 'totally grim'. 'Though perhaps you were hoping to take after your mother? You know, get a job as a cleaner, steal your employer's husband and have *him* buy a flat for you?'

'There'll be no need for her to do that!' Oliver, who obviously doesn't know the finer points of his Glass Family History, looks appalled. 'Not when Charlie will be a perfectly wealthy woman in her own right. If she wants to liquidate any of her assets, that is.'

'But Charlie . . . doesn't have any assets,' Gaby says, slowly.

'Ah . . . that's not quite true. I have a second document here.' Oliver gets up, taking an envelope from his plastic wallet, and – to my astonishment – comes over and puts it in my hands. 'The exact contents are for you to read on your own, Charlie, but I can tell you the gist. Which is that Mr Glass has left his entire share of the business – all fifty-one per cent – to you.'

There's a stunned silence. Gaby is the first to break it.

'*What?*'

'Well, like I say, the contents are for Charlie to read, but I assure you that Mr Glass was very—'

'Open it.' Diana is on her feet again, stabbing a finger at the letter in my hands. The smile has been wiped clean off her face. Evidently the shock of the last twenty seconds has been enough to dislodge, for once, her usual habit of playing Happy Families in front of witnesses.

'I wonder if Charlie might prefer a little privacy . . .'

'Open,' breathes Diana, 'it.'

My hands are shaking as I tear at the envelope and pull out a single sheet of paper. It is written in extremely neat, blue handwriting that obviously belongs to Oliver Winkleman. The voice, however, is Dad's alone.

My darling Charlie, it says. *Well, if you're reading this, I'll be dead and gone, and you're probably sitting somewhere in that monstrous new office with your sisters, waiting on Oliver's every word for my last will and testament.*

'What does it say?' Diana is demanding.

'Let her *finish*, Mummy.'

I carry on reading. *Look, I know I should be saying this to you in person. I should be coming back home today, putting my arms around you the way I used to do when you were little (and when I wasn't stuck in this sodding wheelchair) and telling you this: thank*

111

you, Charlie, and I'm sorry. But I can't. Because I'm bad at saying thank you, and – you know me, Charlie – I don't think I've ever apologised for anything.

'Does he mention me?' Robyn asks, craning over my shoulder. 'Or anything about the horse?'

So I'm telling you now: thank you, Charlie. Thank you for giving up your life to take care of me when nobody else would. Thank you for being the best daughter a man could ever have. Thank you for being better than me. Though how could you not be? After all, you're your mother's daughter too.

I must have let out a noise, because Gaby says, 'What? *What?*' But I carry on reading.

So, my shares in Elroy Glass are yours, Charlie, to do with as you wish. Sell them, keep them, it's up to you. I only ask two more things, if you don't mind, after twenty years of unreasonable demands: first, remember how much I loved the business. Along with your mother, that shoe shop was the love of my life. And second: whatever you do, make it something you want to do, for a change. I've held you back long enough. Consider this a long-overdue leg-up. I love you, Charlie. Dad.

My head and eyes are swimming, so much that I almost can't read the P.S. at the very bottom of the letter.

P.S. If I'm lucky enough to end up in the same place as her, I'll give your very best love to your mother.

'It's true,' I say, when I can speak at all. 'He . . . wants me to have his share of the business.'

'No.' Gaby shakes her head. 'It's a mistake. He wasn't lucid. He always told me the business was mine. Mine and Robyn's.'

'Yes, I think that's what he intended in a much earlier version of his will,' Oliver Winkleman says. 'The version he drew up with Mr Kellaway ten or fifteen years ago. But evidently he had a bit of a change of heart last October. Like I say, it's not uncommon. People fall out, have family quarrels . . .'

Or, quite possibly, people just begin to grow weary, as year after year drags by without their two eldest daughters offering an invitation to Christmas lunch, or popping round for a chat, or bringing over a takeaway to watch in front of *Strictly Come Dancing*, or calling to ask about the news from a worrying doctor's appointment.

I mean, *I* used to get upset that Gaby and Robyn didn't seem to give a shit about Dad and his illness. But I never thought Dad was upset. I never thought Gaby and Robyn could do a thing wrong, in his eyes.

'OK, now I'm *really* confused,' Robyn is saying. 'All I want to know is, which of us is getting this horse that was mentioned?'

Diana starts to laugh. It's a rich, ringing laugh, so different from her usual careful tinkle, and it takes me a moment to realise she's not laughing at what Robyn's just said. She's laughing at me.

'No. No, it's just absurd! Elroy leaving *Charlotte* the business? What the hell is *she* supposed to do with it? She can't even *wear* any of the shoes! I mean, are we supposed to re-brand Elroy Glass? Sell Birkenstock sandals to wear with fat-day tracksuits?'

Oliver is looking disconcerted. As well he might, with Diana apparently unravelling before his eyes. 'Ah . . . anyway, you can sell the shares, Charlie, if you want to, which would certainly leave you with enough capital to buy a new flat and not have to worry about money, probably even for the rest of your life . . . or of course you can hang on to them and—'

'No, no, she'll sell them! Of course she'll sell them,' Diana snaps. 'I'll have the company lawyers draw up all the paperwork we need. We can get this mess sorted out in no time, and then we can all go back to normal.'

Normal.

Normal being fine for everyone here, of course.

Diana can go on running Elroy Glass and Gaby can go on Having It All, and Robyn can go on finding herself billionaire sugar-daddies and having men fall at her feet like adoring skittles whenever she so much as swooshes her hair in their direction.

But what will I go on doing? Fetching cups of tea for people who have perfectly functional arms and legs of their own? Allowing Diana to insult my appearance, my intelligence and the memory of my mother, without uttering a word to stop her? Is that what's always going to be normal for me?

I take a very long, very deep breath, and fix my gaze on Oliver.

'Hang on to them and what?' I ask him.

'Sorry?'

'You said I could hang on to the shares and . . . and what?'

'Well, that would be entirely up to you. You'd have the controlling interest in the company. You could either just sit back and be a silent partner, or I suppose you could start to take an active interest in the day-to-day running of the business.'

'Oh, honestly, Oliver, now you're just being silly,' Gaby says. 'Charlie doesn't know the first thing about the business!'

'But I could learn.' I feel like I'm standing before an aircraft door, just about to leap out into the empty sky beneath me, without even checking to see if I have a parachute. 'I mean, you know, Gaby, that I always wanted to work in the business when I grew up. You know that's even why I started an Italian degree, so that maybe one day I could be useful dealing with the factories in Tuscany. And I know I'm inexperienced, but perhaps I could do something kind of behind-the-scenes . . . run the website, or . . . I don't know . . . deal with customer complaints or something . . .'

Diana is laughing again. 'Wait a minute, everyone! It's just occurred to me *exactly* what Charlotte could do, if she wants to come and work here. We've been having all kinds of problems with the contract cleaners lately – totally unreliable, floors not even getting hoovered – so why don't we get her to come in and

115

take care of the office cleaning? After all, it's in her blood! How about it, Charlotte darling?' She turns to me, a genuinely amused smile on her face; she's really, really enjoying this. 'You don't mind working nights, do you? You'd look ever so fetching in the overalls.'

Somewhere very deep inside me I feel something snap. No – snap is the wrong word. I feel something . . . release. Like a ripcord on the parachute I've never really known I was wearing.

I give Diana a smile of my own. Because this is the most totally, purely joyful I've felt in twenty years. This is the happiest I've felt since Mum died.

'Actually, Diana,' I say, 'I'm afraid I very much do mind working nights. And given that Dad saw fit to leave me the lion's share of the company, I'm pretty sure he intended that I do something more with it than just the cleaning. Wouldn't you agree?'

Diana doesn't agree. Diana stares at me, just as silent as everyone else in the room.

A moment later, Gaby breaks the silence, getting to her feet in a brisk, businesslike manner.

'Oh, now, come on, Charlie. Mummy didn't mean it. Of course you don't have to do any bloody cleaning. But Daddy must have made some mistake – it's perfectly obvious. He wasn't thinking clearly during those last few months, that's all.'

'Gaby,' I say, quietly, 'that isn't true. And anyway, even if it were, how would you know that? You were never there.'

116

'It's true,' Robyn pipes up. 'You *were* never there, Gaby. Daddy felt totally abandoned by you. He told me himself, every time I used to go and see him. Me and Charlie were the only ones who really cared about him, weren't we, Cha-Cha?'

Gaby ignores her. 'All right,' she says, 'I could have seen more of Daddy these past couple of years, I grant you that. But the notion that he'd leave you the business, to exact some kind of revenge on me . . . it's just absurd. And you have to admit, Mummy has a point. I'm not being mean, but this isn't the kind of place someone like you can come to work, behind the scenes or not. It's . . . an image-obsessed business.'

'And I've got the wrong image, you mean.'

Diana lets out a whoop of laughter. '*Finally*, she says something sensible! Yes, Charlotte, you have the wrong image. You're *fat*, my darling, in case you hadn't realised. Your backside is the size of Cambridgeshire. And you have dreary hair, and cheap clothes, and the hands of a charwoman. And you want to come and work at a luxury shoe store? Looking like . . . wait a minute, Charlotte. Where are you going?'

I'm heading for the door, is where I'm going.

En route, though, I cross the room to Oliver Winkleman, and reach out to shake his hand. 'Thank you ever so much, Oliver. Can I call you, if I have any more questions?'

'Ah, certainly. Any time.'

I can hear three voices behind me as I walk out of

117

the office. There's Gaby, high-pitched and incoherent; there's Robyn, still enquiring, petulantly, about her horse; and of course there's Diana. She's yelling after me: screaming, in fact, demanding that I come back this instant. But I'm not listening. I'm heading for the stairs.

And then I'll be heading for my flat.

And then I'll be heading somewhere else entirely.

I scrabble in my bag for my phone, pull it out, and dial Lucy's number. She must be at work, because she doesn't pick up, so when it goes to voicemail, I leave a message.

'Luce? Hi, it's me. Look, can you call me when you get this? I need . . . I need your help on something. Do you think you'd still be able to fix up one of those boot camps you were telling me about? In Vietnam, or California, or anywhere else your boss wants someone to go? Because something has happened, Luce. Something . . . amazing. At least, something that could be amazing, if I give it a chance. If I give *myself* a chance. So just . . . just call me as soon as you get this, OK?'

I slip the phone back into my bag, and I keep striding, all the way past the designer shops, heading southbound down Bond Street.

PART TWO

Chapter Six

Ever since I turned up at the pub near Lucy's office, this group of men standing outside has been staring at me. No, it's worse than that: intermittently staring at me, then retreating into their huddle to whisper and laugh together like a gang of teenage girls.

I can feel myself turning more and more violently red with each guffaw, and with each fresh outbreak of laughter I glance down at my jeans again and wonder: What on earth was I thinking?

I'd just like it on record that this is all Natalie's fault. Natalie was the head trainer at the California desert boot camp I've just returned from, and even though she basically tortured me morning, noon and night for the last ten weeks, we ended up pretty friendly, too. It helped, I think, that I became kind of a member of staff, helping in the kitchens to cover the cost of my stay beyond the two free weeks Lucy could arrange for me. Anyway, Natalie was the one who talked me into buying the jeans. Jeans that are, I should add, the first I've worn in my entire adult life. Not an especially remarkable pair of jeans, I grant you – basic indigo denim things, with a mid-rise waistband and a slight boot-cut – but nevertheless, still a pair of jeans. And as everyone knows, as this gaggle of gossiping men apparently knows, as everyone on the entire planet apart from Natalie knows, if you have a bum the size of Cambridgeshire, you SHOULDN'T BE WEARING JEANS AT ALL.

Because this was the remarkable thing about boot camp. Ten weeks slogging my guts out beneath the Californian sun, and I *still* have a bum the size of . . . well, maybe not the size of Cambridgeshire. The size of a smaller county than Cambridgeshire.

Rutland, perhaps?

It's all the more disheartening because – despite the fact that my flight from Los Angeles only landed this lunchtime – I've really made a huge effort to look nice, seeing as it's my first meeting with Lucy in almost three months. It wasn't exactly fun, let me tell you, fighting my way home to Earl's Court from Heathrow in the morning rush hour, just to spend a solid hour showering, changing and doing full hair and make-up, when all I really wanted to do was crawl under my lovely welcoming duvet and give in to my protesting body clock. But from the way these men keep laughing at me, clearly I still look like I've been pulled through a hedge backwards, through eight time zones, before having my make-up applied by Bozo the Clown and my hair done by Edward Scissorhands.

And – oh, God – one of them is breaking away from the group, and heading my way. He's tall, and probably about forty, and he's wearing a sharp suit and an even sharper smile.

'Waiting for someone?' he asks, as he reaches me.

'Mmm.' I turn away, slightly, to show that I'm not in a mood to be mocked. But this, I should have realised, is a mistake, because all it does is give the remaining blokes in the group a better view of my Rutland-sized bum, and they all start whispering and sniggering again.

'Boyfriend, I suppose?'

'No.'

'Husband?'

'No.'

'Oh.' He adjusts his tie, then takes a gulp from his pint of lager. 'So you're . . . single, then?'

I curse Lucy for being late and leaving me stranded like this, fair game for a smart-aleck businessman to take the piss out of me.

'Yes.' I can feel my face flaring. 'Actually, I have quite a few phone calls to make, so . . .'

'Of course. Sorry I bothered you.'

And he's gone, scuttling back to his group, who by now are all practically wetting themselves with laughter.

Just as I showily take my phone out of my bag, another of the men peels off from the group and comes my way. Actually, make that *swaggers* my way. He's the one who's been pretty much the ringleader in all the looking and whispering and guffawing: he's smoothly handsome, an Alpha male, and he knows it.

'Hey!' he greets me, in an upbeat fashion. 'I'm Alex. Listen, I just had to come over to say how sorry I am about Tim.'

I blink at him. 'Tim?'

'My mate over there. Sorry if he was bothering you. He's a bit of a pest, unfortunately. Always going after the best-looking women and getting shot down.'

I'm soft enough actually to feel sorry for Tim, for a moment, until I clock on to what this Alex guy has just said.

The *best-looking* women?

'We all told him,' Alex carries on, before I can process this any further, 'he stood about as much chance of getting somewhere with you as England have of winning the World Cup. But he persisted, bless him.'

'Er – yes. Bless him.'

'Anyway, the least I can do to apologise for all this infantile behaviour is buy you a drink.' He smiles at me, winningly. 'And one for the friend who's joining you, perhaps? If she's even half as much of a stunner as you, Tim will be hitting on her, too, so I might as well buy her the drink in advance to make up for it.'

My ears popped quite badly as the plane came in over Heathrow earlier, so it's possible that I'm just not hearing this Alex guy properly.

Because it sounded very much as if he's just called me a *stunner*.

And he didn't *look* like he was joking when he said it.

'Glass of wine, maybe?' he's continuing, his air of confidence starting to wobble, just slightly. 'Or a vodka and tonic? I mean, help me out here . . . sorry, I don't know your name.'

'Charlie.'

'Help me out here, Charlie! If I have to go back to my friends and say you wouldn't even let me buy you a drink, they'll take the piss out of me just like they were taking the piss out of Tim.'

'Oh . . . er . . . well, I guess maybe a glass of pinot grigio, or something . . .'

'One for you, and one for your friend! Coming right up!'

There's a noisy cheer from his friends as he spins round and heads into the pub itself, raising both arms in triumph as he goes.

Thank Christ, I suddenly see Lucy turning the corner towards me. I actually break into a brief jog to go and greet her.

'Jesus, Luce, I've never been so glad to see you in my life!' I throw my arms round her, and hug her very tightly. 'I've just had this weird experience with these blokes over there, and I'm thinking maybe it might be a good idea to move to a different pub . . . oh, but we can't now, of course, because he's buying us drinks . . .'

'*Charlie?*'

Lucy's expression is somewhere between that picture 'The Scream' and Macaulay Culkin in the posters for *Home Alone*. Her mouth is wide open and she's actually clapped both hands to the sides of her face.

'I . . . don't believe it,' she adds, rather faintly. 'You've *shrunk*.'

Shrunk may be pushing it but what I think Lucy is referring to is my weight loss. Which is approximately thirty pounds. OK – thirty-two pounds precisely. Fat girls like me don't do *approximate* weight loss. We know about every single pound of podge that we've painfully shed from our bodies.

Lucy prods me, disbelievingly – one finger jabbing my stomach, the other hand squeezing my upper arm.

'But . . . you never said you were going to try and lose . . . *how* much weight have you lost?'

'Um, a little more than two stone?'

'*Two stone*? Charlie! You said you wanted to shift a few pounds so that you could go and work at Elroy Glass without Diana being so horrible to you! You never said you were going to try and lose two stone!'

'That's because I didn't intend to lose two stone.'

Not that I'm going to claim a thirty-two pound weight loss just *happened*. I didn't lose thirty-two pounds down the shower drain one morning, by happy accident. I lost thirty-two pounds through hunger. Stomach-churning, mind-altering, wake-in-the-middle-of-the-night-thinking-about-garlic-bread hunger. Oh, and I also lost it through Natalie's five-mile sunrise runs. And her five-mile sunset hikes. And sit-ups. And lunges. Dear God, so many, *many* lunges. But I didn't plan to lose thirty-two pounds when I first arrived in California. It's just that, once the first six or seven pounds had gone, I began wondering how it would feel if I could pull off that trick of wafting, sylph-like, back into London after all.

'And more to the point, what's the deal with your hair?' Lucy croaks.

Ah, yes. My hair. The other thing Natalie talked me into.

Last weekend, I accompanied her on a drive into San Francisco, where she was going shopping for new jeans (which, thanks to Natalie's persuasion, I ended up doing too) and to have her hair cut and coloured (which, thanks to Natalie's persuasion, I ended up doing too). The woman in the salon trimmed my lank lengths into layers with – for the first time in my life – a long, side-swept fringe, and said she was going to take me 'five shades lighter' than my natural mouse. This didn't sound like it was going to be anything too drastic. But as it turns out five shades lighter than my natural mouse is *blonde*. A glowy, golden shade that the woman in the salon kept calling *honey-blonde*, and that looked great in the warm sunlight of Los Angeles but that I'm a tiny bit concerned, now I'm back in grey London, actually looks more like the silky blonde coat of Heidi, the Labrador Diana had put down when she realised I was getting attached to her.

'Do you hate it?' I ask Lucy, now. 'Do I look like Heidi?'

'Heidi the girl at the top of the mountain?'

'Heidi the Labrador.'

Lucy snorts. 'No, Charlie, you don't look like Heidi

the Labrador. Or Heidi the girl at the top of the mountain, for that matter. You look *incredible*. I mean, properly incredible. I hardly recognise you . . . yes?' she suddenly asks, as Alex reappears from inside the pub, holding an extremely large glass of white wine in either hand. 'Can I help you?'

'I was just buying a drink for you and your friend . . .'

'That's nice, but I'm afraid we have to go now,' says Lucy, linking an arm through mine and hauling me away from the pub, down the street towards Berkeley Square again. '*Charlie!*' she hisses at me. 'What the hell was that? You can't just go accepting glasses of wine from strange men in pubs!'

I could point out that many of Lucy's relationships, long-lasting or otherwise, started when she accepted glasses of wine from strange men in pubs, but all I say is, 'I think he was just being friendly.'

'He was chatting you up!'

'Don't be ridiculous.'

'Oh, I'm sorry, I forgot. Men *don't* go around trying to chat up skinny, tanned blondes. My mistake.'

'I'm not skinny . . .'

'No, actually, you're right on that one.' Lucy stops, ostensibly to cross the road, but actually to give me a bit of a once-over. 'You're better than skinny. You've only gone and got yourself all bloody *toned*. I mean, my God, Charlie, your *bum*!'

'All right, all right, I know. My bum's still massive.'

'Are you insane?'

'Well, it's not small.'

'True.' Lucy contemplates my rear end, concentration etched on her face. 'But who'd want a small bum when they could have one like that? All sticky-out, and firm, and bootylicious . . .'

'Luce, can we please, *please* stop talking about my bum?'

'But Charlie, you should be proud of it! *I'm* proud of it! I'm proud of *you*. You look so incredible. And not just your hair, and that bum . . . it's everything, Charlie. I mean, you know I always thought you were pretty before, but this is a different league. You have cheekbones, Charlie. *Cheekbones!*'

'Let's go in here,' I suggest, hastily, pulling Lucy towards the Starbucks we're just passing, 'and get ourselves a nice cup of coffee.'

'God,' she's still saying, as we join the back of a short queue. 'No wonder that guy was hitting on you at the pub. Ferdy is going to go absolutely *nuts* when he sees you. I still think he thought you were gorgeous before, but . . .'

'Ferdy?' I ask, sharply.

'Yes. Ferdy. You are going to give him a call, Charlie, now that you're back, aren't you?' Lucy fixes me with one of her stern looks. 'You've done all this hard work to make yourself look amazing. It can't just go to waste!'

'It isn't going to waste! I didn't do all this with Ferdy in mind. I didn't do it with men in mind at all. I did it to get a life.'

'It doesn't have to be one or the other. Men are a *part* of life, you know, Charlie.'

'Fine, but as far as my life goes, I don't think Ferdy is going to be a major feature of it.'

'And you know that how?'

I don't want to go into any details right now. Such as the fact that Ferdy didn't email me once the entire time I was away. He didn't reply to my email letting him know I was going away. Nor, indeed, did he reply to any of the three (OK, four) emails I sent after that. I'm sure he was busy with Chill and everything, but if he *really* liked me, the way Lucy seems determined to believe, he would have sent a couple of lines at some point, wouldn't he? Surely he would have found a spare minute to do that?

'I just know,' I say, hoping to put an end to this conversation. 'Anyway, I want to hear all about you! You didn't email me nearly enough while I was away. How's everything been going?' I order two coffees (a delicious creamy latte for Lucy and a miserable, calorie-free Americano for me) and dig in my purse for some British change to pay with. 'With work? With YoHoHo?'

'Work is fine. YoHoHo is *great*.' Her face lights up. 'I had a huge order for a *Pirates of the Caribbean* theme party in Woking just this morning. Oh, and there's another party customer in Croydon who's trying to get me to source them a plank.'

'What on earth for?'

'For walking the plank, I assume. I'm not sure why

they can't just go down to their local timber yard and get any old plank – actually, to be honest with you, I'm a little bit concerned about the whole walking the plank thing at all – but mine is not to reason why. Mine is . . . well, to sell them a plank, I suppose. That's what Pal says.'

'And how is Pal?'

I ask this in an upbeat and breezy tone. I missed Lucy so much while I was away that I decided I'm going to make a huge effort to be Entirely Positive about Pal from now on. If she loves him, it must be because there's something about him worth loving. And because I love Lucy, I'm just going to have to work overtime to find out what that something is.

'Pal's great. Actually, I have a bit of news on that front.'

'Oh, my God. You're not engaged, are you? I mean,' I say, hastily adjusting my tone so I sound Entirely Positive (as opposed to Dismayed and Distraught), 'has he asked you to marry him?'

'No, no. I don't think we . . . well, I don't think *he* is exactly at that point, just yet. It's still such early days, and it's not like either of us is in a hurry. It's not like it's a crime not to be married before you turn thirty, no matter what my annoying little sister . . . um, where was I?'

'You were telling me you have news?'

'Oh, yes.' Lucy takes our coffees from the barista and leads the way to a corner table. 'You have to come to a party this weekend, Charlie.'

'That's your news? That you're having a party this weekend?'

'Well, you haven't heard what kind of party it is yet!' She takes a deep breath. 'It's a flat-warming party!'

'You've found a new flat?'

'Charlie, you're being dense. Pal and I are . . . well, we're moving in together.'

Entirely Positive, Charlie. Entirely Positive, remember?

'Lucy! That's brilliant!' I lean across the table to give her a hug, and start talking a mile a minute, a sure-fire way of covering up any not-so-positive reactions that might sneak out. 'When did you decide? How did it happen? Are you going to look for a new place, or is he just moving in with you? Or are you just moving in with him? No – that doesn't make much sense for you, because he's all the way over in Docklands, isn't he?'

'Well, actually, I am going to be moving in to his place. In fact, I've already done it. Just this past weekend. I didn't want to tell you such huge news over email. Because it *is* huge, isn't it?'

'Of course it is. It's . . . it's terrific, Lucy.' I take a long, too-hot gulp of my Americano. 'Though it's going to be a bit more difficult for you getting to work, isn't it? All the way over from Docklands?'

'Maybe, but Pal works much longer hours than me, so it's really important that he's the one who stays closer to work. And with any luck, YoHoHo will take off, and I'll end up working from home anyway! Or, you know, maybe even further down the line, there might be a baby on the horizon, and obviously then I wouldn't be working at all . . . not that Pal and I have discussed that, of course, with regards to ourselves, but I know he's not a fan of mothers going back to work in general . . .'

God, Pal really does make this Entirely Positive thing difficult, doesn't he?

'. . . and talking of work,' she carries on (by the look on her face desperately trying to find a way out of this conversation), 'I want to hear what you're planning on doing. Not that you need to worry about work now that you're this huge heiress!'

'I don't think *heiress* is exactly the right word.'

'Oh, Charlie, please let me call you an heiress. It makes you sound like someone who runs around town wearing ballgowns and pearls and marvellous hats.' Lucy sounds wistful. 'Someone who goes to posh parties in country houses, and gets cornered in the conservatory by the disreputable son of a duke who does unspeakable things to you behind the papyrus . . .'

Tempting though it sounds to have unspeakable things done to you behind the papyrus, I need to drag Lucy back into the twenty-first century.

'But really, Luce, I'm not an heiress. Yes, Dad left me his shares in the business, but I'm not just going to go and cash those in.'

'Oh.' She looks disappointed, visions of the marvellous hats and the disreputable duke's son vanishing like fairy dust. 'You're not going to sell any of them?'

'No, because that would mean I have less than fifty-one per cent. And if I hang on to fifty-one per cent, that means I'm still the majority shareholder. And that means that it'll make it harder for Diana to push me around when I start working there.'

Lucy plonks her coffee cup down on the table. 'You're going to work there? In close proximity with the High Priestess of Mordor? The woman who can't so much as open her mouth without saying something horrible to you?'

'Well, she can't say I'm disgustingly fat any more, can she?'

'Charlie, you weren't disgustingly fat before, but Diana still kept telling you that you were. And if you're working alongside her every single day, she'll only find something new to torment you about.'

'Which is precisely why I won't be working alongside her.'

'I don't understand.'

'Well, while I was away, I did a lot of thinking about what kind of job I might be able to do for the company. You know, seeing as I'm not very qualified, or experienced, or anything.' I hold up a hand to stop Lucy before she can jump in. 'You know that's true, Luce. I don't know the first thing about the fashion industry, or about marketing, or about sales . . .'

'That doesn't stop half the people who get jobs in the fashion industry, or marketing, or sales,' Lucy mutters.

'Maybe not, but this is a big deal to me, Luce. And

134

I really need to try and play to my strengths, whatever they are. That's what I realised, when I was talking about this with Natalie . . .'

'Who's Natalie?'

'Oh, she was one of the trainers at the boot camp. You'd have liked her. I mean, when she wasn't yelling at you to run faster, or jump higher, or do another twenty lunges on each leg, that is.'

'Right.' Lucy takes a sip of her latte. 'Natalie sounds a barrel of laughs.'

'Well, she kept going on and on at me about how important it is to play to your strengths. Which I've never thought I had, really.'

'Are you crazy? How about the fact that you're an amazing cook? Or that you should really think about going to catering college and getting a job in a swanky restaurant? Or apply to go on *Masterchef*? Or sell your shares in Elroy Glass and use the money to set up your own party catering firm? And, you know, maybe go into business with your lifelong best friend, who just so happens to run a party *supply* firm, and who's starting to think about offering a pirate party catering option to her London customers . . .'

'Lucy, come on.' Tempting though the idea of party catering sounds, pirate-themed or otherwise, I need to focus. 'Dad left me the company he loved. And he really seemed to think I could do something with it. Which is when it occurred to me, Luce, what my strength is. It's Dad!'

Lucy glances nervously over her shoulder, as if she

thinks I've just seen the ghost of my father standing behind her, or something.

'Jesus, Charlie, thanks for freaking me out!'

'Sorry – all I meant was that my *strength* is Dad. Knowing him, I mean. Knowing what kind of company he wanted Elroy Glass to be. Knowing the way he used to run things, before Mum died, and before his Mad Morocco years, and before Diana started getting her claws into everything.'

'You're not actually talking about firing Diana, are you?' Lucy is looking even more freaked out than she did a moment ago, when she thought Dad had popped into Starbucks to do a little light haunting over a cappuccino and a blueberry muffin. 'Because if you have an actual death wish, I think there are probably a hundred less terrifying ways to fulfil it.'

'No, no. God, no. I'm not thinking of firing Diana.' I feel the need to reiterate this, just in case – I don't know – she's got my handbag bugged, or something. 'I wouldn't dream of firing Diana! I mean, I don't even know if technically I *could* . . . even if I did want to, which I obviously don't . . .'

'Relax. I'm sure she hasn't got your handbag bugged. Well, I'm *fairly* sure she hasn't got your handbag bugged . . . honestly, Charlie, you don't need to check.'

She says this because I've reached down to get my handbag. But I'm not looking for a bug (come to think of it, I don't even know what a bug would look like; that's probably something I should check out pretty sharpish). I'm looking for a torn-out magazine page.

'Here,' I say, when I finally find it and hand it over to her. 'I saw this in the *Sunday Times* I bought at Heathrow when I was on the way to America ten weeks ago. In the Style section.'

Lucy glances down at it. 'Er . . . it's a picture of a girl I've never seen before.'

'Yes. Melanie Morgan.'

'And Melanie appears to be . . .' she peers more closely at the page to read the accompanying bits of writing '. . . an assistant hotel manager from Brighton.'

'Yes. It's one of those pieces,' I add, helpfully, 'where they have little interviews with ordinary people who just happen to be quite stylish, and ask them all about the clothes they wear for work, and for going out, and stuff.'

'I see,' Lucy says, though she sounds as if she doesn't see at all. 'And Melanie's favourite outfit for going out is . . . *my Vivienne Westwood hobble skirt, layered vest tops from Urban Decay or Topshop, this Alexander McQueen clutch I snapped up for eighty per cent off at a flash sale on The OutNet, and these amazing Jimmy Choos that my husband bought me for my last birthday.* Huh. Why is Melanie Morgan married,' Lucy asks, pensively, 'and not me? I mean, don't get me wrong, she looks like a perfectly nice girl, but . . .'

'Lucy! Carry on reading!'

'Oh, right. Um . . . *My weakness is designer shoes,*

*which I treat myself to when I can afford them. I
have two more precious pairs of Jimmy Choos at
home, plus one pair of beautiful Gina peep-toes and
some Miu Miu knee boots that my friends are always
on at me to let them borrow. I desperately wanted
to wear Elroy Glass heels on my wedding day last
year – what girl wouldn't? – but they were so heart-
breakingly expensive that even I couldn't justify it!
So I went with a classic silver Jimmy Choo sandal
instead.'*

'So expensive that she couldn't justify it!' I repeat.
'I mean, did you know that these days Elroy Glass
shoes are a minimum of six hundred pounds a pair?'

'Well, yes . . . Charlie, are you telling me *you* didn't
know?'

'I didn't! I'm not even sure Dad knew, to be honest,
although he always got in an awful temper whenever
Diana sent the company accounts through. I mean,
six hundred quid a pair, Luce!'

'I know. It's crazy. Especially when the shoes are
so boring these days.'

I stare at her. 'What do you mean?'

'Oh, come on, Charlie, have you not even noticed
that? Elroy Glass shoes aren't exactly the kind you
swoon over. Not these past couple of years anyway.
I don't even know who's doing the designing right
now.'

'It's a whole bunch of people, I think. Freelancers,
some of them. When Dad got very bad last year, he
stopped even asking to approve the designs. But I

didn't realise . . . you never said you thought they'd got boring, Luce!'

'That's because I'm not really in the market for a six-hundred-quid pair of shoes.'

'Well, Dad never intended his shoes to be totally out of reach like that. You remember the customers who used to come into the store on Saturdays when we were little, don't you, Lucy? Most of them were just ordinary women who'd saved up to treat themselves.'

'Like Melanie Morgan does with her Jimmy Choos.'

'Exactly. And they'd come to the King's Road store, and they'd have a good old browse, and the shop assistants would offer them a glass of champagne even if they weren't necessarily buying anything. And Melanie Morgan got me thinking that maybe I should be trying to resurrect that.'

'Free champagne for a bunch of women who can't afford to buy the shoes?' Lucy snorts. 'Yeah, Charlie, I really think Diana will go for that!'

'No. That I should be trying to resurrect the idea that Elroy Glass shoes are an affordable luxury.'

'Ohhhhhh.' For the first time since I've been talking about this, Lucy actually looks as if she's got what I'm saying. 'Affordable luxury. I like that, Charlie!'

'Natalie says affordable luxury is a big thing these days, what with the economy and sustainability and everything.'

'I like it slightly less now that I know Natalie approves of it.'

I let this go. 'Anyway, I've been putting together this whole idea about launching a cheaper range of shoes within the brand. A kind of diffusion line, I suppose you'd call it. Only a very small range at first. I'd hire a recent graduate to do the designing, so hopefully that part wouldn't cost too much, and Elroy Glass has already got factories in Italy that could do the manufacturing. And I was thinking of calling the range Glass Slippers,' I add, suddenly shy now that I'm actually saying this out loud. 'What do you think?'

Lucy is staring at me. 'I think it's brilliant.'

'And the best thing of all,' I add, 'is that this would be a totally separate project. If I'm starting a new range, and trying to get the King's Road store back up and running, I'll hardly need to see Diana at all. Once I've gone there tomorrow and asked her if I can do this, that is.'

'You're not going to ask her. You're going to *tell* her.' Lucy bangs her hand down on the table. 'You own the bloody company, Charlie! You can march in there and tell Diana you're going to launch a range of moonboots for gerbils, and she can't say a bloody word about it!'

'Actually, I think she can. And I think she probably *should*, if I start suggesting moonboots for gerbils.'

'You know what I mean. She has to listen to you, Charlie, even if you're suggesting something stupid. And as it happens, I don't think Glass Slippers is a stupid idea at all. I think it's a really good one.

Providing you guarantee that I'll be given free samples of these new shoes, that is. In a size five.'

'If this works out, Lucy, you'll get all the free shoes you want!' I stop, because a counter assistant has just appeared at our table, hovering with a tray. 'Sorry, do you want to close up or something?' I ask her.

'No. I'm just bringing you these.' She sets her tray down on the edge of the table and starts unloading two large cappuccinos and two slices of blueberry cheesecake.

'But we didn't ask for . . .'

'They're from the guys over there.' The waitress nods towards a table in the far corner, where two men are sitting. They're wearing gym gear and look freshly showered, and they're grinning at us. 'I think they want me to tell you what nice guys they are, too,' she carries on. 'But the dark-haired one comes in here pretty much every day and he's always really rude to the staff, so in all honesty I can't give him a great character reference. I'd take the free coffee and cake, though. I mean, that doesn't happen every day, does it? At least, not to girls like me.'

I stare at her. Then I stare at Lucy.

'I *told* you men liked tanned, skinny blondes,' Lucy sighs, before turning to the waitress herself. 'If it's all the same to you, could we get those to take away?'

'Good decision,' the waitress says, loading the mugs and plates back on to her tray and heading behind her counter to pour the coffee into takeaway cups and put the cheesecake into paper bags.

'But we can't just take their food and drink and leave without talking to them,' I say. 'It's not polite!'

'And it's not very polite of them to think they'll get anywhere with a girl like you by sending over two smarmy pieces of cheesecake!'

I don't say that actually the cheesecake itself can't be blamed, that it looked totally delicious and not at all smarmy, and that it's been so long since I so much as gazed upon a slice of cake that I couldn't care less why it's being sent my way. I just say, 'Come on, Lucy, they're just . . . generous strangers. Being friendly.'

'Oh, Charlie.' Lucy gets to her feet, giving me the type of kindly, indulgent smile you see on the faces of doting grandparents when their toddler grandchild has just said something adorable. 'Charlie, Charlie, Charlie.'

'What, what, what?'

'You have much to learn, my child. But fear not,' she adds, linking an arm through mine, 'for I have much to teach you. Now that I'm all settled down with Pal, I'm absolutely *gagging* for a bit of action in the romance department.'

Seeing as she doesn't seem to notice the supreme irony of what she's just said, I don't think I'll point it out to her. Anyway, I'm too busy trying to smile pleasantly in the direction of the generous strangers without either Lucy or the waitress noticing. And, as Lucy takes the polystyrene tray of cappuccinos and the bags of cake from the waitress, wondering just how long my sunrise jog is going to have to last tomorrow morning if I eat one teeny little forkful of that cheesecake. Or maybe two.

Because let's face it, if I'm meeting with Diana tomorrow, even a mouthful or two of cheesecake will have nowhere to hide.

Chapter Seven

My paranoia about today's meeting with Diana is spreading like wildfire. It's the reason I was up at five-thirty this morning for an hour-long run along the Embankment, it's the reason I spent a further half-hour doing squats and lunges in the kitchen when I got back from my run along the Embankment, and it's the reason why, a couple of hours later, I'm sitting in the waiting area of this beauty salon, waiting for my name to be called for my threading appointment.

The salon is called Skin Deep, and it occupies a chopped-up bit of the premises in between Dad's old store and Chill. The prices seem pretty reasonable, for a King's Road location, probably because it's tiny, and slightly scruffy, and because (the owner must live in the bedsit above) it feels a little bit like you're sitting in someone's living room. In fact, the more I look around, the more I suspect that this *is* the owner's living room. There are old family photographs on the walls, a couple of birthday cards on the telephone table and, on the arm of the chair I'm sitting in, a copy of this week's *Radio Times*, folded back on itself and with a big red Biro ring around today's scheduled episode of *The Inspector Lynley Mysteries*.

But I'm not going to let any of these things put me

off, not when this meeting with Diana is lurking on the horizon. Lucy's right: even now I've lost two stone, Diana's radar will just zoom around until it finds a fresh weakness to lock on to. I can't predict everything she might choose to terrorise me about, but seeing as she's already roundly mocked me for thinking I could ever work in fashion (terrible hair and charwoman's hands, if I recall correctly?) I can certainly do my level best to match, as nearly as possible, the kind of women to whom I served tea and pistachio macaroons at Dad's memorial.

Hence my appointment here, to try to whip my eyebrows into suitably arched shape.

'Sharlee?' demands a middle-aged woman in white overalls, appearing from the treatment area at the back of the salon. She's burly and well muscled – and just as stern-looking as the family members glowering down from the black-and-white photos – and despite the fact she's running a beauty salon, her only concession to traditional femininity is the slash of glossy crimson lipstick she's wearing. 'For eyebrow threading with Galina?'

'Oh – I think that's me!' Highly likely, seeing as I'm the only person waiting. 'Actually, it's Charlie.'

'But you are here for eyebrow threading?'

'That's right. It's my first time, so—'

'This way, please.'

Galina leads me through a pale-pink curtain and into a small treatment room. It's windowless and faintly claustrophobic, and contains no furniture except for a paper-covered treatment table, a very bright electric lamp, and a wheely table, a bit like a hostess trolley, containing a hot-wax pot, splints of wood, bits of something that looks like dental floss and a couple of pairs of nail scissors.

'Gosh,' I say. 'It looks a bit like an interrogation room in here!'

She turns to look at me, hands on mighty hips. 'I grew up in Lithvania, part of former Soviet Union. Please, no joke about interrogation room.'

'Oh, God, I'm so sorry . . .'

'Father was four years in Stalin's forced labour camp.'

'Again, I'm really, really sorry.'

'You think eyebrow threading is same thing as torture by Soviet secret police?'

'Well, I've never actually had my eyebrows threaded before, but . . . no,' I correct myself, hastily. 'No, I don't think that. Not at all.'

'Good. Please, lie down.' Galina indicates the treatment bed, with its sheet of paper coating, and I hop on. A moment later, she's swung the lamp round, over my face, and is studying me through a large magnifying glass that's attached to it. 'You are never doing eyebrows before.'

'Yes, that's what I said.'

'Is no need.'

'No need to have them threaded?'

'No need to mention is first time. Is very obvious.'

'Oh.'

'And you are also wanting moustache done?'

'Moustache? I . . . I don't have a moustache.' *Do I?* 'They're just downy hairs above my upper lip.'

'Moustache and eyebrow threading at same time is fifteen pound. Eyebrow alone is twelve pound. Other facial tidy-up is five pound per area.'

'Oh . . . so it just makes financial sense to call it a moustache, then?'

She shrugs. 'If is moustache, I call it moustache.'

I'm not sure, as Galina advances on my eyebrows with a taut length of one of those pieces of dental floss, that it would be sensible of me to argue. I've already got on her bad side with the whole Soviet-interrogation thing, and the last thing you want to do is upset someone who's about to do something painful to . . .

Owwwwwwwwwwwwwwwaaaaaaaaaaaaahhhhh.

Painful? Did I just say painful? I was wrong: this isn't mere pain. There has to be a whole new word for this sensation. Even *agony* doesn't cover it. It's like a thousand red-hot needles being inserted into your follicles one by one, but at very high speed, before being twisted, to cause maximum discomfort, and then yanked out.

It hurts so much that I don't even make a sound. My vocal cords seem to have been paralysed.

'Now I do underneath brow. Is more painful than above.'

I can report that Galina is right.

I can also report that by the time she's done

underneath my left eyebrow and above my right eyebrow, the only thing that's preventing me from jumping off her table, running to the nearest police station and having her indicted as some kind of war criminal is the fact that if she doesn't do beneath my right eyebrow, I'm going to look like I'm raising one eyebrow at Diana. Which, obviously, isn't an attitude that she would take kindly to.

'Eyebrows done,' Galina announces finally, peering at them beneath her magnifying mirror for a couple of moments. 'Now your moustache.'

'No!' I find my voice. 'I mean, I've changed my mind about my . . . about the downy hairs above my upper lip.'

'You are finding very painful?'

'I am finding very painful.'

'Is pity. Threading is big improvement.' She reaches into the front pocket of her tunic and pulls out a hand mirror, which she holds up to my face. 'You see?'

It's hard to see, given that my eyes are still watering, but when they start to clear, I realise that Galina is right. My eyebrows do look much better. I'm not sure, yet, that the threading has achieved any 'opening up' of my face, the way the magazines are always telling you it will, nor that it's necessarily made me look five years younger, which is the other thing the magazines are always telling you. But these things may be more apparent when the bright-red colour wears off my skin. I'm just relieved, frankly, that there isn't profuse bleeding.

'You have moustache done next time,' Galina

suggests, standing back to allow me up off the treatment bed. She pulls open the pink curtain and we head out into reception again, where her next victim – sorry, *client* – is already waiting. 'When you are coming back for wax.'

'Er – *am* I coming back for wax?'

I mean, did I accidentally make an appointment, or something? The last two minutes are such a blur that I wouldn't be surprised what I'd agreed to.

Her own eyebrows shoot upwards. (I notice, for the first time, that she doesn't appear to be a devotee of threading herself.) 'You are not *waxing*? You are leaving legs *with hair on*?'

'No, no!' I say, in case the next client overhears and gets the impression I go about the place like a Yeti. 'I shave!'

'Waxing is better. But I tell all clients this. Not just hairy ones.'

The good news is that at least the rest of my face now matches my flame-grilled eyebrows. And the other good news, I guess, is that at least the next client is tactfully burying her head in a copy of *OK!* magazine. I grab a ten and a five-pound note out of my purse, hand it to Galina and mutter at her to keep the change.

'For this price I could have done moustache too,' she calls after me, reproachfully, as I make a dash for the door. 'I wait for your call, Sharlee. For booking next appointment!'

*   *   *

With the help of a few ice cubes, a dab or two of arnica gel, and a careful coating of concealer, my eyebrow area is both deflated and back to its usual colour by the time I arrive at the Bond Street store for my meeting with Diana at four-fifteen.

It's a relief, because it would have been ironic if, after all my other painstaking preparations for this event, bright-red brows had been the thing that blew it for me. Honestly, I think there are Hollywood starlets who put in less grooming time before an appearance on the red carpet at the Oscars than I've just done for this silly little meeting. The starlets are probably less stressed-out about it all as well. As for me, I can't exactly claim I've kept my cool. There was a last-minute panic when it looked like the new-me-sized clothes I'd ordered from ASOS (regular!) weren't going to arrive on time. Then, though they did arrive on time, I panicked again when it looked like the top I was most comfortable in didn't really go with the trousers I was most comfortable in and I had to make an agonising *Sophie's Choice*-worthy decision between top half and bottom. (Bottom half won, because the alternative to the trousers was a new pencil skirt which would have had to be worn with heels, and I didn't fancy the idea of falling flat on my face when I got up to greet Diana.) Then I took much longer doing my hair than I'd allowed for, because I still haven't quite got the hang of the new fringe and all the layers, and it takes me a good half-hour with a round brush and plenty of wrist-ache to blow-dry enough oomph into it. And then, of course, there was the fact that I hadn't factored in extra time to put those careful coats of concealer on my eyebrows before I even started the rest of my make-up.

Still, the final effect of all the effort and panic is . . . well, if a long way from Hollywood starlet perfection, then at least decent enough to make me confident I've got my defences shored up against my evil stepmother.

Well, confident-ish. There's a bottle of Rescue Remedy in my bag that's helping me with that final boost. Though right now, I can't help wishing I'd gone with Lucy's usual technique, and topped up the Rescue Remedy with a dash of Bombay Sapphire.

Because I'm a couple of minutes early, I decide it might not be a bad idea for me to go and have a little look in the store itself. Seeing as I'm, you know, sort of the owner now, and everything.

The Elroy Glass store on Bond Street is a pretty forbidding place. Gaby was responsible for the design, and it's so sleek and minimalist that there are only ever about three pairs of shoes visible, and even those are displayed in a rather off-putting fashion, usually teetering on narrow and extremely high Perspex units that make it clear you have to be almost six feet tall even to catch a glimpse of them. The rest of the place looks more like an art gallery than a shoe shop, with the occasional *photograph* of a shoe popping up on a large expanse of blank wall. I've not, I realise, actually been inside the store since I brought Dad here –

the one and only time he paid a visit – the week after it opened almost five years ago. Dad, of course, hated the new store in the way only Dad could hate things – simmering volcanically for weeks afterwards, with the occasional terrifying eruption – and I have to say I don't blame him.

Courage sufficiently plucked up, I open the door and go inside.

The sales assistant pounces as soon as I go in.

'Hello! Can I help you?'

'Oh, sorry, I'm not here to buy shoes.' I feel the need to apologise, because there are, in fact, no other customers in the place. This is in stark contrast to all the other shops I was glancing in as I walked along Bond Street just now. 'I'm here for a meeting with Diana.'

'Diana Forbes-Wilkinson?'

'Yes. Unless there's another Diana working here that I don't know about!'

The sales assistant just stares at me, her expression a mixture of blankness and mild hostility.

'Um, yes, Diana Forbes-Wilkinson,' I say, feeling foolish now. 'But I didn't want to bother you or anything. I was just popping in to have a little look at the latest collection.' (Which, by the way, doesn't look as if it's going to take me very long. As expected, there are only four pairs of shoes on display: three metallic strappy sandals and a pointy high-heeled court in nude patent leather.) 'Maybe I'll just go on up to the office, and . . .'

'*Charlie?*' This comes from Gaby, who's just appeared from the back of the store.

'Gaby!' Despite myself, I'm pleased to see her. Pleased, too, to see that she's abandoned her customary black, presumably as a concession to the warm day, and is wearing a pale-grey linen shift dress that makes her look almost winsome, for a change. On her feet are the nude patent courts that are displayed on one of the Perspex units in the middle of the shop. 'You look lovely!'

'And you look . . .' It would be an exaggeration to say that her mouth opens and closes like a goldfish – this is Gaby we're talking about, after all, and I'm not sure she's done anything like a goldfish one single time in her entire thirty-three years – but it certainly opens involuntarily before she gets control of it. 'My goodness, Charlie!' she manages, after a moment. 'That's quite the dramatic makeover! I thought you were just going travelling these past couple of months.'

'Well, you know. I thought it was a good opportunity for a bit of self-improvement.'

'You don't say!' Her gaze is sharp, now, as she gives me a keen once-over. 'You've lost weight!'

'Yes.'

'And your hair . . .'

'Yes.' Having already been through all this, and in precisely the same order, with Lucy, I'm not all that keen to go through it again. I know I was tired of being invisible before I lost weight, but it's not like I want to replace that with a minute level of scrutiny every time I run into someone I know. 'I'm here for a meeting with your mum!' I say, attempting to change the subject.

'With Mummy?' Gaby frowns.

'Yes.'

'This afternoon?'

'Yes.'

'Now?'

'Yes . . . look, Gaby, is there some kind of a problem? Is Diana out or something?'

'No, no, she's here. She's upstairs, in fact. In the boardroom.' This seems to remind her of something, and she turns her attention to the sales assistant. 'Pippa, does it *really* take you fifteen minutes to produce a pot of coffee? Are you roasting the beans yourself? Flying off to source them in Nicaragua like the man from the bloody Kenco ads?'

'No, I'm really sorry, Gaby . . . I got distracted by talking to this lady.'

This is pretty unfair of Pippa, because she's only been talking to me for the past minute, and she's not even doing a particularly stellar job of that. (I make a mental note, though, that the sales assistant is meant to be fetching coffee for Gaby. I mean, doesn't she have a PA of her own to do that?)

'Well, get a move on, will you? You know what my mother gets like when she's kept waiting for something.'

This is enough to send Pippa scurrying, at roughly the speed of Usain Bolt, in the direction of the little kitchen out the back of the store.

'Is Flora on holiday?' I ask Gaby.

'What?'

'Flora. Your PA.'

'Oh, no, Flora's left. Gone to get married, or have a baby, or something . . .' Gaby demonstrates, with a wave of her hand, the level of interest she has in the lives of her employees. 'Pippa is helping me out these days.'

'But she's the sales assistant.'

'What do you want me to say, Charlie? We're streamlining. Everyone has to make cutbacks every now and then.' Visibly irritated, she turns back towards the door that leads up to the office floors, holding it open so I can follow her. 'Well, if you're absolutely sure Mummy said four-fifteen, I suppose you'd better come up. But you are aware that everyone's here, aren't you?'

This doesn't sound good. '*Everyone?*'

'The company directors. Well, the ones who could make it at short notice. Mummy only called the meeting at three days' notice.'

Of course she did.

Three days ago is when I emailed Diana to ask if she could meet me some time today. And I'm quite sure her very next move, after replying to my email, was to get straight on the phone to the company directors and summon them all to a meeting at the very same time.

God, I'm such an *idiot*. I should have remembered that ritually humiliating me is one of Diana's very

155

favourite activities. But then I think my brain prefers to block out the memories of her stunts in the past. Such as the time she 'forgot' to mention that the window-cleaners were coming the same morning that she'd suddenly and unexpectedly suggested that I might like to treat myself to a Jacuzzi bath in her marble bathroom . . . Or the time she kindly coached me in a few basic German phrases to try out on Gaby's visiting exchange partner Karin, and I only realised I'd been duped when Karin herself very nicely took me aside and said that she was very sorry I was still wetting the bed every night at the age of twelve, but that it might make things easier for me if I didn't keep going around telling people about it.

And now Diana is trying to set me up all over again, springing a room full of intimidating, important company directors on me with absolutely no notice.

She'll have it all planned out: the sly put-downs, the poor-dear-you-aren't-really-following-are-you looks, the questions specially designed to make me look hopelessly out of my depth. This is the opening salvo in her war against me; a war of attrition that she hopes – no, she *assumes* – is going to end swiftly and with my total capitulation. The whole thing is designed so that I'll barely even make it to the end of the day without begging Gaby and Robyn to take my shares off me, and for a knock-down price at that.

And yet . . . well, if this is a war, I've got the potential for a bit of a stealth attack of my own, haven't I?

I mean, Diana's expecting me to creep into the boardroom looking overweight and under-groomed. And what was the whole purpose of the past ten weeks – the running, the lunging, the constant, gnawing hunger – if it wasn't to give me at least the external appearance of someone who *isn't* hopelessly out of her depth?

A phrase of Natalie's suddenly pops into my head, one she was fond of yelling at us as we dragged our exhausted bodies into the gym for a post-jog round of circuits: *fake it 'til you make it.*

Gaby glances back at me as she leads the way past the open-plan first floor and up on towards the boardroom on the floor above.

'You know,' she says, rather abruptly, 'if you'd rather just skip the meeting . . .'

'No. I'm fine.' I take a deep breath. 'As a matter of fact, there are a couple of things I'd like to talk to the directors about.'

'*Really?*'

'Well, *a* thing,' I say, a bit less confidently. 'Just the one, really. But still, a very definite . . . er . . . thing.'

Gaby gives one of her usual tetchy shrugs, makes the kind of face that generally goes with the expression *it's your funeral*, and pushes open the door to the boardroom.

Chapter Eight

The first thing I think is: *They're all men.* Half a dozen of them, sitting around the long mahogany table. But, of course, they're not *all* men, because there's a woman at the head of the table: Diana.

She's the first one to glance up as Gaby and I come in.

She's presumably been anticipating my arrival because for just half a second her face is fixed in its usual icy, superior smile.

And then she actually sees me. Which is when something else happens to her face. It contorts – so fleetingly that if you'd blinked, you'd have missed it – but it most definitely contorts. There's Diana in all her true colours, for the briefest of moments, her face all twisted up with the hatred she's usually so expert at concealing.

But there's something else there, alongside the hatred. Something even I don't think I've ever seen in her face before.

Is it my imagination or does she look *scared* of something?

If she does, she certainly doesn't for long. She's up on her feet already, the icy, superior smile safely back on her perfectly powdered face.

'Charlotte! My goodness!' This, it's instantly clear, is the closest she's going to get to openly acknowledging my new appearance. She comes to greet me, placing a kiss – purely for the benefit of her audience – in the vicinity of each of my cheeks. She smells, as usual, of Guerlain's Les Meteorites powder – a sweet, violet-heady scent that, thanks to her, I can't abide – and the Elnett hairspray that keeps her chignon in place. She's back in her high heels, of course, after February's bunion surgery, and looking somehow taller and more imposing than ever. 'We weren't expecting you.'

'You told me to come at four-fifteen.'

'Yes, but four-fifteen tomorrow.'

'You said Thursday.'

'Well, it can be difficult to get these things right, especially when you're not used to having to come to meetings, and so forth.' She slips one arm round my shoulders. 'In fact, this is why I purposely didn't ask you to come to this meeting today. I know it's a world away from the kind of thing you've been doing for the past few years . . .

'Charlotte's been such an angel,' she suddenly announces, to everyone sitting at the table, 'playing nursemaid to my late ex-husband, Elroy. There aren't many people who'd do the awful, undignified jobs she's had to do, let me tell you. Pureeing Elroy's vegetables, helping him in the bathroom, pushing him around the place in a wheelchair . . . I'm sure you all appreciate how difficult these things can be. Even if it *sounds* terribly simple and basic.'

159

It's the first battle of the war, and she's won it. Won it, in fact, without me getting off so much as a couple of shots of answering fire.

'Well, seeing as you're here, I really should introduce you to everyone.' Keeping one arm around my shoulders, Diana points to a large man with a shock of salt-and-pepper hair, who's sitting to the immediate right of her own place at the head of the table. 'This is Alan Kellaway, not only a director of the company but also our much-loved and terribly distinguished lawyer.'

'I know Mr Kellaway,' I say. I haven't seen him in years (his falling out with Dad – a falling-out that I now realise must have been due to Dad's last-minute alterations to his will – meant that he didn't come to the funeral), but I can see that he's not changed in all that time. I'm quite sure he's still wearing white Y-fronts and Argyle-pattern socks beneath his suit. I nod in his direction, but – knowing that he's got both his feet placed very much in his long-term mistress Diana's camp – I can't quite bring myself to smile.

'And I know Charlotte, of course,' Alan Kellaway says, nodding back at me. 'Though you've changed rather a lot since the last time I saw you, I must say . . .'

'So, who's next?' Diana carols, cutting Alan off before he can draw attention to my makeover. She waves a hand in the direction of two more of the men, both a good deal younger than Alan, and both of whom are staring at me so fixedly that I'm suddenly concerned I've got watercress from my low-fat

160

lunchtime soup all over my teeth. 'This is James Sadler and James Butterfield. They're from the private equity firm that loaned us the capital to build this very store five years ago. And this gentleman here,' she goes on, graciously indicating the last of the directors, an overweight and rather grouchy-looking man in a pinstripe suit, half-moon glasses and what looks like a cricketclub tie, 'is Terry Pinkerton. Of course, you'll recognise his name, Charlotte.'

There's no *of course* about it.

'Terry Pinkerton?' Diana repeats. 'Of Pinkerton French Gibbon? The investment group that have owned fifteen per cent of the company's shares for the last twenty years? Oh, dear, Charlotte – don't tell me you haven't so much as glanced over any of the company files I've sent you?'

'You haven't sent me any company files.'

Diana shoots an embarrassed, apologetic look at Terry Pinkerton of Pinkerton Dutch Baboon, or whatever his investment group was called. 'Well, Charlotte, you mustn't worry. It's perfectly all right to admit that you're still struggling to get to grips with all of this. Nobody would think any the less of you if you were finding it harder being the chief shareholder than you thought it was going to be!'

'Actually, you haven't sent *me* the latest files either.'

This voice comes from the corner of the room, and I realise there's another man in here who isn't sitting at the table, but stuck away at a lonely chair by the window, as if Diana is punishing him for something.

161

And she almost certainly is punishing him, because it's Oliver Winkleman, Dad's solicitor, who put her nose so permanently out of joint at the will-reading.

'Oliver!' I beam at him. I'm relieved beyond belief to see a single friendly face. 'Hi! How are you?'

'Oh, yes, I forgot. You two are great pals, aren't you?' Diana can't entirely keep the sour note from entering her voice. 'Was that why you were so keen to join us today, Mr Winkleman, even though you're not a director? Because you wanted to catch up with Charlotte after her travels?'

'But according to you, Charlie was meant to be coming to a meeting with you tomorrow.' Oliver gives Diana a pleasant smile. 'So it would have been odd for me to have been expecting to see her here.'

Diana, who didn't expect to find such implacable opposition in someone who looks so incredibly mild (she's not the only one), is too shocked to reply. Before she can gather herself, however, there's a knock at the boardroom door, and Pippa comes in with a tray of fresh coffee. I attempt to use this distraction to scurry over to where Oliver is sitting and grab the chair next to him, but Diana is having none of it.

'Oh, Charlotte, no!' she says, as I make a move towards Oliver's lowly corner. 'You're the most important person in the room now. You should be seated at the head of the table.' She steers me there and practically manhandles me into her own seat. 'Don't you all agree, gentlemen,' she adds, appealing to the rest of the table, 'that the new chief shareholder should really be the one running this meeting, now that she's graced us with her presence?'

'Mummy, come on,' Gaby begins, only to be interrupted by Terry Pinkerton.

'Actually, Diana, I think we'd all really just like to get on with the meeting, full stop.' His voice sounds about as grouchy and impatient as he looks. 'After all, Moscow could do with some more discussion . . .'

'Absolutely it could.' With a great show of humility, Diana scuttles back down to the far end of the table and slips into an empty seat. 'Charlotte, why don't you give us your thoughts about Moscow?'

'Moscow?'

'Yes.'

'My thoughts?'

'Yes!'

Time seems to stand still. Alan Kellaway, the two Jameses and Terry Pinkerton are all staring fixedly at me. Gaby is staring fixedly at the screen of her iPad. Diana is still smiling. Beaming, actually – she's positively triumphant at the imminent victory, her second in almost as many minutes, that she's about to chalk up on her scoreboard.

If I let her.

Stall for time: that's what I need to do. I pick up the pen in front of me, and pull a blank sheet of paper towards me, with a purposeful expression on my face.

'We're all waiting!' Diana sings. There's a joyous, mocking undertone to her voice that she's always seemed to reserve for her moments of special cruelty towards me.

It's this mocking sing-song that does it.

Fuck her. I mean, seriously. Fuck her. Who the hell does she think she is, setting up this whole elaborate scheme with the sole purpose of humiliating me? Wasting the time of everyone in this room, just to have the maximum possible number of witnesses there when I make a total idiot of myself.

I hold up a hand to silence her. 'Hold on one moment, please, Diana. I just have to think something through.' I write down the letters *ABCDEFG*, then the numbers *1234567*, all the while trying to look deep in thought. 'In fact, Diana, if you could possibly fetch me a cup of coffee, that would be much appreciated.'

Down the other end of the table, Gaby lets her iPad slip from her fingers. It thuds, gently, on to the table.

'Black, please. No sugar,' I add, when Diana doesn't move. I'm not meeting her eye. I write *Peter Piper picked a peck of pickled peppers* on the sheet in front of me, nodding sagely as I do so. 'Just a small cup will do.'

The temperature in the boardroom, by my reckoning at least, has fallen about ten degrees. I still refrain from looking up, but after a moment I hear Diana get to her feet and move, her heels tap-tap-tapping ominously, towards the coffee table.

Now I glance up, look directly at Terry Pinkerton and clear my throat.

'I think Moscow is a very interesting proposition,' I say. 'But obviously I don't want to tread on any toes. I'd very much like to hear your thoughts about it.'

'My thoughts?' He peers at me over his half-moon glasses. 'Well, I don't suppose it's the worst idea in the world to channel funds into opening a new flag-ship store in Moscow.'

Of course. A *new store* in Moscow. I write the words *new store in Moscow* on my sheet of paper, already feeling better than I did ten seconds ago.

'It does seem as though sales in the Russian Federation countries are up,' Terry Pinkerton continues, in his growly voice. 'And frankly, they're the only sales that *are* up, as you probably know.'

'Actually, Charlie may not know that,' Oliver Winkleman says, suddenly, from behind me, 'because she's not been given any of the relevant paperwork. And I'd just like to say that I am being fobbed off every time I try to get hold of any company docu-ments that I think Charlie ought to be allowed to—'

'Oliver, for the love of God!' Alan Kellaway turns round in his seat to glare at him. 'Will you stop banging on about company documents? Charlie is more than welcome to see any documents she wants. Isn't that right, Diana?'

'Of course.' Diana is heading my way, with a coffee cup in her hand. She doesn't look as if she's actually about to fling it into my face, but she certainly looks as if she'd like to. 'Here's your coffee, Charlotte.

Do let me know if there's anything else I can get you. Anything at all.'

I will myself not to flinch at the sarcasm. 'Thank you, Diana. But just the coffee is fine. Now, I was hoping to pick up on something we were just discussing. About sales being poor everywhere except Russia.'

'Sales aren't *poor*!' Gaby snaps.

'They're not brilliant,' one of the Jameses mutters, though he seems to regret putting his head above the parapet when Gaby turns on him, her eyes spitting fire.

'Sales are down *across* luxury brands, as it happens! I'm sure the struggling economy isn't something you've noticed in private equity, with your big, fat bonus cheques at the end of every fiscal year, but people aren't exactly champing at the bit to pay a fortune for a pair of shoes these days, what with their mortgages and their petrol bills to pay.'

Which is an opening for me to talk about something I *do* actually have a clue about, instead of getting bogged down in this Moscow stuff.

'Actually, that's something I'd really like to discuss,' I say.

My voice has gone a bit wobbly with nerves, but I try to distract everyone from this by leaning down to my handbag to get out the file I've been assembling.

'Um, perhaps I should start by telling you about a girl called Melanie Morgan . . . no, no, forget that!'

I say, hastily, as I see Terry Pinkerton's face crease further into grouchiness. I take a deep breath and start again. 'OK, look, what I really want to say is this. I think Elroy Glass shoes have become far too expensive. I think we're pricing ourselves out of the market. I know for certain that my father never intended for his shoes to be unaffordable by anyone but the trophy wives of Russian oligarchs. So what I'd really like to do is launch a small diffusion range of better-value shoes, and sell them in the old King's Road store.'

OK, it's not exactly the way I'd envisaged my presentation, but I think I got everything in there that I wanted. And nobody – yet – is getting up and leaving. Or laughing.

Well, not openly, anyway.

'Oh, and I'd call it Glass Slippers,' I croak, finally. 'In case anyone was wondering.'

'Hmmm,' Terry Pinkerton says, after a moment. He looks at both the Jameses. 'What do you think? Because that doesn't sound like a totally ridiculous idea to me.'

It doesn't?

'I think, Terry,' the other of the Jameses (James II) replies, 'that we'd want to see some sales projections. And a proper business plan. And of course we'd need to know how much it would cost . . .'

'I can tell you the answer to that right away!' Gaby is looking indignant. 'Too bloody much, that's what it would cost!'

'But I thought we'd be able to keep origination costs down by using some very new designers,' I say, 'and obviously you've already got all the production capacity necessary with the factories you've contracted for manufacture. And the old store is just sitting empty . . .'

'Because we haven't leased the place to anyone else right now. The moment we do, it goes back to bringing in a grand a week!'

'Sure, but a grand a week isn't going to keep the business afloat, if sales really are that bad.'

'I've already said –' Gaby slams her hand down on the table '– sales *aren't* bad!'

There's a bit of a silence.

A silence during which I suddenly notice that Diana is staring at me. She has the kind of expression on her face I imagine Marie Antoinette was wearing when a bunch of grubby revolutionaries stormed into her palace, packed her off to the Bastille and then started helping themselves to the best bits of furniture.

'Well!' she says, after a moment. 'It all sounds very noble to me! Now – am I right, Charlotte – you seem to be suggesting that we turn ourselves into some kind of . . . charity? Some well-meaning philanthropic organisation, dedicated to providing cut-price shoes for penniless unfortunates?'

'That's not what I said.'

'Should we rename ourselves, do you think?' Diana is in full flight. 'Stilettos for the Starving? Peep-toes For Paupers?'

'Oh, for heaven's sake, Diana. I don't believe that's what the girl's suggesting at all.' Terry Pinkerton is already getting to his feet, popping his half-moon glasses in the top pocket of his pinstripe jacket. He turns to me. 'Look, why don't you put together that business plan, like James suggested? Get something a bit more concrete on paper? I'm sure we'd all like another look at your proposal when you've taken it further.'

'Yes, of course I can do that . . .'

He nods. 'Good. Then I think we can leave today's meeting there. We can discuss all this – and the Moscow issue – at the AGM in a few weeks' time. I think a properly scheduled meeting will be far more valuable than a last-minute one,' he adds, with a meaningful look at Diana. 'Don't you?'

She nods, mute with fury, as Terry Pinkerton and the two Jameses start, with visible relief, to pack up their things and leave the boardroom. There's a bit of general chit-chat, between the men at least, and James II leans across the table to shove a folded piece of paper in my direction. When I open it, I see that it's a mobile-phone number, with the words *Drink some time?* scrawled above it in black Biro. I shoot him what I think is a polite (but Lucy would no doubt describe as over-encouraging) smile before he leaves, James I at his heels.

As the door closes behind them, Diana turns on me. Now that the main part of her audience is gone, she isn't looking so much like Marie Antoinette facing down the revolutionaries as Marie Antoinette a moment after the swish-thwack of the guillotine.

'Thirty. Five. Years,' she says. Her voice is deathly cold. It perfectly matches her expression. 'Thirty-five years I've run this business. And now I'm being lectured to in my very own boardroom?'

'Diana, I wasn't lecturing you.' I swallow. 'I'm sorry if that's what you thought I was doing. All that's happened is that I've come up with an idea, and I thought it was worth a mention.'

'Worth a mention in front of all the other directors? Before you'd even had the courtesy to bring it to me first?'

'I tried to bring it you,' I say. My desire to be treated with fairness trumps my usual fear of disagreeing with her. 'I was bringing it to you for our meeting at four-fifteen today. I wasn't to know you'd scheduled a directors' meeting for exactly the same time.'

'Look.' Alan Kellaway is getting to his feet. I'd almost forgotten he was still here, but now he's heading for Diana as if he's keen to hustle her out of the boardroom before she launches herself at me and starts scratching my eyes out. 'Why don't we just call it a day for the time being? Like Terry said, we can discuss it all again at the AGM. In the meantime, Charlotte –' he bestows on me a rather condescending, if not actually unpleasant, smile '– you can be getting on with fleshing out this little idea of yours.'

I have no time to reply, *What are you calling a*

'*little idea*', *you pompous windbag?* before he's opened the boardroom door for Diana.

'There's really no need for any kind of a scene,' he says.

Diana seems to be about to say that there is, very much, a need for a scene. But in the same moment it also seems to occur to her that she's probably just as able to make a scene with me another time in the near future. Probably – her preferred style – when there are no witnesses.

'Fine,' she spits. 'Let's go down to my office, Alan. That is, if it hasn't already been razed to the ground by Charlotte's zealous campaigners for freedom, equality and cheap ankle boots.'

'I'll see you back at the office,' Alan Kellaway says over his shoulder to Oliver Winkleman, before the door closes behind them.

Gaby, who has been studiously gathering up her papers and her iPad, turns to me the moment they've gone.

'Bloody hell, Charlie. Thanks for giving me fair fucking warning!'

'But, Gaby . . .'

'You said it was just a *thing*. You didn't say it was a suggestion to revolutionise the entire fucking *brand*. Which, as the brand's bloody PR director, you might think I'm entitled to a bit of a heads-up about!'

'I'm sorry, Gaby. I really didn't know Diana was going to . . . well, ambush me like that.'

'And whatever Terry said,' she goes on, as if I

haven't spoken at all, 'this Glass Slippers idea of yours isn't going to work.'

'Is it a bad idea?'

'I didn't say that. I said it isn't going to work.'

'But maybe if we just—'

'Don't –' she eyeballs me, looking uncannily like Diana for a moment '– tell me how to do my job, Charlie.'

'I'm not, Gaby. I'm really not. I just want to give this a shot.'

'Yes, well, you can give it all the shots you like – you can pepper it with machine-gun fire for all I care – but I'm not giving it so much as a bloody minute of my own time. I have an overloaded schedule already, you know, Charlie. I have a husband, and two children, and three stepchildren, and a nanny who wants to go back to Romania, and overdue bunion surgery that I can't find room for in my diary.'

Good grief: Gaby has bunions too? Is this something she's inherited from Diana, or is it simply the inevitable result of squeezing your feet into the kind of eye-watering shoes they both wear on a daily basis?

More to the point, is it a product of squeezing your feet into Elroy Glass shoes? I mean, I know Dad used to worry that manufacturing standards were slipping these past few years . . . but surely if you pay six hundred quid for a pair of shoes, you ought to be confident that they're not going to increase your risk of developing a painful and unsightly foot deformity?

'But, look, you're the chief bloody shareholder, lest

we forget,' Gaby continues. 'I'm not going to try and stop you. Just don't come and badger any of my staff. Everyone's far too busy already.'

'I wasn't going to. I'm going to take the lead on this myself, Gaby. Well, apart from the designing, obviously . . .'

'And, before you ask, no, there *isn't* anyone on the design side with the time to knock up some pretty pictures for you. Mummy's just sacked one of the freelancers we were using, and there aren't many others left who'll work for her.'

'Right.' At that I can't help feeling a little pang of worry that actually, things at Elroy Glass are worse even than I thought. 'If you wouldn't mind, though, Gaby, there is just one small favour I wanted to ask . . .'

'*Here* we go.' She rolls her eyes.

'May I have the keys for the King's Road store?'

'Oh. Well, I suppose that's fine. I can have my nanny drop them round to you, if you like.'

'If she doesn't go back to Romania first, that is!'

'What?'

'Well, you just said . . . never mind. That would be great. Thank you, Gaby.'

She snorts, unwilling to accept my thanks, and marches from the boardroom. The door bangs shut behind her.

'Well!' says Oliver. 'That went brilliantly, I thought.'

He's got such a lovely twinkle in his eye that I want to throw myself at him for a long, relieved cuddle.

'Oliver . . .'

'Olly.'

'Olly.' I take a step towards him. 'Thank you so much for helping me out!'

'It was nothing.' He's buckling up his briefcase. 'Somebody had to make it clear you were coming into the meeting entirely unprepared. And the way your stepmother is obfuscating all my attempts to get her to give you the up-to-date company accounts . . . well, it's nothing short of a disgrace!'

'I'm really grateful, Olly, for everything you're trying to do on my behalf.'

'Your father would have wanted it.' He gives me a shy smile. 'And, you know, you really did rather well just now. Honestly, Terry Pinkerton did seem genuinely impressed by your suggestion. For what it's worth, I think Glass Slippers sounds a terrific idea.'

'Thanks, Olly.' I open the door for him and we start down the stairs. 'I can't say how pleased I was to see you when I got here.'

'Well, I was pleased to see you. You're looking really . . . really brilliant.'

'That's nice of you to say.'

'Well, it's true.' In typical lawyer fashion, he seems to feel the need to back up his statement with a solid wall of indisputable facts. 'Your hair is different. Your clothes are different. You seem to have lost a good two or three stone . . . not that you needed to or anything!' he adds, obviously panicking when he realises how that just sounded. 'I only mean . . . well, you look nice,' he says, rather dismally, as we reach the bottom of the stairs. 'That's all.'

'Thank you.' I can feel myself getting flustered. Which is crazy, because I don't even fancy Olly, for Christ's sake.

Though I probably should, come to think of it.

I mean, I should probably *try* to.

Maybe it's just because I'm on a bit of a high, relieved that Diana's horrible ambush didn't come off (and did I really ask her to fetch me a cup of coffee?), but I'm suddenly thinking that Lucy might be right about men being an important part of life. Maybe I should be trying to make some kind of progress on this front.

'Olly, would you like to come with me to a party tomorrow night?' I hear myself say, all of a sudden. 'I mean, if you're not busy already, that is. Though it might not even be that much of a party, come to think of it. There are going to be quite a lot of serious Scandinavians there . . .'

'That sounds great.'

'Really?' I blink at him. 'What, even with the serious Scandinavians?'

'Oh, I've never let a serious Scandinavian put me off doing anything. Besides, this is a party thrown by your friend Lucy, right? The one I met at your flat? The one with the Norwegian boyfriend?'

'Yes.'

'Well, she seemed lovely.' Is it my imagination, or

175

is Olly turning ever so slightly pink in the cheeks? 'I'd love to come, Charlie.'

We swap mobile numbers, agree to text to make meeting-up plans tomorrow and then part, outside the store, to walk our separate ways, Olly towards his office on Brook Street and me towards the Tube at Green Park.

Chapter Nine

Admittedly I've not been on many actual dates before, so I'm not exactly an expert. But if this is what dating is, then it's great. I should have been doing more of it a long time ago.

I met Olly at Wapping station a little after seven, and we quickly repaired to a nearby wine bar where we found an outside table overlooking the river, drank glasses of nicely chilled rosé and had a lovely chat.

The only thing, I think, that would make it a really, *really* perfect date is if I actually started to fancy him, just a little.

It's stupid of me, because he is, I'm realising, quite good-looking, especially now that he's out of his work suit-and-tie combo. So while he's been chatting away I've been looking at different bits of him and trying to get myself all giddy and excited about the prospect of them touching different bits of me. You know, the way I can't seem to help doing whenever I see Ferdy, or that I couldn't help doing that time I met Jay 'sex-on-legs' Broderick. I stared at Olly's arms and tried to crank up a sweeping-me-on-to-a-horse fantasy, and when that failed I stared at his mouth and tried to spin a kissing-every-inch-of-me fantasy, and when that failed too (and when I think I started to make him a bit uncomfortable with all the staring) I gave up and just concentrated on listening to his stories about his sweet, funny-sounding family instead.

Anyway, now we've finished our drinks, and left the wine bar, and we've just got to Pal's building – which, I suppose, is now Lucy's building too. I press the buzzer for apartment 918, which is on the ninth floor.

'You'll really like Lucy,' I tell Olly, while we wait for her to answer. 'She's the nicest person I know.'

'Well, she seemed terrific when I met her briefly at your place.'

'Oh, she is. She's really terrific. She's funny, and sweet, and—'

'Hello?' comes Lucy's voice, over the intercom. There's some background noise: music and people talking. 'Charlie, is that you?'

It must be one of those video-entry systems. I wave at the intercom. 'Yep, it's me!'

'Well, who the hell is that with you?'

'It's Olly.'

'Olly?'

'You met him that time you came round for dinner. Dad's solicitor? Remember?'

'Oh, for Christ's sake, Charlie! He's not your *date*, is he?'

I'm slightly regretting the fact that I've just been describing Lucy as funny and sweet and the nicest person I know.

'Er . . . well, you didn't say I shouldn't bring anyone . . .'

'That's because it never occurred to me you *would* bring someone!'

'If it would make things easier,' Olly says, rather nervously, from behind me, 'I'm perfectly happy just to make my way home.'

There's a brief silence from the intercom, while I wait for Lucy to laugh and say he mustn't be ridiculous and to buzz us on up.

'Well, actually,' she says, after a moment, 'if you haven't come from too far away, or anything . . .'

'Lucy!'

'All right, all right.' There's a buzz and the door clicks open. 'You'd better both come up.'

I spend the entire lift journey apologising for Lucy's odd behaviour, while Olly spends the entire lift journey insisting that I mustn't worry about it. When we reach the ninth floor and get out of the lift, Lucy is waiting for us.

At least, I think it's Lucy. I have to blink a couple of times to be absolutely certain. I guess this is because I was expecting her to be wearing some version of her usual party outfit: something sparkly, perhaps, and rather small. Certainly not something a primary school teacher might wear for her first ever parents' evening, which is what she appears to be wearing right now: a below-the-knee navy-blue dress, prettily accessorised with a puff-sleeved cotton bolero and nude ballet pumps.

'Sorry if that sounded rude, just now,' she says to Olly.

'That's OK, I really didn't—'

'Yes, look, I need to have a quick word with Charlie,' she interrupts him, starting to usher us both towards an open door just along the corridor, which I assume is Pal's flat. 'So can you go and find someone to chat to for a bit? Everyone's perfectly friendly. I mean, quite a lot of them will be speaking Norwegian, which I know can be a bit off-putting at first, but if you butt into a conversation, they'll all be very happy to switch back into English instead.'

'Lucy, I'm not just going to abandon Olly to a room full of strange people!'

'Oh, for God's sake, Charlie, only *some* of them are strange.' Lucy shuts the door behind us. She grabs a full wine glass from a tray that's sitting on a console table in the tiny hallway, shoves the glass into Olly's hand and shoves *him* in the direction of one of the two doorways that lead off the hall. 'Even the Norwegian ones are mostly normal, when you actually get talking to them.'

'I meant *strangers*. I wasn't implying your guests were a bunch of weirdos.'

'Well, he'll be fine either way. Won't you, Olly?' Lucy doesn't wait for an answer before giving him another little jab towards the party. Then she grabs my hand and pulls me through the other doorway, which opens into the kitchen. 'Charlie!' she hisses at me, as soon as we're alone and the kitchen door is closed behind us. 'What on earth are you playing at?'

I stare at her. 'What on earth are *you* playing at?'

'Bringing a date! You never said you were bringing a date!'

'He's not a date. He's just a . . . new friend.'

'Bollocks.' She waves a hand, taking in my outfit. I'm wearing a new pencil skirt from ASOS, teamed with a black sequin top and black knee-boots with a safe, two-inch heel (well, I figure I've got to start somewhere on the high-heels front). 'You're dressed up all sexy for him.'

'Well, forgive me for trying to look nice for a party! Unlike . . .' I stop myself before I say anything about her own parent-teacher evening outfit. 'Look, I don't even fancy Olly, as it happens,' I say, but lowering my voice, just in case he's not found anyone to talk to, and is shyly hovering in the hallway outside with his wine glass pressed up to the door, or something. 'He really is just a friend. And he isn't even going to be that, any more, if you keep trying to get rid of him!'

'I'm not trying to get rid of him. I'm trying to clear a path.'

'Clear a path to what?'

'To you!'

OK, now I'm totally lost. The wine I drank earlier is making me foggy in the head, and the super-bright kitchen spotlights aren't helping either. In fact, the kitchen itself is freaking me out. And it would freak you out too, if you'd ever seen any of the kitchens in the various flats that Lucy has lived in before now. Not being the world's most enthusiastic cook, she tends to use her kitchens for general storage: books piled up on the counter, make-up strewn across the table, shoeboxes (I'm not making this up) stacked up in the oven. And things got more chaotic after she started up YoHoHo. There was a very good chance you'd wander into her kitchen to make a cup of tea and find the kettle and, indeed, most of the mugs were filled with bits and bobs of plastic 'loot' and brassy-gold 'doubloons'.

But here, in Pal's flat, the galley kitchen is pristine. Even though Lucy has only just moved in, there's not so much as a packing box anywhere on the spotless granite surfaces. Not only that, but there is evidence that the oven is being used for actual *cooking*, rather than the storing of footwear: there's a light on inside and warming-bready smells coming from within.

'Oh, shit, my blinis!' Lucy suddenly gasps, grabbing a nearby tea towel and yanking the oven door open. 'Do you think they're all right, Charlie? Not over-warming?'

I peer at the blinis. For a moment, I'm hit with a sudden craving – not just for the blinis themselves, which are exactly the type of food I can never, never eat again, but more importantly for the act of making them. I used to make great blinis: proper, full-sized buckwheat ones, whipped up to Dad's Aunt Esther's original Russian recipe, then layered with thick-cut smoked salmon and dollops of luscious, lemon-spiked sour cream. I'm going to miss cooking that way. I already miss cooking that way, now that I actually think about it. Although I helped out in the kitchen at boot camp, that wasn't so much Cooking as Shredding Raw Vegetables. And since I've been back, the most exciting thing I've done in the kitchen is whizz up some wilted watercress in the blender and turn it into something you'd have to be generous to call 'soup'.

'They're not overcooking at all. Actually, they could use a few more minutes,' I tell her, just preventing myself from actually salivating over them. 'God, Luce, did you actually make them yourself? Not just open up a packet, I mean?'

'Yes, but they were perfectly easy. Well, by the sixth trial run they were perfectly easy. It's Pal's mother's recipe,' she adds, looking a little bit pleased, as she bangs the oven door shut again, 'which was really nice of her, letting him give it to me, don't you think? I'm going to write her a thank-you card *in Norwegian*. Is that a nice idea, do you think? I've been thinking it's probably time to start learning a few words of it anyway . . .'

'I think that would be very nice, Luce – the card, that is.' I don't comment, in the spirit of being Entirely Positive, on her plan to start learning Norwegian. 'But can we get back to what we were just saying? About you clearing a path for something?'

'Not something. Someone. I just can't bear the thought that you're going around the place looking like a million dollars, but still being too shy to *do* anything about it.'

'Do anything about what?'

'About you and Ferdy.'

'Lucy, there isn't any me and Ferdy.'

'Well, not right now. But that could all change. If – say – you were to run into him at a party. Or something.'

'That's hardly likely. We don't go to the same parties. I'm not friends with anyone he's friends with.'

'That's not true. You're friends with me.'

'Yes, but you're not friends with Ferdy . . .' Something, very slowly, is starting to dawn on me. '*Are you?*'

'I wouldn't say we're exactly best buddies . . .'

'You only met him once!'

'Well, maybe he just happened to remember that I worked for The Bespoke Planet, and maybe a few weeks ago he started to plan a surprise fortieth wedding anniversary cruise for his parents, and maybe he gave me a call, and maybe I've been sorting out that cruise for him, and maybe when he came into the office the other day I asked if he wanted to come to my house-warming party tonight . . .'

'Lucy, stop saying *maybe*. Did all those things happen, or didn't they?'

'Yes. They did.'

'So . . . Ferdy is coming here tonight?'

'Yes! Now you see why I don't want this Olly person cluttering up the place! Unless . . .' She grabs my arm, her eyes suddenly shining. 'You know, maybe it's a *good* thing you brought Olly along with you. Maybe it'll make Ferdy a little bit jealous! Maybe he needs to realise there are other men going after you. Come to think of it, maybe I should go and introduce you to a few of Pal's friends, for you to start flirting with before Ferdy gets here. Well, OK, not *flirting* – in fact, Charlie, you have to absolutely promise me you won't attempt to flirt with anyone at all, not even Ferdy. Just be yourself, and—'

I cut her off, before she can insult my flirting skills any further. 'I can't believe you've gone behind my back like this!'

'But it had to be behind your back. You'd only have chickened out of coming otherwise.'

'I wouldn't have chickened out.' (Not true: I probably would have chickened out.) 'I just think it's going to be horribly awkward, that's all. I mean, he obviously doesn't have any interest in me, even as a friend, or he'd have kept in contact while I was away.'

'Well, that simply proves that the two of you are just as hopeless as each other,' Lucy decides, optimistic as ever. 'We all know he already liked you . . .'

'*You* know that, Luce. I'm not sure anybody else does.'

'Come on, Charlie. Would he really have given you all that help when your dad was ill, if he didn't like you?'

'He's a good person.'

She ignores this. 'It's so obvious just how much you like him . . .'

'It's not obvious.'

She ignores this, too. '. . . and when he sees how

185

incredible you look now, he's not going to be able to keep his hands off you! All I'm doing is facilitating the inevitable.'

Lucy seems so sure that I'm actually starting to wonder if she might be right. If there really *is* a chance that Pal's pristine, rather chilly flat could be the unlikely scene of my misty-moor fantasy; that any moment now, the kitchen door will fly open and in will come Ferdy, looking tall, broad and appealing; that his jaw will drop open and his eyes will light up; that he'll stride across the granite floor tiles and sweep me up into his arms . . .

I get the surprise of my life when, all of a sudden, the kitchen door *does* fly open.

But sadly it's not Ferdy standing in the kitchen doorway. It's Pal.

'Lucy, I thought we agreed you'd have the first round of hot canapés ready at quarter to nine . . . oh, hel*lo*,' he suddenly says, his mouth upending itself into a smile when he sees there's someone else in the kitchen with her. 'You must be one of Lucy's friends! I don't think we've met.'

'Pal!' Lucy gives a nervous laugh. 'This is Charlie!'

'Oh, you have two friends called Charlie?'

'No, I have one friend called Charlie.'

'No. You obviously have two friends called Charlie. The fat one, and this one.'

'I am the fat one,' I tell him, crisply, before turning back to Lucy. 'Luce, actually, I think you might need to get those blinis out now . . .'

'Shit!' She grabs her oven glove again and pulls the oven door open. The blinis within are just starting to brown, marginally too much, around the edges. 'Are they salvageable?'

'More than salvageable. A little bit of crunch makes them even tastier, in fact. Look, why don't I help you get them topped with smoked salmon and sour cream?'

'No! You have to go out and start, you know, *enjoying the party*. Before other people get here.' She shoots me a meaningful look. 'Actually, there are one or two people I'm sure Pal would like to introduce you to. Why don't you go and take Charlie to meet Stefan, babe?'

'Stefan? Are you crazy?' Pal looks irritated. 'After what he did to Britta Jensen at Erik's Christmas party?'

'Charlie will be fine.' Lucy is fussing over her blinis. 'You can handle yourself, can't you, Charlie?'

I shoot her a look that says this may depend on exactly what Stefan *did* do to Britta Jensen at Erik's Christmas party.

'Oh, Stefan's harmless,' Lucy says (which is precisely the word people use on the TV news when their next-door neighbours have just been arrested for burying dozens of dead bodies beneath the patio). 'Look, I just need peace and quiet in here for a couple of minutes, OK?'

The rising tone of her voice suggests I should probably obey her instructions. Anyway, I don't really have a choice, because Pal is opening the kitchen door and ushering me out towards the living room.

This is where the party is really happening. Though 'happening' is a bit inaccurate. In all honesty, 'party' is a bit inaccurate.

There are about two dozen smartly dressed, mostly blonde and more-than-averagely-tall people standing around in Pal's neat, grey-toned living room, sipping glasses of white wine and nibbling neat little rounds of rye bread with pretty toppings, and engaging in what, if I spoke Norwegian, I could probably identify as extremely serious conversation. There are strains of something Vivaldi-ish coming out from a set of Bose speakers on a side table.

I may not have managed to get out to many parties while Dad was ill, but I do remember the parties Lucy used to throw, back in the old days, and this looks absolutely nothing like them. Lucy's parties were usually inspired by a general theme – Mexican Fiesta, Mafioso Wedding, Barbados Beach Barbecue – to which she would fit whatever lethal cocktail she'd made up for the night, and whatever takeaway food best matched it. She was good at inviting an entertaining mix of people, too, chucking in old schoolfriends and new university friends with a few random neighbours and a couple of long-lost cousins for good measure.

I suppose it is *possible* that Lucy picked Scandinavian Accountants' Conference as her theme for the night. But it doesn't seem terribly likely.

'Let me get you a glass of wine, Charlie,' Pal says, steering me towards the table that's been lined with perfectly aligned rows of glasses and bottles of white wine encased in those foil chiller sleeves. 'Unless you're not drinking tonight?'

'Why would I not be drinking?'

'Well, you've obviously lost a *lot* of weight. So maybe you're training for something. And I never drink when I'm training for something. Alcohol is just empty calories.'

'I'm not training for anything. And, yes, I would like a drink. A large one.'

Which is probably a very bad idea, because alcohol really *is* nothing but empty calories: empty calories that will almost certainly go straight to my bum. My blood runs cold, momentarily, at the mere thought of the number of lunges I'm going to have to do to get rid of them. And I know how crazy it is to be depriving myself of so much as a single blini when I'm perfectly happy to knock back booze by the bucketload. But this is Lucy's fault. If she hadn't invited Ferdy, I wouldn't be feeling the need to knock back booze, by the bucket or any other kind of load.

'White wine?' he asks, lifting an open bottle.

'Red, please, if you've got it.' (Red is higher in alcohol, so I can consume fewer empty calories but still get comfortably sloshed; you can't say I'm not being creative here.)

'No, it's white only.' He starts pouring me a glass. 'I can't trust Lucy to go about the place pouring red wine for people! She's such a . . . what's that English expression . . . butterfingers?'

With an enormous effort, I manage not to take the glass from his hand, upend it over the pale-grey carpet, and say, *Is that what you mean by butterfingers?*

'So, you must be doing some pretty hardcore gym work,' he continues. 'Are you running . . . are you rowing? It's hard to get that kind of lean muscle mass without putting in the hours on the treadmill.'

'Actually, Pal, I think I'd better go and find the friend I came with.' I can see Olly again now, as a gap opens up between groups. He's engaged in conversation with a pair of absurdly tall men, one of whom is wearing – without irony or embarrassment – an actual neckerchief. Olly is looking slightly desperate, bless him, though he shoots me a brave smile and gives me a little wave, much in the manner of a doomed soldier being sent off to war. 'But thanks for the drink . . .'

'Now, what I've been doing in the gym lately –' Pal either hasn't noticed I've spoken, or (more likely) has just unilaterally decided that what I've said isn't as important as what he's about to say '– is some very intense fartleks.'

This is far, far more information than I want from him.

'Right. Oh, dear. Have you been eating more beans than usual, or something?'

'*Fartleks*,' he repeats, pouring himself a very small glass of wine and leaning back against the wall, as if he's settling in for a long chat. 'It's a kind of interval training, developed in Sweden. Haven't you heard of it?'

'No, I can't say I . . .'

'I start out with a steady ten-minute jog on the treadmill, followed by a five-minute recovery phase, and then I start a repetitive series of very fast one-minute sprints, interspersed with one-minute brisk walks . . . oh, I think you know those people who are just arriving,' he says, suddenly, nodding over my shoulder towards the door. 'Weren't they at your flat the time I came round for that dinner party?'

I turn round to look.

Lucy is coming through the doorway, carrying a platter of smoked salmon blinis and wearing an expression of sheepish fury. Behind her, holding hands, are Ferdy and Honey.

Holding hands.

'I suppose you'd better come and say hello to Charlie,' Lucy is telling them. 'Charlie, look who it is! And look who he's brought with him.'

'Well, he really had to bring me with him!' Honey says. She looks, if anything, even more adorable than the last time I saw her, wearing another of her little skater skirts with an I Heart New York T-shirt, her blonde hair in a springy ponytail. 'I am his girlfriend, after all!'

I'm not sure who looks the most shocked: me and Lucy, on hearing this declaration from Honey; or Ferdy and Honey, as they come face-to-face with the brand-new me.

'Oh! My! God!' says Honey, after a moment. '*Charlie?*' She turns to look up at Ferdy, pulling on his arm like a little girl attracting attention. 'This is the same Charlie whose dinner we went to?'

'Yes.' Ferdy's mouth is half open. Though not, I have to say, in a very good way. He looks less like a man in the throes of desperate lust and more like a man suffering from severe constipation. 'Yes, this is that Charlie. At least, I *think* it is . . .'

'Yes, it's me.' I beam at them both, brightly, to make up for the fact that Lucy is still scowling. 'It's . . . great to see you both!'

'I had no idea you were back,' he says, looking more constipated than ever.

'Well, you didn't even tell *me* she'd gone away!' Honey says, reproachfully. 'One of your very best friends, Ferd, and you didn't bother to mention that she'd gone somewhere.'

I'm not sure how Honey has formed the (inaccurate) impression that Ferdy and I are close enough to be described as 'very best friends', but it certainly can't be because of anything Ferdy himself has said to her. After all, the fact that he didn't mention that I'd gone away, coupled with the fact that he didn't reply to any of my emails, is pretty convincing proof that he barely thinks of me as any kind of a friend at all.

'And you know I'd been wanting to get in touch with Charlie,' Honey continues to scold him, 'to thank her for being the one who got us together!'

This is news to me. 'I got you together?'

'Yes! It was that night we came to your flat for that amazing dinner! I was all upset about my cat, remember? Well, we got so much closer after that night that honestly, Charlie, if it weren't for you and that dinner, it might never have happened!'

'Oh, I'm sure you'd have found a way,' Lucy mutters. 'Blini?' she adds, shoving her platter under Honey's and Ferdy's noses, with not inconsiderable violence.

'Er . . . Yeah, I guess I'll have a blini,' Ferdy says, sensibly accepting.

'So, Charlie,' Lucy goes on, 'do you think Olly would like a blini too? Olly's the guy Charlie came with,' she goes on, before I can even answer. 'See – that good-looking guy over there, talking to the guy in the . . .' she stops, seemingly unable to utter the word *neckerchief*. '. . . scarfy thing.'

'Oooh, *Charlie*, you've got a new *boyfriend*!' Honey squeals.

'He's not my boyfriend. We're just friends.'

'Friends with *benefits*,' Lucy says, with a meaningful look at Ferdy. 'If you know what I mean.'

'*I* don't know what you mean,' Pal says, irritably. 'What kind of benefits are you talking about? Does the guy work for Social Services, or something?'

'Hey, isn't he the guy who came round when we were all having dinner?' Ferdy asks, craning his neck to see Olly across the heads of the tall people surrounding him.

'Exactly! He's been after Charlie for ages,' Lucy says. 'Though of course he's only at the front of the queue. A *very long* queue.'

I know Lucy's trying to help, but she's managing to make me sound like a bit of a slut. I don't know if this is better or worse than the last time she tried to Talk Me Up to Ferdy, and succeeded in making me sound like Mother Teresa.

'Well, I'd love to go and say hi to him!' Honey says. 'Find out all the gossip about him and Charlie!'

'Oh, brilliant, I'll take you over there.' Lucy sounds more friendly towards Honey than she ever has before. In fact, she even hands Pal her platter of blinis, just so that she can slip an arm through Honey's and start to lead her towards Olly. 'Babe, would you mind taking those round before they get cold? You're an angel, thank you.'

Which means – thanks, Lucy – that Ferdy and I are left alone.

We just sort of blink at each other, in silence, for a couple of moments.

I note that he does, as expected, look tall, broad and appealing. He's wearing nice jeans, and a dark-grey T-shirt that matches the colour of his eyes, and his dusty-brown hair is all sticking up in its usual haphazard tufts, making me wish I could just reach out and rearrange it.

'Um,' I begin, just as Ferdy also speaks.

'So!'

So is, obviously, a lot more promising than *um*, so I give him the floor.

'It really is . . . it's good to see you, Charlie.'

'You too.'

'And you look so . . .'

I wait, with bated breath.

'. . . different!'

I know, in an instant, that Lucy was right.

Because I know, right now, that I didn't do this big makeover *just* because I wanted to make something of my career. It must have been a little bit because of Ferdy, too, if this crushed, miserable feeling I'm getting right now is anything to go by.

Obviously I didn't really think he was going to do that Roger Rabbit, eyes-on-stalks thing, no matter what Lucy was insisting earlier. And obviously, now that he's actually got a girlfriend, that's even more unlikely.

But I can't deny that I was secretly hoping for something a little bit better than *you look so different*.

'I honestly don't think I'd even have recognised you,' he carries on. 'I mean, I was hoping that when you got back, you might be able to come to the new parlour and taste-test a few of the new flavours I've been working on. Mint Crisp. Coconut Choc-chip. But you don't look like you've been doing too much ice-cream tasting these past couple of months.'

'No.' I don't want to admit that I'll never actually be able to eat ice cream again. That merely thinking about Coconut Choc-chip ice cream is enough to make me gain a stone. 'Not much.'

'And it's not just . . .' He stops. 'It's the hair, and the tan . . . is that *fake*, by the way?'

'Um, no, as a matter of fact. It was pretty sunny in California.'

'Of course. Sorry. I just assumed . . . I mean, Honey's always sloshing on fake tan, so I thought maybe . . .'

'Hey, talking of Honey . . .' If nothing else, so that we don't have to talk about fake tan any longer. 'What brilliant news that you've got together! I'm really happy for you. She seems such a great person.'

'Yes. But how about you and this . . . Olly, is it?'

'Oh, God, no, we're really not together!'

'I know, I know, you're just – what was it Lucy said – friends with benefits?'

I'm about to mount a strenuous denial of this when I realise that Ferdy is looking at me a bit oddly. He's gone from looking constipated to looking as if he's just eaten something that's disagreed with him.

Either Lucy's home-made blinis are less successful than they look, or – can this possibly be? – Ferdy is more bothered by Olly than I thought.

Well, I guess the only way I'll know for sure is if I test out the waters. I attempt to look coy, and take a little sip from my wine glass.

'Well, you know how it is,' I say. 'Trying to navigate that tricky area on the edges of the friend zone!'

(*The friend zone* is something I read about in that same copy of the *Sunday Times* Style magazine as I read about Melanie Morgan and her luxury-shoe habit.)

Ferdy just blinks at me and repeats, rather blankly, 'The friend *zone*?'

'Yes, you know – the, er, zone where you're stuck being friends?'

'Hang on – is that the same thing as the queue?'

'It isn't a *queue*,' I explain, patiently, 'it's a *zone*.'

'No, I meant that Lucy was talking about there being a queue of guys lining up to get their hands on you . . .'

'Oh, that! No, no,' I say, hastily, 'there's no queue.'

'I thought not.' He seems to relax visibly, as if the room has been spinning on its axis and now it's mercifully righted itself again. He even smiles properly, for the first time since he's arrived. 'I mean, a whole queue of guys? I really don't see it, Charlie.'

Which makes me feel, just a little bit, like finding the nearest quiet corner, curling myself up into a ball and dying.

I mean, it's bad enough that Ferdy so obviously doesn't fancy me himself. But now he's implying – no, he's out-and-out *saying* – that he doesn't think other men are going to fancy me either.

'There may not be a queue,' I hear myself say, coldly, 'but there's certainly a . . . a string.'

Now his smile broadens. 'A string?'

'Yes! A string! A string of . . . of suitors.'

He presses his lips together, clearly trying not to laugh.

'I'm sorry,' I snap, 'if that seems so terribly amusing to you.'

'Charlie, I'm not amused. It's just a funny expression, that's all . . .'

'Because I'll have you know, I'm practically beating them off with sticks at the moment, Ferdy. Only the other day, I had men offering me glasses of pinot grigio in the pub, and buying me slices of cheesecake at Starbucks!'

'I hope the stick you were beating them off with wasn't too big, then. Because that could have made a nasty mess of the cheesecake if you weren't careful.'

I glare at him. 'I said I was *practically* beating them off with sticks. Obviously I wasn't actually . . .' I break off, because I can see that Honey is heading back our way. 'I thought you were going to talk to Olly,' I say, as pleasantly as I can, when she reaches us.

'I did, for a bit, but I wanted to ask him all about you, and he's kind of stuck in this really boring conversation with those tall guys. I think they're talking about the differences between Swedish and Norwegian. Your friend Lucy seemed really interested, though, so I left her to it!' Honey dimples at me. 'But you two seem to have been having a good old catch-up! Lots to talk about, I can see!'

'Oh, not much,' I say, at the exact same time as Ferdy speaks.

'We were just chatting about work, and stuff.'

No, we weren't.

Unless I've been hallucinating for the past five minutes, we weren't talking about work at all.

I give Ferdy a bit of a look, trying to understand why he's suddenly got that constipated expression back on his face again, but he isn't quite meeting my eye.

'Oooh, yes, Lucy just told me you'd inherited your dad's whole business!' Honey's blue eyes are wide. 'So are you the boss now?'

'God, no. That's still my stepmother.'

'But you must be doing *something*?'

'I'm just trying to set up a very small new range, that's all. It probably won't even get off the ground.' I don't quite know why, but I feel the need to make everything sound slightly silly. Maybe Honey's techniques are rubbing off on me. 'There's loads of ways it can go wrong. I have to find a designer, and get the King's Road store refurbished, and—'

'King's Road? The one next door to Ferdy's new ice-cream parlour, you mean?'

'It's next door but one,' Ferdy says. He says it quickly, and firmly, as if he's worried I'm going to be popping in for cups of coffee every five minutes. 'Not next door.'

'Even so, you'll practically be neighbours! Gosh, how nice for you both!'

'Well, we'd better let Charlie go and spend at least some of the evening with her . . . with Olly,' Ferdy says, rather abruptly. 'And we can't stay much longer anyway.'

'We have to be at Ferdy's parents early tomorrow morning,' Honey informs me. 'We're all getting the train to the coast for a beach picnic to celebrate his dad's birthday.'

So things are already that serious between them, then?

'That reminds me,' I blurt, in an attempt to cover any hint that I'm a bit disconcerted. 'I haven't seen your dad for ages, Ferdy. Not since Dad's funeral. I really must give him a call to wish him a happy birthday!'

'So you *know* Martin and Maria?' Honey looks disconcerted herself, for a moment.

'Well, I know Martin.'

'Oh, my goodness, then you should come along with us tomorrow!' She grabs Ferdy's hand. 'Wouldn't that be nice, sweetie?'

'Charlie's very busy. With work and everything,' Ferdy says. He doesn't look at me. 'Aren't you, Charlie?'

'But it's a Sunday,' Honey says. 'She can't be working on a Sunday.'

'Ferdy's right. I am very busy. Work, and . . . and Olly . . .' I catch his eye across the room, which is harder work than I'd like, seeing as he's engaged in what looks like a fairly intense discussion (about Norwegian and Swedish? *Still?*) with Lucy and Neckerchief Man. 'I should really go and rescue him, and let you two be on your way!'

We all troop over to Lucy, so that Ferdy and Honey can say goodbye and apologise for their appearance being so brief, and so that I can inveigle Olly away before Ferdy asks him any pointed questions about being in the friend zone, or anything.

I lure Olly back to the drinks table on the promise of a refill of white wine, and I've just started to ask him if he's having as awful a time as I suspect he is when we're rejoined by Pal and three assorted Scandinavians, all looking for wine refills themselves, and all eager to discuss the scintillating, party-appropriate topic of the looming British pensions crisis, and how this upcoming disaster has been avoided in the Swedish and Norwegian economies.

Chapter Ten

Gaby doesn't send the nanny over with the keys to the store until Monday evening, so it's already Tuesday morning when I head to King's Road to take a proper look. I'm a few minutes away when my mobile starts ringing. You'll understand my shock (because it's only just gone half-past nine in the morning) when I see that it's Robyn calling.

'Robyn!' I answer the phone. 'Are you *up*?'

'Are you *skinny*?' she snaps back at me.

'Sorry?'

'I've literally just got back from a long weekend in Miami with Yevgeny, and Mummy has left a message on my landline telling me you're back from your travels and you're skinny!' She sounds distraught. '*How* skinny, Charlie? Are you, like, *model* skinny? Are you skinnier than Gaby? *Are you skinnier than me?*'

'Robyn, calm down. I'm not skinny at all.'

'But Mummy said . . .'

'I've lost a bit of weight.' I leave aside, for the time being, the interesting fact that Diana has been leaving messages for Robyn about my new appearance. Especially since she seemed so iron-clad in her determination not to mention it to my face, when I turned up for the meeting last week. 'I promise you, Robyn, I'm not skinny.'

'Well, what size are you? Are you an eight? A six?'

I have to stop myself from laughing out loud. 'Yes, Robyn, I'm a size six.'

'OH MY GOD!'

'I was joking!' I kick myself for such a stupid, rookie mistake. 'I'm nothing like a size six, Robyn. Or even an eight.'

'Just tell me the truth, Charlie.' There's a loud, sorrowful sniff. 'I can handle it.'

'Look, I'm a size twelve, OK?' Which is a pretty neat way of being able to average out the fact that I'm a ten on the top and closer to a fourteen on the bottom. 'Boring, average twelve.'

'And you've had to work really, really hard at it? The weight didn't just, like, fall off?'

Now she's actually sounding rather tearful – I think with relief as much as anything, though I also remember that Robyn's biggest pet peeve is her friends turning up for a night out looking thinner than when she last saw them, and then, to add insult to injury, claiming that the weight has 'just fallen off'.

'No, Robyn, it did not just fall off. I had to exercise, and eat very little, and I'm going to have to carry on exercising and eating very little if I want to stay this size.'

'Oh. OK.' There's another loud sniff, but she sounds calmer already. 'Well, I'm really happy for you, Cha-Cha. I bet you feel amazing. Which I'm glad *someone* does, by the way, because I feel shit. I just had the worst weekend of my entire life, in case you're interested.'

'A bad weekend on the beach in Miami?'

'Yes.'

'With your billionaire boyfriend?'

'He's not a billionaire. He's only got, like, a few hundred million, or something.'

'Jesus. It's worse than I thought.'

She's not listening. 'And he's not my boyfriend, as it happens. Do you know why?'

'Because he won't leave his wife?' I joke.

'Oh, no, I already knew he wasn't going to leave his wife.'

'Robyn! I had no idea he was really married . . .'

'What he actually told me – right after he'd just bought me half the fucking Tiffany store – was that he isn't going to leave Sophia.'

'Sorry – who's Sophia?'

'His other girlfriend!' she spits. 'He said he was going to break up with her and spend more time with me, and now he's decided there's . . . what did he say? . . . room in his life for both of us. Can you fucking believe it?'

No. I really, really can't believe it.

'And how dare he try to soften the blow with a load of Tiffany jewellery? I mean, is that what he thinks of me? That I'm nothing more than some shallow gold-digger who can be bought off with a handful of fucking diamonds? *God*, Charlie,' she says, impassioned now, as if she's standing up in the United Nations to give a rallying call against world hunger, 'I'm so sick and tired of people thinking I'm only interested in men for their money. I mean, all right, *some* of my boyfriends have been well off. But that's only because I think it's nice when they can buy me nice things, and take me to nice hotels and stuff. It's not because I actually love *money*, or anything. Like, fifty-pound notes and stuff. It's just little bits of *paper*, isn't it?'

'Well, when you put it like that . . .'

'I mean, so fucking *what* if Yevvie wants to buy me a Porsche for my birthday . . . or rather, *wanted* to buy me a Porsche for my birthday,' she adds, dramatically. 'Because it's all over now. I told him where he could stuff his yellow-diamond charm bracelet. *And* the matching earrings.'

'That's great, Robyn. I'm really proud of you.' And I am, in a strange kind of way. 'But look, I have to go right now. I'm on my way to the King's Road store.'

'King's Road?'

'Yes. I'm . . . well, I'm thinking of doing it up a bit. I'll tell you about it next time I see you.'

'Oh, well, I might jump in a cab and head over there a bit later this morning. If I'm still too upset to go to sleep, that is.'

'You do that,' I say, suspecting that she probably won't be too upset to go to sleep. (Though, on the other hand, her desperation to make absolutely

100 per cent sure I'm definitely *not* thinner than her might be enough, on its own, to propel her towards the nearest taxi.) 'Good to talk to you, Robyn. And . . . well, don't be too upset about Yevgeny, will you? You can honestly do better than a man like him.'

I'm at the store by now, so I rifle in my bag for the keys Gaby's nanny dropped off, slot the right one in the lock, push the door wide open and step inside.

Those fashionistas who turned up for Dad's memorial service might not have been the friendliest bunch, but with the benefit of hindsight, they certainly brightened this old place up a bit. Now that it's empty of that glamorous, twittering crowd . . . well, it's just empty, full stop. The walls still smell faintly of fresh paint, the blown-up photos of Dad are stacked up, in painfully casual fashion, on an IKEA-type table at the back, and where the occasional ray of sunlight peeks through the whitewashed windows it only serves to highlight the amount of swirling dust particles that are filling the stuffy air.

It takes me totally by surprise when I feel the sharp prickle of a sob at the back of my throat.

'Excuse me?'

The voice behind me takes me even more by surprise. I let out an actual shriek as I spin round to come face-to-face with . . .

Oh, my God. It's Jay Broderick.

'I'm so sorry!' He holds up both hands, making a calming gesture. 'I shouldn't have snuck up on you like that. I *wasn't* sneaking up on you, actually. At least, not deliberately! I saw the door was open, and I just thought . . .' He stops. He puts his hands back down. A smile spreads across his face. 'Hi,' he finishes.

I catch my breath for a moment. Which is easier said than done, because he looks incredible. He's wearing grey jeans, battered leather trainers, and a dark-blue hooded top, half-unzipped to show a V-necked T-shirt and a tantalising hint of light-brown, muscular chest beneath. He's got a day's worth of stubble, and his hair is slightly damp, and his sooty eyes are fixed on me now in a penetrating fashion, presumably because he recognises me from somewhere but can't quite put a name to the face.

'Hi,' I repeat, when I can find a voice that isn't a squeak.

'This isn't an antiquarian bookshop,' he observes.

'This . . . isn't an antiquarian bookshop,' I repeat.

'Why isn't it an antiquarian bookshop?' he asks.

'Why isn't it an antiquarian bookshop?' I repeat exactly what he's just said, for the third time in a row. 'Er . . . because we don't sell books. Antiquarian or otherwise. I think you must be looking for the book dealership that used to lease the premises.'

'Ah. I think I must be.' He looks around at the empty space in front of him, before looking back at me, more keenly than ever. I suspect he's just about to put two and two together and work out where he's seen me before. 'So, I won't be able to purchase a first edition of *Silas Marner* for my father, then?'

'I'm afraid not. Well, not here.'

'Though it doesn't look like I'd be able to purchase anything at all here, to be honest with you. Are you a front for some kind of drugs business?'

'No, I'm a front for a shoe business. I mean, I'm an *actual* shoe business. What I mean is—'

'I'm Jay,' he suddenly says, taking a step forward. His face lights up with a grin and he extends a hand to shake mine. 'By the way.'

'I'm Charlie.'

'Charlie.' He repeats my name, shaking my hand as he does so. His eyes are fixed more intently on me than ever. 'A pleasure to meet you.'

To *meet* me?

Hang on: so he *doesn't* recognise me?

I mean, I know it's possible – after all, Lucy barely recognised me the first time she saw me after I lost the weight and went blonde, and she's spent a million times longer in my company than Jay Broderick has – but if he doesn't recognise me, I don't understand why he's looking at me in this kind of . . . *probing* manner.

Oh, dear God, I haven't got some of my revolting breakfast muesli stuck in my teeth, have I? It would be odd, given that I only eat about three teensy spoonfuls of it, and so I can pretty much account for every single (tasteless, dry) sunflower seed and every single (tasteless, chewy) dried cranberry in there, but it would definitely explain the intense staring.

'Charlie,' he repeats after a moment, as if trying the word for size. His voice is suddenly soft, and slightly lower than before. 'Is that short for anything?'

'Charlotte.' I'm assuming that this will be the point at which he puts two and two together, and works out that I'm the same Charlotte who came for a job interview and subsequently dislocated his shoulder a couple of months back. But when he doesn't – when, in fact, he just carries on staring at me – I feel the need to fill the silence with, 'It'd be a bit weird if I was actually christened Charlie, after all! People would think I was a boy, or something.'

'I very much doubt,' he says, still not taking his eyes off me, 'that anyone could possibly think that.'

There's a brief silence. Jay leans one shoulder against the door and folds his arms. He pushes the sleeves of his hoodie upwards, displaying forearms that are smooth and strong and capable-looking, and make me think, instantly, of what it would feel like to run my hands along them, up over his biceps and towards his shoulders . . . then place my hands either side of his face and pull him towards me so that I could kiss those soft lips and feel him kissing mine . . .

'So, Charlie,' he says, thankfully interrupting my fantasy before I start having him (mentally) press me up against the door and (mentally) unbutton my shirt. 'An empty store, jumpiness when approached by strangers . . . are you *sure* you're not a drug dealer?'

'I'm positive.'

'Then are you running some kind of covert surveillance mission? For MI6, perhaps? If I make one wrong move, are you going to inject me with something from a syringe concealed in the heel of your shoe, then finish me off by garrotting me with my own shoelaces?'

'I . . . don't work for MI6.'

'To be fair, Charlie, that's exactly what an MI6 operative *would* say.'

'Yes, but . . .'

'Hey.' He stops leaning against the door, reaches over and touches me, lightly, on the shoulder. It's just for a moment, but my skin feels like it's lightly sunburned where he's touched me, even if it was through the fabric of my T-shirt. 'I'm joking. I don't really think you work for MI6.'

I send up a hasty, desperate prayer to the Gods of Witty Banter, asking them to bless me with the ability to say something pert and perky. Not for ever: I don't want miracles. I'd just like to be able to return Jay's banter for the next couple of minutes, until he calls an end to this little rendezvous and heads off to find that first edition of *Silas Marner* elsewhere.

'Well, if I *did* tell you,' I say, all in a rush, 'I'm afraid I'd have to kill you.'

He laughs. It's not a smile, or a fleeting grin, it's an actual *laugh*.

Yes! The Gods of Witty Banter have heard my prayers after all!

'Probably safest,' he says, 'if I stop asking so many questions, then.'

'Probably.'

'Pity. Because I did have just one more question,

as it happens.' He tilts his chin up, his sooty eyes fixed on me. 'This job of yours – running a shoe shop, gathering top-secret counter-intelligence data for the secret service, whatever it is you actually do – does it keep you busy on Friday nights?'

'Friday nights?'

'Yeah. Specifically, will it be keeping you busy this coming Friday night? And if not, how would you feel about using this coming Friday night to attend my birthday party?'

'That's . . . more than one question,' I say. I've been abandoned, again, by the Gods of Witty Banter. More than that: it appears that I'm so shocked by what's just happened (correct me if I'm wrong, but has Jay Broderick just invited me to his birthday party?) that I've even been abandoned by my basic good manners.

Jay blinks. 'That's true.'

'I mean . . . sorry, that sounded really rude . . .'

'Look.' He holds up both hands, in a gesture of surrender. 'If you've got a boyfriend, or something . . .'

'I don't!' I yelp.

'Oh. Well, I was about to say that you should bring him along to my party too.' Jay grins. This time there's more than a hint of devilishness in it. 'But you know what, Charlie? I liked what you said better.'

OK. Let's just take a deep breath here. Before I go getting totally swept away in this moment, and all its many marvels, let's just keep a clear head and try to take a calm, rational view of what's just happened.

211

1) Jay Broderick has just asked me to come to his birthday party;
2) Jay Broderick has just asked me if I have a boyfriend; and
3) Jay Broderick has just appeared to express satisfaction that I don't have a boyfriend.

I'm really, really trying not to put two and two together and make five, or anything, but when you set out the facts like that . . .

It's literally the worst time in the entire world for what happens next to happen. Which is that the shop door suddenly opens and Robyn walks through it.

'Hi, Cha-Cha, I thought I'd just pop . . . oh, my *God*! *Jay*!'

Right, well, even if I was putting two and two together correctly, and Jay Broderick *was* implying he might, just might, fancy me a tiny little bit, that moment is over. Because Robyn is here, and because Robyn is wearing minuscule denim shorts and a sexy, sloppy sweatshirt with a big set of red lips printed on it, and because Robyn could take an Olympic gold medal in flirting, if flirting were an Olympic sport, and – most of all – because Robyn evidently knows Jay, and because Jay evidently knows her.

She's flinging her arms round him and kissing him on both cheeks.

'What are you *doing* here?' she demands, doing one of her little hair-swooshy things, plus (and only someone who knows Robyn like I know Robyn would notice this move) dropping one shoulder, ever so slightly, so that her sweatshirt slips sideways to reveal a hint of hot-pink bra strap. I can't help noticing, too, that she's sporting a huge pair of yellow-diamond earrings and – when I glance at her wrist – a matching yellow-diamond charm bracelet. (Evidently when she told Yevgeny where he could stuff them, the place she was meaning he could stuff them was inside her jewellery box.) 'I haven't seen you in *ages*!'

'Yeah, it's been a while.'

'It's been *ages*!' Robyn reaffirms. 'I never see you in Shropshire any more!'

'Well, I don't go there much.'

'Even so . . . I don't think I've seen you since Eddie Methuen-Campbell's engagement party.'

'I wasn't at Eddie Methuen-Campbell's engagement party.'

'Yes, you *were*. I did vodka shots with you and Jamie Ackroyd on the tennis court. Actually –' she does another little hair-swoosh, and runs her tongue over her lips to make them look more alluring '– I think I might have done a little bit more with Jamie Ackroyd on the tennis court than that!'

'Right.' Jay nods, pleasantly. 'Well, it sounds a great night. Shame I missed it.'

'Oh, *Jay*!' She giggles, and gives him a playful swat on the shoulder, while I study the floor and try to ignore the unpleasant bubbling sensation in my innards. (Could be searing jealousy, could be chronic hunger pangs, most likely a mixture of both.)

'Don't be silly! You must remember. I was wearing that little pink dress, the really short one that was cut away, like, literally all the way at the back . . .'

'Wait a minute.' Jay's voice is deadly serious. 'Was it a Versace dress?'

'No, it was Alexander McQueen . . .'

'Ah.' He shakes his head, almost sorrowfully. 'Then no, I'm sorry. I don't remember.'

It suddenly occurs to me that he might be taking the piss out of her. Not in a cruel, mocking way . . . but not necessarily in a flirtatious way either.

'Then you're a very forgetful boy.' Robyn pouts. 'And you still haven't told me what it is you're doing here.'

'He was just looking for *Silas Marner*,' I say, hastily, although I don't know why I feel the sudden need to explain away Jay's presence. 'I mean, the book. Not the *actual* Silas Marner, obviously . . .'

'Charlie!' Robyn has only just noticed me. 'Fucking hell! I hardly . . .'

But she stops herself before adding the words *recognised you*. She may not be the sharpest tool in the box, my sister, but when it comes to men, she's 100 per cent switched on. And she's not going to draw attention to my appearance, new or otherwise, when a guy like Jay Broderick is around.

'Wait – you two know each other?' He looks surprised.

'Well, of course we do!' Robyn gives him another playful swat. 'We're sisters!'

'You're *sisters*?'

I know I'm pretty well accustomed, after all these years, to people looking amazed that Robyn and I are related, but I suppose I'd hoped my makeover might have taken away just a little of that amazement. But Jay is looking more than just amazed. He's looking flabbergasted.

'That's right!' Robyn trills. 'Robyn and Charlie, the Glass sisters!'

'But I thought . . . isn't your sister called Abby, or Gaby, or something?'

'Ugh, *Gaby*. You don't want anything to do with her, Jay. She's a moody old cow. And married these days, by the way. Gazillions of bratty children. Whereas me and Charlie are the fun, single sisters!'

'Single?' Jay raises an eyebrow in Robyn's direction. 'Last I heard, you were going out with Yevgeny Lysenko.'

He says it in a light but pointed tone of voice, making me wonder two things. First, how does he know so much about Robyn's love life? And second, why does it sound as though he cares?

'*God*, no. That's all over. Yevvie was, like, literally a total pig to me this past weekend. *Anyway*,' she continues, moving a little bit closer to Jay and 'adjusting' her bra strap, so that he can see how sexily pink it is, and so that he can start thinking about the beautiful breasts it's holding up, 'now that I'm not with Yevvie any longer, you can invite me to your birthday party on Friday night!'

'I can?'

'Of course! I've been hearing all about your party from, like, literally *everyone*. Now, don't worry, I wasn't offended that you hadn't invited me – I know some people can be a bit wary of Yevvie, especially after that episode with his security people and Jamie Ackroyd at Eddie Methuen-Campbell's engagement party – but you don't need to worry about that kind of thing now.'

'Well, that's good to hear.'

'Isn't it? Anyway, look, you don't need to send me an official invite, or anything. Just pop me down on the guest list.'

Just as I'm about to die of mortification, on Robyn's behalf, Jay nods.

'No problem, Robyn. I'll put you down on the guest list.'

'Excellent! I can't wait—'

He cuts her off, turning to me. 'And I'll put you on there too. OK, Charlie?'

There's an awkward silence. Robyn stares at him. Then she stares at me. Then she stares back at Jay again.

'You're inviting *Charlie* to your party?'

'Well, I've already established that she isn't going to be busy on surveillance duty that particular evening . . .'

'Huh?'

'. . . or getting dropped behind enemy lines for a covert mission in Taliban-occupied Afghanistan. So yes. I am inviting Charlie to my party.'

'But . . . Charlie doesn't go to parties.'

'Doesn't go to parties?' echoes Jay. 'Good God, Charlie – do you have some kind of party allergy, or something?'

'Don't be ridiculous!' Robyn snaps, before I can answer. 'Nobody has a party allergy.' She thinks about this for a moment. '*Do* they?'

'Oh, yes. It can develop at any time, apparently.' Jay is wearing an expression of the utmost seriousness. 'And it's known to run in families. So if Charlie's got it now, Robyn, there's a pretty good chance you could get it too.'

'He's only joking,' I say, quickly, when I see her face fall. 'And no, Jay, I'm not allergic to parties.'

'Good. So you'll be there, then, on Friday night?'

His eyes are fixed on mine again, burning into me with such intensity that I'm suddenly worried I might accidentally catch alight, or something. I'm certainly feeling extremely hot, now I come to think of it; in fact, I'm only just noticing that sweat has started to collect at the base of my spine, where of course there's a nice, handy place for it to pool, in the shape of my shelf-like bum.

'Um, yes. I'll . . . be there.'

'We *both* will.' Robyn suddenly links an arm through mine. 'And who knows, Jay – I might even wear that pink dress again!'

'Right. Good.' Jay answers her, but he's still looking at me. 'Looking forward to it.'

Which is the last thing he says before he opens the shop door and heads back out on to King's Road.

'Oh, my *God*!' Robyn squeals, the moment he's out of earshot. 'I have to call Lulu and Jules and tell them Jay Broderick just personally invited me to his birthday party! They're going to, like, *literally* die of jealousy! But hang on – I need to call Richard Ward first . . . I'm going to need to get in for an emergency colour and cut on Thursday, and a blow-dry on Friday morning . . . and then of course I'll need a morning at the Mandarin Oriental spa – maybe a whole day, if I'm going to fit in a slimming treatment as well . . . oh, and I'll need a pedicure . . . though my feet look utterly disgusting thanks to my bloody bunions, so I'm just going to have to hope Jay isn't into toe-sucking, or anything.'

'You have bunions too?'

'There's no need to make me self-conscious, Charlie!' she snaps. '*Everyone* has bunions.'

'Oh, right.'

'. . . and I'll need a showgirl wax, obviously.'

'A what wax?'

'*And* I have to get in a mega Net-à-Porter order, too!' She's already scrabbling for her iPad. 'I've got literally nothing to wear, and they've got a shed-load of gorgeous new Valentino I need to try on. Though everything's bound to look hideous on me at the moment because I'm so fat and pale . . . Cha-Cha, will you call Richard Ward and the Mandarin Oriental for me and get all those appointments fixed up while I get these dresses ordered? But don't book anything earlier than eleven on Friday morning!' she screeches.

'If I'm going to pull Jay Broderick at his party, I need my beauty sleep the night before!'

'*Are* you going to pull Jay Broderick at his party?' I ask, before I can stop myself.

Robyn stops stabbing at her iPad and stares at me, hand on one hip. 'Hel-*lo*! Didn't you *see* the way he was looking at me?'

I didn't, actually, but you don't tell Robyn that kind of thing.

'And he's had a crush on me for, like, literally *ever*. I mean, I've known him since I was nineteen or twenty. His family have this, like, totally incredible house a few miles from Mummy's in Shropshire. God, Mummy will just *die* of excitement if I get together with him!'

'Right. But it just seems so soon after Yevgeny . . .'

'Charlie, this is *Jay Broderick* we're talking about. Jay-gazillions-in-the-bank-Broderick.'

'I thought,' I say, more pointedly than I'd intended, 'you weren't interested in money.'

'Have you *seen* him? He could have, like, literally *nothing* in the bank, and I'd still be dropping my knickers and begging him to shag me senseless over the railings on his hundred-foot yacht. Oh, though I guess if he had nothing in the bank, he probably wouldn't have the hundred-foot yacht, would he? Well, I'd just find another railing somewhere. I mean, Hyde Park has railings and stuff, doesn't it? And you can get into Hyde Park for absolutely free.'

I feel myself turn pink, not just because I'm always embarrassed when Robyn gets quite so graphic, but because this image isn't a million miles from some of the fantasies I've been having about Jay myself.

'Oh, don't be such a prude, Charlie,' Robyn scoffs, when she sees my cheeks redden. 'I'm only describing exactly what I happen to know he did to Cassia Connelly last summer in Cap Ferrat.'

'Cassia Connelly . . . the supermodel?' I feel a strange, tight sensation in my throat, as if I'm wearing a polo-neck a size too small. 'Jay went out with Cassia Connelly?'

'Well, I don't think they did too much *going out*, if you know what I mean!'

I do know what she means, and the strange, tight sensation in my throat is getting even stranger and tighter.

What kind of a fool have I been to entertain the notion, these past fifteen minutes, that Jay Broderick might have fancied me a little bit? Never mind that I'm thinner now, and blonder now, and never mind that I've furnished myself with the regulation eyebrows.

It would be laughable, if I weren't feeling quite so miserable right now.

'But then, Jay's such a playboy, he's practically always got some stunning supermodel draped round him,' Robyn is saying. 'Which is why I have to lose *at least* five pounds before Friday . . . especially if I'm going to go to the party with you, Cha-Cha, you bitch. I used to look *really* thin when I stood next to you, and now I'm only going to look a *bit* thin.' She looks properly put out, and without the slightest notion that what she's saying might sound rather rude. 'Though I suppose,' she adds, generously, 'that it'll be nice to go to a party together for once. Hey, I know – you can come over to mine to get ready before we go! When was the last time we did that, Charlie?'

'Well, let me see. I think that would be . . . never?'

'We'll put on music,' she's continuing, unembarrassed, 'and drink champagne, and you can help me do my hair and make-up . . . it'll be brilliant, Cha-Cha! Just like the old days! Oh, I have to take this!' she suddenly adds, as her phone rings loudly. 'It's Lulu! *Hi*, darling,' she says into the phone, shooting me an excitable wink and opening the door, already on her way out. 'You'll never guess who *I've* just run into! *Or* where I'm going on Friday night . . .'

I watch her for a moment as she strides away, the red soles of her Christian Louboutin ankle boots flashing as she does so.

Chapter Eleven

Galina may not actually curve her crimson-painted lips into a welcoming smile, but there's a glint of triumph in her eyes as I settle into her chair on Friday morning.

'So, Sharlee. You are wanting me to do something about moustache.'

'I'm wanting you to do something about the downy hairs on my upper lip.'

She nods. 'Moustache.'

'Well, I still think it's not exactly . . . all right, all right,' I surrender. 'Yes, please, Galina. I would like you to do something about my moustache.'

'You will not regret. Will be much better without it.'

'Well, I hope so. I've got this party tonight, you see, and . . .'

'So you want also wax? Leg, Brazilian, Hollywood, showgirl . . .'

There's that word again, the one Robyn mentioned.

'Galina, what exactly *is* a showgirl wax?'

'Is legs, arms, armpits, Brazilian bikini, face, toes . . .'

'*Toes?*'

'Toes are getting hairy sometimes. You want?'

'Do I want hairy toes?'

'Do you want,' she asks, patiently, 'showgirl wax?'

'Oh, I see! Oh, God, no. No, I don't want any kind of a wax at all, Galina. I'm perfectly happy just shaving.'

She shrugs. 'Nice men prefer wax. Nice men prefer smooth all over. You are wanting meet nice man at this party, no?'

'No, I'm not. I mean, OK, the host happens to be a nice man, and I know for a fact that he prefers smooth all over, seeing as the only people he dates, apparently, are top international supermodels . . .'

'Then you are not having snowball chance in hell,' she points out, charitably. 'Now, keep mouth still, please.'

I won't dwell on the details of the next two minutes, because (unlike Galina) I'm not some kind of pain freak who revels in reliving the experience of eye-watering agony. All I really need to report is that there are clearly even more nerve endings in the upper-lip region than there are in the eyebrow area, and that the hairs there are even less happy about being wrenched from their follicles by a large Lithuanian with a sadistic streak. And I know for sure she has a sadistic streak, because the second she's finished my upper lip, she's already asking, 'Now I do also sideburns?'

'I . . . don't have sideburns.'

A scoffing noise. 'You are having sideburns.' She strokes the sides of my face, beneath my ears, as though she's a judge in an Elvis lookalike contest and I'm one of the hopeful contenders for the Best Female Elvis title. 'For you today I include in price of moustache.'

'But I really didn't think I had . . . I mean, nobody's ever mentioned . . .'

She thrusts a magnifying mirror into my hand. 'You look. You see.'

I turn my head to see if I can spot these so-called sideburns in the mirror.

Well . . . I suppose she *may* have a point. Calling them sideburns is pretty extreme, but under the very bright light, there is the faintest whisper of soft, downy hair beneath my ears that I've never really noticed before. And I don't think anyone else is going to notice it either. Unless Jay Broderick's required standards of female grooming are so *very* sky-high that you're refused admission to his parties until a security guard has given your face the once-over with a magnifying mirror and a high-powered torch.

'I suppose maybe you'd better do my sideb— those areas.'

'You will not regret. Will help you meet nice man.' Satisfied by my capitulation, Galina is tearing off a new length of twine. 'And next time you come, you will be dating. And you will be wanting showgirl wax. And eyelash dye. You would not regret eyelash dye. Make eyes look less piggy.'

'Do I *have* piggy eyes?'

She shrugs, neither confirming nor denying this. 'Eyelash dye make them look bigger. And who does

224

not want eyes looking bigger? Why not improve appearance, wherever is possible? Is small effort for big reward.'

'Small effort?' I put my head back down on the headrest and grip the chair's arms as Galina approaches my so-called sideburns with her fresh piece of floss. 'Well, if you say so, Galina. If you say so.'

I don't, in fact, have the slightest intention of getting ready at Robyn's before the party this evening. This isn't because I don't secretly yearn after some idyllic vision of sisterhood, where Robyn and I prance round her flat in bathrobes and face masks, singing mid-eighties Madonna at the tops of our lungs before settling down to a girlie hour of mani-pedis and helping each other pick out the right accessories to go with our outfits. I've secretly yearned after that scenario plenty of times over the years. No: it's because I'm smart enough to know that the reality wouldn't be that idyllic at all. The reality, let's face it, would involve:

1) Robyn throwing a temper tantrum because she's got it into her head that there's the vaguest suspicion of a hint of a suggestion of the beginnings of a spot on the underside of her chin;
2) Robyn conducting a fashion show with every item in her wardrobe, getting me to take pictures of her in every dress, from every angle, and then listing *ad nauseam* the many different ways in

which everything she owns makes her look fat and
disgusting;
3) Robyn (having decided she's fat and disgusting)
burying herself under her duvet and refusing to
go to the party until very, very gently coaxed over
the course of roughly ninety minutes; and
4) Robyn getting me to help with her make-up and
insisting that I try out smoky eye after smoky eye
until eventually there's no time left for me to do
my own make-up and I have to daub it on in the
back of a taxi.

Look, I'm not suggesting that I need to primp and
perfect myself for hours before this party, in the hope
that Jay notices me amongst the crowds of international supermodels. But I think I owe it to myself
at least to *try* to turn up looking like I've made an
effort. Instead of looking exhausted and frazzled from
the full Robyn Treatment, and wearing make-up that
would shame even The Joker from Batman.

So this is my alternative plan: I'm going to get
myself ready in blissful peace at my flat, *then* go round
to Robyn's at the designated time so that I can still
perform all the required soothing/coaxing/smoky eye-
perfecting without having to worry that I'm barely
dressed and made-up myself.

Blissful peace, unfortunately, hasn't quite materialised.

The trouble is that I was so red and sore after
this morning's threading/torture appointment with

Galina that I had to delay my planned late-afternoon run along the Embankment and half-hour of lunges until I was sure that the sweat wouldn't make me all red and sore again. So now I'm in a colossal hurry. I'm showered, at least, but the last hour has been entirely taken up with blow-drying my hair (*Damn* this blasted fringe! *And* these sodding layers!) followed by several minutes of sitting immobile by my open bedroom window until I'm cooled down enough from the blow-drying to think about starting my make-up.

So when the doorbell rings I ignore it, and carry on rubbing in my tinted moisturiser and brushing on my blusher. It'll only be a pizza delivery for one of the other flats, ringing my bell by mistake to taunt my starving stomach with the scent of yeasty pizza dough, sweet tomatoes and tangy pepperoni. Anyway, my phone has just started ringing, too, so I'd better grab that . . . oh, it's Lucy.

'Luce? Sorry, I can't talk. I'm running seriously late . . .'

'I'm upstairs.'

'What?'

'I'm upstairs, outside your flat. I just rang the door-bell but you ignored me. And I know you're in because I can see the lights on.'

'I wasn't ignoring *you*, I was ignoring the pizza delivery person I thought you were . . .' I'm already scurrying up the stairs to let her in.

When I open both the inner and the outer front

doors, she's standing on the steps with a bottle of red wine.

'I thought,' she says, 'you might like an evening in with a glass or three of this and a repeat episode of *Peter Andre: The Next Chapter.*'

Evenings in with wine and *Peter Andre: The Next Chapter* have, for better or worse, long been a popular way for the two of us to spend time together. Though never usually on a Friday night – Friday night is almost always Lucy's date night with her current boyfriend. Pal must be fartlek-training this evening, or something.

'Oh, no, Luce, I can't! I have to go out!'

'So I see.' She comes into the flat, deposits her wine bottle on the old telephone table and folds her arms, perusing me closely. 'Your hair looks gorgeous. And you smell yummy. You're not . . . going on a *date*, are you, Charlie?'

'No! It's just this party I've been invited to.'

'Whose party? And why haven't you told me about it?'

'Because,' I point out, 'I haven't been able to get hold of you all week. I've left messages.'

'Oh. Yes. Sorry about that. I've been busy at work, and Pal isn't keen on me making calls when I get home in the evenings . . .'

I'm too stressed to give any energy to being Entirely Positive about Pal right now, so I dredge up some old advice that Mum used to give me: if you can't say anything nice, it's better to say nothing at all.

'Look, Luce, I'm running really late, so can you come downstairs and we'll talk while I finish getting ready?'

'I can do better than that. I can actually help you get ready.' There's a bit of a bounce in Lucy's step as she starts down the stairs ahead of me. Never having had to put up with Robyn-style antics over the years, she loves getting ready for parties almost more than she loves parties themselves. Though this has probably changed now, seeing as I suspect that getting ready for the parties she goes to with Pal involves little more than a brisk shower and a handful of milk thistle capsules, to line the stomach before one too many sips of chilled white wine. 'So, what kind of party is this, then? Where is it? What are you wearing?'

'Well, I think it'll be fairly smart.' Feeling suddenly shy, I reach into my wardrobe for the new dress I've bought from ASOS. 'So I thought a nice cocktail dress would be the right sort of thing . . .'

When I turn round, Lucy has made a great show of falling on to my bed and snoring, in mock-slumber.

'Fine. You think it's a boring dress.'

'Not true.' She sits up. 'It's *such* a boring dress, Charlie, that I have literally no thoughts about it at all.'

'You've barely looked at it!'

'I don't need to look at it. It's black, right? With wide straps and a square neckline, right? With an A-line skirt to hide your bum. Correct?'

This is, in fact, correct.

'Actually,' I say, feeling a bit disgruntled, 'it also happens to have a very nice little sparkly belt that you can put round the waist . . .'

'Saints preserve us from nice little sparkly belts!' Lucy gets to her feet and grabs the dress from me, holding it up against my body and pulling the kind of faces plumbers make when they're about to diagnose your boiler with a fatal fault, or that doctors make when they're about to tell you that your symptoms require an urgent colonoscopy. 'Come on, Charlie! You've worked so hard to look this good, and now you're choosing to go to a party in something so . . . unspectacular?'

'Well, I apologise for not having the kind of clothes budget that allows me to order half a dozen spectacular dresses on Net-à-Porter.' Which reminds me . . . Robyn. I reach for my phone, which is somewhere amongst the cache of open make-up pots on my dressing table. 'I have to text Robyn, tell her I'm going to be a bit late.'

'You're going to this party *with Robyn*?'

'Yes. It's a long story.'

'Bloody hell, Charlie. It's not a party for one of her obnoxious friends, is it? Miffy Tallulah-Fudgington or Hector van Codswallop-Sissingthorpe?'

'No. And I'm not certain either of those people exist. Well, not Miffy Tallulah-Fudgington, anyway.'

'Oh, God, then it's not that scary Russian bloke she's been going out with?' Now Lucy looks genuinely concerned. 'I read about him in the papers sometimes, and all I'll say is, I'd steer clear of the canapés unless you happen to have a handy pocket-sized Geiger counter stashed away in your handbag.'

'It's not Yevgeny's party, no.' I finish sending the text to Robyn and then sit back down at my dressing table to get on with applying a hasty line of eyeliner and a layer of mascara. 'Anyway, he was Ukrainian, not Russian. And Robyn isn't going out with him any more.'

'Charlie Glass! Why are you avoiding the issue? Why won't you just tell me whose party it is?'

'Lucy, it's no big deal, honestly.' I do my best to make my voice sound super-casual, the way it would if I popped to the newsagent over the road and passed the time of day while buying the Sunday paper. 'It's just that Broderick bloke I was telling you about, that's all.'

'*Jay* Broderick?'

'Mmm.'

'You're going to *Jay Broderick's* party?'

'Mmm.'

'And you're *really* planning on wearing this dreary bit of cloth?' She shakes the ASOS dress at me, furiously. 'Do you have any idea how glamorous this party is going to be, Charlie?'

'Do *you* have any idea how glamorous it's going to be? I mean, for all you know, it's going to be a . . . a charity fund-raiser for . . .' I struggle to think of the least glamorous charity I possibly can '. . . search and rescue in the Brecon Beacons. It could be full of earnest mountaineers in Day-Glo walking gear.'

'It's not going to be a party to raise funds for lost hikers, Charlie. This is Jay Broderick we're talking about. The party's going to be full of racing drivers, and international supermodels.'

'You don't,' I mutter, almost stabbing myself in the eye with my mascara wand, 'have to remind me.'

'Probably, in fact, full of racing drivers *having sex* with international supermodels.' Lucy is sounding almost wistful, all of a sudden. 'In one glorious, torrid, drunken orgy . . .'

I set down my mascara. 'OK, I don't think I want to go to this party after all.'

'Well, now you're just being ridiculous. I'd give my eye teeth to go to a party like this, Charlie! I mean, seriously, when you compare it to some of the parties Pal takes me to, with all his work colleagues standing around sipping sparkling elderflower and talking about the latest thrills and spills in the world of tax-accounting . . .' She stops herself before she says too much. 'Anyway, all I'm saying is that you absolutely can't go to the party in something boring and black from ASOS.' She throws the dress, with nothing short of contempt, on to the bed, and starts rifling through my open wardrobe. 'Seriously, Charlie, I'm not letting you be a wallflower tonight.'

'I'm not being a wallflower. But I won't really know anyone there apart from Jay Broderick, and he isn't going to notice me . . .'

'Well, obviously not. He'll be draped in about half a dozen Victoria's Secret Angels all night.'

'Thanks,' I mutter, 'for reminding me.'

'Hey, don't take that personally, Charlie, I'm just saying that Victoria's Secret Angels are more Jay Broderick's type. Anyway, you haven't explained how you even got invited to his party at all. This isn't anything to do with that interview you went for a few months ago, is it?'

'Christ, no. It's . . .'

'Oh, my God.' Lucy stops rifling through my wardrobe and pulls out a hanger. 'This is *it*.'

The hanger she's clutching is holding Mum's dress. The floaty silk, kimono-style dress she used to wear for her fabulous dinner parties. I keep it hanging in my wardrobe, though I haven't so much as looked at it for years.

I deliberately don't look at it, in fact. It just reminds me, painfully, of what I used to do for months after Mum died. Which was to bury my face in the soft silk and try very, very hard, to breathe in a fading hint of Anaïs Anaïs.

'This is Yves Saint Laurent,' Lucy says, peering at the label inside. 'I never knew you had a vintage Yves Saint Laurent dress hanging in your wardrobe, Charlie.'

'Neither did I. I mean, I didn't know it was Yves Saint Laurent.' I reach out and touch the silk. It's pale grey and hand-painted with a deep-red cherry-blossom print. It has a low, cowl neckline and full-length floaty sleeves that remind me of a medieval princess's gown. 'Mum used to wear it when they had fancy guests for dinner. I think Dad bought it for her in Paris.'

'Oh, *Charlie*! That's so romantic.' Lucy's looking wistful again, though in a rather sweeter way than she was when she was talking about the racing driver/ international supermodel orgy. 'I wish I had a man who'd do things like that for me.'

'You have Pal!' I say, and promptly wish I hadn't, because both of us know that Pal isn't the type of man to buy vintage designer dresses, in Paris or anywhere. 'Anyway, I can't wear Mum's dress, because it isn't going to fit. Mum was slim.'

'*You're* slim.'

'Well, Mum didn't have a bum the size of a small county.'

'It's bias-cut,' Lucy says (not actually bothering, I note, to deny that I still have a bum the size of a small county). 'It'll skim over your bum. Cling to it in all the right places. In fact, it'll make your bum look a darn' sight better than that horrible, blah A-line monstrosity will.'

I don't bother defending the ASOS dress any longer, though I think calling it a monstrosity is a little bit unfair.

I'm being drawn in, slowly but surely, by the power of the incredible Yves Saint Laurent. Even though it's over two decades old – and come to think of it was probably vintage when Dad bought it, so it might well be a good deal older than that – the silk has this shimmering, almost glowing effect, and the draping of the cowl neckline is so perfect it makes you want to weep.

Comparing it with the ASOS dress is like trying to compare a vintage Aston Martin with a fresh-from-the-factory Nissan Micra.

And seeing as Jay is a man who must know a good car when he sees one, there's probably more chance of him noticing me if I turn up at his party in an Aston Martin of a dress than if I turn up wearing the sartorial equivalent of a Nissan Micra.

'All right.' I take the dress from Lucy. 'I'll try it.'

She knows me well enough not to say anything when I scuttle into the bathroom, for privacy. I'm shy enough about stripping off at the best of times, and right now all I'm wearing under my dressing gown is the nude bra and thong set I bought yesterday afternoon. I close the bathroom door behind me, shrug off my dressing gown, hang it on the peg on the back of the door and then oh-so-carefully step into Mum's dress.

It's a bit of a wriggle to get it up over my hips, but nothing like the struggle I thought it was going to be, and easy enough to slide the sleeves up over my shoulders. I don't quite dare to take the dressing gown all the way off its peg, which would give me a clear view in the full-length mirror on the back of the bathroom door. But I push the dressing gown to one side, and take a quick, nervous glance.

Oh, my God.

I look . . .

Could I actually go so far as to say *beautiful*?

The glowy grey silk is reflecting light up on to my

face, the cowl neckline flatters my bust, my arms look astonishingly toned and slender through the peekaboo magic of the sheer sleeves. Most incredibly of all, the bias cut of the skirt is – as Lucy predicted – clinging to my curves in all the right places. I scarcely dare look at the back view for too long, in case what I'm seeing turns out to be a trick of the light, but it looks like my bum is miraculously less shelf-like than normal. Not the size of a regular bum – let's not get ahead of ourselves – but most definitely not the size of a small county. A small county *town*, perhaps. Melton Mowbray, maybe. Or Leamington Spa.

I'm not being vain – at least, I'm not trying to be vain – and I'm certainly not trying to claim I look as beautiful as Mum did when she wore this dress. But after so long being completely invisible, it's a heady, giddy rush to feel that I might not be invisible tonight after all.

I won't be the belle of the ball, but I don't think I'll be the beast either.

There's a little knock on the door, and Lucy is sticking her head round.

'Can I see? Does it fit?'

'Yes . . . it definitely fits . . . but is it too dressy, do you think? Or too long? I mean, I'd already planned to give Mum's crystal stilettos another go . . . I've been practising walking in them for the last three days, and I'm confident that I'm no danger to any passing Sachertorte . . . well, as confident as I'll ever be . . . oh, my God, Lucy, are you *crying*?'

I don't even know why I ask, because it's pretty obvious that she's crying. Tears are actually streaming down her cheeks.

'You look like a mermaid!' she howls.

'In a . . . bad way?'

'No! In a good way!'

'But, Luce, you don't usually cry when you think people look good.'

'I do! I cried when Kitty put on her wedding dress the morning she got married, didn't I?'

I don't point out that this was, really, just a continuation of the crying Lucy had been doing ever since her sister had announced her engagement six months previously. Because there's something in the way she's crying right now that reminds me, exactly, of the way she was crying on Kitty's wedding day.

'Lucy . . .' I grab the toilet roll and hand her a huge wodge of it. I'd instinctively go to put an arm around her, but I'm horribly conscious of what would happen to Mum's glowy grey silk if it got tears and mascara on it. 'Is everything OK? I mean, were you coming round tonight to talk about something?' I take a deep breath. 'Like, I don't know, things between you and Pal, maybe?'

'What? No! Why would I need to talk about that? Things are brilliant between me and Pal!'

'OK, so maybe you wanted to talk about how . . . brilliantly things are going. Either way, if you want to talk, Luce, I won't go to this silly party.'

'Are you crazy?' She blows her nose, loudly, on the

toilet roll. 'You'll pick watching *Peter Andre: The Next Chapter* with me over partying with a billionaire?'

'He's not a billionaire,' I say, immediately hating myself for sounding a bit like Robyn – and anyway, I'm not even sure I'm right about that. 'And yes, Lucy, of course I'd pick staying in with you over that.'

'Well, you're not going to. You're going to go to this party if I have to drag you there myself. You look ridiculously beautiful, Charlie – that's all I was crying about.'

'It's not me. It's the dress.'

'Oh, Charlie. I think it's a little bit you.' She reaches over and tucks a few strands of my hair behind my ear. 'You know, if you weren't so blonde, you'd look exactly like your mum right now. I bet she wasn't much older than you when she last wore this dress.'

Which is all I need, frankly, because now I can feel tears welling up as well. Thank God there's a distraction in the form of my mobile, which I can suddenly hear vibrating, with a text message, on my dressing table.

'That's bound to be Robyn . . .' I gulp, darting out of the bathroom and back into the bedroom.

HURRY UP CHA-CHA FOR FUCKS SAKE AM HAVING A CRISIS I MEAN IT THIS IS SERIOUS

Which is my cue to finish getting ready as quickly as possible, so I can get out on to the street and find a taxi to take me to Robyn's flat, in Westbourne Grove.

*   *   *

My legs and bum, worn out from the run and all the lunges, are howling at me in protest when I get to the fourth floor in Robyn's building, where her flat is situated. It doesn't help that I have to take the four flights of stairs i-n-c-r-e-d-i-b-l-y slowly and gingerly, to be sure of not treading on the hem of Mum's dress.

When I finally reach the right floor, Robyn is already waiting for me, leaning out of her front door wearing nothing more than a black lace push-up bra, a titchy black thong that makes my own nude thong look like a pair of Bridget Jones's Big Pants, an absolutely huge diamond-studded cuff, and a tearful, furious expression on her fully made-up face.

'Charlie? What the fuck has taken you so long?'

I can tell, immediately, that she's in the throes of a fully fledged pre-party paddy. I know these paddies well, and I also remember that there are many possible reasons behind them. It could be a paddy about her fringe looking wrong, or her arms looking fat, or her feet looking big. It could be a paddy about her eyeliner 'looking a bit too Cleopatra-ish' or it could be a paddy about her pre-party champagne tasting 'a bit too champagne-y'.

'I'm here now, Robyn,' I say, not quite able to bring myself to apologise for the fact that I'm all of three minutes later than I said I'd be. 'Tell me what's wrong.'

'*Everything's* wrong!'

'That can't possibly be true.'

'I hate my shoes!' she wails at me, now. 'They're too pointy and they hurt my *fucking* bunions.'

'Well, maybe you could wear a different pair?'

'But they're the only ones that go with my dress! *And* I hate my dress! In fact, I hate *all* my dresses! I've got, like, literally nothing to wear! I mean *literally*! And I hate all my earrings and I hate all my necklaces! The only thing I own that I even *like* –' she holds up an arm, brandishing it violently in my face '– is this cuff. And I can't wear it because it's so obvious that Yevgeny gave it to me and I don't want Jay to be reminded of Yevvie when he's trying to pull me. And because I think there's a chance Yevvie might have had his jeweller put a tracking device in it somewhere, and I don't want him turning up and causing a scene like he did at Eddie Methuen-Campbell's engagement party.'

'Robyn, I'm absolutely sure you've got something lovely to wear.' I put a soothing arm round her shoulders and guide her back into her flat, which is huge, and split-level, and extremely white, from the thick, snow-coloured carpet to the faint sprinkling of crystalline powder (oh, *no*, Robyn) that I can see on the large Perspex coffee table. 'Let's go to your bedroom and have a proper look.'

'I'm telling you!' she shrieks. 'I don't have anything lovely! I don't even have anything halfway *decent*!'

'But you got a few things from Net-à-Porter, didn't you?'

'Only a couple,' she says, as we go up the flat's winding spiral staircase into her bedroom, which looks – I'm not exaggerating – pretty much the way I imagine the Net-à-Porter dispatch facility must look. There are black Net-à-Porter bags everywhere: small bags, medium-sized bags, large fold-over bags that are actually more like suit-covers, and which I assume are used to package the most expensive designer dresses they deliver. The floor is practically ankle-deep in black Net-à-Porter tissue paper. And on every surface – the super-kingsize bed, the armchair, the dressing table – are flung brand-new dresses, in every shade of the rainbow.

'This is the one I was planning to wear,' Robyn says, grabbing an outrageously small piece of gold lamé, holding it up to herself for a moment, and then throwing it aside with even more disgust than Lucy was chucking my ASOS dress about with earlier. 'See? It makes me look *disgusting*. Jay Broderick isn't even going to notice me. Well, he probably will notice me, but it'll only be to vomit on the floor because I look so foul . . .'

'Robyn, you're being ridiculous. You could turn up to the party in a bin liner and all the guys would still fancy you.'

'Jay wouldn't.'

I swallow, hard. 'Of course he would. Now, come on, let me help you choose something. What about this?' I pick up a short, sparkly dress in pillar-box red. 'It's Valentino, Robyn! You always look great in Valentino.'

'I do,' she says, modestly. 'But not that one. Net-à-Porter sent the wrong fucking size. It looks like a sack on me. Which is, like, literally the worst thing that's ever happened, because I pull every single time I wear Valentino, and I know Jay likes girls in red, because every time I saw him out with Cassia Connelly she was wearing . . .'

'All right, then what about this?' I grasp at a heap of midnight-blue silk, which turns out to be a rather stunning baby-doll-style dress, with an Alexander McQueen label in the back. 'This would be gorgeous on you!'

'I *suppose* . . . hang on, Charlie.' Robyn is suddenly reaching over to me, pulling at the lapels of my coat. 'What's that you're wearing under there?'

'Oh, it's just a dress.'

'I know that,' she snaps. 'Let me *see* it.'

Suddenly shy, I unbutton the long winter coat I'm wearing (yes, I am a bit hot on this warm summer's evening, but I decided I'd rather overheat than run the risk of sitting on something sticky in the taxi and ruining the dress for ever) and open it so that Robyn can see.

Her mouth falls open. 'Is that . . . *vintage YSL?*'

'Yes!' I'm impressed. Though with the amount of time Robyn spends thinking about clothes, it would probably be amazing if she *didn't* recognise an Yves Saint Laurent dress when she saw one. 'It was my mother's. Is it OK, do you think?'

'Well, take off that bloody awful coat and I'll tell you!'

When I do (take off that bloody awful coat, that

is), Robyn just looks at me, one hand placed on one jutting, bony hip.

'Hmmmmm,' she says, after a long moment of silence.

'Don't you like it?' I feel panic rising in my gullet. It's all very well for Lucy and I to think I look nice. We're not exactly cutting-edge fashionistas. Under more professional scrutiny, maybe the effect of Mum's dress isn't so miraculous as I thought.

'It's not that I don't *like* it . . . I mean, it was your mother's, of course, so I don't want to be rude . . . but I just . . . hmmmmm.'

'Robyn, please, stop saying *hmmm* and tell me what you think!'

'Well, I don't want to be rude . . .'

'You've already said.'

'. . . but I think the print is way too loud. And you do realise that, like, literally nobody else at the party will be wearing full-length?'

'Nobody?'

'Nobody. You'll stick out like a sore bum!'

'Thumb,' I correct her. I'm starting to feel sick with nerves. 'But, Robyn, I don't have anything else to wear!'

'Well, *that's* nothing to worry about! Now you're all skinny, you can just borrow something from me.'

'I'm not as skinny as you!'

'True . . . oh! Wait a minute, Charlie. Didn't you tell me you were a size twelve now?'

'Yes, but . . .'

She holds up a hand to stop me, using the other to delve into the pile of dresses on the bed and pull out the sparkly red Valentino one. 'This is a size twelve! They sent me the wrong one, remember?'

I stare at it, aghast. 'Robyn, I can't wear that.'

'Are you insane? Of course you can wear it! You're not all fat and blobby any more, Cha-Cha!'

I choose to ignore the word *blobby*. I'm too focussed on the dress, which – despite Robyn's claim that it looked like a sack on her – still looks pretty small to me. It's strapless and has a short, straight skirt that probably wouldn't come down much further than my mid-thigh region. It looks like the kind of thing Joan from *Mad Men* might wear if she was on the prowl for a hot, rich, single man to take her mind off her enduring passion for Roger Sterling. Actually, scratch that: it looks like the kind of thing Joan from *Mad Men* would wear if she lost her job as a super-secretary and had to make ends meet by street-walking instead.

'Isn't it *sexy*?' Robyn breathes, fondling the fabric in a manner that's 180 degrees the opposite to the way she was sneering at all her dresses earlier. '*Pleeeease*, Cha-Cha, just try it on! It'll really brighten you up. And don't forget what I said: all the other girls will be wearing short dresses.'

I have a sudden vision of a scene that wouldn't be out of place in a Jane Austen novel: a roomful of gamine fillies in fashionably short frocks, all whispering behind their fans/coming to a shocked halt in the middle of their stately quadrilles/swooning into the arms of a passing Regency buck at the sight of me, committing the ultimate social faux pas and daring to turn up to a party in something below the knee.

I mean, it *is* a Valentino that Robyn's offering to lend me, for Christ's sake. It's not the cheap and cheerful ASOS 'monstrosity' Lucy was so unenthused about earlier.

And then there was that thing, of course, that Robyn said about Jay and girls in red dresses . . .

'OK, but I really don't think it's going to fit . . .'

'Brilliant!' Robyn whoops. 'Let's get this old thing off you.'

'Oh, I'll just go and change in the bathroom . . .'

'For fuck's *sake*, Charlie, I'm your *sister*. I've seen you naked like literally bazillions of times.'

She hasn't, in fact. I've made sure of that. But she's already pulling at the zip on the side of Mum's dress, sliding it down over my shoulders, and shaking it down around my knees for me to step out of. Then – in an astonishingly brisk manner that reminds me of Gaby – she's whipped off my bra and is holding out the sparkly red Valentino for me to step into. I wobble a couple of times in my spindly heels, but this is the least of my worries.

'Robyn, I told you,' I say, as she hauls the dress up my legs, where it stops dead halfway up my thighs, 'it isn't going to fit . . .'

'It's meant to be snug.' Robyn seizes the sparkly

fabric and begins to yank it, inch my inch, up towards my hips.

It's quite a feat of upper-body strength for someone so skinny. In fact, I don't think I've seen her put so much physical effort into something since she ripped Gaby's Classical Civilisation project into a hundred tiny pieces (terrible revenge for Gaby saying Robyn's new bikini made her twelve-year-old stomach look 'pregnant').

'Just grab on to the door handle,' she gasps, edging the dress's panels over my burdensome bottom, 'and breathe in.'

I briefly have time to wonder how I've somehow ended up playing the role of corset-wearing Victorian to her gimlet-eyed lady's maid. But that's about all I have time to wonder, because at this moment Robyn heroically gets the dress up past my bum. From this momentous development it's relatively easy to wiggle it past my middle and over my boobs, and then with one last almighty effort, she cranks the zip all the way up one side until it closes under my armpit.

I'm seeing stars. There's a whooshing sound in my ears. With some difficulty, I turn to glance at myself in the mirror.

'See! Told you it would fit! And it looks great! Look at your *boobs*!' Robyn adds, as an afterthought.

Which is ironic, because in this dress my boobs are not an afterthought. They're jutting out, way up above my poor, crushed ribcage, as though I'm presenting them for some kind of prize-melon award at a village fête. They're the main event. The chief exhibit. At least, this is what I think until I turn to look at my rear view.

My bum, once again, is the size of a small county.

A small county that's been swaddled in skin-tight, fire-engine red Valentino. With spangles on.

'Robyn! You . . .' I have to choose my words carefully, because I know I'm only going to be able to manage to utter about six of them '. . . sure . . . size . . . twelve?'

'Of course I'm sure! It fits, doesn't it?'

'Depends . . . definition . . . fits.'

'Well, I think you look great. *Very* sexy. Oh, that'll be the taxi,' she adds, as her intercom suddenly buzzes. 'Go down and tell him to wait two minutes, will you, Cha-Cha?' She grabs the midnight-blue baby-doll dress from the pile on the bed. 'I guess it'll have to be this one.'

'Will you . . . hang . . . Mum's . . . dress . . . so won't . . . crumple?'

'Yes, yes, I'll do all that. Just go and tell the taxi to wait, Charlie, please, or he'll think there's nobody here and drive off.'

Going down to the taxi is easier said than done, because in this dress (which I'm starting to think is only twenty per cent dress, and eighty per cent boa constrictor) I can't exactly make rapid progress, especially not when there are stairs involved. All I can do is kind of mince forward, rather like some over-enthusiastic extra playing Chinese Peasant Woman

Number Three in an amateur pantomime of *Aladdin*. These blasted shoes don't help, either: I may have been able to stride around my flat without wobbling off them, but now I'm taking these tiny, faltering steps, they're that much harder to balance in.

I suppose I should be gratified, when I do make it down the stairs and out into the street, that the waiting taxi driver's eyes are out on stalks (exactly the way I wanted Ferdy's to be last weekend), but frankly I'm too worn out to care. And anyway, this isn't necessarily proof that I actually look *nice*, or anything. It's perfectly possible that this taxi driver just happens to be an enthusiastic cultivator of prize melons, and he's interested in the fact that I seem to have strapped two of them to my chest.

'Sister . . . down . . . two . . . minutes,' I manage to tell him, before collapsing into the back of his taxi.

'No problem, darling . . . Off out to a glamorous party, are you?'

'Yes.'

'With your sister?'

'Yes.'

'That's nice . . . oh, is this her now?'

I peer through the window to see where he's pointing.

It is indeed Robyn coming out of her building.

Robyn, wearing Mum's Yves Saint Laurent dress.

She's a good couple of sizes too small for it, but this doesn't matter, partly because she's slipped a skinny diamante belt around the waist, and partly because – like I should have realised before I let her talk me out of wearing it – the dress is so brilliantly cut, the fabric so beautiful, that it flatters pretty much whatever kind of body is under it.

'You don't mind, do you, Charlie darling?' she's saying, as she clambers into the taxi beside me, bestowing on me her prettiest smile. 'I just thought it was such a divine dress, it would be an awful shame for *nobody* to wear it.'

'But . . . you said . . .'

'Oh, come on, Cha-Cha, you're not going to be a pain about it, are you?' She pouts. 'Besides, *you're* wearing one of *my* dresses. That's the nice thing about being sisters, now that we're almost the same size. We can do swapsies with our clothes!'

I don't have anything to reply to this. The Valentino boa constrictor dress had already taken away much of my physical ability to speak; now Robyn has taken away pretty much all the will.

I'm kicking myself for being so completely and totally bamboozled.

'Please . . . be careful . . . very delicate . . .'

'Well, for fuck's sake, Charlie, what do you imagine I'm going to do? Chuck glasses of red wine all over it and rip off the hemline by trapping it in a car door?'

I hadn't, actually, imagined either of these things, but now, of course, I'm really worried.

Robyn puts a hand on my shoulder, her eyes wide. 'I'll guard it with my life, Charlie, I promise. The only bad thing that could *possibly* happen to this dress this evening is Jay Broderick ripping it off me in a fit of passion . . . God, I'm *joking*, Cha-Cha, there's no need to look like you're about to be sick! Just along the road to Holland Park, please,' she instructs the taxi driver, who's now openly ogling the pair of us (not just this pair of mine) in his rear-view mirror. 'I promise, if I *do* shag Jay, I'll get totally naked before I let him so much as get a hand on me, OK?'

I say nothing, and concentrate on re-educating myself in the skill of breathing as the big, posh houses of Notting Hill gradually become the even bigger, even posher houses of Holland Park.

Chapter Twelve

When we get out of the taxi in front of the Broderick house, the first thing I notice is the thudding bass-line coming from somewhere inside.

The second thing I notice is that the gates are manned by two burly security guards, wearing dinner jackets, earpieces, and stern expressions, as if they've been tasked with presidential security for the evening, and there's a very real chance we might be the descendants of Lee Harvey Oswald, smuggling Russian-made rifles inside our party dresses. (As if I could smuggle *anything* inside this dress. For Christ's sake, there's barely enough room for my essential organs in here.)

Standing in between the security guards, looking leggy and efficient as ever in black leather leggings and a cropped, tight blazer, is the leggy and efficient Annabel.

'Good evening, ladies.' She smiles, briskly, then glances down at her clipboard. 'Could I get your names?'

'Robyn Glass.' Robyn has adopted the haughty, disdainful expression she favours when talking to Staff. 'I expect I'll be listed in the VIP section.'

'Robyn!' I hiss, embarrassed for her. 'This is a

birthday party, not a club.' (I've learned that if I speak very softly and quite slowly, I can manage to get out entire sentences all in one go.) 'There won't be a VIP section.'

'Of course there will,' she scoffs. 'Everyone has a VIP section at their birthday party! I had one at my last birthday party, remember?' (She seems to have forgotten that her last birthday party was at her then-boyfriend's beachside home on Capri and that neither I nor Gaby was invited.) 'This is my sister Charlie,' she adds, to Annabel. 'She's probably down in brackets next to my name, or something.'

I freeze as, for one awful moment, it suddenly occurs to me that Annabel might remember my surname. But evidently her efficiency doesn't extend to this (either that or she just can't countenance that a Charlotte Glass she met three months ago could be the Charlie Glass who's in front of her right now) because she doesn't blink an eyelid as she glances down at her clipboard.

'Yes, you're both down here, ladies. And you are in the VIP section, as it happens. So if you'd just like to follow me . . . ?'

I'm a bit stunned that there is such a list after all – I mean, if you invite people to your house for your birthday, shouldn't they *all* be VIPs? And what does it say about Jay Broderick that he's hosting a two-tier party like this? – but Robyn is excitedly linking her arm through mine and hauling me after Annabel as she starts to lead us through the open gate.

I'm managing to speed up my mincey pantomime walk enough to keep pace across the driveway, even if it does mean that my thighs are chafing against each other. Annabel is barking orders into her walkie-talkie, and when we reach the house itself, the wide oak front door opens for us as if by magic.

'Two more VIPs,' she tells the waiter who's opened the door and is standing behind it with a drinks-laden tray. 'Show them through to the library, please.'

The lobby looks rather different from the last time I saw it. There's a five-piece jazz band and a full cocktail bar complete with flair barmen, and the lift (sensibly) has been cordoned off with a single red-velvet rope. There's an extremely loud volume of chatter coming from the library, and there are people to-ing and fro-ing across the lobby to help themselves to the cocktails that are being snazzily made by the barmen.

'Oh, my fucking *God*!' Robyn shrieks, slipping her arm out of mine the moment she spots a pair of extremely skinny blonde girls in (natch) extremely short party dresses, who are helping themselves to cocktails before heading towards the staircase. 'Chloe! Zoe! I didn't know you were coming!'

Chloe and Zoe both squeal with excitement and I stand back and watch, not quite certain what to do, as the three of them start giving each other the once-over.

'Have you lost weight?' Chloe/Zoe demands of Robyn.

'No! I'm huge. *You've* lost weight. I hate you.'

'Well, I was ill for a few days last week and I couldn't eat. The weight just fell off.'

Robyn visibly winces.

'But you look *fab*,' Chloe/Zoe continues. 'That dress is *amazing*.'

'Oh, it's just something I picked up last time I was in New York. Vintage YSL, I think.' Robyn puts one hand on her hip, striking a pose. She has, at least, the grace to avoid meeting my eye. 'Do you think the birthday boy will like it?'

'God knows. He's being a real old misery-guts tonight,' Zoe/Chloe pipes up. 'He's barely even spoken to me, which is pretty fucking rude seeing as Mummy is, like, best friends with his stepmother and everything.'

'He's in a mood because Cassia Connelly hasn't turned up, I expect,' Chloe/Zoe says. 'Tragic, really, especially when you see how insanely hot he's looking tonight. Anyway, it's deathly dull in the VIP section so we were about to go up and see what's happening on the first floor.' She gestures up the stairs, which is where the thudding bass-line is coming from. 'There's better music, and loads of food stalls, apparently, and I'm pretty sure we'll be able to find someone to give us a bit of coke.'

'Oh, brilliant . . . I'll just tell my sister I'll see her in the VIP section in a few minutes.'

'You came with *Gaby*?'

'Ugh, no. My other sister. Charlie.'

'I didn't know you had another sister!'

'Yes, that's her right here, in the red dress . . .' Robyn turns round and gestures for me to come and join them. 'Cha-Cha, these are two of my very best friends, Chloe and Zoe. Chloe and Zoe, this is my sister Charlie.'

'Hi!' I smile, and wave, which I regret when Chloe and Zoe stare back at me, neither smiling nor waving.

'Hi,' Chloe/Zoe says, and then after a moment, in an accusing tone, 'You're really *pretty*.'

'Oh, well, she doesn't usually look this good!' Robyn says, before I can reply. There's the faintest tinge of green to her skin all of a sudden, but that might just be the lighting. 'But I lent her this dress! Which was, like, really nice of me, because it's a brand-new Valentino.'

'It's a nice dress,' Zoe/Chloe says, in a similarly accusing tone, before glancing down in the direction of my feet. 'Oh, my *God*. Those shoes! They're incredible!'

It's the first genuine-sounding thing she's said, so I try out another smile.

'Thank you! They're vintage ones, by my dad—'

'*Our* daddy,' Robyn snaps. She silences me with a glare, looking – for one terrifying moment – exactly like Diana. 'Anyway, Charlie, I'm going to pop upstairs with Chlo-Chlo and Zo-Zo. I'll see you inside the party, OK?'

Which is just bloody great, because now I *really* don't know anyone at this party. But as Robyn heads for the stairs (Chlo-Chlo and Zo-Zo trailing in her wake) there's not much for it but to grab one of the Martinis the waiter is proffering and mince into the library, where hopefully I'll be able to loiter, looking as if I'm between conversations, until Robyn and her friends stop stuffing coke up their noses and come back down to join me.

Or – I know – maybe I can just try to look busy on my mobile phone! God knows, I'd rather get involved in a text-chat with Lucy than stand around amongst all the smart, glamorous people – sorry, *very important people* – who are shrieking away at each other in large gangs inside the dimly lit library. Yes – I'll find somewhere to sit down and text Lucy. The taxi ride over here led me to the conclusion that sitting down, in this dress, is A Good Thing.

I spot the little chaise-longue where I sat waiting for my interview, which has been helpfully tucked away in a kind of alcove between two tall bookshelves, and teeter over there, clutching my Martini with both hands, for ballast.

I've not been there thirty seconds, and not even managed to get past the first few words of a text to Lucy (*You were right about glam; not seen anyone in Brecon Beacons mountain gear yet*) when someone suddenly plonks themselves down on the chaise beside me.

'*Christ* almighty, that was a lucky escape. You don't mind if I sit here for a moment, do you?'

It's a stunning dark-haired girl, wearing a very small

tangerine-coloured dress (that displays her ample frontage even more than mine does), clashing fuchsia sandals and a spectacular pair of aquamarine earrings.

'Er – no, not at all.' I extend a hand – though carefully, just in case the movement makes my own ample frontage make a break for freedom. Still, at least my conclusion about sitting down was right – it does seem to free up my poor, crushed ribcage by a crucial couple of millimetres and make it easier to talk. 'I'm Charlie.'

'Huh?'

'My name. It's Charlie.'

'No, it's not. It's Anastasia.'

OK – either she's been overdoing what Robyn and her friends are upstairs doing right now, or she's just plain nuts and in the throes of some weird obsession with a missing Romanov princess. Either way, I don't want to risk disagreeing with her.

'Oh, come on, you must recognise me!' she goes on. 'I'm Maggie! Maggie O'Day! We worked together on that shoot in the Negev Desert, remember?'

'I'm, er, not a photographer.'

'Well, of course not. You're a model.'

I actually laugh out loud. 'You think I'm a *model*?'

'Oh, come on, Anastasia! I'm Maggie! The stylist! I styled that desert beauty shoot you were in last summer, for *Elle* magazine.'

'I've . . . never been in any desert beauty shoot for *Elle* magazine.'

'Oh, well, maybe it was *Grazia*. I lose track of these

things . . . Oh, my *God*,' she suddenly shrieks, glancing down at my feet. 'Your shoes are *gorgeous*! God, models always nick the best things from shoots . . .'

'I didn't nick them! They're mine.' I watch her face as she gazes, covetously, at my feet, with much the same intensity as Chloe/Zoe was just doing. 'You really like them?'

'I *love* them,' she breathes. 'Are they vintage YSL?'

'No.' I shut down the pang of bitterness about the *actual* vintage YSL I should have been wearing tonight. 'They're vintage Elroy Glass.'

'They're *not*!'

'They are.'

'But Elroy Glass shoes are really blah . . . oh, though come to think of it, I'm fairly sure my mum used to wear Elroy Glass in the olden days. And *she* wasn't blah. She once shagged David Bowie on Concorde to New York.'

'That's . . . nice.'

'Or maybe it was Adam Ant . . . They look like a size six. Can I try them on?'

It takes me a moment to realise she's talking about the shoes.

'Um, sure.' On the basis that if she's not worried about the possibility of contracting a verruca, or anything, then why should I be, I unbuckle my shoes and pass them to her.

'Oh, my *God*,' she repeats, although semi-orgasmically this time, as she slides her feet into them. 'How can a pair of shoes this gorgeous be this comfortable?'

'You think they're *comfortable*?'

'Well, not compared to my ancient UGGs, perhaps. But compared to these bloody things –' she kicks one of her own fuchsia sandals in my direction, indicating that I should try it on '– you might as well be walking on air.'

I put my right foot into the fuchsia shoe and – when I have to double-check that I've not accidentally tried to put on the left one of the pair, or something – realise that Maggie is right. Here I've been assuming that Mum's crystal-covered shoes were the most painful footwear experience known to womankind. But trying on this fuchsia sandal is a whole new level of agony.

No wonder 'everyone' is suffering from bunions, if this is the kind of shoe 'everyone' is wearing.

'So, did you find them in a vintage store or something?' Maggie is asking.

'No, I . . .' I realise it's going to be very long-winded to explain all about Dad, especially when there's so much noise from the chattering crowds and that thudding bass-line from upstairs. And when she's convinced I'm a model called Anastasia. 'Kind of a vintage store. Yes.'

'Well, you have to tell me where. I'd literally *kill* for a pair of . . . oh, mother of God, incoming, *incoming*!' Before I can work out what she's talking about, Maggie is kicking off my shoes, pulling her own back on and scrambling to her feet. 'Sorry to ditch you, Anastasia, but I need a new hiding place.'

'Hiding place from whom?' I ask, slightly alarmed that a chainsaw-wielding madman is about to hove into view.

But it's too late, because Maggie-the-stylist has shot off like a nervous deer, blending into the crowd of equally beautiful people in a manner James Bond himself would be proud of.

I realise who she's fleeing from about two seconds later: Hamish.

He's just appeared at the edge of my little alcove, clutching two full champagne glasses. His face is still shiny and roughly the same colour as uncooked bacon, and his shirt collar is still too tight, causing a ridge of bacon-hued flesh to ooze downwards over the starched white fabric.

'Hel-*lo*,' he says, when he sees me.

'Hello.'

'You're looking pretty lonely over here all by yourself.' He manoeuvres himself down on to the chaise-longue next to me, in the space that Maggie has just abandoned, and puts the champagne glasses on the bookshelf behind us. 'I'm Hamish.' He extends a hand and takes mine before I offer it. His palm is damp, with the texture of warm Play-Doh. 'I'm Jay's best friend.'

I'm not that surprised by the fact he doesn't recognise me – this is pretty much to be expected, apparently, by now – but I am a little taken aback by his claim to be Jay's best friend. I mean, *really*?

'You know, I'm pretty sure we've met before, but

you're going to have to tell me where.' He's leaning in a bit closer, close enough that I can see a sheen of sweat on his forehead. 'Have you been to one of the parties at my country house in Wiltshire?'

'No . . .'

'Do you work near the Ferrari showroom in South Kensington? I've been in there quite a lot recently, picking out a new car.'

'No, I don't work near—'

'Oh, I know – do I know you from Davos? I take a ten-bedroomed chalet there for three weeks every Christmas, hire a Michelin-starred chef and throw some pretty raucous dinner parties, Cristal as far as the eye can see . . .'

'No. I've never been to Davos.' And I'm not entirely sure why Hamish is apparently so keen to list all his luxury possessions and hint at his vast entertaining budget. I pull my shoes back on, the better to make my exit. 'I've never been skiing at all.'

'Never been skiing? Well, I suppose that makes sense.' A smile passes across his shiny lips (I have a sudden feeling that he's wearing a light layer of clear lipgloss) and I wait for him to say something obnoxious about me not looking the athletic type, or make some crack about my breaking the ski-lift. 'You wouldn't want to risk the damage, would you, not with a body as incredible as yours?'

I stare at him. I'm dimly aware that my mouth has dropped open. Being mistaken for a model was one thing – it is pretty dark in this corner after all.

But having Hamish telling me that my body is incredible, after (only three months ago) calling me a heifer . . .

OK. I think I've just cottoned on to why Hamish was so keen to shoehorn in all those little hints about his bank balance.

I think he's coming on to me.

If Lucy were here she'd get all excited and tell me that I need to behave like Julia Roberts in that scene in *Pretty Woman* where she goes back, transformed and elegant, to visit the snooty shop assistant who refused to serve her when she was looking all trashy, and revels in rubbing her face in it.

But I don't feel like replicating that scene right now. Because in *Pretty Woman* the snooty shop assistant wasn't pressing her thigh unpleasantly hard against Julia Roberts's thigh, nor placing a sweaty, Play-Doh hand on Julia Roberts's bare shoulder. Nor was she fixing her eyes on Julia Roberts's prize-melon breasts as though she had an insatiable fruit craving and they were the last thing for sale in the greengrocer's.

'Look, how's about this for a plan?' Hamish is saying. 'Why don't you and me get out of here? Go and grab a drink somewhere. My flat in Mayfair, for example.'

'But there's plenty to drink here!' I waggle my Martini glass at him before hastily downing the contents. 'In fact, I need to go and get myself a refill!'

He stops me from getting up by pressing his hand down more firmly on my shoulder.

'Actually, I meant somewhere more cosy. Wouldn't that be nice?'

'Oh, well, I'm not really a fan of cosy. Cosy isn't really my cup of tea. In fact–' a bright idea occurs to me '– talking of cups of tea, I suddenly have this horrible feeling I've left the kettle on at home . . .'

'No need to worry about the kettle. Leaving an iron on is the only thing you have to worry about.'

'But my kettle is . . . is wired up to the iron! I had a very peculiar electrician,' I add, when Hamish frowns at this. 'He took an extremely cavalier approach to wiring. If I leave the kettle on, my whole flat is in danger of burning down.'

'Tell you what, gorgeous.' Hamish's hand slides damply downwards, from my shoulder to my wrist, and interlocks its fingers with mine. 'If your flat burns down, I'll buy you a new one. In the meantime, I've got a bit of blow in my pocket.' He's breathing, hotly, right into my face. His breath smells of booze and – oddly – fresh horseradish. 'Why don't you and I go up to one of the bedrooms and start a little private party of our own?'

'But I don't blow. I mean, I don't *do* blow,' I correct myself, hastily. 'And it would be pretty rude, I think, to start a party of our own when this one's still going on.' I give my hand a sharp pull, succeeding in freeing it from his grasp, and get to my feet. There's a worrying creak from the seams of the Valentino dress, but I choose to ignore it. I'd honestly rather bust out of this dress altogether than stick around with Hamish a moment longer.

'Oh, no, you're not going anywhere!' Hamish gets to his feet, too, making him literally at eye-level with my prize-melon cleavage. 'We've only just started getting to know each other . . .'

I'm about to say that I'm perfectly happy knowing Hamish exactly the amount that I do right now, and no better, when something unexpected happens.

Jay Broderick appears, quite suddenly, at Hamish's shoulder.

He's wearing a midnight-blue suit and a crisp white shirt. His hair (still) looks as if he's just rolled out of bed after a night sleeping the wrong way on it. His cheekbones are more razor-sharp than ever in the sultry lighting. He looks, in the words of Chloe/Zoe, insanely hot.

'Hamish,' he says. 'Everything all right here, mate?'

'Oh, Jay.' Hamish can barely hide his irritation. 'Actually, mate, I'm a little bit busy right now. Mind giving me some privacy?'

'No problem, except that I think Charlie's had just about all the privacy she wants for one evening.' Jay fixes his sooty eyes right on mine. 'Right?'

'Well, I do have a . . . er . . . friend I wanted to talk to . . .'

'Sure.' He reaches right around Hamish and takes my hand. It's possible that this might just have created a couple of sparks of electricity; at least that's what it feels like. I'm a bit too dazzled by his proximity to pay much attention to the finer details. 'Let's go and find her.'

'Oh, come on, mate.' Hamish is looking furious. 'Don't do this to me. I saw her first.'

'Wrong.' Jay flashes a rather dangerous smile in Hamish's direction, before his eyes lock on to mine again. 'I've been waiting for her all night, as it happens.'

'All right, all right.' Hamish gives a rather mirthless laugh. 'It's your party, mate. Don't let me cramp your style.'

'I won't.' Jay interlaces his fingers with mine. It feels absolutely nothing like the way it felt a couple of minutes ago when Hamish interlaced his fingers with mine. Mind you, it's so indescribably wonderful that it doesn't feel like *any* feeling I've ever felt before. 'Come on, Charlie. Let's go and get a breath of fresh air, shall we?'

And before I can say another word, Jay has led me away from my corner, weaving through the crowds without stopping. We go out into the lobby and towards the lift, where he pushes aside the velvet rope, presses the button and stands back to let me through the lift doors as they open.

'Come on up. I've got a surprise for you.'

It occurs to me, about three seconds before the lift doors open again, that he could be taking me to a bedroom. Probably *is* taking me to a bedroom, in fact. We're certainly not stopping off at the first floor, where the main party is, but going two . . . no, three floors up above that.

I'm torn between incredible, pulsating, over-whelming desire (for Jay to throw me on to a bed and take me to heights of pleasure I never knew were possible) and total terror (because I haven't done any heights-scaling with a man, pleasurable or otherwise, for roughly 80 per cent of the last decade).

Oh, and gut-wrenching regret that I didn't get that showgirl wax Galina was bugging me about this morning.

'Hey, it's OK,' Jay says, just as the lift doors open. (Thank *God*, we don't seem to be stuck between floors.) 'I'm not taking you away to be ravished, or anything.'

I manage to cobble together a little laugh – tricky, from within the Valentino rib-crusher – and try not to look too disappointed.

'Oh, one more quick question.' He stops, just as we're halfway out of the lift. 'You're not scared of heights, are you?'

Of pleasure?

'Charlie?'

'No, no, I'm perfectly fine with heights.'

'Great.' He grins, and squeezes his interlocked fingers gently around mine as he leads me out of the lift. 'Then I hope you like it.'

'Like wh—'

Stupid question.

We're standing on the edge of a roof garden. It's about the size of my kitchen, and beautifully land-scaped with a single magnolia tree in the centre, and

266

lilac bushes growing all round the sides over waist-height railings. There are fairy lights strung from the lilac bushes and Chinese lanterns hung from the branches of the magnolia, and in the far corner there's a low, Arabian Nights-style sofa, plump with garden cushions. Beside the sofa is a little cast-iron table, bearing a tray with a glistening silver ice bucket, a bottle of champagne, and two glasses. There's a second, lower table that has another tray set on it, this one with three or four plates of elegantly arranged canapés, bite-sized pieces of fruit and cocoa-dusted chocolate truffles. From some unseen place, speakers are playing light jazz, something that Dad would have been able to identify at 100 paces, but that I can only guess is Miles Davis.

Is this . . . has Jay set all this up . . . for *me*?

'I took a chance you'd like champagne,' he is saying. He lets go of my hand and heads for the tables, where he takes the bottle out of the ice bucket, deftly pops the cork, and starts pouring the contents into the champagne glasses. 'Though I'm afraid I didn't know if you like rosé . . .'

'I love rosé.'

'. . . which is why I played it safe and stuck to white.' He glances up at me and smiles. It's one of the devilish smiles I first noticed him giving to Annabel, but softened with something more . . . angelic, perhaps? 'My apologies, Charlie. I'll sort out the pink stuff for next time.'

Next time? I'm not even sure my heart is going to

make it through *this* time. Now that we're here, in this personally catered roof-garden idyll, I can feel it starting to hammer, nineteen to the dozen, inside my chest. If I'm not careful, the extra movement is going to put my prize-melon boobs in danger of wobbling right out of the top of the dress. I need to sit down again. I mince over to the sofa and lower my spangly red bum all the way down towards it.

'One glass of plain champagne coming up.' Jay turns to me, both glasses in his hand, and looks rather surprised when he sees I'm already attempting to sit. 'I'd thought you might like a look at the view first. You can see all the way to Big Ben from up here.'

'Oh!' I stop myself, mid-lower, before my spangly red bum hits the sofa cushion, and start cranking myself back upwards again. 'Of course!'

'On second thoughts . . .' He's moving towards the sofa himself. 'I can show you the view later. After all, Big Ben isn't going anywhere. Please, Charlie, have a seat.'

I realise that, thanks to his dratted perfect manners, he isn't going to sit down until I do, so to make sure I get a decent head start, I begin winching myself back down towards the painfully low sofa cushions again, talking while I do so to cover any giveaway creaks from my seams.

'Did you know you can go up Big Ben? On a guided tour, I mean. I never realised that until a couple of years ago, when my best friend Lucy took her godchildren out for the day, and . . .'

I can stop. I've finally parked my bottom on the Arabian Nights cushions and don't have to worry about covering up creaking seams any more.

Jay looks at me for a couple of moments, politely waiting for me to finish my story, but when he realises I'm not going to, he sits down (with enviable ease) on the cushion next to me.

'So,' he says, chinking the edge of his glass against the edge of mine. His eyes are fixed on me again, just the way they were down in the library. 'You made it. I was starting to wonder whether you were going to come at all. And then I saw you trapped in that corner with Hamish . . . I hope you didn't mind, by the way?'

'Being trapped in the corner with Hamish?'

He lets out a shout of laughter. 'Well, I assume you minded *that*, from the desperate expression on your face. No, I meant that I hope you didn't mind me riding to the rescue. It's just that Hamish has a bit of a reputation with girls. Especially with a girl like you. You know – a nice girl. A girl who's too polite to tell him to back off.'

Oh. Well, it's nice that he thinks I'm nice. And polite. That's never a bad thing to hear, is it?

But I can't deny I'd have liked it even more if he'd – for example – taken my face in his hands and said, *A girl like you, Charlie, who's so drop-dead gorgeous that I can scarcely look at her without wanting to tear off her suffocatingly uncomfortable Valentino dress and caress every sinful curve of her body.*

Just for example.

'And, of course, Hamish has a *really* bad reputation with girls who are breathtakingly, devastatingly, mind-bogglingly sexy.' Jay takes a sip from his champagne glass. 'Girls like you, Charlie, as it happens.'

Which is about a million times more exciting than what I was just fantasising he might say.

When I realise that Jay is still just looking at me, and that I've got no idea how much time has elapsed since he last spoke, I swallow to moisten my throat, then open my mouth to speak.

'Do you . . . think I'm sexy?'

Brilliant, Charlie. Just brilliant. Of all the things you could have said in this moment – that you think Jay is pretty fucking breathtaking too, for example – you choose to quote the lyrics of a Rod Stewart song.

'Nah, not really.' Jay casts an amused eye around the roof garden. 'I quite often go to this kind of trouble to impress a girl I find only mildly attractive.'

'Oh, right . . .'

He laughs again then shifts a couple of inches on his cushion so that he's closer to me. 'You have to double-check if I think you're sexy? Doesn't the private party in the secret roof garden tell you *anything*?'

'It might just be another VIP section,' I point out.

Jay groans. 'Oh, God, the VIP section. It's awful, isn't it?'

'A bit,' I admit.

'OK, in my defence, I didn't know a thing about

any VIP section myself until about an hour ago, when I started wondering why lots of my friends didn't seem to be turning up to the party. Then I found out that the party planner had unilaterally drawn up a VIP list, and that most of my friends weren't actually on it . . . But, no, Charlie – in answer to your point, this isn't another VIP section. This is just for you and me.' He gets up to retrieve the bottle of champagne and tops up both our glasses. 'And here . . . try one of these.' He reaches for the plate of canapés and picks up a little puff-pastry goat's cheese tartlet, which – before I can refuse – he's popped into my mouth. 'Good?'

I nod, unable to speak until I've swallowed, and partly just unable to speak because the canapé is not just 'good', it's the most delicious thing I've tasted in months. The pastry is buttery, the goat's cheese is sharp and creamy, and it has actual *texture*, unlike the no-fat yogurt and vegetable soup that has formed the entirety of my diet since mid-March. Even though I know the Valentino dress is going to punish me for this, I have to reach out and help myself to another. (And then, when Jay turns his back to put the champagne bottle down again, yet another.)

When he sits back down, he's a little closer than before. There's barely a hand's width between us.

'So,' he says. 'Charlie Glass.'

'Jay Broderick,' I reply, because that seems like the only thing I *can* reply.

'The mysterious Charlie Glass.'

Which I have absolutely no response to whatsoever. So I just take a couple of small sips of champagne instead. I'm hoping this will confirm his (entirely mistaken) belief in my mysteriousness.

'Where have you come from?' he asks, softly.

'Um, Earl's Court?'

He lets out his third shout of laughter. 'You kill me, Charlie, you know that? Are you always this funny?'

'Not intentionally.'

He even seems to find this funny, because he laughs for another moment or so before continuing. 'Anyway, all I meant was that you seem to have come from out of thin air. I've never met you at a party, or out anywhere with friends . . .'

OK, now I definitely need to stay as silent as possible. I can hardly tell Jay that I haven't *been* to any parties for almost ten years, or that while everyone else I know was out with friends, I was at home being fat and lonely and taking care of Dad.

Still, with any luck he'll interpret my silence as yet more of my apparent mystery.

'And then there's the other thing about you. You don't seem that impressed by me. I mean, I wait all night for you, and pull the whole knight-in-shining-armour move, and bring you up here and tell you how totally irresistible you are . . . and you barely say a word!'

Shit. I've taken the mysterious-silence thing too far. Now I'm obviously on the verge of being just plain rude.

'Oh, I'm really sorry . . .'

'Don't apologise. I love it.' He moves closer – only an inch or so, but close enough so that I can feel the warmth of his strong, solid body. 'Most girls would have been all over me by now. Most girls are all over me no matter what I do. And mostly because I happen to have a couple of quid in the bank. But not you. It's like you're . . . immune to me.'

I don't feel the slightest bit immune to him right now. Quite the opposite: my heart is thudding and my stomach is flipping like a pancake on Shrove Tuesday. It flips even more when he places one hand on the side of my face. His little finger strokes, very gently, the nape of my neck beneath my hair.

'Jesus, Charlie,' he whispers. 'How can you turn up to my party looking like a goddess, and not even seem to realise that you're the hottest thing I've ever seen in my entire life?'

Suddenly, without any warning, we're kissing.

We're kissing! I haven't kissed anyone in years, and now here I am, kissing Jay Broderick.

I just have to say that again, to be sure it's actually happening: here I am, kissing Jay Broderick.

It's even better than I imagined. His lips taste of champagne, and his hands are in my hair, and his chest is pressing, firmly, against my prize-melon breasts. I can hardly breathe. I don't think I've felt so helplessly turned on by anything, ever, in my entire life. I may not have much experience in this area, but I'm fairly sure that Jay is – quite literally – the best kisser on the entire planet. But then he would be, wouldn't he, with the amount of women he must have been involved with? All those beautiful girls who are lining up in droves to let him do whatever he wants to them . . .

I can't do this.

Before I know what I'm doing, I'm pushing him away.

'Hey, I'm sorry!' He pulls himself off me, eyes wide with surprise. His lips are rosy where I've been kissing them, and his hair is more mussed up than ever. 'Let's take a break. I was moving too fast.'

'No. I mean, you weren't . . . it's not you,' I blurt, 'it's me.'

Which isn't quite true, because it's not me either. It's all those other girls – a veritable string, you might say – who are suddenly crowding into my head. It's Cassia Connelly, with the peachy, perfect bottom and the breasts sculpted by the Gods. It's the international supermodels. It's Chloe and Zoe, and Maggie O'Day, and all the fabulous, glamorous women here tonight who are far more in Jay's league than I'll ever be. It's *Robyn*, for Christ's sake, who would throw me from the top of this roof if she could see what I'm doing right now.

'I'm sorry,' I mumble.

'Don't be sorry! It's OK. Look –' he gets to his feet to fetch the champagne bottle again '– let's just have another drink, cool things off for a few minutes.'

'No, I can't. This is . . . it's all wrong.' I start hauling myself up from the low sofa . . .

. . . which is when I feel my seam split.

And not just any seam. The seam at the back of the skirt. The seam that, up to this point, has barely been holding the spangly red fabric together over my county-sized, thong-clad bum.

OK. Game over. I have to get out of here.

'Water!' I yelp, as Jay turns back towards me with a glass of champagne. 'I . . . I'd actually really like a glass of water.'

'Water?'

'Yes, water. I'm feeling . . .' I sit back down, very suddenly, which I realise is going to be the best way to hide the calamitous split until I can make an escape '. . . a bit dizzy all of a sudden.'

'Oh, my God, are you OK?' Jay crouches beside me, concern on his handsome face. 'Do you need something else to eat? Another canapé?'

'Mmm, yes . . . I mean, no! No, just that water.'

'Of course.' He goes into his pocket, presumably for his phone. 'I'll call Annabel, have her get one of the staff bring up a bottle—'

'No! You have to go and get it! What I mean,' I carry on, when he looks rather startled, 'is that I'd rather nobody else came up here. It would . . . ruin the atmosphere.'

'OK. I'll go and grab some water and come right back.' He straightens up and heads for the elevator. 'I'll be two minutes, Charlie, that's all.'

'No hurry. Take as long as you need!'

The moment the lift doors close behind him, I'm scrambling back up to my feet again.

OK – I have to think fast. There has to be another way down from here that doesn't just involve waiting for the lift to creak its way back up, probably with Jay already in it. Or, I realise, as I peer over the edge of the railings, down to the ground four floors below, one that doesn't involve my suddenly developing the power of flight . . .

Oh, a drainpipe! Thank God, there's a drainpipe!

I've been pretty good with drainpipes ever since my teenage years, when Diana would ban me from going to any party she knew I particularly wanted to go to, then go out for the evening herself and lock me inside the house without a key. Admittedly I haven't shinned down a drainpipe for roughly twelve years, nor have I ever done so from quite such a height, nor have I ever done so in a skin-tight minidress and heels, with my basically bare bum peeping out the back . . . But beggars can't be choosers. And if I'm really trying to look on the bright side, I weigh a good two stone less than I did the last time I went down a drainpipe, with thighs strengthened to near-steel by all those painful hours of squatting and lunging.

There's a narrow ledge on the other side of the railings that I need to get to before I can lower myself on to the drainpipe, and I can't possibly risk wobbling off it in my spindly heels. With shaking hands, I unbuckle my shoes, take them off and grip the narrow ankle-straps between my teeth. Then I clamp my clutch bag under one arm while – easily enough, now that my skirt is split open at what was previously the tightest point – kicking first one leg, then the other, over the railings.

It's only a couple of (extremely) careful paces along the ledge until I reach the drainpipe. I lower myself to my knees, hold on very, very tightly to the railings, then slide my legs over the edge of the ledge and around the sides of the drainpipe.

Jesus, it's high up here. I start to inch my way down the drainpipe: knees first, then hands, knees again, then hands again. It's slow going but steady, and when I've inched my way down a couple of storeys, I get up the courage to glance down for a moment. About ten feet below me – on the floor where that bass-line has been thudding from all evening – I can see that there's a jutting balcony that would break my fall if I were to slip at this very moment. Which is good news! I mean, I'm not so jaded by this evening's (myriad) disasters that I can't recognise good news when I see it.

The bad news, however, is that there's someone standing on the balcony, looking up at me. More precisely, let's face it, looking up at my great big, mooning bum.

'Er – madam? Are you OK up there?' the someone calls up to me, through cupped hands.

I don't say anything. I can't say anything, because I've got my shoe-straps clenched between my teeth.

So I just make a kind of *hhnngggg* noise, which is meant to mean *I'm perfectly fine, thank you, no need for any concern!*

'Oh, God . . .' The someone has clearly mistaken *hhhngggg* for *save me, save me, I'm semi-naked and stuck halfway down a drainpipe.* 'Look, I'm going to go and get some help, OK?'

'No!' This time I open my mouth, so I can speak properly. I regret it when my shoe-straps slip out of my mouth, sending the shoes dropping to the garden below. 'I'm perfectly fine! Nothing to see here!'

'Er – actually, there's quite a lot to see here.'

This is when I realise that the someone on the balcony has an extremely familiar voice.

Heart thudding more than ever, I risk a proper glance downwards. Which is when my suspicions are confirmed. The someone on the balcony is none other than Ferdy.

'*Ferdy?*' I blurt, before I can stop myself.

'How do you know my . . . oh, my God.' He's clearly recognised my voice, too. (Well, there's no way he could have recognised me by my bum. Is there?) '*Charlie?* Is that you?'

'Yes. Hi, there.' I try to sound nonchalant, as if I've just bumped into him in the deli aisle at Sainsbury's. Hopefully this will trick him into thinking this isn't quite so mortifying after all. 'So! I didn't realise you knew Jay Broderick.'

'I don't. I'm here with a Chill stall. The party planner read about us in *Time Out* a few weeks ago, and she called and asked if I could . . .' He stops, almost certainly realising that we're not, in fact, in the deli aisle at Sainsbury's, and that it's utterly absurd to be holding this conversation when I'm ten feet above him, clinging to a drainpipe, with my bum hanging out. 'OK, Charlie, this is ridiculous. We need to get you down from there. I mean, for crying out loud, what are you even doing shinning down a drain-pipe in the first place?'

'Well, I went up to the roof garden with Jay, and then my dress ripped . . .'

'*He ripped your dress?*'

'No, no! I ripped my own dress! Look,' I carry on, a bit desperately, 'can you just turn your back for a moment, please, while I come down the rest of the way? I mean, I'm sure you can't have failed to notice that I'm slightly under-dressed in the skirt department, and . . .'

'Hey! Excuse me!' There's a sudden shout, coming from the top of the house.

It's Jay, leaning over the edge of the roof garden. I panic, for a moment, that he's seen me, but I think – God, I *hope* – he can only see Ferdy from this angle.

'Mate,' he goes on, confirming my hope, 'I don't suppose you've seen a girl down there, or anything?'

I flatten myself against the side of the house.

'A girl?' Ferdy shouts back up to him.

'Yeah. Blonde. Red dress. Stunning.'

'*Stunning*, you say?' echoes Ferdy, in a deliberate

tone that I know is meant for my benefit rather than Jay's.

'Yes. In a red dress,' Jay calls. 'Kind of short.'

'Wait – the girl is short or the dress is short?'

'The dress!'

'You've mislaid a stunning girl in a short red dress?' Ferdy calls. 'God, I'm really sorry. Sounds like a pretty bum deal.'

Part of me almost – *almost* – laughs out loud. The part of me that knows I'll find all this funny in about thirty years. The rest of me – the part of me that's clinging to a drainpipe, hiding from a devastatingly sexy man who I'd quite like to be getting off with right now – remains steadfastly unamused.

'Yeah, I thought she might have gone down the drainpipe or something, because there's no other way . . .' Jay sounds truly perplexed. 'Well, never mind. Thanks anyway, mate.'

'No problem!'

A moment later, Ferdy hisses, in a theatrical whisper, 'I think we're alone now!'

'Turn round again!' I hiss back, as I start to shimmy, as fast as possible now, down the drainpipe towards the balcony. When I reach that level, it's only a short stretch to be able to get my hands on the balustrade, and then I can swing my legs over on to the balcony itself.

It's only now that I realise that Ferdy is wearing a weird, red-and-white-striped blazer, a red bow tie, and a funny little straw boater hat. It's bizarre and, in the shadows that are being cast from the rooms on the other side of the balcony, rather creepy.

'The uniform for the night,' he says, when he turns round and realises that I'm staring at him. 'All the food stall-holders are wearing it. As decreed by Broderick. Sorry – by your close personal friend and expert bodice-ripper. You know – *Jay*.'

'He's not a bodice-ripper. I told you, I ripped the dress myself. Or rather, my bloody great bum did.' I don't even care any more about drawing Ferdy's attention to my least-favourite body part. After all, he's had a pretty good eyeful of it tonight. And I'm so suddenly, savagely, miserable about everything that's just gone so horribly wrong, after such dizzying heights of glory just a few minutes ago, that I don't even care. 'My bloody great bum, busting through the seams like . . . like the second coming of Christ!'

Ferdy presses his lips together for a moment. Then he says, 'Well, I'm not a religious man, Charlie, but don't you think you ought to inform the Church about this?'

'It's not funny!'

'I mean, the second coming of Christ is a pretty big deal. They might want to set up a shrine to your bum, organise some kind of formal pilgrimage . . . OK, OK, I'm sorry.' He's slipping off his stripy blazer and putting it over my shoulders. 'There. To protect your modesty.'

'Thank you.' I put my arms through the sleeves of

the blazer, which is so huge on me that it does, thank God, cover my exposed backside. 'And thank you for covering for me just now. With Jay, I mean.'

'It's no problem.' Ferdy is gazing down at me. 'I didn't even know you knew Jay Broderick, Charlie, let alone well enough to go cavorting with him in rooftop gardens.'

'We weren't *cavorting*! We were just chatting.'

'Ah, yes. I'm sure Jay Broderick does a lot of chatting in rooftop gardens. I mean, that's the kind of thing they enjoy, these super-rich playboys – having a really good chat.'

I pull the blazer around myself, suddenly wanting to hide my prize-melon breasts. 'He's not a playboy.'

'Says the girl with the smudged lipstick and the bedhead hair,' he says. Ferdy says it lightly, and with a teasing smile on his face, so I'm not sure exactly what to respond, but fortunately he carries on. 'Anyway, I imagine you're going to need my help getting out of here.'

'Only if it's not too much trouble. I mean, I know you have your Chill stall to run, and everything.'

'Oh, that's OK. My assistant Jesse is helping me. Anyway, your friend Jay's pals don't seem all that big on ice cream, if you can believe it. Or gourmet hot dogs, or organic kebabs. But the guys on the sushi stall are doing an absolutely roaring trade.'

Before I know what he's about to do, Ferdy has hopped on to the balustrade, swung his legs over, and dropped down the six more feet or so to the ground.

He lifts his arms up and indicates that I should climb over too. 'Come on. I'll catch you.'

'I'm too heavy . . .'

'You're not too heavy.'

'I am. I'm twice the weight of Honey.'

'What's Honey got to do with anything?' He sounds cranky. 'Come on, Charlie. Any minute now, your Jay is going to be out here with sniffer dogs and the FBI, tracking down the only woman on the entire planet who'd shimmy down a thirty-foot drainpipe to get away from him.'

Even though I'm not at all sure that Jay is going to be too bothered about trying to find me (I mean, I sent him for water and then did a bunk; the rudeness knows no bounds), I don't want to risk it. So I do as Ferdy suggests and clamber over the balustrade. Then I slip down to the ground below as carefully as I can, ensuring that he absolutely doesn't need to catch me.

'All right, then.' He sounds a bit miffed as he makes a start for the front of the house. 'Let's go and find you a cab.'

Again, I don't argue, because I'd rather run the gauntlet of Annabel on the front gate with Ferdy than without him. But as it turns out, there's no need to run any Annabel gauntlet, because she's no longer on the front gate. It's just the two security guards, who remain blank-faced and impassive when Ferdy asks if we can go past them on to the street, where – in well-organised fashion – there's already a line of black cabs waiting.

'Do you have enough money to get home?' Ferdy asks, approaching the first cab in the line and opening the door for me.

I dislodge my clutch bag from beneath my arm – it's a tiny bit sweaty, now, from my armpit – and peer inside to check that I've still got a twenty in there. 'Yes. Plenty.'

'Good. Anyway, I really should get back to the stall. Jesse could be struggling to contain the crowds. There might be two whole people waiting for ice cream now. Maybe even three.'

'Sorry, of course. Will it be OK if I hang on to your blazer, though? Just until I get home.'

'Sure. I mean, it's not even mine. You can return it to Jay Broderick, when you're done with it, if you want.'

I don't say that I won't be seeing Jay ever again, to return a cheap staff blazer to him or otherwise. There's something else that's suddenly on my mind, and I don't want to wait until I get home to check it out.

'Actually, Ferdy, could you just do one more thing for me? Could you look down the back of the blazer and see if you can see the label in my dress . . . and tell me what it says?'

He looks puzzled, and not all that keen, but he does what I ask. 'Valentino,' he says, after a moment.

'No, sorry – I mean, could you tell me what *size* the label says?'

'Oh . . .'

I can feel his breath, very lightly, on the back of my neck, and I can feel the gentle brush of his finger-tips as he lifts my hair out of the way to get a better look at the label.

'It says UK eight.'

'*Eight?*'

'Yes. Eight.' He lets my hair fall back again and steps away, swiftly. 'I gather from Honey that a size eight is a good thing.'

What's Honey got to do with anything? I almost ask. But I don't, because I'm still trying to digest what Ferdy has just read on the dress label.

Size *eight?*

Robyn did say they'd sent her a size that was too big . . .

But then, anything over a size six would have been too big for Robyn. And she didn't say anything about it being (allegedly) a size twelve until she was trying to talk me into wearing it.

The question is, did she deliberately talk me into wearing a dress that she knew was two sizes too small simply because she wanted to wear the Yves Saint Laurent dress? Or was she trying to make me look silly too?

I shiver, suddenly, although the night is still warm.

'Charlie, I really need to go . . .'

'Sure. Thanks again, Ferdy. Thanks so much.' I pull the cab door shut and ask the driver to head for Earl's Court.

When I glance back over my shoulder, a moment

after moving off, Ferdy has already disappeared back through the gates.

I'm halfway home before I realise that my feet are bare. That my shoes – Mum's beautiful, crystal-embellished shoes – are somewhere at the bottom of a drainpipe in the Broderick family garden.

Chapter Thirteen

When I wake up, the morning after Jay's party, the very first thing I remember about the night before is that I did a runner from the most attractive man I've ever met, just as things were starting to get really interesting.

The second thing I remember is that I lost Mum's shoes when I was shinning down that drainpipe.

The third thing I remember is the touch of Ferdy's fingertips when he lifted my hair up from my shoulders to check the label in the back of my dress.

And then, just when I'm wondering how Ferdy has popped into my mind (I mean, up against the thrill of kissing Jay Broderick, you wouldn't think there'd be room in my head for Ferdy at all), I remember a fourth thing.

Maggie O'Day, the stylist who mistook me for a model. And that conversation I had with her, about Mum's (now-lost) shoes.

I think about this conversation while I haul myself out of bed to go for my loathsome Embankment run, and I think about it while I'm eating my breakfast (three meagre eggcup-fuls of sugar-free muesli and a blob of no-fat yogurt; I have to atone for those delicious goat's cheese tartlets somehow).

I'm also thinking that the reason I went on this ghastly health kick in the first place was to help my career, not so that I could waste my time canoodling with men like Jay Broderick. I'm thinking that if I'm going to so spectacularly mess things up with men like Jay Broderick, the least I can do is focus on that career. On Elroy Glass. On what Dad wanted for me. On worthwhile, meaningful, *positive* ventures that don't come to a nasty end with me halfway down a drainpipe, inadvertently mooning half of West London.

So I put Stage One of my plan into action: call Olly Winkleman's number and, when he answers, besiege the poor guy with a barrage of property-ownership questions he surely couldn't have anticipated when he picked up his phone at ten o'clock on a sunny Saturday morning. He's as obliging as ever, though, hmm-ing and hah-ing in his thoughtful way at every question I ask, and then suggesting we meet later on in the day when he's had the chance to pop into the office and dig deeper into the box-files of Dad's paper-work he keeps there. We agree to meet at the King's Road store at three, which gives me plenty of time to execute Stage Two: going on to the internet to track down Maggie O'Day.

It takes a few minutes to ascertain that she has a Twitter account, and quite a few minutes more to set up my own Twitter account so that I can tweet her. Then, after a tense half-hour wait, Maggie O'Day is actually calling my mobile, after which we chat, for a good long while, as (look at me, multi-tasking) I also use the time to get the day's quota of lunges under my belt.

Then, as soon as I'm finished on the phone, I'm out of the flat and heading to the store, even though it's a good couple of hours until I'm actually due to meet Olly. Stage Three is too exciting to postpone, even for just a couple of hours. And I'm so wrapped up in Stage Three, in fact, that I don't hear Olly coming into the store and up the stairs to the stockroom until his head appears in the doorway, and he says, cheerfully, 'Knock, knock.'

'Olly!' I scramble up from where I've been squatting in the middle of the stacked packing cases – packing cases that I've now opened up and begun carefully to divest of their contents. I would go over and give him a hug, but I'm suddenly aware that I haven't showered or changed since this morning's loathsome run, and that now my rapidly staling sweat is sealed in by the fine layer of dust that's been gradually raining down on me ever since I started going through the cases. 'Thanks so much for coming!'

'It's no problem at all. Glad I can help.'

'Well, at least let me buy you a coffee.' I brush the worst of the dust from my arms and reach for my bag, which is now buried beneath half a dozen pairs of slightly dubious hand-painted clogs, one of Dad's less successful design experiments. 'There's a café over the road.'

'Actually, I passed a rather nice-looking ice-cream parlour just a couple of doors along . . .'

'No!' The last thing I want, after last night's drain-pipe débâcle, is to run into Ferdy. But I think I've startled Olly, so I add, 'I don't think they've opened yet.'

'It looked pretty open. Lots of people queuing.'

'Oh, well, in that case, we'd definitely be better off avoiding it. Nothing worse than queuing for ages for ice cream.' I make a start for the stairs, before Olly can – quite reasonably – come up with roughly half a billion things that are worse than queuing for ice cream. 'Anyway, I could really do with some caffeine!'

'But I think the ice-cream parlour also does coffee—' Olly finally gives up trying to persuade me to join the line at the lovely looking, retro ice-cream parlour, and after I lock up the store, follows me happily enough over the road to the dodgy, fly-blown caff instead.

I insist on buying the coffees (black for me; a creamy cappuccino and a delicious KitKat for lucky old Olly) while he grabs a table as close to the open doors as possible.

As soon as I sit down at the slightly sticky Formica, I remember that I owe him another round of apologies for the housewarming party/Scandinavian Accountants' Conference I subjected him to last weekend.

'But, Charlie, I didn't have that bad a time!' he assures me, midway through my apology. 'Honestly! I learned a lot about the differences between Swedish and Norwegian – who's to say that won't come in handy, somewhere down the line? – and it never hurts to know more of the ins and outs of pension funds.'

I suspect that it *could* hurt, actually, but he's being so polite that I don't want to disagree with him.

'Well, thanks again, Olly, for coming with me. I was the only friend of Lucy's there, so it's a good thing you helped me stick it out. For her sake, that is, not for Pal's.'

'Yes. Pal. I must admit, I found him . . . hard work. Still, maybe it's just a language barrier. He seemed ever so keen to tell me that he farts lots.'

'It's *fartleks*, I think. Something to do with interval training.'

'Ohhhhhh. That does make more sense. He kept telling me he was doing it in the gym, and I kept wondering why they hadn't asked him to revoke his membership. For the sake of all the other gym-goers, if nothing else.'

This makes me laugh so hard that coffee comes shooting out of my nostrils, and Olly has to go and get a napkin for me to mop it up.

'Anyway,' he goes on, tactfully changing the subject while I dab the Formica and try not to die of embarrassment, 'it was a perfectly nice evening. Good to see your friend Lucy again. Oh, and that other chap. Fergie, is it?'

'Ferdy.'

'Ah. I think I may have called him by the wrong name.' Olly looks mournful. 'That might have been why he wasn't all that friendly to me.'

'He wasn't?' I realise that I've jumped on this with far too much interest, so I ask again, more casually, 'I mean, *wasn't* he very friendly?'

'Well, maybe I just imagined it. After all, he was perfectly affable when I met him the first time, at your dinner party. No reason why he wouldn't have been equally affable when I saw him this time.' Not realising the significance of what he's just said, Olly has started rooting round in his briefcase for the paperwork we're actually here to discuss. 'So! We should talk about why you called me this morning. Selling your dad's old shoes . . .'

'Well, it'll be a bit more than just that,' I say, hastily, wanting to disabuse Olly of the notion that what I'm actually planning to do is flog a load of old shoes at Sunday-morning regional car-boot sales, or something. 'What I really want to do is use Dad's old shoes – his *vintage* shoes – as part of the Glass Slippers project.' I sit forward in my chair, buzzing with enthusiasm again, exactly the way I was when I discussed this with Maggie O'Day earlier. 'After all, Glass Slippers is meant to be a range that brings back the glory days of Elroy Glass, and it occurred to me last night: why not focus on the vintage aspect of it all?'

'And vintage is a good thing, yes? I mean, it's not like the jumble sales my mother runs for the church fund-raising committee?'

'Vintage is a very good thing indeed. Which is why I'm thinking that Glass Slippers should be a vintage-inspired line. And what better way to launch a vintage-inspired line than to start off by selling much-coveted, *actual* vintage Elroy Glass shoes – shoes that don't hurt so much you want to die, shoes that don't give everyone bunions – in the original Elroy Glass store?' I take a slurp of watery coffee, then break off a tiny bit from one of Olly's fingers of KitKat, just to take the taste away. 'I've been discussing it with a fashion stylist, and she's going to help me pick out the best ones to put on sale. Assuming I *can* put them on sale, that is . . .'

'Which is where I come in.' Olly nods. 'Well, I've managed to check out the deeds to the store, and you're in luck. On that front, at least. The contents of the store belong to the company.'

This doesn't, in fact, sound like I'm in luck at all.

'To the company? But not to me?'

'Yes.'

'So . . . I *can't* sell them?

'No, no, it doesn't mean that at all! It simply means that you'll need permission from your fellow directors before you do sell them. But as the profits will be going back into the company, I can't imagine any of the directors will have a problem with that . . .' He stops, suddenly. 'Ah. Though I'd forgotten that, of course, Diana *is* one of the directors . . .'

I stare at him in dismay. (Dismay doubled by the fact that, I've just realised, I've somehow eaten an entire finger of KitKat, and not just the little piece I intended.) 'She's never going to give me permission!'

'Oh, I'm sure she would. After all, selling the shoes

would be a direct revenue stream into – what seems like, frankly – a struggling company.'

'Olly, I promise you, I could come up with an idea that would net Diana a cool million pounds in personal profit every year from now until Doomsday, and she'd still reject it out of hand if she thought the idea was important to me. If it was something I might actually enjoy doing.'

He thinks about this in his usual careful, considered manner for a moment before apparently deciding he can't really deny it.

'Well, there's still no need to despair, Charlie. Diana is only one of six directors. Her vote carries no more weight than anyone else's.'

'Maybe not, but Gaby will just do whatever her mother tells her to do, and as for Alan Kellaway . . . sorry to be rude about your boss, Olly, but he was shagging Diana when I was younger, and if he's not *still* shagging her, I'll eat my hat.'

'True, but I'm sure you'll have no problem getting permission from Terry Pinkerton or James I. And James II seemed rather taken with you, if I recall, so I can't believe that will pose any sort of a problem.'

'But it'll be three against three.' I squirm, uncomfortably, in my seat. 'Which means I'll have to take the casting vote.'

'And . . . ?'

I can hardly believe he's asking this. '*And*,' I say, heavily, as I help myself to another finger of KitKat (look, it's medicinal now, OK?), 'that'll just be one more opportunity for Diana to conclude that I'm defying her. I don't know if you've noticed, Olly, but my stepmother isn't big on people defying her.'

'Really, Charlie, this isn't insurmountable. What we need to do is . . .' He breaks off, because something on the other side of the street has, apparently, just caught his eye. 'Oh,' he says, wistfully and with a touch of envy in his voice. 'Nice *car*.'

On the other side of the road – right outside Dad's store, in fact – a sleek, dark-blue sports car has just pulled up. The driver's door opens, and Jay starts to climb out.

'Oh, my God!' I duck, just in case he turns his head and sees me through the caff window.

'Are you OK?' Olly asks, with concern.

'Yes, it's just . . . someone I know.'

'The chap with the Aston Martin?'

'No, don't look!' I yelp, ducking even further, and throwing down what's left of my second finger of KitKat. 'He's only looking for me because he's annoyed with me.'

'Are you sure?' Ignoring my express orders, Olly is peering out through the window. 'It looks like . . . hang on,' he whispers, which is probably strictly unnecessary unless, to add to all his many other impressive physical attributes, Jay has supersonic hearing too '. . . he's carrying something . . . it looks like a shoebox, actually.'

'Mum's shoes!' I'm so relieved that I almost pop my head up for a moment. 'He found them!'

'He's gone up to the shop,' Olly reports, now starting to sound a little bit like David Attenborough hiding out in a camouflaged tent and commenting to camera on the hunting habits of the rare Afghan mountain snow leopard. 'He's trying the door . . . he's trying it again . . . now he's looking around . . . oh, now he's heading for the beauty salon next door . . . maybe he's going to ask in there if anyone's seen you . . .'

'No!'

I have to stop this in its tracks before Jay tries the next store along from Galina's, which is Chill (I don't fancy the prospect of Jay running into Ferdy any more than I fancied the prospect of running into Ferdy myself), or – even worse – heads over to the caff. The trouble is that, even if I weren't too much of a coward to go and actually face Jay after the stunt I pulled last night, there are some pretty major issues with my appearance which make facing him a total no-no. The issues being that, 1) I'm still in the sweaty (and now dusty) leggings and baggy T-shirt that I wore for my loathsome run this morning; 2) I'm wearing, precisely, *zero* make-up; and 3) a large and unsightly spot is swelling, slowly but surely, probably thanks to the stress of last night, in the dead centre of my chin.

'If it would help at all, Charlie, I could go over and take the shoes from him.'

'Oh, Olly! Would you do that?'

'Of course.' He's already pushing back his chair.

'Unless you're avoiding him because he's dangerous or something?'

'No, no. He's not dangerous.' At least, not in any kind of a way that Olly might be imagining.

'Then you're avoiding him because . . . ?'

'It's a long story,' I say, since I'm not especially keen to relive the Great (Drainpipe) Escape again, and certainly not right now, when I need Olly to go and get my shoes from Jay. 'Please, Olly, if you could just go and . . . well, intercept him.'

He's off, taking his polystyrene cup of coffee with him but – damn him – leaving behind the remains of the KitKat. I've just broken off a bite-sized piece from it, to calm my rattled nerves, when I hear my phone start to ring inside my handbag.

I grab it extra quickly when I see that it's Olly calling.

'Olly, hi!' I daren't peek over the edge of the window. 'Has he gone yet?'

'Gone where?'

It's Jay's voice.

I silently curse Olly, who – now that I risk that peek out of the window – is at least looking slightly sheepish. He's outside Dad's store, standing next to Jay, who has slid the shoebox under one arm so he can talk to me on Olly's phone.

'Jay!' I quickly adopt the sunniest, most carefree tone I possibly can. 'Hi there!'

'Hi there,' he repeats. He doesn't sound angry with me. In fact, he sounds rather amused. 'I hope you don't mind but I asked this Olly guy if I could call you on his phone. To prove that he's a friend of yours like he claims, I mean. For all I know, he could be working for them.'

'Working for who?'

'For whoever it is that's kidnapped you.'

OK, now I'm lost.

'Well, I'm assuming that's what happened last night,' he goes on. From my secret vantage point, I can see him moving a little way away from Olly. When he speaks again, he lowers his voice, slightly. 'Because I've racked my brains to think what other explanation there could possibly be for you doing a bunk while I was kissing you. I mean, I'm pretty sure I don't have BO, and I'd been extra-specially careful brushing my teeth . . .'

I can't see clearly, because a queue of three passing double-decker buses has just cut off my sight-line across the road, but I think from the sound of his voice that he's grinning.

'And, of course, I immediately ruled out the possibility that you just didn't fancy me. So quite obviously,' he continues, 'the only explanation is that while I was off looking for a glass of water, you were carted off by a bunch of kidnappers. Now, just tell me what ransom they're asking for, Charlie, and I'll shell it out, every red cent. Ten million, twenty . . . ?'

'Jay . . .'

'Because did I happen to mention, Charlie, that I'm absolutely loaded? I mean, if that changes the way you feel about me at all? I'm not proud. I have no dignity. If my money is the only reason you might want to go out with me, Charlie – I don't care.'

He's joking – at least, I assume he's joking – but I'm too dazed by the charm offensive to laugh at the joke.

I mean, is he really – *really* – still interested in me? After the way I behaved last night?

And more to the point: did I mishear, or did he just say something about *going out* with him?

I clear my throat and try to sound cool. 'But I thought you said you were tired of girls only wanting you because you . . .' what was the phrase he used yesterday? ' . . . have a couple of quid in the bank.'

'Ah, yes. But that was before you rejected me. *If* you rejected me, that is. Because I'm still pretty certain that kidnapping is the only explanation here.'

'Excuse me.' The café owner (a small but terrifying Cypriot woman who looks as if she could be a distant relative of Galina's) has suddenly appeared at my table. Hands on hips, she gestures down at my empty coffee cup and the leftover fingers – OK, half a finger – of KitKat. 'You finished?'

I gesture frantically at her to be quiet, but evidently she's not quite aware of the magnitude of this situation.

'Because if you're not ordering anything else,' she continues, more irritably than ever, 'I have people waiting to use this table. It's Saturday afternoon, you know,' she adds, returning to her counter, satisfied she's put sufficient pressure on me. 'King's Road is full of shoppers.'

Which – brilliantly – has just alerted Jay to the fact that I must be on King's Road.

'Ah,' he's saying now, 'so you're being held on King's Road somewhere, then? Tell me where, Charlie, and I'll come right down and rescue you. Teach those kidnappers a thing or two. I mean, I don't know if you've happened to notice, but I'm six foot two and in phenomenally good shape. Not to mention the fact that I've still got shedloads of upper-body strength from the time when I was this hotshot Formula One driver . . .'

'World Champion,' I blurt, before I can stop myself.

Jay is silent for a moment, before saying, in a more amused tone than ever, 'Been checking me out, by any chance?'

'No! My friend just happened to mention . . .'

'So you've been discussing me with your friends! Even better! What did they have to say about me? Do they reckon, for example, that you should come out to dinner with me one night next week?'

'Dinner?'

'Yes. It's a meal, Charlie. People generally eat it at the end of the day, sometimes with friends, sometimes in a place called a restaurant . . .'

I can see him lean, casually, against a postbox on the other side of the street, and rake a hand through his hair in a way that makes my stomach lurch with desire.

'Anyway, you have to see me sometime, Charlie,' he adds, 'if you're ever going to get your shoes back. You know – the ones I found, funnily enough, at the bottom of a drainpipe.'

'God, yes, thanks so much, Jay. They were my . . . well, I'm really grateful you found them.'

'Look. Charlie.' His voice is suddenly lower. He sounds more serious. 'Joking aside, if you don't want to see me, then please just say so. I can handle rejection. I'm not *used* to it,' he adds, 'but I can handle it.'

'Jay, you've got it wrong.' I grip the edge of the sticky Formica table, to prevent myself from jumping to my feet, running out of the café, leap-frogging buses and throwing myself into his strong, sexy arms. Which would be heavenly, and very dramatic. But probably not advisable, for the road safety of the general public as much as anything else. 'I'd love to see you again.'

'Really?'

'Really,' I say.

His face lights up with a grin and he gives the top of the postbox a thump of triumph.

Seriously: would it be *that* bad an idea for me to reconsider the whole leap-frogging-the-traffic thing? Because with Jay as attractive as he is right now, I'm sorry, but the road safety of the general public is very low down on my list of priorities.

Then I remember the sweaty, dusty leggings and the looming zit, and come to my senses.

'Excellent,' he says, sounding – deliberately? – a lot more blasé than he looks. 'Does Monday night suit you?'

Monday . . . OK, is that enough time to fit in at least two more ninety-minute workouts, deal with the spot in the epicentre of my chin, get one of those spray tans, get a professional pedicure, work up the courage to ask Galina to do that showgirl wax she's been threatening me with . . . ?

I brush aside, hastily, the realisation that I'm sounding a bit like Robyn. After all, the endless preparations she wanted to make before Jay's birthday party were, for her, just unnecessary icing on the cake. For me, they're the cake itself. (Though it's very important, right now, that I STOP THINKING ABOUT CAKE AT ALL.)

'Um, actually, Tuesday would be better.'

'Tuesday it is. So can I get this very nice Olly bloke to give me your number?'

'You can,' I tell him, 'get that very nice Olly bloke to give you my number.'

'Good. I'll call you, then, to arrange what time and where I'm picking you up.'

'God, no, there's no need to pick me up!' I feel, for the first time ever, ashamed of my little flat, at the wrong end of Old Brompton Road (at the wrong end of the whole mansion block, if we're being really honest about it). 'I'll meet you wherever we're going for dinner.'

'Charlie, I'm picking you up. If you don't want me

to know where you live – if you really do lead as much of a double life as it seems – then I'll pick you up right here, OK? At your so-called shoe store on King's Road.'

It's thrillingly masterful – not to mention a perfect suggestion – so I agree.

'Great. Then I'll see you on Tuesday, Charlie. Assuming you've managed to escape from the kidnappers by then, that is.'

This time I manage a flirty little giggle – well, my version of a flirty little giggle; Lucy would be falling over herself to stop me if she were here – and then I quickly hang up before I do or say anything to destroy the moment.

Outside on the street opposite, Jay peels his insanely hot body away from the postbox and heads over to Olly to return his phone. A moment or so later he's climbing back into that sleek, dark-blue sports car and driving away – just a fraction too fast – down the King's Road.

Chapter Fourteen

I'm starting to see why Robyn never appears to do a day's work and why Gaby, who does do a day's work, is always looking so stressed. It's the grooming. How could I not have realised, at the age of almost twenty-nine, that grooming is pretty much a full-time job? And I'm not even talking about the optional extras: facials, and Botox, and laser skin resurfacing, and all the other things I haven't the time, money, or inclination to get involved in. I'm just talking about the basics. Or rather, what seem to be the basics, nowadays, for any self-respecting woman wanting to walk down the street without being chased down it by angry villagers bearing flaming torches and pitchforks.

You need hair without visible roots. You need a thorough wax, seeing as it's summer. You should have a pedicure, for feet that won't shame your sandals. You need non-bushy eyebrows. You need to be free from any hint of (what I'm still reluctant to call) moustache and sideburns. And all of this is to be fitted in around a workout schedule that would make an Olympic athlete weep, and on an energy-sapping, low-carb, low-fun diet that's starting to make me feel like weeping, too.

I'm actually starting to think that there should be

some kind of government subsidy for basic female grooming needs. Or at the very least, that it'd be nice of them to make it tax-deductible.

Not to mention the fact that it's just so bloody difficult to *schedule* it all. I have to fit in enough of those Olympian workouts (vital, because I'm not going out for dinner with Jay Broderick feeling like the largest potato in the sack), which puts paid to any notion of getting a pedicure until I can stop stuffing my feet into my trainers. I'm too busy to go to Galina for the wax until tomorrow morning. And this lunchtime – Monday's – is spent, for two-and-a-half boring and heinously expensive hours, flicking through old magazines at the hairdresser's while a very nice girl called Louisa obliterates any pesky hint of mousebrown root from my newly blonde hair.

I'm almost starting to wonder if going out with Jay tomorrow night is worth all this faff and hassle.

I said *almost*.

Anyway, it's not like I haven't got about a million better things to do with my time than whirl endlessly round on this carousel of beauty upkeep. I've already spent the morning unpacking every single pair of Dad's shoes from the packing cases in the storeroom, photographing them and cataloguing them all in a file on my computer. I need a full inventory of what's actually available to show to Maggie – and to the directors, of course, if the project ever gets that far. And not only this, but on the (safe) assumption that Diana is going to put every possible spanner in the

305

works to prevent Glass Slippers from selling Dad's vintage shoes, I've decided that it would be a good idea to start work on the vintage-inspired line that would, anyway, follow.

Maggie has put out some feelers and found three or four freelance shoe designers who are young, talented, but – most importantly of all, if I'm going to win over my fellow directors with this project – cheap. A couple of them are meeting me for a chat at the store this afternoon, so as soon as the Hair Appointment That Time Forgot is over, I jump on the bus and head for King's Road.

I'm just opening up the door to the store when there's a tap on my shoulder and I turn round to see someone I haven't seen in ages.

It's DI Wright. I mean, *Martin*. Ferdy's dad.

He's a tall but lean man (Ferdy once told me he gets his own chunky build from his Italian mother) who, with his kindly, concerned face and thoughtful manner, always looked more like a genial maths teacher than a senior policeman. He looks more like a maths teacher than ever today, in fact, as he's wearing a rather battered corduroy jacket and what you might call 'Dad' jeans. (I wouldn't call them this, because my own dad, as befitting of his status as a grandee of the design world, would never have worn such cosy, unflattering denim; wax-coated Japanese skinnies were more Dad's jeans style until he got too ill to hoik himself into them, and bright-coloured silk pyjamas after that). Martin looks, also, rather surprised at my own appearance – as well he might, seeing as the last time he saw me I was a fat brunette – but years on the force have left him with an inscrutable air that means you never know quite what he's thinking.

'Charlie,' he says.

I don't need to decipher his tone of voice to know why he's here.

I mean, I've known what date it is ever since I woke up this morning. Known what date is approaching, however resolutely I try to ignore it, for the past few weeks.

'I hope you don't mind,' he says, 'the surprise visit. But Ferdy told me you were setting up shop here and so I thought I'd pop by the next time I was in the area. You know, to see how Ferdy's new premises are doing.'

'On July the sixth?'

'On July the sixth.' He clears his throat. 'Just to see how you're doing. But you look very well. You look . . . blossoming, actually.'

'You look great, too.' I realise, suddenly, that I haven't given him a hug or kiss hello, so I do this now. He smells of Pears soap, exactly the way he's always smelled. Exactly the way he smelled twenty-one years ago today, in fact, when he sat next to me on a sticky plastic chair in a hospital waiting room and tried to get me to play him at noughts and crosses to distract me, while a few feet away two doctors and a nurse explained to Dad how Mum had died. I have to swallow back the lump that forms in my throat as the clean, soapy smell brings back that evening to me as if it were yesterday. 'I've been meaning to call you for ages, I'm so sorry . . .'

'You've been busy, Charlie love. Don't worry about it.' He nods at the Cypriot café over the road. 'Shall we pop and get a cup of tea? If you have the time, that is?'

I tell him that I have just a few minutes – which I do, before Maggie's prospective shoe designers arrive – and so we head over to the café, order a pot of tea between the two of us and take it over to a quiet table.

'Well!' I say, busying myself with tea-pouring. 'I'm really glad I can finally get to wish you a belated happy birthday! Honey mentioned it,' I add, when Martin's brow creases.

'Ah. Honey. I wasn't sure if you knew her or not.'

'Yes. Well, no. I mean, I don't *really* know her. I've met her a couple of times when she's been with Ferdy, that's all.'

'Ah,' Martin repeats. 'A common occurrence these days. And getting more common by the day! Honey being with Ferdy, that is,' he explains, when I look confused myself. 'I was saying to his mother, only the other day, that I'm starting to wonder if Honey has patented some invisible technology that means she's actually managed to surgically attach herself to Ferdy without him realising it.'

This is such a Martin-like thing to say (this is a

man, after all, who has devoted much of his retire-
ment to reading science-fiction novels and pottering
around in his shed trying to improve on classic inven-
tions like tin openers and Sellotape), not to mention
such an accurate description of Honey, that I have to
laugh. It intrigues me, too, because . . . well, is it just
me, or does this sound as if Martin doesn't like Honey
all that much?

'Don't get me wrong,' he continues, as though he's
read my mind, 'she's a . . . a lovely girl. Don't you
think?'

'Oh, yes! Lovely.'

'I just . . . well, Ferdy's mother and I . . . well, it's
hard to say, isn't it, if your children have found the
right partner or not?'

'Um, I imagine so, yes.'

My phone rings, quite suddenly, inside my handbag.
When I grab it, I see that it's Lucy calling. Despite
the fact I've already been forced to ignore three calls
from her today (hairdresser) I decide to let it go to
voicemail and that I'll call her back later. This conversation about Honey is too intriguing to interrupt.

However, the ringing phone has obviously broken
the moment, because when I put it back in my bag
and look at Martin again he just says, in an apparent
non-sequitur, 'Ferdy was rather upset when you
dropped out of touch a few months ago. You were
in . . . America, was it?'

'America, yes. But I didn't drop out of touch!' I
can't help feeling rather outraged at Ferdy for telling

Martin this. 'I mean, I emailed him! Several times, in fact! I just assumed he was too busy to reply.'

'Well, he certainly works too hard, that's for sure.' Martin takes a sip of his tea. 'I hope you and he still find the time to chat occasionally?'

'I've been pretty busy myself lately,' I say, hastily, not wanting to make Martin any more wary of Honey by indicating that Ferdy seems to have had a bit of a personality transplant since starting his relationship with her, and that I'm not sure he and I will ever 'chat' again. 'I don't know what Ferdy's told you, but Dad left me his entire share of Elroy Glass in his will. So I'm doing my best to bring a bit of Dad back into the business.'

Martin looks pleased. 'That sounds terrific, Charlie! And I'm so glad your dad did that for you, in his will. Of course,' he adds, with a kindly pat of my hand, 'I'm sure it doesn't compensate you for all those years when he wasn't much of a father to you.'

I blink at him. 'Martin, he was terminally ill with motor neurone disease for the past ten years. How was he supposed to be any more of a father to me than he actually was?'

'Er . . . I'm not talking about this past ten years, Charlie. I'm talking about the ten years before that.'

This still isn't making very much sense. 'But he had a total nervous breakdown. He was grieving for Mum.'

'In Turkey. Yes.'

'Morocco.'

310

'Morocco. I apologise.'

There's a rather awkward pause for a moment or two, before he continues.

'Anyway, Charlie, while we're on the subject of your mum.' He sets his mug down. It's time, I can see from the expression on his face, for his customary annual update on the case. 'As ever on . . . on this day, I want to let you know that I'm still making sure the file on the accident is kept active. Obviously I can't claim there's a huge amount of police resources devoted to it! But I check in every now and then with a couple of my old colleagues who are still working at Battersea police station. And I drop in on old Jane Brearly every once in a while, too, see if there's anything fresh she might have remembered. Of course, she's past ninety now, so I'm not sure how much longer I'm going to be able to do that.'

Jane Brearly is the only witness to Mum's accident, and very far from an ideal one. If, God forbid, you should ever get into a bad accident, the kind of witness you want is some spry young person with twenty:twenty vision and a trigger-happy finger with the camera on their mobile phone. Either that, I guess, or functioning CCTV in the area. What you don't want is a seventy-one-year-old lady with dodgy eyesight and an even dodgier memory. What you don't want is Jane Brearly. She was sure about one thing only: that the sports car she saw speeding off after colliding with Mum was 'Cadbury's Dairy Milk-purple'. She couldn't be any help at all with the make or model, seeing as she

311

kept making the vague claim that the car was 'definitely named after a planet', but whether Mars, Mercury or Venus, she could never be completely certain. Not that it mattered which, seeing as – like Martin kept trying to gently remind her, back then and many times over the years – there *are* no sports cars named after planets.

'That's OK, DI Wr— Martin. I mean, I appreciate your trying, and everything.'

'Well, I don't want you to give up hope, Charlie.'

'No. Absolutely.'

Because I'm not going to tell him that I gave up hope years ago. That would just be rude, under the circumstances, wouldn't it? Besides, I don't know that it would make so very much difference if we ever *did* find out who'd hit Mum and not bothered to stop. Justice is all very well, but it isn't going to bring her back.

'Old cases like these are being solved all the time! Though obviously quite a lot of them,' Martin says, looking like he wishes he'd not started down this optimistic road now that he's actually thought about it, 'are cases that involve DNA testing.'

'I know. It really is fine, Martin. I'm realistic about this.' I can see, over the road, that a guy and girl in head-to-toe black and with matching John Lennon glasses have just arrived outside the store and are trying the door. They have to be Maggie's fledgling shoe designers. Nobody but serious fashion people would be dressed in black on a warm day like this.

'Actually, Martin, sorry, but I really need to go now. The people over there have just arrived for a meeting with me . . .'

'Of course.' He looks rather solemn, as he always does when his duty has been done for yet another year. I think we both prefer the non-anniversary occasions, when he can just chatter away happily about the latest Ray Bradbury short story he's just discovered, or about his recent strides in the race to create Ultimate Sellotape. 'It was good to see you anyway, Charlie love. Why don't you try to come over to the house with Ferdy some time? I know Maria would love to meet you after all these years, and I'm sure Ferdy's told you what a superb cook she is.'

'That sounds lovely,' I say, making no mention of the fact that it might be a little bit awkward, seeing as Ferdy and I don't really seem to be friendly any more. I get to my feet and lean over to give him a hug. 'Great to see you, Martin. Are you heading over to Chill?'

'I'll just stay here for a bit, I think.' He reaches into the pocket of his corduroy jacket and pulls out a paperback with Isaac Asimov's name on the cover. 'Finish my tea. I think Ferdy is at the Soho branch today anyway.'

Which pretty much gives away the fact that he wasn't just 'in the area', and that he came all the way over here just to mark the date of Mum's death.

I bend down again and give him a kiss on the cheek, before promising again that I'll see him soon. Then I leave the Cypriot café and head over the road to meet the couple in the matching John Lennon glasses.

I'm pounding the pavement this evening – my second run of the day, though a different route than along the Embankment this time – when Lucy's number pops up again on my mobile.

Shit – I haven't had the chance to call her back today. After she called when I was with Martin at the café, she called a further two times while I was with Leo and Suzy at the store.

Leo and Suzy, by the way, being Maggie's prospective shoe designers: a sweeter-than-sweet pair, once you got past their burning intensity. They're coming up with sketches for six vintage-inspired pairs of shoes for me and Maggie to approve in time for the directors' AGM, a few weeks from now.

'Drainpipe?' Lucy demands, when I breathlessly answer her call. '*Drainpipe?*'

'Sorry, how on earth do you . . . ?'

'I called Ferdy this afternoon, just to give him a heads-up on where I've got to with the bookings for his parents' anniversary cruise. And wouldn't you know it? He just so happened to give *me* a heads-up on how he spent his Friday night. Which, you know, it might have been nice if someone else had given me instead.'

She sounds annoyed. I can't really blame her – I'd be a bit put out if she'd snogged a gorgeous man, escaped from him down a drainpipe, and then left me to find out all about it from a third party instead – but it's not like I've been deliberately trying to avoid telling her.

'Sorry, Luce, but I've been manic all day today! And in fairness, I did text you on Sunday asking you to call me . . .'

'You did. And I tried you as soon as I had some time to myself, without . . .' She breaks off before adding the word *Pal*. 'But all you said in your text was, *Call when you get a chance*. You didn't say, *Call me urgently because I have incredible news about my snogathon with a hot billionaire* . . .'

'He's not a billionaire!'

'Aha! But you don't deny you had a snogathon! And what was all that Ferdy was telling me about a torn dress? He didn't rip your mum's Yves Saint Laurent off you, did he?'

'No, Ferdy didn't rip anything off me.'

'I meant,' she says, sounding confused now as well as annoyed, 'Jay Broderick.'

'Oh!' Of course. 'No, he didn't rip Mum's dress. I wasn't wearing it, for starters . . .'

'Charlotte Aibhilin Glass!'

'No, no, I wasn't naked, either!' I say, hastily, realising she's got the wrong end of the stick. 'Robyn conned me into wearing this too-small Valentino dress of hers, and then Jay had set up this really low sofa in this private roof garden, where he took me for champagne—'

'Oh, my *God*!' She's so excited at this new

information that she's forgotten to sound annoyed. 'He took you off for private champagne?'

'Yes. And it was so wonderful, Luce, I can't even describe it.'

'I bet! Is that why you're so out of breath right now?'

'No, no, that's because I'm running.'

'*Running?*'

'Yes, Luce, running. So that I don't burst out of any more clothes when . . .' now I can't keep the excitement out of my own voice '. . . when I go out with Jay again tomorrow night.'

There's silence at the other end of the phone. It goes on so long that I assume I've accidentally switched it off, or something. 'Lucy?'

'You have to give me a minute, Charlie.' She's sounding pretty breathless herself. 'I need this to sink in. You're going on a *second date* with Jay Broderick?'

'Is it a second date? I'm not sure the party counts as a first date. I mean, seeing as I pulled my whole Incy Wincy spider act, and all that.'

'Where's he taking you?' she starts firing at me. 'And what are you wearing? Because if you're planning on giving that ASOS monstrosity another airing . . .'

'I'm not. And I thought I'd just go casual. Jeans and a blazer.'

'And sexy lingerie! You have to be prepared, Charlie, for all eventualities.'

'Not *that* eventuality.' But I can feel myself getting

warmer, and it's not just the fact that I'm still running.

'Oh, come on. What if, instead of taking you to a restaurant, he drives you to a helipad, and whisks you off for a night in Paris? The Hotel Georges Cinq, I bet, and a huge suite, all covered with red rose petals . . .'

'That's not going to happen! And even if it does, who's to say that means I have to . . . to get down to my undies?'

'Charlie, I know you haven't had sex in a while, but surely you remember that it does kind of help if you get down to your undies?'

'I'm not going to have sex with him!'

'Oh, go on, love,' a passing jogger tells me, with a cheery wink. 'Whoever he is, it'll make his day.'

'Well, that's just stupid,' Lucy carries on, while I speed up and try not to die of embarrassment. 'What else are you going to do in a Paris hotel room?'

'I'm not going to a Paris hotel room! That's only happening in your head!' I hiss. 'Besides, let's just say he *did* take me to a Paris hotel room. Would that mean I *had* to have sex with him? I mean, is that what the suffragettes were fighting for?' I blank out, conveniently, tomorrow's appointment for a top-to-toe showgirl wax, which I'm not at all sure the suffragettes were fighting for either. 'Are women *obliged* to sleep with a man, just because he takes them to Paris and covers a bed in rose petals?'

'Charlie, nobody's saying you should feel *obliged*

317

to sleep with him. But it's *Jay Broderick*. Why the hell wouldn't you *want* to sleep with him?'

It's neither the time nor the place for me to go into all the reasons why I don't want to sleep with him.

Or rather, why I desperately *do* want to sleep with him (leg-melting lust, heart-pounding desire, loin-burning yearning, to name but three) but why there's one VERY BIG reason why I won't. The same VERY BIG reason that explains why I'm out running for the second time today, in the gathering dusk and a light drizzle. The same VERY BIG (you've probably worked it out now) reason why I took my life in my hands to flee from him the other night.

It's certainly not the time or place to confess to Lucy that, despite all that leg-melting, loin-burning lust, I'm sort of secretly hoping that Jay Broderick might be the kind of man who's not really all that into sex after all. That he might be the kind of (red-blooded, adult) male who actually *prefers* a clothes-on kiss and fondle to clothes-off, legs-akimbo, body-parts-revealing sex.

It's *possible*. Isn't it?

'I bet he's amazing in bed,' Lucy is saying now, rather dreamily, and making me hope she's not still in the office. (Or back home with Pal, come to think of it.) 'I bet he knows exactly what he's doing, and exactly how long to do it for . . . *I'd* have no problem thinking of stuff to do in a hotel room in Paris with Jay Broderick, let me tell you. Oh, not that I've got any complaints about my sex life, by the way!' she adds, hastily, clearly realising she might have sounded too wistful by half. 'No complaints at all. And anyway, even if I *did* – have any complaints, that is – Pal is really sensitive to my needs. I mean, OK, it's a bit of a faff to actually go through the whole complaints procedure . . .'

Am I hearing this wrong, or has Lucy actually just admitted that Pal runs their sex life like the John Lewis customer services department?

'Um, complaints procedure?'

'Yes, it's just this thing we do, since we moved in together, if either one of us has something to say about the other that's getting on their nerves . . .' She's sounding slightly sheepish. 'Not just sex stuff. Like, Pal finds it annoying when I don't wipe the shower down with the squeegee thing. And he doesn't like it when I forget to switch the coffee machine off after I've used it. Writing it down in black-and-white is a much better way to bring it up than having a blazing row. I mean, Pal's parents do it too. And their marriage has lasted forty-one years.'

The thought of forty-one years with Pal makes me feel so suddenly and profoundly depressed that I actually have to stop running.

'Luce,' I hear myself blurt, 'isn't there anything Pal does that gets up your nose?'

'What?'

'Well, you said he hates it when you don't use the squeegee, or turn off the coffee machine. And he told me at your party that he can't trust you with red wine because you're so clumsy . . . and I'm just wondering if you ever tell him *he* does anything annoying?'

'I tell him plenty of things that annoy me!'

'Really? It just seems, sometimes, like . . .'

'What are you saying, Charlie? That I'm a wimp about confrontation?' Lucy's tone is tetchy again, the way it was right at the start of this phone call. Actually, it's more than tetchy. She sounds downright annoyed. 'Because I don't think I'm a wimp about confrontation at all, as it happens. I was perfectly happy to call you just now, wasn't I, and tell you how offended I was that you didn't bother to share the details of Saturday night with me? I'm quite happy letting you know that I'm actually quite pissed off about that.'

'That's not what I mean. Anyway, I did try to get hold of you! But I've just been too—'

'Too busy. Yeah. I know.'

'It's true! I met this fashion stylist at the party, and she gave me this idea about maybe selling Dad's vintage shoes, and I've been talking to Olly about the legal side of all that, and I had a meeting with these designers today—'

'Oh, well, then I'm amazed you've had the time to take my call at all! What with stylists and designers and heaven knows what other glamorous people you're chatting to.'

There's an awkward silence, which – for some unfathomable reason – I choose to bring to an end by mumbling, 'Olly's not glamorous.'

There's another awkward silence.

'Fair point,' she says, after a moment.

'Luce, look, I really am sorry . . .'

'It's OK. I'm sorry too. Forget about it. I need to go now anyway. I'm still at the office, and Pal doesn't like it if . . .' She stops. 'Well. I should get going, is all.'

I don't want to end the conversation still unsure if things are OK between us. We don't usually bicker like this. In fact, the last time we had a proper bicker was probably about two decades ago, when we seriously fell out over ownership issues surrounding a Mark-from-Take-That poster.

'Can I call you tomorrow? Before I go out with Jay Broderick, I mean?'

'Don't be an idiot, Charlie. Obviously you can call me before you go out with Jay Broderick. But only if you promise to call me right afterwards, too.'

'Of course I will, Luce.'

'And I warn you, I'm going to want every detail. Rose petals and all.'

'Rose petals and all,' I say, because I don't want to get into another quarrel about the likelihood of every aspect of her Jay Broderick Fantasy Date coming true.

'And death-defying escapes down drainpipes?'

'And death-defying escapes down drainpipes.'

'Good. Can't wait. Speak tomorrow, Charlie.'

'Great. Speak tomorrow.'

It's only about thirty seconds after the call has ended before a text message pops up on my phone. It's from Lucy.

Btw I haven't forgotten. I know what the date is today. But I know you prefer not to mark it. Just saying am here if you need me. Lx

Which is lovely. But inaccurate. It's not that I prefer not to mark the day of Mum's death. It's just that, for all these years, I've preferred to do it alone.

This evening's one-off new jogging route comes to an end, only a couple of minutes later, when I reach the outer gates of St Mary's Catholic cemetery, all the way up in Kensal Green. The same as every year on this date, on Christmas Day afternoon, and on Mum's birthday, I buy half a dozen pink roses from the man outside the gate, then head into the cemetery itself.

It's only when I'm actually here, making my way through all the headstones, that I start to regret my decision to run here. When I made the plan, I had this silly notion that I wanted to show Mum the new me: bouncy, perky Charlie, full of beans and vim and vigour.

But now that I'm almost at her grave, that all feels wrong.

I know this is really illogical, but I just have this uncomfortable, unsettling feeling that Mum isn't going to recognise me.

This was a bad, bad plan.

Three rows away from her grave, I deposit the half a dozen pink roses, instead, at the headstone of a Much Loved Husband, Father and Grandfather named William Austin. Then I turn round and head back towards the gates, starting to run again as soon as I'm out on the Harrow Road.

Chapter Fifteen

Galina, when I shuffle shame-faced into Skin Deep at lunchtime on Tuesday, can scarcely contain her glee.

'You are here for showgirl wax!'

'Well, yes, that's right, Galina.'

'You are meeting nice man at party? You are going on date with him?'

'As I matter of fact, I am.' I follow her through the curtain and into the torture chamber. 'I'm going out to dinner with him.'

'You are taking knickers off.'

'No! Absolutely not, Galina, not on a first date – I don't care how sexy he is. Tonight is just dinner.'

'I mean you are taking knickers off now, please,' she says, rolling her eyes and waggling a pair of paper knickers at me. 'I am wanting to start with Brazilian.'

'Oh. I see.'

My hands are trembling with (what I assume are) pre-wax nerves, as I fumble with the zip on my jeans and pull them off. Shy of nudity as ever, I manage to get my knickers off and the paper ones on while Galina's back is still turned, fiddling with her pot of burning-hot wax. Still, there's very little point being shy of nudity in these circumstances, I realise as soon as I've got the paper knickers on and am clambering up on to the treatment table. Being shy of nudity in this situation is, I suspect, one of those things that gets categorised in the same bracket as shuffling deck-chairs on the *Titanic*.

'You are making right decision,' she says. 'You are getting properly prepared for all eventuality.'

Good grief, not *another* person who thinks I ought to be whipping my clothes off the moment Jay picks me up this evening. Performing a little impromptu burlesque, perhaps; offering him a full menu of the sexual options available to him tonight before we've even had the food menu handed to us at the restaurant.

'Sure, but I'm not getting prepared for any . . . *eventuality* in particular.' I lie back against the crackly roll of paper. 'I'm only getting this wax so I feel properly groomed. For my own personal sense of self-esteem.'

'Self-esteem is good. Self-esteem attractive to men. Men more likely want to go bed with girl when she has self-esteem.'

'Galina, I've already said. I'm not *going* to go to bed with him!'

'Ah. I am understanding now.' She nods, sagely, still stirring her wax pot like it's a witch's brew. 'You are phobic of the sex.'

'No! I'm not phobic of the sex. I just . . . haven't done it in a while.'

She turns round, dripping spatula in hand, and

stares at me. More precisely, at the paper-knicker-covered portion of me. Her eyes widen in sudden and theatrical horror.

'Is very clear you have not done it in while! Is like Enchanted Forest down there.'

I feel my face flooding with colour. 'Well, I think that's a bit of an exaggeration.'

'Is not. If I am looking hard enough, I think I am finding Sleeping Beauty!'

She chuckles at her own joke. I remain grimly offended.

'But is no problem, Sharlee. I am growing up near Kazlu Ruda forests in Lithuania. If is anyone who can be hacking way through, is me.' She brandishes her spatula at me in Churchillian fashion before leaning down, uncomfortably close to bits of me that I usually avoid letting people get close to, hoiking up one side of the paper knickers and starting to paint a hot layer of wax beneath. 'So, before date you are thinking also eyelash dye? Spray tan?'

'No, thanks, Galina. I'll just stick with using mascara for now. And I think I'm still just about tanned enough from being in LA.'

She shrugs, unconvinced, and paints a large area of my inner thigh with molten wax. 'You are paler than when I see you last week. Pale is not so good as tanned. Tanned is looking more slim.'

'*Really?*' I'm kicking myself, now, for not realising this. 'Oh, God, Galina, then I'd better get a spray tan, too!'

'Is good decision. I will fit you in for spray tan tomorrow lunchtime.'

'Oh, no, that's no good. I mean, do you have any time today? Can you fit it in after the wax, for example?'

She laughs, ringingly. 'You cannot be getting spray tan on same day as wax! Tan will collect in open pores! Will be looking ridiculous! Anyway, skin will still be red and sore from wax until tomorrow.'

I stare at her. 'Tomorrow?'

'Yes.'

'But . . . I'm going out on my date *tonight*!'

Galina falls silent.

'Then this is *big* mistake,' she says, after a moment. She's regarding, with great sorrow, the portion of me that she's just slathered hot wax all over. 'Tonight you will still be looking like plucked chicken.'

'What?'

'Men are not finding plucked-chicken lady-parts attractive.' She ponders this. 'In fact, nobody is finding plucked-chicken lady-parts attractive. Probably not even other chicken.'

I lift my head so I can see where she's already put the wax. It spreads, a thick and yellow crust of it, all the way down one side of my ill-fated 'lady-parts'. 'And is there . . . any way of getting this off without the plucked-chicken effect?'

She shakes her head. 'Is not.'

'Oh, my God!'

'Maybe is better to be quitting while we are ahead.'

'*How?* I can't turn up for my date with . . . with *half* a Brazilian wax!'

'But you are saying he is not going to see this area on first date,' she says, rather slyly. 'You are saying is just dinner.'

I'm too appalled to reply.

'OK. We are not doing rest of showgirl wax today, perhaps. You are shaving rest of excess body hair instead. But now am starting Brazilian, I think I am having to finish. Unless you are having chutzpah to tell him half-Brazilian is new trend.'

I look up at Galina. Galina looks down at me.

'You are not having chutzpah,' she decides. 'I am having to finish. But don't worry. Will be OK. Maybe you are just turning lights out before you get in bed with him.'

'*I'm not getting in bed with him!*'

'Then is nothing,' she says, bracing herself to pull the cooled wax away, 'for you worry about.'

I brace myself too, gripping the sides of the treatment table in anticipation of the agony to come. But before she rips the wax off, she's suddenly distracted by something several inches further down, below my hips.

'You are having orange-peel skin on thigh,' she says, with interest. 'When you are coming in for spray tan and eyelash dye, Sharlee, I can be giving you cellulite treatment for that.'

Seven hours later, my poor, plucked-chicken lady-parts – and the rest of me, of course, still (just about) attached to them – are gingerly placed in the bucket seat of Jay's midnight-blue Aston Martin. All of us – lady-parts, Jay, the Aston Martin and me – are roaring, at speed, westbound along the M4.

Yes, I did say the M4. The myriad restaurants of London, one of which I assumed we were going to be eating at this evening, are a dim memory in the Aston Martin's rear-view mirror. And I'm starting to get this anxious, slightly sweaty sensation that Jay might be kidnapping me, or something.

That's if we get there at all. Because he is driving at almost 100 miles an hour – as far as I can tell from my nervous peeks at the speedometer – and he's only got three fingers of one hand balanced casually on the wheel. I know he was a racing driver, and so anything under 150 miles an hour is probably a snail's pace to him. But let's not lose sight of the fact that he *was* a racing driver. Emphasis, that is, on the 'was'. OK, so the old newspaper reports I've Googled are full of the fact that his career-ending smash into the crash barrier on the Japanese Grand Prix circuit was down to a mechanical fault rather than driver error. Still, the journalists who wrote those newspaper reports aren't the ones currently hurtling along the M4 in the bucket seat beside Jay, not knowing if they're going to meet their end a) in a high-impact multi-vehicle pile-up or b) hacked into little pieces in a ditch in Berkshire.

'All OK there?' Jay asks, casting a glance in my direction. He's not said too much since we hit the motorway, probably all the better to concentrate on driving three inches from the rear of all the slow-coaches and fuddy-duddies who are sticking to a brisk eighty-five in the fast lane. 'Not too cold? Too warm?'

'No.'

'Too fast?' He shoots me a grin. 'I know a preparing-to-meet-my-maker face when I see one.'

'No, no, not at all!' I fib, because I really don't want to seem like a pathetic scaredy-cat who can't handle a bit of speed.

'It's OK, Charlie, honestly. I promise you, you're safe. I did drive pretty fast for a living, you know, back in the day. And I wasn't bad at it, either.'

'Oh, I'm not worried!' I give a little laugh. 'I mean, I love driving fast! Love it. The faster, the better, as far as I'm concerned. The only thing I worry about –' I notice, with horror, that the speedometer is creeping up past the 100 mark '– is your driving licence. If you get points. Isn't this part of the M4 choc-a-block with speed cameras?'

'I know where the cameras are. But we appreciate your concern.'

'We?'

'Me and my driving licence.' He grins at me again, before expertly slicing through the middle and slow lanes of traffic so that we can shoot off the motorway at junction nine. 'So, you haven't asked where I'm taking you.'

'I assumed you wanted it to be a surprise.'

'You assumed right!'

He looks delighted, but then he looks pretty delighted by everything I say. Everything I *do*, come to think of it: even getting into his car, back at the store, and clicking my seatbelt into place made him look like I'd just offered to cook him his favourite dinner of all time while simultaneously performing Astounding Erotic Feats with a potato-masher and a pair of oven gloves. Still, at least his admiring glances have made me confident that I've scrubbed up OK. On the surface, at least. Because any of those wild rose-petal fantasies Lucy was spinning (and that I might have been secretly hoping for myself) have pretty comprehensively gone out of the window thanks to the Galina-inflicted Brazilian wax disaster that is currently lurking beneath my jeans.

'Not that it's exactly a very exciting surprise,' Jay is continuing, barely bothering to slow down as we shoot round a roundabout. 'It's only a pub. But it's a really nice one, and it's owned by an old friend, and I thought you might fancy getting out of town for the night. Well, for the *evening*,' he corrects himself. 'I'm not suggesting we stay over, or anything. Though this particular pub does have some lovely little rooms . . . and I could promise you a nightcap in front of a cosy open fire and a romantic four-poster bed . . . but I get the feeling that a guy has to work a lot harder than that with Charlie Glass.'

I give a half-smile, and try to pull off that mysterious look he seemed so keen on back on the roof terrace, in order to conceal the fact that every part of my being is howling, *Not you, Jay Broderick! You don't have to work a single iota harder than that! A romantic four-poster bed, you say? Then please, feel free to throw me down on that bed, tether me to all four of those posts and do whatever you like with me!*

In the dark, of course. And gently, so as not to make my red-raw nether regions any more uncomfortable than they already are.

But within reason, whatever you like!

Five minutes later, and a few miles along an increasingly quiet and rural B-road, Jay expertly slings the Aston Martin around a hairpin bend and comes to a halt outside a mellow stone building calling itself the King's Arms.

He starts unfastening his seatbelt. Then he reaches over to help me with mine, just as I start to undo it myself.

Our fingers touch. I hear him catch his breath – or maybe it's me catching mine. Either way, we both just sit and stare at our touching hands for what feels like roughly three days, but is probably more like three seconds. I'm the one who breaks the silence.

'Do you get manicures?'

'No, Charlie.' He grins at me. 'I don't get manicures.'

'Oh. Right. It's just that your hands are nicely groomed. So I wondered if you have them manicured. Or if you just use a good hand cream, or something . . .'

Thank *God* Jay puts an end to my nervous prattling (Manicures, Charlie? Seriously?) by sliding his hand further over mine. His skin is cool. The pads of his fingers caress the base of my fingernails. I mentally add *Fingernails; base of* to the list of erogenous zones Jay Broderick seems capable of creating in me.

'You have lovely hands, too,' he says, softly.

'Thank you.'

'*Very* beautifully manicured.'

'Thank you.' I swallow. My throat is dry. I've no idea what to say next. 'I . . . get pedicures, too.'

He laughs. 'You're hysterical, Charlie.'

I'll take *hysterical*. *Hysterical*, let's face it, is better than *weird blabber-mouth who seem to want the world to know intimate details of her foot-care habits*.

'Come on then, funny girl,' he goes on, opening his door and getting out of the car before coming round to my side to open the door for me. 'Let's go and get something to eat.'

He takes my hand and leads the way to the King's Arms entrance, pushing the door open with one magnificent shoulder.

He's right. It's a really nice pub. Though it's still just about light outside, inside the pub it's dimly lit and cosy, with a flagstone floor and not one but two gently crackling open fires, to take the chill out of the British midsummer evening. Content-looking regulars are nursing pints and halves at polished wooden tables and snug corner booths. A beaming middle-aged publican appears from around the other side of a well-stocked bar and greets Jay like a long-lost son.

I gather from their conversation that he's a former mechanic who used to work on the cars Jay drove, but he's evidently almost as much of a fanatic about cricket as he is about motor racing, because there's a pretty lengthy chat about England's form in the last test match before he finally leads us both away from the bar and towards the snuggest booth of them all – tucked away in privacy at the very back of the room, close to the larger of the two log fires.

'Shepherd's pie on the menu tonight,' the beaming publican tells Jay. 'Linda made it specially for you, when you called and said you were coming. Shall I bring one of those, and maybe just a salad for the lady?'

'Bring the lady a shepherd's pie, too, Andy,' Jay suggests, sliding into the booth next to me. 'And let's have a bottle of something red. If that's all right with you?' he asks, as Andy scurries to do his bidding.

'Red wine? Yes, lovely.'

'And the shepherd's pie? I thought you'd prefer that to a salad. It's just that Andy's used to me coming here with some borderline-anorexic girl who gets the vapours at the mere thought of carbs. But if salad is what you'd prefer . . .'

OK, this is a tricky one. Shooting through my head are several competing thoughts:

1) Andy has mistaken me for borderline anorexic (good, in a twisted sort of way);

2) Jay *hasn't* mistaken me for borderline anorexic (bad, in an even more twisted sort of way);
3) shepherd's pie shepherd's pie shepherd's pie shepherd's pie;
4) shepherd's-pie consumption will require many extra hours' loathsome running tomorrow to prevent it forming disgusting fat cells and sticking limpet-like to thighs and bottom for all eternity;
5) who are these (borderline anorexic) girls that Jay has brought here before me?; and
6) shepherd' s pie shepherd's pie shepherd's pie shepherd's pie.

Greed and hunger crowd out all the other thoughts.

'Shepherd's pie is perfect!'

'I haven't brought many girls here, by the way,' Jay says, making me wonder if he can read my thoughts. (I hope to God he can't, because right now he'll basically just be hearing me say *shepherd's pie* on an endless loop.) 'It's not the kind of place I'd bring most of the girls I know.'

Oh, God. Now I'm really lost. Is this a good thing or a bad thing?

'It's a good thing!' he reassures me, either because he really can read my mind or just because I'm looking a bit dismayed by what he's just said. 'I don't get the impression, Charlie, that you're the kind of girl who only wants to go out to the most expensive restaurants and the most exclusive nightclubs. I get the impression, in fact,' he adds, reaching for my hand again and entwining his fingers with mine, fixing his inky eyes on me as he does so, 'that you may just be the most beautiful girl in the entire world who's happy eating shepherd's pie and drinking iffy Chianti in a little pub in the middle of nowhere.'

I'm prevented from falling down in a gibbering heap on the flagstone floor by the fact that Andy reappears in our cosy corner, bearing said bottle of iffy Chianti and a couple of glasses.

'It's what I find so refreshing about you, Charlie,' Jay continues, after Andy has sidled off again, pouring us each a glass of wine and chinking his against mine. 'That you'd rather eat shepherd's pie than salad. That you're naturally gorgeous, without having to go to any effort.'

I choke on my mouthful of wine, and have to pretend it's gone down the wrong way.

But really – *naturally* gorgeous? Without having to go to any effort? If only Jay knew about the eight solid hours of exercise I've put in since Saturday, and the three separate face masks I put on while I was getting ready this evening, and the crick in my neck I've got from half an hour examining my eyebrows for stray hairs in the magnifying mirror, and the full hour it took to do my make-up, and the thousands of buttock-clenches I was doing in my chair at the Hairdressing Appointment That Time Forgot, and, of course, the Hairdressing Appointment That Time Forgot itself, and the agonies and indignities of Galina . . .

Actually, thank Christ he *doesn't* know.

And if the reason that he fancies me is because I'm a breath of fresh air compared to his usual type, then it's in my interest to have him *not* knowing for as long as humanly possible. Frankly, I'll mainline shepherd's pie if that's something he finds attractive about me. I'll go about the place wearing a nosebag of the stuff. I won't even complain about all the additional hours of loathsome running I'll have to do (clandestinely, of course), if it means that he keeps gazing at me with those incredible, sexy eyes, and clasping my hand in his the way he's doing right now.

'Anyway. Now that I've finally persuaded you to come out with me, how about telling me a little bit more about yourself?' His handsome face creases into a grin. 'All I really know about you so far is that you work for MI6, you've recently suffered a nasty bout of kidnapping, you prefer shepherd's pie to salad, and that you hate my driving.'

'I don't hate your driving!'

'Charlie. Your nails have left a permanent imprint on my passenger seat.'

'Well, at least they were nicely manicured nails,' I quip.

He throws back his head and lets out such a loud shout of laughter that several of the regulars glance over in our direction. 'Good point. And I don't mind, by the way, that you hate my driving. Obviously, you should know that driving means absolutely everything to me. But don't worry, I'll try not to take it personally.'

336

'Tell me about your driving career,' I say. I'd much rather talk about him than myself, for one thing, and for another, I'm in danger of being rendered speechless by the fact that he's taken his hand out of my hand and placed his whole arm, instead, around the top of the booth behind me. It's as close as we've got, this evening, to a repetition of him putting his arms around me the way he did when we were kissing the other night. 'I'd love,' I croak, 'to know more about it.'

'What is there to know that people don't know already?' He smiles, devastatingly, and takes a sip of his wine. 'Winner of one world title, runner-up in two more. Some people thought that was spectacular over-achievement, some people thought that was spectacular under-achievement. Quite a lot of people thought I only got as far as I did because of my father's money. But it wasn't my father's money driving the car the year I won the Formula One World Championship. Mind you, it wasn't my father's money driving the car when I ploughed it into the crash barrier on the sixth lap of the Suzuka circuit either.'

'I'm sorry,' I say, because he isn't smiling any more.

'It's OK.' He shrugs. 'Shit happens. I wasn't badly hurt. Just a couple of fractures and a dislocated shoulder.'

'That . . . must have been painful.'

He shrugs again. 'You have to keep it in perspective – or so people are always telling me. I could have been killed, I suppose . . .'

'Exactly!' He looks so bleak, all of a sudden, that I want to be one of those people who try to help him put it in perspective. 'Honestly, Jay, there are worse things that can happen in a car than that! My mother was killed by a hit-and-run driver, so—'

'Jesus!' He sets his glass down on the scrubbed-pine table-top and stares at me, appalled. 'That's . . . my God, Charlie. That's awful.'

OK, I think my attempt to put things in perspective has gone a little too far. In fact, I might just have killed the moment. For my next trick, maybe I should tell Jay all about Dad's lingering and unpleasant illness, or my miserable childhood spent being tormented by my evil stepmother.

'Don't apologise. It was twenty years ago. Ooh, here comes the shepherd's pie,' I add, seeing Andy mercifully approaching with two steaming plates on a wide wooden tray. 'Looks delicious.'

Actually, massive is what it looks. Forget shepherd's *pie*: it looks as if Andy is, in fact, serving up an entire shepherd.

'There's more where that came from!' he threatens, setting the plates down in front of us, before heading back towards the bar.

Jay is surveying his plate, bleakly. 'I can't eat this.'

'Oh.' I'm disappointed. After all, if he doesn't eat the shepherd's pie then I can't exactly tuck in. 'Well, I suppose we could just get some of that salad Andy mentioned . . .'

'No, I mean, I can't eat.' He shoves his plate away.

'Because of what I just told you about my mother, you mean?' I stare at him. 'Jay, that's sweet, but you . . . you don't have to care that much!'

'I don't have to care about the fact you've just told me your mother was killed by a hit-and-run driver? When you were – what? – six?'

'Eight,' I say, unable to suppress my tiny thrill that – really? – he thinks I'm twenty-six.

'Fuck.' He gives his plate another shove. This time it knocks into mine, and a blob of mashed potato falls off the side. 'Well, aren't we a couple of peas in a pod?'

'Sorry?'

'My mum died when I was eight, too.'

Now it's my turn to look appalled. 'Oh, Jay.'

'Cancer.' His handsome face has darkened, as if there's a thunderstorm about to pass directly over it. 'She was thirty-four. Only a year older than I am now.'

'Jay, I . . .' For once, I feel my own childhood tragedy dwarfed by someone else's. It makes me want to put my arms around him and never let go. But he's not looking like he'd appreciate that, so I try reaching for his hand instead. 'I'm so sorry. It's awful, isn't it?'

'What, watching your mum die from stage-four breast cancer? Nah.' He pulls his hand away. He looks, suddenly, like a little boy – specifically, a very, very sad little boy who won't let himself cry, and who certainly won't let himself be comforted. 'It's delightful.'

I know from my own painful experience that there's

nothing I can say right now. Besides, his mood is actually making me feel distinctly upset. Not because he's sitting here, hurt, angry and unable to eat, when we'd just been having lovely, flirty banter only three minutes earlier. But because I recognise only too well this precise kind of hurt and anger. It's the hurt and anger of an eight-year-old who has just lost their mother. It's the hurt and anger I had to swallow every single day after Mum died because there was no place for it at Diana's house. She was always crystal-clear about that.

'Let's get out of here,' Jay mumbles, getting to his feet and pulling out his wallet. He chucks down two fifty-pound notes – surely way too much for a bottle of red and two (uneaten) plates of shepherd's pie – and heads for the door.

I follow, stumbling slightly in my knee boots, and get to the car as fast as I can. This time, needless to say, Jay doesn't open the door for me. He simply starts the engine, before I've actually managed to close my door, and roars, faster than ever, back along the road we came on.

I could cry. In fact, I'm very close to crying.

On the bright side, at least I don't need to worry, any more, about how to prevent him from encountering my disastro wax. He isn't going to come near my disastro wax with a bargepole, after what I've just done. Seriously: make sweet love to the girl who's just inadvertently reminded you of the worst thing that's ever happened to you? Sensuously caress the body of someone who brought the sensitive topic of dead mothers into the conversation?

No wonder he's driving back towards London, now, even faster than he drove us here. And it's even worse, because there's no chatting to take my mind off the fact that we're doing well over a hundred, and that Jay is flashing his headlights at other drivers in the fast lane to make them get out of his way.

There's not a word at all, in fact, until we're back over the Hammersmith flyover, and slowing down to a mere fifty along Cromwell Road.

'Where am I taking you?' he asks, yanking the gearstick down a couple of notches. 'And don't tell me I can drop you at King's Road,' he adds, before I can say exactly this. 'Just let me take you to your actual home, Charlie, for Christ's sake. I'm not going to care two hoots if you live in some kind of slum, or something.'

'It's Earl's Court.'

'God. *Worse* than a slum.' He glances at me when I don't say anything. 'That was a joke, by the way. Not that I'd expect you to realise I can still make jokes. Not when I've been such an arsehole this evening.'

'You haven't been an arsehole. It's completely understandable to get upset about your mum. I still do too, sometimes.' I glance out of my window. 'I shouldn't have said anything.'

'It wasn't your fault.' He reaches across the gearstick and puts his hand over mine again. 'You've been perfect. Direct me from here?'

So I do direct him, off Cromwell Road, all the way down Earl's Court Road and then a right turn (where, as Diana pointed out, the seventy-four bus passes so close I could reach out from a window and touch it) on to Old Brompton Road. Jay pulls the Aston Martin up where I tell him, on a single yellow line on the opposite side of the road to my flat, and turns the engine off. He turns towards me, and I'm expecting him to say something else – about the shepherd's pie we abandoned (my stomach is still rumbling) back in Berkshire; about the fact that the newsagent's we're parked outside is security-shuttered, at ten-forty-five, despite its bold signage claiming it's OPEN TIL MIDNIGHT; about the fact that it's been fun while it lasted but that it's probably better if we don't see each other again. But he doesn't say anything at all. He just pulls me towards him and starts to kiss me.

It takes me a good couple of minutes to stop being stunned into immobility and start kissing him back. At which point (look, the past hour has been really stressful, for one thing, and let's not forget that Jay is officially the best kisser in the world, for another) I can't prevent myself from letting out an actual, wild-animal moan.

'You too, huh?' Jay pulls away. He's looking delighted again, which suggests I don't need to be quite so mortified by my unwitting moan as I thought I did. 'I don't know about you, Charlie, but I'm seri-ously regretting abandoning those four-poster beds at the pub right now.'

'I know,' I mumble.

'Well, I could always come up to your flat . . .'

'No!'

'OK, OK.' He holds up his hands, grinning. 'I get the message, Charlie, don't worry! You don't have to do anything with me that you don't want to do.'

'No, it's not that!'

It really, really isn't: I want to do *everything* with him, then go right back to the start and do everything all over again. I don't even care, any more, that I live in a gloomy basement flat, or that – now I come to think of it – I've left tights and bras drying all over the banisters. And I'm not sure I even care, any more, that I'm not Cassia Connelly, or any of the anorexic salad-munchers he usually goes to bed with. Frankly, I'm so limp with desire for him that I'll happily run the risk that he flees, after the sex, and never calls me again, just so long as it's *after the sex*, that is. But how – *how?* – can I possibly do the sex parts without getting sufficiently undressed to reveal the mortifying plucked-chicken lady-parts? Admittedly there are probably all kinds of moves to get around that . . . but I don't *have* any moves! And I'm not sure that even Jay has enough moves for the both of us.

'Look, honestly, Jay, it's not that I don't want you to come in . . .'

'It's just too soon?'

Too soon after my Brazilian wax? 'Yes,' I reply, honestly.

'You'd rather know me better before . . . well . . . *you* know?'

'Mmm.'

'Then how's this for a plan?' He leans closer and puts one hand, gently, on the side of my face. 'Why don't we spend this whole weekend together? Just hang out for a couple of days, get to know each other better? Hey, I know! We could go to my place in Shropshire. I chill out there like nowhere else. Fresh air, good food . . . and I keep a lot of my cars there, so we could put a couple of them through their paces.'

He's inviting me to spend an entire weekend in his company? When my red-raw thighs will be back to normal? And fit (as they'll ever be) for close-quarters contact . . .

'We could make a proper house-party of it, if you fancy,' he's going on, fired up with enthusiasm by the prospect of a hearty weekend of good food, country air, extreme speed . . . and me. 'I'll see which of my friends is free . . . and why don't you bring some friends along, too? That way,' he adds, with one of his devilish grins, 'they can check me out on your behalf. Let you know whether they think you ought to be falling into bed with me or not.'

I can feel myself flush hot-pink. I'm too flustered to think straight. 'I suppose I could invite my best friend Lucy . . .'

'Lucy. I like the sound of her already. Now, just give me a heads-up – is she susceptible to bribery, in any way? If I accidentally-on-purpose leave a Cartier bracelet in her room, do you think she'll be more or less likely to give me the thumbs-up as a candidate for her best friend's affections?'

I'm about to laugh, but then I remember one problem. 'Oh, dear. I forgot. She's got a Norwegian boyfriend.'

'So she'll be in Oslo this weekend? Or busy eating whale meat? Or otherwise engaged at an a-ha concert?'

This time I do laugh. 'No. But I don't think her boyfriend will let her out for the weekend.'

'Wow. He sounds a barrel of laughs. Well, invite him along. There's plenty of room at the house. The more the merrier.'

'Not in Pal's case.'

'And maybe I can bribe him, too. With a first-class cruise along the fjords. And a Morten Harket T-shirt.'

Barrel entirely scraped of Norway-stereotype gags, Jay gets out of the car to come round and open my door again. He accompanies me across the road to the steps outside my flat, then puts his arms around me and kisses me, once more, firmly on the lips. It's incredible, and intoxicating, and – thank God – as if the whole horrible comparing-dead-mothers episode has never happened.

'So I'll pick you up Friday afternoon,' he says, when he comes up for air. 'And I'll text you details of where we're going in Shropshire, so you can tell your friends where to meet us.'

I watch him while he crosses the road again, back to his car. Then quite suddenly – and I don't, honestly, know what possesses me – I dart back over the road myself and tap on his window just as he starts the car engine. He winds the window down, and when it's all the way, I lean through it and kiss him – again, I don't know what possesses me – softly on the forehead.

He looks rather startled, though not displeased. 'What was that for?'

'Just a thank you,' I hear myself say. 'For a really lovely evening.'

He lets out a low chuckle, then blows me a kiss of his own as he starts to manoeuvre the car away from the yellow line. 'You're a very unusual girl, Charlie Glass,' he says, just before he roars away, again, at twice the speed limit. 'Very unusual indeed.'

I don't go into my flat. I nip up the road to the late-night Tesco, and get there just before it closes its doors at eleven. Once there, I do a whip-round with my basket, finding my way effortlessly to the right shelves and sections despite the fact I've bought nothing but no-fat yogurt and blueberries here since I've been back. Tonight I buy minced lamb, a bag of potatoes, then carrots, celery and onions, and – glancing over my shoulder as I do so – two packs of creamy, unsalted butter.

Half an hour later, I'm back in my basement kitchen, sautéing my perfect little dice of carrot, celery and onion in some of the butter, and chopping more of it into cubes ready for the mashed potato that will form the topping of my shepherd's pie.

It's not even that I want to *eat* a shepherd's pie, as such, although I can't deny that it's been on my mind (and deep in the soul of my rumbling belly) ever since Andy the publican first mentioned it a few hours ago. It's more that I want to cook it. That I just want to cook, full stop. To fill my kitchen with the soothing smells of softening vegetables and browning meat, to enjoy the gentle rhythm of chopping, and mashing, and stirring. I used to make a lovely shepherd's pie in the old days, for Dad, and seeing as (again) it was one of Mum's favourite recipes, cooking it always made me especially happy.

Not that I'm not happy in other ways, these days. Who wouldn't be happy when they've just had a glorious makeout session with a man like Jay? When they've just been invited for a weekend with him in the countryside? When they're thin, and well-dressed, and even more well-coiffed: everything a girl is supposed to be.

Obviously I'm happy.

It's just that I miss some of the stuff that used to make me happy, too. I miss shepherd's pie.

It's funny, but now that I've started cooking, I can't seem to stop. As soon as the shepherd's pie is browning in the oven, I take some butter and flour and egg yolks, and start to make pastry. I find a serviceable tin of golden syrup in the cupboard, locate a couple of lemons, and realise I can make the pastry into a treacle tart. I'm tempted to make fresh custard to go with it, but by the time the tart is in the oven, the shepherd's pie is ready to eat, so I sit down at the table, help myself to a proper-sized portion – OK, maybe more like two – and dig in.

After all these weeks of rabbit food (in amounts that would annoy any self-respecting rabbit) the taste is, quite literally, ambrosial.

Jay is going to have to be even better in bed than I think he is to give me an experience that will top this.

Despite eating slowly, and savouring every delicious mouthful, my plate is empty before I know it. I clear the kitchen while waiting for the treacle tart to brown, then, when it's ready, cut a respectable slice, put it on to a plate, and go to sit on the banquette beneath the skylight, for maximum sensory enjoyment.

Truly maximum sensory enjoyment, though, calls for a scoop of ice cream.

Luckily I didn't throw out every single one of Ferdy's polystyrene containers when I cleansed the flat of (almost) all temptation after I got back from America. I happen to know that there's a carton of his Scratchy Umbrella ice cream lurking behind the frozen peas; not the absolute perfect pairing with treacle tart, perhaps, but beggars can't be choosers.

Not, as I sit back down beneath the skylight with my plate of treacle tart and my scoop of ice cream, that I feel all that much like a beggar. I feel sated, and content, and at ease with myself in a way I'd almost forgotten.

All right, there aren't enough miles along the

Embankment for the loathsome run I'm going to have to endure to work this off. There isn't a pair of trainers sturdy enough for the amount of lunges I'm going to have to do, between now and Friday, to prevent this gourmet late-night snack from taking up permanent residence on my thighs and bottom.

But right now, I'm just glad to feel like Charlie again, for a while.

Chapter Sixteen

'Oh, my *God*. You're inviting me to a weekend in Shropshire?'

'Yes, Lucy. For the third time, in fact, yes.'

'With you and your hot new billionaire boyfriend?'

'He's not my new boyfriend. And he's not a billionaire.'

'But he is extremely hot, though.'

'Yes. He is extremely hot.'

Hence the Amazon page I've got open on my laptop right now, from where I'm preparing to order every sex manual I can get my hands on. I'm still mortified, even the following morning, by the fact that I *kissed Jay on the forehead* last night. Seriously, what the hell was I thinking? Not content with turning down the prospect of more than mere kissing at his birthday party and then again last night, I also seem masochistically determined to make him think of me as motherly and chaste. Whereas what I really want him to think is that I'm dynamite in the sack and up for anything.

'Have you ever tried tantric sex?' I ask Lucy now, peering at the cover of a book called *Tantra for Beginners* on Amazon.

'You mean, like Sting?'

'Oh, God, I don't want to do anything if it's painful.'

'No, like Sting the singer. Isn't he supposed to be indulging in tantric sex every five minutes. Or, more to the point, every five days?' She sniggers, Muttley-fashion, because she's at work and can't be seen to be having too much fun in case her boss Duncan realises she's not on the phone to a client. Mind you, if Duncan has overheard her talking about tantric sex, he'll probably cotton on to the fact that she's not on the phone to a client anyway. (Unless The Bespoke Planet has started offering some very, very bespoke holidays indeed.) 'Why are you reading about tantric sex, anyway? You don't need to have tantric sex with Jay Broderick, Charlie. I think he'll be more than happy with plain old vanilla.'

At the word *vanilla*, my stomach lurches with hunger. This is mostly because it reminds me of the fact that all I ate for breakfast (and all I'm planning to eat for lunch) is a miserable pot of vanilla Müllerlight. After last night's overdose of shepherd's pie and treacle tart, I'm in self-enforced starvation mode in order to shed valuable ounces in time for the weekend. But also, if I'm being really honest, because on my way into the store half an hour ago, I walked past Chill, where a blackboard sign outside was advertising the flavour of the day as Thriller in Vanilla. I remember Thriller in Vanilla from back when I was still taste-testing Ferdy's ice creams: the smoothest, most luscious real vanilla ice cream you've ever tasted, flecked with thousands of speckly vanilla seeds and best served, on

Ferdy's recommendation, with warm dark-chocolate sauce and a sprinkling of chopped nuts. The mere thought of it – especially after the sugar-and-cream hit from the Scratchy Umbrella last night – makes my saliva glands ache with desire. Actually, it makes my entire body ache with desire.

I can remember Ferdy pottering around my kitchen the evening he brought that ice cream over, breaking up the Lindt chocolate bars he'd brought with him and chatting while he melted them over a simmering pan of water. When the chocolate was melted, he added double cream, and a tiny shot of rum, and the merest pinch of sea-salt, and then he poured the whole glorious concoction over large scoops of the ice cream . . . he ended up with this cute little ring of dark chocolate around the edges of his mouth, and I spent the rest of the evening alternating between being too shy to mention it and being only another shot of rum away from vaulting the table and removing the chocolate marks with my own lips . . .

'Anyway, look, just say you'll come to Shropshire, Luce, please,' I beg her now, following Amazon's *Customers Who Bought This Also Bought* link to a veritable smut-fest of erotica. My fingers hover, for a moment, over clicking on *The Kama Sutra*, before I decide that I'd be crazy to try running before I can walk. Or rather, from the look of the couple on the cover, getting both legs behind my ears before I can barely manage one. 'Jay's going to have friends there, and I don't want to be outnumbered.'

'Charlie, I'd love to, honestly, but Pal doesn't—'

'He's invited too!'

'Oh!'

'I know he might not want to drag himself all the way to the country for the weekend, but there'll be fresh air and loads of space for him to do his training . . .' I don't add that actually I suspect that the minute Lucy mentions this weekend to Pal, he'll be packing his bags and jumping on the fastest train to Shropshire. And that it'll have far more to do with his desire to mingle with a multi-millionaire than his desire to do his fartlek training in the open countryside.

'Well, he'd probably really enjoy that . . . I'll ask him, OK?'

'Brilliant, Lucy. Thanks.'

'But hang on – you still haven't told me about last night! Did Jay take you somewhere amazing? Did he kiss you again? Did he . . . ?'

'I'll tell you everything later,' I promise. Because, let's face it, the whole shepherd's pie/blighted child-hood saga is a bit tricky to go into over the phone. Anyway, Maggie O'Day is getting to the store in five minutes, and I need to go over the road to the Cypriot café and get some coffees and croissants in readiness for her arrival.

There's a problem with this plan, however: the Cypriot café is closed. A handwritten sign attached to the inside of the glass door declares, in large letters that are somehow as bad-tempered as the owner herself, *CAFÉ CLOSED POWER CUT*.

The nearest Starbucks is a five-minute walk away, the nearest Pret A Manger even further than that. *Dammit.* This is the first time Maggie's been to the store, and I wanted to be a decent hostess. I guess I'll just have to nip to the newsagent's on the next block and get some bottled water and (not for you, Charlie, NOT FOR YOU!) KitKats instead.

Oh, hang on. There's always Chill.

I know it's open, thanks to the Thriller in Vanilla sign out the front, and I know they do coffee. Which, if I know Ferdy, is probably really excellent coffee. I know I've been avoiding it, because I've been avoiding him, but maybe if I just saunter past, I'll be able to tell if he's there or not. There's only a maximum three-in-one chance that he *is* there. He could be at either of the other two stores, or elsewhere at a meeting . . .

I think I'm in luck! I can see through the glass windows that there's only a skinny young guy behind the counter. So I decide to take the risk, stick my head through the doorway and ask him, in a bright and breezy tone of voice, 'Is Ferdy in this morning?'

'Nah,' he replies.

Perfect! I go in and close the door behind me.

It's the first time I've been inside the branch since it opened, and I have to admit that Honey's done a pretty nice job on the decor. The colour scheme is pistachio-green and strawberry-pink, already getting the tastebuds geared up for a full-on ice-cream experience as soon as you walk in. There's a small customer seating area, mostly furnished with comfy pistachio-green booths and one or two bistro tables, and the entire back section of the shop is taken up with the huge freezer and a green-and-pink-painted counter, where you can sit at a high stool to drink coffee or just to pick out your ice cream. The flavours are printed in swirly lettering on a large menu mural on the back wall: everything from the Thriller in Vanilla that was getting my stomach growling earlier to Lemon Meringue Crunch and – my heart gives a funny little flip as I notice this one – Mint-choc *Stracciatella*.

'Was Ferdy expecting you?' the skinny guy behind the counter asks now. He's wearing a tag on his crisp white T-shirt that informs me his name is Jesse. The same Jesse, presumably, who was helping Ferdy out with the stall at Jay's party. 'I can try his mobile and see where he is, if you like?'

'Thanks, but no need. I'll just try and catch him later,' I fib. 'In the meantime, can I have two cappuccinos, please?'

'His girlfriend's around,' Jesse offers, 'if you want to speak to her instead?'

'Honey? Oh, no, no, no. Just the coffees . . .'

'Honey?' He's stuck his head through the doorway behind him, and is calling up the stairs. 'Someone here for Ferd!'

'But I'm not! I'm not here for Ferd at all! Actually, I think I'll forget about the coffees, too!'

But it's too late. There are fairy-light footsteps

tripping down the stairs, and a moment later Honey appears at the bottom of them.

She's looking sweeter (and more Disney princess-like) than ever, in pale-pink skinny jeans and a grey marl T-shirt with a print of a rainbow on it, her blonde hair freshly washed and fluffy.

'Charlie!' she squeals, when she sees me.

'Honey! Er – hello!'

She bounces across the shop floor and throws her arms around me in an excitable – and astonishingly tight – hug.

'I didn't expect to find you here,' I puff, when she lets me go.

'Oh, I'm helping Ferdy do up the upstairs. He's turning the first floor into an office and hoping to let the top floor out as a little flat. But more importantly, what are *you* doing here?'

'I just popped in to get some coffee . . .'

'She was looking for Ferdy,' Jesse helpfully explains. 'I told her I could try his mobile if she liked.'

'No, I wasn't looking for Ferdy. I just wanted some coffee for this meeting I'm having at my store in a few minutes.'

'Charlie, don't be silly!' Honey wags a finger at me. 'You know, if you came here to see Ferdy, you should just say so!'

'I would, if that was really the reason I came, but—'

'There's no need for you to feel you need to lie to me about that kind of thing!'

'Well, I'm glad, but I'm really not lying . . .'

'Fibbing, then!'

'No, not fibbing either.'

'Oh, *Charlie*!' Her smile broadens. 'Really, this whole situation would be so much easier if you just felt able to be honest with me about it!'

'Honey, I am being honest. Now – er – if I could possibly just get two cappuccinos to go, I'd really—'

'I know you were hanging out with his dad the other day.'

'What? No! I wasn't *hanging out*. It was just a . . . a special day for both of us, that's all.'

'Right. Well, I think I ought to be informed, don't you, if you're sleeping with my boyfriend?'

I'm too stunned to reply.

Behind us, showing a commendable degree of maturity for one so young, Jesse takes a couple of large steps backwards, and disappears out of sight in the direction of what must be a stockroom.

'Well?' Honey's smile widens. It's an effect, coupled with her scarily blank baby-blue eyes, that reminds me of Chucky the evil doll from those terrifying horror movies. 'It's a perfectly straightforward question!'

'Honey, are you . . .' I stop myself, just in time, before saying the word *insane*. Just in case she actually *is* insane – properly, quantifiably insane – and takes offence at the close-to-the-bone slur even more than she's taken offence at the absurd notion that I'm sleeping with Ferdy. 'Are you crackers?' I say instead, with a laugh. This, I'm hoping, will be the right approach: light-hearted, gently joshing bemusement. 'Of course I'm not sleeping with your boyfriend!'

'Are you planning to?'

'No, I'm not planning to!' My cheeks are suddenly heating up, which is diabolically bad timing. I *really* don't fancy trying to explain to Honey that though I'm ABSOLUTELY NOT planning to sleep with Ferdy, I have *entertained the notion* of such an event in the past. I'm not sure she's in the mood to laugh with me, just now, about Fantasy Ferdy appearing on his Fantasy Horse from across a windswept moor. Let alone Fantasy Me and my torn corset. 'Honey, seriously, why are you even asking all this?'

'Why are you blushing?'

'Because you're embarrassing me! I only popped in for a cappuccino! Not the third-degree.'

'It's not the third-degree, Charlie. I just want to know what's going on between you and Ferdy.'

'But there isn't any me and Ferdy.'

'A little hard to believe, when he talks about you the way he does!'

'How does he talk about me?'

OK – that question was a big mistake.

Honey's eyes are filling, immediately, with huge, watery tears.

'Oh, God, Honey, please don't cry! All I mean is . . . look, I don't believe he talks about me in any particular way at all. Honestly! I'm not even sure we're friends any more.'

'Why? Because something happened between you?'

'No, because he seemed pretty pissed off with me after what happened at the party the other weekend.'

'Lucy's party?'

'No, the party he was working at in Holland Park. The weekend after Lucy's party. He must have told you about what happened? The drainpipe? And how he had to help me escape when my dress split open?'

'He didn't,' Honey whispers, looking more stricken than ever, 'even tell me you were there.'

'Oh, well, I'm sure it was just an oversight. Not because he's keeping secrets from you, or anything . . .'

But it's no good. Honey (who I think may have been taking lessons from Robyn on the drama-queen front) lets out a blood-curdling wail and dashes back towards the stairs, scurrying up them as if her life depends on getting away from me as quickly as possible.

'Honey?' I call, helplessly, after her. 'We really should talk about this . . .'

Obviously, there's no answer. And I don't want to risk following her up the stairs, just in case she's waiting at the top to pour a vat of boiling oil over me, or something.

'Was that two cappuccinos?' comes Jesse's voice, as he reappears from the back of the shop, just as seamlessly as he vanished in the first place. 'Or just the one?'

'Neither. I . . . forget about the coffee. I'm sorry.'

I'm shaking a bit, with the shock of it all, as I hurry two doors along and back to the store. When I open the door, realising too late that I've forgotten to lock it, I see that Maggie has already arrived, and is sitting with her long legs up on the table, waiting for me.

'Charlie Glass!' she says, a mock-horrified look on her face. 'You bad, bad girl! What *have* you been up to?'

'What? I wasn't doing anything! Honey's got totally the wrong end of the . . .' I break off, as Maggie turns my laptop round to face me. '*Oh!*'

Thanks, presumably, to my recent search parameters on Amazon, an X-rated video pop-up has appeared in the top right-hand corner of the screen. It features a three-second loop of a grimacing naked man doing something frankly disturbing to an (and I don't blame her) even more grimacing naked woman.

I dart to the computer and click on the X to close the pop-up, mid-grimace.

'A friend was just asking me about . . . about tantric sex . . .' I avoid Maggie's eye, even though she's grinning in an understanding sort of way. 'And you know what the internet is like, when you're searching for something . . . all kinds of dodgy things pop up out of nowhere.'

'Dodgy things popping up out of nowhere?' She gives me a big, lascivious wink. 'Sounds all right to me! And, you know, if there's anything you want to know about tantric sex, you only have to ask. I used to do it sometimes with an old boyfriend. He used to go out with a girl who'd been a backing dancer on tour with Sting, and obviously Sting knows a thing or two about tantric sex . . .'

'So I gather.' I don't want to delve into the manner in which Sting communicated his tantric sex Top Tips to one of his backing dancers. Nor, frankly, do I want to hear any more about tantric sex at all. Or Sting, for that matter. The ghastly grimacing couple on my computer screen are refusing to go away, popping up again like a virus – oh, *God*, I've given my computer a virus, haven't I? – every time I click on the X in the corner of their box to get rid of them. 'I really am so sorry about all this,' I mumble, feeling just about ready to die of embarrassment. Not only have I failed to provide so much as a dribble of coffee or a crumb of croissant, but now I'm lowering the tone of the meeting before it's even begun. 'I know it must all look very unprofessional.'

'Hey, that's perfectly OK, Charlie. I have a sky-high sex drive, too. Honestly, if you could see the kind of thing I watch on *my* laptop . . . Oh, hey, isn't that your sister I can see out there?' she goes on, gesturing towards the street with her Evian bottle. 'The snotty gold-digging one who's always coked to her eyeballs whenever I see her at parties?'

I'm too surprised to even, as usual, defend Robyn – it has to be Robyn that Maggie is talking about – from accusations like the one she's just made. Because she's right: Robyn is indeed outside on the street. White van men hang out of their windows and bus drivers leer from their cabs, while Robyn, strutting at speed towards us in spray-on jeans, a cropped vest, and heels even higher than Maggie's sex drive, rudely sticks up a middle finger at them.

A moment later, she's stalked through the door and slammed it behind her with far more vitriol than Honey managed only a few minutes ago. She points a furious finger in my direction.

'You're shagging Jay Broderick, you absolute bitch!'

I bid a final farewell to the last dregs of my professionalism. I'm not sure I could look any more unprofessional now, to be perfectly honest. And it looks like this is going to be the second Nasty Scene of my day so far. I'm starting to wish I'd never got up this morning.

'Robyn!' I put down my treacherous computer and hurry over to her. 'Do you think we could have this conversation another time, please?'

'Hah! So you don't deny it? You *are* shagging him!'

'Yes! Yes, I *do* deny it. And *no*, I'm not . . . shagging him,' I say, completely truthfully.

Robyn emits a derisive snort. 'Bollocks. Lulu called me just now to say she'd been talking to Poppy Gregory, who's going out with Caspar Blake-Ashby . . .'

I blink at her, none the wiser about who any of these people are, or how they fit into the issue of me and Jay. Shagging or otherwise.

'Well, *obviously* Caspar works with Ben Mortimer! Jay's best friend! And Ben told Caspar that Jay called him this morning to invite him to bloody Shropshire for the weekend! With *you*! How could you *do* this to me?'

'You know, that's pretty much the question I asked myself when I saw the size eight label in the back of that Valentino dress you lent me.'

'What? Oh, *that*.' Robyn tosses her head, contemptuously. 'That was just a little joke, Charlie.'

'Talking me into wearing a dress without telling me it was two sizes too small?'

'Well, it all worked out pretty well for you in the end, didn't it? Wiggling your giant boobs under Jay's nose all night! Was that why you disappeared at his party? So you could give him a private viewing of what was going on beneath my brand-new Valentino?'

I bite back any remark about split seams, because the last thing I want is Robyn charging back home and spitefully destroying Mum's Yves Saint Laurent dress, which – it now occurs to me – is still in her possession. In fact, it also occurs to me that, now she's found out about me and Jay, it's probably a good idea for me to get the hell over to her flat as fast as my legs will carry me and stage a daring rescue mission on Mum's dress before she spitefully destroys it anyway.

'Look, Robyn, I really would prefer to talk about this another time . . .'

'Oh, Maggie won't care!' Robyn glowers in her direction. 'When it comes to Jay Broderick, she's just as much of a slut as you are.'

I turn round, startled, to glance at Maggie. She

shoots me an eye-roll before saying, dangerously sweetly, to Robyn, 'And lovely as ever to see you too, Robyn darling. Hey, how are things going with that very nice Ukrainian boyfriend of yours? The one who's the very nice Ukrainian boyfriend of lots of other women, too?'

'*Ugh!*' is Robyn's only reply to this, though whether it's directed at Maggie, at Yevgeny, or at the memory of Yevgeny's other girlfriends, it's hard to tell. 'Well, I hope you feel *good* about yourself,' she spits, turning back to me, 'betraying your *own sister* like this. Especially when I'm due to have *life-threatening surgery* any day now.'

'My God, what's wrong?'

'My bloody bunions is what's wrong!'

I have to talk fast, to cover Maggie's snort. 'But, um, that isn't exactly life-threatening surgery, Robyn. I'm sure you'll be absolutely fine.'

'I hope I *die* on the operating table! That'll show you.'

'Robyn, don't say that—'

'And I hope you have a *horrible time* in Shropshire this weekend. And I hope you get all fat before you go . . . no, I hope you get *even fatter*!'

With this, her Carabosse-worthy curse on me (and on Jay's sexuality), she turns and stalks back out of the door, sticking up her middle finger at a bus driver who hasn't even had the temerity to leer at her yet.

'Well!' says Maggie, as the door slams behind her. 'Isn't she just a ray of sunshine?'

Oh.

Maggie.

I compose my face as carefully as I can before turning back to look at her again.

'And, yes,' she says, before I can bring myself to ask the question. 'Robyn's right. About one thing, anyway. I used to go out with Jay Broderick.'

Of *course* she did. She's chic, and glamorous, and incredibly pretty, and she was a VIP guest at his birthday party. I don't know why it didn't occur to me before.

'And, yes,' she adds, with yet another of her cheeky winks, 'he was the one I tried the tantric sex with. Just in case you were wondering!'

I hadn't been wondering. But now, naturally, it's all I can think about.

'Hey, don't look so worried! It was, like, five years ago! And it was only for a couple of months. Our boy Jay can't stay interested in anyone for very much longer than that!'

Suddenly, I feel this morning's vanilla Müllerlight rising up my gullet, eager to make a reappearance.

'Are you all right, Charlie?' Maggie asks, staring at me with concern. 'Do you need to sit down, or something?'

'No,' I croak. 'I'm OK.'

'Well, I'm not surprised you're feeling a bit rubbish, after that stupid cow yelling at you like that.' She comes over to me and holds out her water bottle. 'God, Charlie, did she *really* lend you a Valentino dress that was two sizes too small?'

'Mmm. It split.'

Now Maggie looks really cross. 'That's just a waste of a good Valentino.'

I force myself to laugh – even though I think she might have been deadly serious – and take another sip of water. 'Well, again, I'm really sorry about all these interruptions . . . let me take you upstairs to the stockroom, so you can have a proper look at all Dad's old shoes.'

'Sure. Let's go and do that first, shall we?'

I hand her back her bottle and I'm just about to lead the way towards the stairs when she stops me by touching my shoulder lightly.

'Charlie – you weren't upset by what I said just now, were you? About Jay Broderick? And the two-month thing?'

'What? No!' I can hear in my own voice how defensive I sound. 'Not at all, Maggie!'

'OK. But your sister was right, was she? You are going out with him?'

'I don't know.' This, at least, is honest. 'We have *been* out . . . and I am going away with him for the weekend.'

'To his place in the country?' She nods, looking impressed. 'You're already higher in the pecking order than I ever was! He never offered to take me there. I think it's only for special people.'

This cheers me up slightly – as I think, bless her, it was meant to.

'Well, you'll have a great time,' she adds. 'Jay's the

master of a good time.' She nudges me, nodding down at my sex-mad computer. 'And it looks like you're planning to show him a pretty good time, too, Little Miss Tantra!'

Which I don't think was ever officially one of the Mr Men or Little Miss books. Though obviously I haven't spent long enough trawling through Amazon to be absolutely sure.

I start up the stairs hoping that a good hour or so with Maggie going through Dad's shoes will block out the increasingly uncomfortable vision in my head: a vision of Jay, somewhere in the recent past, having hour after hour of athletic virtuoso sex with one of Sting's most lithe and bendy backing dancers.

I'm just locking up the store at five o'clock, ready to head home for a fun-packed evening of Loathsome Running and squats and lunges, when I hear my name being called from a little way along the street.

'Charlie! Hey!'

It's Ferdy. He's coming out of Chill and heading my way, a rather grim expression on his face.

I hold up my hands, automatically. 'Look, I'm sorry, but I really, really didn't mean to make Honey cry . . .'

'Charlie, I'm coming to apologise to *you*.' He looks grimmer than ever. 'For Honey's . . . little moment this morning. Jesse told me about it. I gathered that it was about . . . well, that it was something to do with me.' He's looking rather flustered. 'Look, I know what Honey is like, when she gets a bit paranoid about stuff. And I'm just sorry that you had to deal with it.'

'That's OK.' I put the keys into my bag and zip it up. 'Is she all right now?'

'She's fine,' he says, in a voice that suggests quite the opposite. In fact, he looks far from fine himself: pouchy-eyed and more drawn than usual, his tufty hair even more in need of a comb. 'Just a touch of the green-eyed monster, that's all.'

'About . . .' I swallow, and start again, trying to sound casual. 'About you and me?'

'About you.' Ferdy shoves his hands into his pockets. 'You know. The way you look, and everything.'

'That's ridiculous.'

'Hey, I didn't say it made any sense!'

Ouch.

I stare at him, hurt beyond measure. 'Is there something *wrong* with the way I look?'

'I didn't say that.'

'But you said—'

'I didn't *mean* that.' He jiggles his hand in his pocket, looking exasperated. 'I only meant . . . oh, here we go,' he mutters, as right out of nowhere – as you'd expect, from the speed it's travelling at – Jay's dark-blue Aston Martin *vrooms* up to the kerb beside us. 'Here comes lover boy!'

I would deny that Jay is anything of the sort (I'm sure that, technically speaking, you probably have to have had sex with someone before they can be called your lover boy) but I'm seized with a burning desire to let Ferdy know that there are *some* men out there who find me attractive, even if he doesn't. Some *extremely desirable* men, as it happens. Plus I'd actually quite like to end this conversation before Jay joins us, just in case Ferdy gets it into his head to mention anything about drainpipes, or ripped dresses, or incredibly visible panty-lines, or anything.

'Well, it was nice catching up with you, Ferdy.'

His eyebrows rise, just for a moment. 'Are you trying to get rid of me?'

'No! I just . . .'

'Don't worry. I don't want to cramp your style any more than you want me . . . cramping it.' He turns to walk back to Chill, but has to pass right by the Aston Martin to do so and is blocked for a moment as the driver's door opens and Jay gets out of it.

'Hi!' Jay says to him. His brow furrows. 'Wait – don't I know you from somewhere?'

'Don't think so.'

'Yeah, I do . . . you're the ice-cream guy!'

'Yes. I'm the ice-cream guy.'

'That's right. I thought I recognised you.' Jay takes a step in my direction. 'Hey, there,' he says, leaning down to plant a kiss on my lips before turning back to Ferdy, with a smile. 'So, you two know each other?'

'Nearby premises,' I offer, by way of explanation, just as Ferdy replies at the same time.

'We're old friends.'

'I didn't know that! Hey, if I'd known, mate, I'd have invited you to my party as a proper guest, not just as one of the catering staff.' Jay slips an arm, casually, around my shoulders. 'You didn't tell me you were friends with the ice-cream guy, Charlie!'

'I didn't know he was going to be at the party,' I say, but I'm interrupted by Ferdy again.

'I think Charlie was pretty busy that night anyway.' He's looking directly at Jay, and (deliberately?) not looking at me. 'Far too busy to come and hobnob with the catering staff.'

There's something about the way he says *catering staff* that makes the hairs on the back of my neck rise up, slightly, the way that's supposed to happen with wild animals when they scent danger. Though I don't know what could possibly be dangerous about this situation: just the three of us, passing the time of day on the pavement. Still, it's not just me. I'm pretty sure Jay has sensed it, too, because there's a similar edge to his voice when he next speaks.

'Yeah, Charlie *was* a bit busy that night, actually.'

'So I hear.'

'We both were.'

'Imagine,' says Ferdy, 'my surprise.'

There's a bit of a silence. Jay and Ferdy stare at each other over the top of the Aston Martin's open door. Jay is still smiling, though rather less pleasantly than before, and Ferdy is still wearing an expression that – I think – is meant to imply cold contempt. Trouble is, because his face is accustomed to looking gentle, thoughtful and incredibly sweet, he looks less like he's feeling coldly contemptuous and more like he's staying very, very still in order to avoid being stung by a particularly nasty-looking wasp.

I'm annoyed with him and embarrassed for him in equal measure. What does he think he's doing, getting all shirty with Jay like this? I'd assume it was something more than just some weird *Upstairs, Downstairs* chip-on-the-shoulder act – something to do with me, for example – if it weren't for the fact that Ferdy has just made it very clear he doesn't find me remotely attractive. That actually, quite possibly, he finds me more than a little repulsive.

'Anyway!' I say, as brightly as possible, and hoping to put an end to this uncomfortable encounter. 'Good seeing you, Ferdy!'

'Yes, of course, don't let me keep you.' He nods at the car. 'You obviously have places to get to.'

'What, in this old banger?' Jay laughs, and gives the top of the car an affectionate thump. 'Fan of Aston Martins, are you?'

'Not particularly.'

'Oh, mate. You're seriously missing out! But then,' Jay shrugs, 'I guess if you aren't a car kind of a guy . . .'

'I didn't say I wasn't a car kind of a guy.' Ferdy is turning slightly pink. 'I said I don't particularly care for Aston Martins.'

'Well,' I say, getting that hair-prickling feeling again, and this time worse than before, 'each to their own, obviously! How else would that explain all those people buying those horrible black Range Rovers, when there's—'

'I'm more of a vintage Jaguar kind of a guy,' Ferdy interrupts me, still looking directly at Jay, 'actually.'

Jay nods, approving and disdainful in equal measure. 'Who *isn't* a vintage Jaguar kind of a guy? I've got a beauty, as it happens . . . well,' he adds, with a grin, and dropping a kiss on the top of my head, 'I guess you could say I have *two* beauties. And only one of them has a modified stroker crankshaft and red-leather upholstery.'

I'd be thrilled to my cotton socks that Jay has just called me a beauty if it weren't for the fact that Ferdy has just shot him a look that – radiating goodness or not – suggests he'd quite like to push him under a passing vehicle. And that he wouldn't care if that vehicle were an Aston Martin, a vintage Jaguar or the number eleven bus. Clearly Jay's car talk is playing even more into that *Upstairs, Downstairs* sense of inferiority than I realised.

'It's a 'sixty-seven E-type,' Jay is continuing, fixing his own gaze firmly on Ferdy. 'Series one. Four-point-two litre engine. All-synchromesh four-speed gearbox. Open headlights.'

Ferdy (who apparently has a lot more idea what all this mumbo-jumbo means than I do) actually looks interested for a split second, before covering it up with deliberately unimpressed blankness again.

'I have a 'fifty-nine XK one-fifty,' he says, 'as it happens.'

I blink at him. 'You have a *vintage Jaguar*?'

It's the first time he's looked back at me in this entire conversation. 'Yes, Charlie. As a matter of fact, I do. I just don't go around bragging about it.'

'I didn't mean—'

'The Roadster, huh?' Jay nods. Unlike Ferdy, he's actually allowing himself to look impressed. 'Wow. That's a nice car, mate.'

'Well, I like it.'

'I bet you do . . . hey, you know what? You should join me and Charlie in Shropshire this weekend! Bring the Roadster!'

'Oh, no, I don't think Ferdy will be able to do that,' I say, trying not to sound as horrified as I feel. 'He's got three ice-cream parlours to run, and it's going to be a sunny weekend!'

'Exactly. A perfect time for tooling around the glorious Shropshire countryside in an XK one-fifty! *And* my E-type,' he adds, with another smile in Ferdy's direction. 'I'd let you have a good go behind the wheel, mate. If you think you can handle it, of course.'

'No, really, Jay, I think Ferdy's far too busy to—'

'Yeah, that sounds good, actually,' Ferdy interrupts me to tell Jay. 'Shropshire, you say?'

'Yes. My family has a place about five miles south of Ludlow.'

'But there won't be room!' I've given up trying not to sound horrified. 'Lucy's already coming, with Pal, so . . .'

'There's plenty of room. Anyway, my friend Ben

and his wife were meant to be joining us but they're busy with family this weekend, so they won't be able to make it after all.' Jay's hand gently strokes the nape of my neck. 'Relax, Charlie. It'll be fun.'

'I don't think Ferdy's girlfriend will think so,' I say, desperately trying to come up with a way that he can get out of the invitation. He can't actually *want* to come, can he? Not when he so blatantly regards Jay as a couple of rungs lower, on the scale of worthwhile human beings, than Osama bin Laden and Adolf Hitler. 'I doubt she'll be at all happy about Ferdy leaving her behind for a weekend, especially not when . . .'

'Oh, you've got a girlfriend?' Jay looks surprised. 'Well, bring her along too, mate. The more the merrier!'

I wish he'd stop saying that. Besides, if Honey comes too, it's going to be more like The More, The Scarier. The More, The More Psychopathically Paranoid and Prone to Unnerving Fits of Hysteria.

'Well, I'll ask her,' Ferdy says. He's looking a bit uncomfortable himself for the first time in this whole uncomfortable conversation. 'See if she fancies it.'

'I'm sure she will. And you'll be wanting the address, won't you? That's what I came here to give Charlie, as a matter of fact.' Jay looks down at me. 'For your friend Lucy.'

'I thought you were just going to text me that,' I say.

'True, but you know what?' He grins at me, so sexily that – despite the fact that we're very much not alone right now – I actually feel my heart skip a couple of beats. 'I asked myself why on earth I'd send you a text when I could come down here and see you in person.'

Ferdy emits a noise that's part cough, part sneeze. 'So, can I have the address too, then? Unless you'd rather have an excuse to come back again tomorrow?'

Jay shifts his head to one side and regards him for a moment. 'Oh, I don't need an excuse, mate. Don't worry about it.'

'I wasn't worried.'

'Glad to hear it.'

'And I'm glad that you're glad.'

OK, this is just getting silly. Not only are we right back where we started, the two of them staring at each other across the car door like the Aston Martin is no-man's-land and they're dug into opposing trenches, but I'd actually quite like to prevent Ferdy from embarrassing himself any further. Honestly, if I don't step in, I think there's a good chance he'll produce some Socialist Workers' Party leaflets from his pocket and start noisily berating Jay about the evils of capitalism and the rights of the working man.

'Well,' I say, 'maybe we'll see you on Friday, Ferdy!'

'Any time after six-ish,' Jay says, holding out his iPhone so that Ferdy can see the address written on the notepad there. 'Whenever you can get away from town. I have someone who cooks for me there, so I can guarantee you a decent dinner on arrival.'

'Sounds good.' Ferdy types the address into his own phone, then slips it back into his pocket. 'Looking forward to it.'

'And bring the Roadster, yeah? I've got a bit of land set aside for racing there. We can put it through its paces, see what it can do.'

Which is just great. As if I didn't have enough to worry about this coming weekend – Pal; Honey; how to bluff my way through a tantric sex session – I now have to worry about Ferdy breaking his neck on Jay's 'bit of land set aside for racing', just to prove that his vintage Jag is worthy of comparison with Jay's vintage Jag. Just to prove that he can score points off a former Formula One driving champion. Just to prove that he's not impressed by Jay's wealth or status at all.

'Can I give you a lift home?' Jay is asking me, now, as Ferdy turns and starts to walk the short distance back towards Chill. 'Or even better, can I give you a lift to a pub or bar of some kind, where we can get a couple of drinks?'

'I'd love to,' I say, which is entirely true, 'but I have loads of work to be getting on with.' (This isn't entirely true. I have loads of pre-weekend preparations to be getting on with. On this precise evening, if memory serves, that'll be one loathsome run, a good half-billion lunges, roughly seventeen pints of detoxifying dandelion tea, and a couple of hours in the bathroom pummelling my thighs into submission with a body brush, a tub of Fat Girl Slim and my brand-new Bliss spa 'slimulator'.) 'But I'll take that lift home, if you're still offering it.'

'Well, it's a poor second best, but it'll do.' Jay steers me round to the passenger door and opens it for me.

'Nice guy,' he says, nodding in the direction of Chill as I start to get in. 'Ferdy, is it?'

'Mmm. He is nice.' I could – but don't – add *usually*.

'I'll have to keep my eye on him this weekend though, I can tell.'

'Sorry?'

'Come on, Charlie!' He gives me another of those heart-skipping grins. 'The poor bloke's obviously nuts about you. Why else do you think I stood there like some kind of flash git, going on about my half-million quid Jag? That's me being jealous!'

'Of *Ferdy*?'

'Of the guy who couldn't more obviously have the hots for you if he was walking the streets with a huge sign around his neck saying, *I have the hots for Charlie Glass*.'

I stare at him. 'He . . . has a girlfriend.'

'Ah,' Jay says, with a solemn nod. 'Well, that settles it, then. People are never nuts about someone when they're going out with someone else. That must be why nobody ever breaks up, and why the divorce rate in this country is so incredibly low . . .'

He's still expounding on this theory, and I'm still politely laughing, when he starts the car up and *vrooms* it away from the kerb again, past Chill's wide glass windows. Obviously we're already going so fast that I can only see through them for a second. But I can see that Ferdy is back behind the counter, and leaning down to serve ice cream to a small child who's just gone in with its mother.

He doesn't look like he's nuts about me. He looks like he's just getting on with his job.

It's sweet of Jay to be jealous. But it must be because he's just the jealous type. In a protective, Alpha-male way, not in a *Fatal Attraction,* Honey-this-morning kind of way.

Oh, and talking of Honey, there's something very, very important that I want to check out with Jay, right this very minute.

'Your place in Shropshire,' I ask, as casually as possible, 'it does have locks on the bedroom doors, does it? Sturdy ones? That nobody can . . . er . . . pick? And creep into your room in the dead of night, for example?'

'Don't worry.' Jay slides his hand across the gearstick and places it, gently and tantalisingly, on the lower and outer quadrant of my right thigh. 'We'll have plenty of privacy at the house this weekend, Charlie. No matter how many of your friends are staying there too.'

Which is great, but isn't quite what I wanted to know. Still, if I'm really lucky, maybe it'll be a moot point. Maybe Honey will let Ferdy out of her sight for the weekend, and I won't have to worry about being murdered in my bed – come to think of it, I realise, with a lurching in my stomach, *Jay's* bed – after all.

Chapter Seventeen

The drive to Oxley Manor, a journey that Googlemaps assured me would take two hours and forty-eight minutes, is accomplished in a fraction over two hours. When you take into account the fact that there was Friday afternoon traffic heading out of town, you'll probably begin to realise just how fast Jay was driving.

'Home sweet home,' he says, as – in the middle of the lush green countryside now – he spins his Jaguar through an open set of gates, up a gravelled driveway and towards a part-timbered, part-stone Elizabethan manor house that's such a beautiful sight, in the late-afternoon sunshine, it almost makes me want to weep.

Of course, there's also the little matter of the fact that I'm already pretty much weeping anyway. I finally succumbed, yesterday, to Galina's insistence on dyeing my eyelashes ('You will not regret. Is better look for piggy eye than smudged mascara') and I can only assume I'm having some kind of allergic reaction to the dye she used. I woke up this morning with what looked like the beginnings of conjunctivitis in my left eye, by lunchtime the same thing was happening to my right, and mere moments before Jay came by the flat to pick me up, I had to do an emergency dash to Boots on Earl's Court Road to pick up eyedrops and a cheapy pair of sunglasses to try and hide the swelling. I'm still having to surreptitiously dab watery tears off my cheeks every five minutes, though.

As soon as I get a bit of privacy, I'm going to try and call Galina and see if there's any remedy she can suggest that might improve the situation. I don't think she'll mind the out-of-hours call, especially since she and I have become rather touchingly close these past few days, as Operation: Get Naked In Front of Jay has ramped up several gears. We're certainly close enough (after Tuesday's showgirl wax, Wednesday's – truly agonising, by the way – cellulite treatment plus eyebrow/moustache/sideburn maintenance, and yesterday's all-over spray tan plus ill-fated eyelash dye) that she rather sweetly texted me, during the warp-speed motorway journey, to say, *Enjoy country weekend ps don't forget take tweezers and magnifying mirror. Also tea-tree oil in case ingrown hair pustules. G xx*

'Oh, Jay.' I gaze up at the manor. 'It's gorgeous.'

'Glad you like the look of it!' Braking the Jag to a stop, Jay switches off the ignition and undoes the seatbelt that I begged him to put on somewhere between junctions four and five of the M40. 'And just wait until you see the gardens round the back. There's a pear orchard, and a knot garden, and a diddy little lake that's just big enough to swim in . . . hey, if the weather stays like this, we can have a dip tomorrow. I hope you brought your bikini!'

My gut reaction – hollow, disbelieving laughter, followed by the question *don't you know me at all?*

– is fortunately overridden by a more measured response.

'Such a shame! I didn't pack a swimsuit.'

'Oh, that's easily remedied. I'm sure there'll be a spare bikini lurking around the house somewhere.' Jay gets out of his side of the car and comes round to open my door for me. 'Besides, finding a spare bikini is Plan B.'

'What's Plan A?'

'Now, come on, Charlie.' He grins at me. 'I'll bet you're a girl who wouldn't say no to a spot of skinny dipping.'

He's right, in one sense. I *am* a girl who wouldn't say no to a spot of skinny dipping. I'm a girl who'd *scream and yell* no to a spot of skinny dipping. I'm a girl who'd quite possibly turn to extreme violence as a way to avoid skinny dipping.

'Well, that sounds wonderful, of course. But we can only hope the weather holds.' I gaze up into the (cloudless, azure-blue) sky and give a little bit of a shiver, hoping Jay won't notice that it's a balmy twenty-three degrees at six in the evening. 'The forecast I saw was pretty ropey.'

'Really?' He closes the car door behind me, loops his arms around my shoulders and presses me back against the shiny cream Jaguar, moving his body very close to mine as he does so. 'Then we'll just have to find some other reason to take our clothes off this weekend, Charlie, won't we?'

'We certainly will,' I reply, in a voice that – I happen

to know – is croaky with nerves, but that Jay evidently thinks is husky with lust. He moves closer still and places the lightest of kisses on my lips.

'I can't even tell you,' he murmurs, 'how insane you've been driving me ever since you got in the car this afternoon.'

From the look in his eyes, I can only assume that what he means is that I've driven him insane *in a good way* i.e. with desperate lust, rather than something to do with the way I kept fiddling with the air conditioning or squeaking in terror when the speedometer crept up past 120.

'Take these off,' he murmurs, reaching for my sunglasses, 'so I can kiss you properly.'

'No, no, I'm perfectly OK!' I clamp my own hand on to the sunglasses, and hold on for dear life. 'These will just make it more . . . mysterious, won't they?'

'Will they?'

'Oh, absolutely! Look . . .'

Before he can attempt to take the glasses off again, I launch myself into a kiss of such passion that he seems rather taken aback for a moment. But only for a moment. Once he's stopped being surprised, he starts kissing me back with similar abandon. After a moment, he presses me even harder against the side of the car, and I wrap my left leg around his right, and it's all so completely marvellous that neither of us hears the gravel crunching beneath the wheels of another approaching car until it stops only a few feet away from our entwined bodies.

For a moment, I think it must be Ferdy, but then I realise that the car is a banged-up Ford Sierra taxi with *Ludlow Cabs* written on the side, not whatever fancy-schwancy Jaguar Ferdy is going to be arriving in. And that the doors are opening to let Lucy out of one side, and Pal out of the other.

'Hey, there! Did we come at a bad time?' Pal, dressed in chinos, a shirt, and a jaunty-looking cravat that he must have borrowed from his neckerchief-wearing buddy, and looking more cheerful than I think I've ever seen him, heads towards us. He stretches one hand out to Jay, who's pulling himself away from me with a lot less embarrassment than I feel disentangling myself from him, and then kisses me heartily on both cheeks as if we're long-lost buddies. 'Splendid to see you, Charlie! And splendid to finally meet you, Jay! I'm Pal Kjaerstad. I think you know my sister-in-law, Marit?'

'Marit . . . ? Oh, yeah, of course! She used to cook for my father and stepmother.'

'Well, yes, but I think she became very much a friend of the family, too, if you don't mind my saying. In fact, I almost feel I know you already. Marit used to tell me all about your family, what delightful people you were . . .'

I can't stick around to witness this display of sycophancy, and anyway I've just noticed that Lucy, charmingly abandoned by Pal, is struggling to get the bags out of the car and pay the taxi driver at the same time. I hurry over to her and grab the larger of her bags while she fishes in her handbag for a tenner.

'Interesting way to greet our arrival,' she whispers at me. 'Full-on hanky-panky on the driveway . . .'

'There's a lake,' I interrupt her, talking out of the side of my mouth like a Mafioso in a spoof mobster movie.

'Sorry?'

'A *lake*!'

'A lake. Right. And that's a disaster because . . . ?'

'I can't let Jay see me in a bikini!'

'Er, you do realise that if everything goes to plan this weekend, he'll be seeing you in a lot *less* than a bikini . . . hey, Charlie, it's OK! There's no need to cry about it!'

She's obviously just noticed the tears dribbling down my cheeks. This *bloody* allergic reaction.

'I'm not crying! It's my eyelash dye!' I yank off the sunglasses to show her the result of Galina's ministrations. My heart sinks into my five-inch wedges when Lucy recoils in horror. 'Oh, God. Is it that awful?'

'Well . . .'

'It is, isn't it? *Shit*. How am I going to take my sunglasses off when we . . . you know . . . get down to it, if I look like one of those things playing the saxophone in that bar scene in *Star Wars*?'

'You mean the Mos Eisley Cantina?' Lucy puts her head on one side, studying me for a moment while she actually thinks about this. Hence the fact that I'm not terribly reassured when she says, 'No, no, honestly, it's not *that* bad! Anyway, Jay's probably a huge *Star Wars* fan. Almost all men his age are.'

'That's my best hope? That Jay won't flee in terror when he attempts to undress me because he's *probably a huge* Star Wars *fan*?'

'Look, it'll probably calm down if you take an antihistamine, or something. I might have some Zirtek in my bag . . .'

She stops talking, suddenly. I shove my sunglasses back on, because I can tell from her expression that Jay is coming up behind me.

'You must be Lucy! Great to meet you.'

'And you must be Jay.' She beams up at him. 'Charlie's told me so much about you!'

'Only the good things, I hope.' Jay swoops in to give her a kiss on either cheek. 'Why don't you guys come on inside? I'll show you to your bedroom and we can all get settled.'

'Why don't *I* show Lucy to their bedroom?' I suggest. Because I'm mindful of the fact that the next step after Jay showing Pal and Lucy their bedroom is for him to take me to *our* bedroom, and that unless I'm very much mistaken, this will be my cue to start getting down to more of what Lucy has just called the hanky-panky. And until I can take these bloody sunglasses off without reminding him of favourite sci-fi adventure movies from his childhood, I'd really rather avoid any situation that might lead to either hanky or panky. 'You can . . . er . . . show Pal your car!'

'Oh, now, that would be splendid. Absolutely top-hole,' says Pal, who seems to have got himself thoroughly prepared for his Traditional English Weekend in the Country by reading volumes of P. G. Wodehouse and watching *Downton Abbey*.

Jay's eyebrows knit closer together, quizzically. 'How will you know your way to the right bedroom?' he asks me.

'Well . . . oh, didn't you say there's a housekeeper? I'll just ask her.'

'Hannah? Sure, if you dare.' He looks amused by the whole thing, as if he's rather enjoying my sudden presumption that it's OK for me to act like the lady of the manor. 'She's on her way out now, actually.'

He's right: a middle-aged woman (who seems to have undergone similar preparations to Pal's, and modelled her entire appearance on the Scottish housekeeper in *Downton*, right down to the grey cardigan and grim facial expression), is coming out of the house now and heading towards us with a purposeful air.

'Great! I'll get Lucy settled, you boys can talk about . . . about gearboxes and horse-power, and we'll all meet again when it's time for dinner!'

I grab Lucy's hand and pull her towards Hannah and the house, before she can do anything to resist.

A few minutes later, Hannah has led us through a breathtaking, flagstone-floored Great Hall and up a flight of narrow stairs to the bedroom she's allocated Lucy and Pal for the weekend. She's keen to continue along the corridor and show me to my bedroom, too, but I'm just desperate to get rid of her so Lucy can give me the Zirtek she may or may not have in her bag.

'That's really kind,' I tell her, while Lucy 'ooohs' and 'aaahs' her way around the charming, wooden-beamed bedroom, 'but I'll find my way there a bit later!'

'How?' Hannah wants to know. 'Have you been here before? Are you the one he brought here the weekend before Christmas, when I was off on holiday? The one he filled the bath with champagne for?'

'No . . .'

'Then are you the one who came here last summer? Kept sunbathing nude in the Knot Garden?'

'No! Absolutely not.'

'No. I didn't think I recognised you. Mind you, it could just be that you looked different with your clothes on.' Hannah casts an appraising eye over my sundress-clad body, before clearly deciding that I can't possibly have been the nude sunbather. 'Fine, though,' she eventually sniffs, 'if you want to find your bedroom yourself. I've put you in the one at the far end of the corridor. It's Jay's favourite when he brings a girl to stay. Super-kingsize four-poster bed. Decent sound-proofing—'

'Terrific, Hannah, thank you!' I practically bundle her out of the room, no longer simply keen to have my Zirtek moment alone with Lucy, but also desperate to put a stop to her disapproving references to all the other floozies Jay has brought here for filthy weekends before me. 'I'll manage from here!'

'God, this *place*!' Lucy says, emerging from the en-suite bathroom as Hannah closes the bedroom door behind her. 'You have to see the size of the shower, Charlie! Oh, and by the way, why didn't you warn me just how ridiculously hot Jay is in real life?'

'Did I not?'

'No! I mean, bloody hell, Charlie. That body! That smile! Those eyes!'

Eyes. This reminds me. I whip off my sunglasses, take a deep breath, and risk a peek in the mirror on the wardrobe door.

Dear God, I was right. I'm *Star Wars*-tastic. My right eye, in particular, has puffed up to golfball-like proportions, and is the sickly pink of undercooked sausage, and my left eye, though less swollen, is unpleasantly shiny and oozing more of those tears than ever. It's grotesque. *I'm* grotesque. And, as Hannah the housekeeper has just so helpfully reminded me, Jay isn't accustomed to bedding grotesque women.

'Seriously, I'm sick with envy,' Lucy is saying, 'that you get to have sex with that beautiful man tonight. You only have to look at Jay to know he must know exactly what he's doing in the bedroom department. I mean, *exactly*. I bet he'll have all kinds of moves. I bet he'll pick you up, and throw you down on the bed, and . . . er, Charlie? Are you all right?'

'No,' I croak. 'I'm not. I can't do this, Luce.'

'Can't do what?'

'Any of it. Champagne baths. Nude sunbathing.' This is precisely how I felt that night up on the roof terrace at Jay's party, only this time magnified by about a hundred. And this time, I'm not sure there's any equivalent of a handy drainpipe to shin down. 'I'm out of my depth. No, it's worse than that: I'm not even sure I know how to swim! I *haven't* swum in ten years, and even then I pretty much used to stick to the real basics. A bit of backstroke. Doggy paddle . . .'

'OK, OK. Let's just take a deep breath here.' Lucy seizes my hand and pulls me towards the bathroom, where she sits me down on the loo seat while starting to rifle through her washbag for the Zirtek. 'Now, I assume all this talk about swimming is really about sex, right?'

I nod, unable to form words at the moment.

'And you're having a bit of a freak-out because you've suddenly realised you don't want to have sex with Jay after all?'

'No! I do want to! Of course I want to!'

'Oh, thank God.' Lucy is visibly relieved. 'I thought you might have really cracked up there, for a moment. Aha! Zirtek!' She pulls a foil packet out of her washbag, pops out a tablet and hands it to me before turning to the basin to fill the tooth-mug with a splash of water. Then she hands the mug to me and perches on the edge of the bath herself. It's a gorgeous bath – one of those cast-iron, claw-foot ones – in keeping with the general theme of gorgeousness throughout the entire bathroom. It's tastefully fitted out in swish white marble and glittering grey granite, with subtle daylight-effect lighting, and mirrors lining every single wall, except for a spot to the left of the shower where there's another small door, perhaps leading to a separate dressing room, or something. 'OK. The Zirtek should solve the problem with your eyes. Now, why don't you tell me what the real problem is?'

'The problem is that I'm not a supermodel. Who may or may not have been the luscious specimen who was sunbathing nude here last summer. The problem is that I'm not Maggie O'Day. Or a devotee of tantric sex.'

'Charlie, you're not making any sense.' Lucy glances down at the foil packet she's just handed me a pill from, presumably to double-check it isn't accidentally some kind of hallucinogen that might make someone start raving on about apparently such unconnected matters as Sting's backing dancers and naked sunbathing. 'And what's all this tantra stuff again? You're not seriously planning to have tantric sex with Jay, are you? Because if that's the case, Charlie, no wonder you're panicking! I mean, that's all a bit . . . advanced.'

'No, I'm not planning to have tantric sex with Jay.' I take another swig of water from the tooth-mug. I wish to God it was vodka. 'Frankly, if I can get through any kind of sex with Jay without hideously embarrassing myself, I'll count it a victory.'

'*Get through* sex? With Jay? Charlie . . .' She takes a deep breath. 'Call me a lunatic, but don't you think you ought to be trying to actually, you know, enjoy it?'

I see my own blank reflection, gargoyle eyes and all, reflected back at me in the mirror opposite.

'And why would you embarrass yourself?' Lucy continues. 'Because you're not a super-bendy super-model?'

'Don't remind me.'

'Charlie, don't you think that if Jay *wanted* to have sex with a super-bendy supermodel, he'd have brought one of them away for the weekend, instead of you?'

'But he might change his mind. When he sees me . . . with nothing on.'

'Charlie. Believe me. There's not a man on earth who is going to change his mind when he sees you with nothing on, as you so quaintly put it.' She takes a rather deep breath. 'You know, you do seem to have got a bit . . . well, obsessive these days. About your appearance, I mean.'

'I'm not obsessive!'

'OK, OK. Overly concerned, perhaps.'

'I'm not overly concerned, either!'

'I'm not criticising, Charlie. I'm just saying, you don't have to be so determined to make everything absolutely perfect.' She takes a second deep breath – deeper, even, than the first this time. 'I mean, just because your dad abandoned you when things were less than perfect in his own life, it doesn't mean all men are—'

'Dad didn't abandon me!' I'm not sure whether to be more astonished by this pronouncement or by the fact that the conversation has segued, somehow, from tantric sex into amateur psychoanalysis. Has Lucy formed some kind of a league with Ferdy's dad, or something? To try to brainwash me slowly into accepting their chosen view that Dad, while charming and great company, was a sure-fire cert for any Bad Father of the Century award that might be knocking about. 'What on earth are you talking about?'

'OK, maybe *abandoned* is too strong a word.'

'It's too wrong a word!'

'Look, I'm just saying that maybe your obsession . . . your *concern* . . . with being so perfect for Jay, maybe it's less to do with Jay's liking for bendy supermodels and more to do with the fact that you're scared he'll do a runner if the smallest thing upsets or offends him.'

'Dad didn't *do a runner*. He had a breakdown.'

'Hundreds of miles away. Leaving you with—'

'And it wasn't a small thing that upset him. It was Mum dying.'

Lucy holds up her hands, either in surrender or just to bring an end to the topic. 'Fine. I'm just saying, your grooming regime looks pretty hard core to me.'

'It's just the basics,' I say, glad to be back on the (much less) thorny issue of my hard-core grooming regime.

'It's a hell of a lot of the basics! Not to mention the six-mile runs . . .'

'Well, excuse me for not wanting to get disgusting and fat again.'

'You were never disgusting,' she says, gently.

'Says you. And anyway,' I carry on, before she can try to claim that I wasn't fat, either, and lose all credibility with me, 'tonight isn't just some fantasy, Luce. Some beautiful, innocent fairy tale, with Prince Charming sweeping me into his arms and carrying me away to his castle. I've *actually got to get naked* with Prince Charming. And Prince Charming is accustomed to going out with supermodels and tantric-sex experts.'

'So you keep telling me.'

'My point is that I wouldn't be here with him now if I still looked the way I used to.'

'Maybe not.' Lucy shrugs. 'But you definitely *don't* look the way you used to. Nothing like it, in fact. So if you can't let your old hang-ups slide just long enough for you to have a rip-roaring time in the bedroom with a man like Jay Broderick, then that's just plain wrong. I mean, if you knew the kind of workaday, unsatisfactory sex most women have to have with their boyfriends, desperately trying to get them to do something more exciting than a quick fumble under the duvet every second Thursday, and once on Saturday mornings . . .' She stops talking, quite suddenly, and gets up from the side of the bathtub, busying herself with re-zipping her washbag.

'Er, Luce?' I'm concerned by what she's suddenly saying. 'Are you . . . talking about Pal?'

'What? No! I'm talking about men *in general*.'

'OK. It's just—'

'I mean, obviously Pal and I have been together for an absolute age now, so of course our sex life isn't what it used to be. That's just totally normal. And he's so busy with work, and training at the gym . . . and, you know, it's actually pretty offensive of people to assume that just because he's Scandinavian, he must have this insanely high libido.'

'I wasn't assuming that.'

'It's the *Swedes* who are constantly up for it, with their naked saunas and their dodgy birch twigs. *Norwegians* actually have very low sex drives, Pal says. So I don't mind at all, or get upset or anything, when it looks like he just isn't interested in having sex with me. I mean, as long as he fancies me enough to make me pregnant one day, way in the future obviously . . .' Her face is pink now, and almost as shiny as my left eye. 'Anyway, weren't we talking about you? Because you're the one who really needs to chill out about all this sex stuff, Charlie. Let go of all these ridiculous inhibitions. I mean, you're primped and plucked to absolute perfection, as far as I can see. You're risking permanent injury to your sight. You're *jogging*, for crying out loud. What's the point of all that, if you can't just shag Jay Broderick senseless—'

Quite suddenly, the little door next to the shower, the one I thought must lead to a dressing room, opens up, and Ferdy's head appears around it.

'Oh!' all three of us gasp in unison.

'Shit!' Ferdy carries on, turning beetroot-purple, though whether because he's just walked in on two girls in a bathroom, or because one of those girls was talking about shagging his host to the point of insensibility, I don't know. 'I mean, I'm really sorry! I thought this was our bathroom.'

'Oooh, are we *sharing* a bathroom?' Lucy heads over to give Ferdy a hug hello, and peers over his shoulder into what clearly isn't a dressing room, but a guest bedroom that also adjoins this bathroom. 'God, that could be awkward after one too many drinks this evening! And I should, er, warn you that Pal might make quite a few strange-sounding noises when he's getting ready in the morning. He does these special stretching exercises that make him, well, grunt a bit . . . oh, God, that's my YoHoHo phone!' she suddenly yelps, as a mobile rings her 'Life on the Ocean Wave' ringtone from out in the bedroom. 'I promised Pal I wouldn't bring it this weekend . . .'

Ferdy is staring at me, now we're alone, in this intense, fixated kind of way that almost makes me start to wonder if Jay could possibly be right about his feelings for me after all.

He takes a deep breath. 'Charlie . . .'

'Where's Honey?' I chirrup, partly to break the intensity of this moment, and partly to remind him that he has a girlfriend. More to the point, a borderline psychotic girlfriend, who could, at this very moment, be lurking behind him with a blunt instrument.

'She gets car-sick on long motorway journeys. I'm picking her up at Ludlow train station in half an hour. Charlie . . .'

'Oh, what a shame! It must have been fun driving

along the motorway in your sports car! I'm dying to see it, Ferdy, and I know Jay is—'

'Charlie.' He comes through the doorway now, right up to me, and gazes down at my face. 'What's happened to your eyes?'

Ohhh. My *eyes*. That's why he's been staring at me so intently. Not because he's secretly in love with me, but because he, too, is subconsciously experiencing all kinds of flashbacks to happy childhood video nights in the company of Chewbacca and R2D2.

'Oh, I'm fine! Just an allergic reaction to some dye.'

'You've been *dyeing your eyes*?'

'No, no! My eyelashes! You know, just so you don't have to waste time faffing around with mascara and stuff.'

'Ah. I didn't know about that, actually. Just think, all these years I could have practically halved my morning beauty routine if I hadn't been layering on the mascara.'

I laugh. Ferdy grins. Then I remember I'm still looking swollen and shiny, so I stop laughing and shove my sunglasses back on.

'They don't look that bad, honestly, Charlie. Not so much so that you need to hide away behind your sunglasses.'

'Well, I don't want to put anyone off their dinner later! Anyway, it's only until the Zirtek has had time to work.'

'You mean the hayfever tablets? Actually, Charlie, I think you'd be better off with something like Piriton.

That's for more general allergies, if I remember correctly.'

'Oh, no!' I'm dismayed. 'I've taken the Zirtek now! Anyway, I'm not sure anyone will have any Piriton around here.'

'Well, don't worry, is all I'm saying. It'd be a shame to ruin your . . . uh . . . romantic weekend with Jay over something like a little allergic reaction.'

'It's not a romantic weekend!' I say, hastily. 'I think the weekend is much more about the car stuff now, to be honest. And why didn't you ever tell me you owned a vintage sports car, Ferdy? This is a whole new side of you I never knew existed!'

'It's just something I tinker with from time to time. My dad's uncle Mike left it to me in his will a few years ago. Honestly, Charlie, I'm a complete amateur on this whole front. I hope you'll warn your boyfriend of that before he insists on challenging me to time trials!'

'Oh, I'm sure he won't do anything like that.'

'He mentioned it the moment I pulled up on the driveway.'

'Well, I'm sure he doesn't mean it *seriously*.'

'He wants a seven o'clock start tomorrow morning.'

'Probably just so there's all the more time the rest of the day for relaxing in the garden.'

'You're determined to be positive about this, aren't you, Charlie?'

'Afraid so!'

He grins. 'Then how can I possibly argue?'

It's the most relaxed I've felt around him since getting back from LA; almost back to the days of the great ice-cream trials. All we need, it feels like, is a huge carton of Scratchy Umbrella and a couple of spoons, and the awkward frostiness that's existed between us ever since the night of Lucy's house-warming party might continue to thaw.

'Charlie? Do you know if this place has WiFi?' Lucy has appeared in the other doorway of the bathroom again, looking somewhat wild-eyed and panic-stricken. 'This customer claims the website keeps crashing! I think it's just her connection, but I really need to check, and Pal's going to be so irritated if he thinks I've brought YoHoHo stuff away with me for the weekend . . .'

I say that I'll go and ask Jay, just as Ferdy glances at his watch and mumbles something about really needing to go and collect Honey. So we all disperse from the community bathroom and head down the stairs towards the driveway, where Ferdy folds himself behind the wheel of a little green sports car, and I extricate Jay from where he's talking to Pal over the open bonnet of his cream Jaguar, so that I can find out the answer to the WiFi question without activating Pal's YoHoHo radar.

The Zirtek, thank God, appears to have done its job. By the time I've showered (in the even more huge and beautifully appointed bathroom that's attached to the even more huge and beautifully appointed bedroom

Hannah has put me and Jay in for the weekend), changed into my dress for dinner, and done my make-up, my eyes have receded to almost-normal proportions and almost-normal colouring. I'm still dribbling the occasional tear, but if I'm quick on the draw with the tissues I've stuffed into my bag, I'm hopeful that nobody is going to notice. Anyway, with any luck nobody is going to notice even if I'm *not* quick on the draw, thanks to the fact that, only an hour into supper, we're all – to a greater or lesser degree – what is technically known as Absolutely Hammered.

Before supper even began, Jay's groundsman Pete (who apparently doubles up as a barman when he's not doing whatever it is that groundsmen do . . . tending the ground, I guess, in a manly sort of fashion) mixed us round after round of Martinis while all six of us sat out on the terrace, admiring the view over the gardens. Then, as the sun began to dip behind the horizon, and we moved from the terrace into this gorgeous wood-panelled dining room, we switched to refreshing ourselves from the many, many bottles of wine that Hannah had put out for us.

Now, as I drink deeply from what must be at least my fourth glass of red, on top of the three super-strength Martinis I knocked back earlier, I'm actually starting to wonder what all my earlier panic was about. I mean, stressing out about sleeping with Jay Broderick? Getting into a tizz about the terrible hardship of having to go to bed with this absurdly handsome and sexy man who's sitting beside me?

What the hell was I thinking? The prospect of following up Lucy's recommendation, and shagging Jay senseless, is becoming more and more attractive with every sip of this delicious Merlot. Though in all honesty, I'm so tipsy that pretty much everyone around this table is starting to look more and more attractive and delightful.

There's Lucy, for example, almost directly opposite me on the other side of the round table: my lovely, beautiful best friend Lucy, dressed rather dowdily again but nevertheless looking almost like her old self as she chatters away to Ferdy, glass of white wine in hand. And there's Ferdy, of course, looking . . . actually, I think I'd better not dwell on how Ferdy looks. Ill advised, I think, to sit here staring at him, thinking about how handsome he looks in that pale-blue shirt, thinking about what it might feel like to run my hands through that dusty, tufty hair, when his girlfriend is sitting to his right, and to my own boyfriend's left. Speaking of Honey, the booze that's slowly making its way through my system is even making me feel warm and fuzzy towards her. I mean, obviously it would be even nicer if she weren't regarding me with a crushed-puppy expression every time I smile in her direction. But you can't have everything. Anyway, with Jay by my side, I feel like I pretty much *have* got everything.

He leans over to me now, ostensibly to refill my wine glass but also to whisper in my left ear.

'You look amazing tonight, Charlie.'

'You don't,' I whisper back, 'look so bad yourself.'

'I can't wait for dinner to be over,' he murmurs. 'Seriously, Charlie. I can't wait.'

By which I'm assuming he means that he can't wait for dinner to end so that he can take me up to the bedroom and do all kinds of wonderful things to me. Though there's just as good a chance, I admit, that he can't wait for dinner to end so that he can escape from Pal. Pal is sitting on my right-hand side and – I can only assume – attempting to impress Jay by name-dropping pretty much every human being he's ever been friends with, or accountant to, or – as far as I can tell – bumped into by accident on the escalators going down to the Tube, in the hope that one of them might provide him with common ground with an influential billionaire.

'And I don't know if you know Jack Samuelson?' he's asking Jay now, tucking heartily into his plate of lamb navarin with pommes Lyonnaise, as though he's completely forgotten that only three months ago he sat in my flat fretting about his cholesterol level and spurning pretty much exactly the same dish.

Tonight, by the way, I'm the one doing the spurning. I don't care how delicious the lamb smells, or how heavenly Hannah's perfect circle of pommes Lyonnaise looks, oozing its little pool of butter on my plate. I'm fast approaching the culmination of Mission: Get Naked In Front of Jay Broderick, a mission that has been weeks and hundreds of pounds in the making, and I'm not about to let unnecessary things like carbs and fat put me off my stride.

A pea or two is probably OK, though, isn't it? Just a dainty forkful of these exquisite, garden-fresh peas, which admittedly are pretty much drenched in sweet melted butter but which, you have to admit, are probably also packed with all kinds of fantastic nutrients that will give me the energy I need to keep up with Jay in the bedroom. In fact, with that in mind, a *little* taste of the Lyonnaise potatoes might actually be a good idea, rather than a bad one. After all, shagging someone senseless requires a fair old amount of effort, if memory serves. Jay's not exactly going to be too impressed if I just lie there, exhausted from lack of nutrients. So, a taste of the potatoes it is. For the nutrients. Very important. Vital, you might say.

'Jack Samuelson of *the* Samuelsons?' Pal is continuing, leaning around me to better address Jay. 'I wondered whether your family might be friends of his family? Lovely guy,' he goes on, without actually bothering to wait for Jay's reply. 'He's been a client of ours for years. As a matter of fact, I'm due to go to Ascot with him next weekend. The Royal Enclosure, obviously. Will you be there at all?'

'Nope. Not really into horse racing.' Jay, with the patience of a saint, shoots Pal a polite smile. Then he shoots me a much less polite smile (frankly, it's bordering on the filthy) and leans over to murmur in my ear again. 'Have I told you already how much I love watching you eat, Charlie? The way you just go for it . . . it's so sexy.'

Which is when I realise that my little forkful of

402

potato has somehow become an entire serving. And that I've polished off my peas and made pretty solid inroads into my lamb.

Oh, sod it. It's all nutrients, remember? And when my gluttonous appetite is making Jay smile at me the way he's smiling at me now . . . well, I can face the consequences tomorrow morning, can't I? I've brought my hateful trainers and hateful running kit in my weekend bag. So what if I have to be up with the lark, squatting and lunging my way around the knot garden that former girlfriends have used for nothing more strenuous than topless basking? It'll be worth every bite. I *want* Jay to think I'm this lusty, sexy, sins-of-the-flesh kind of girl, rather than the kind who's just had a bit of a meltdown in her friend's bathroom because she's terrified of getting naked. So I smile at him in (what I hope is) a flirtatious manner, and lustily reach for a refill from the pommes Lyonnaise dish. I'm rewarded by one of those filthy smiles back, and the sudden touch of his hand, as he rests it – lightly, tantalisingly – on my thigh.

'Well, maybe I could ask Jack if he has any spare tickets for the Royal Enclosure.' Pal is persistent – you have to give him that. 'I'm sure you'd have a splendid time, Jay.'

'Oooh, don't go to Ascot.' Honey shudders, her blue eyes widening. 'It's really cruel! All those poor horses, breaking their legs and dying.'

'That's the Grand National, sweetheart,' Jay tells her, kindly.

'Ascot is the posh one, Honey. With the Queen and everyone in big hats,' I add.

'All *right*, Charlie!' Honey's voice is querulous, and she looks as if she might actually be about to weep girlish tears all over her own pommes Lyonnaise rather than eat them. 'There's no need to make me look stupid!'

'Sorry . . . I mean, I wasn't . . .' But I break off, distracted by Jay's hand drawing a slow, sexy figure of eight, an inch or two above my knee. Which is a fatal error, because the lull gives Pal the opportunity to swoop again.

'I was also wondering,' he asks Jay, 'if you'd ever had any dealings with Adrian Halliday. You know, of Halliday Freeman Burke? Adrian's brother-in-law is a colleague of mine – well, more of a friend, really – and he's terribly keen for me to join him the next time he goes out to the Hallidays' ski chalet in Colorado . . .'

Jay makes the catastrophic mistake of admitting that he does, indeed, know Adrian Halliday, which causes Pal to launch into a long explanation of precisely how he first came to know the blasted brother-in-law. I grab my wine glass and take a large gulp, wondering if I can find anything to say to Honey that isn't going to make her accuse me of being mean to her. When I decide that there isn't, I start eaves-dropping on Lucy and Ferdy's conversation, across the other side of the table. Ferdy is raving, with a passion bordering on the messianic, about a *torta*

Caprese he ate in a trattoria the last time he was visiting his aunt in Rome.

'. . . and I keep trying to recreate it at home,' he's saying, 'but it never comes out quite right. If it's not too dry, it's collapsing in the middle. And the last time I tried it, it didn't seem to cook at all.'

I open my mouth, ready to lean over the table and say that it's probably just because he's misjudging the quantity of almonds, and that if he liked, I could try to dig out an old recipe for a very *Caprese*-like chocolate almond cake I used to make for Dad. But I'm distracted by Jay's hand, which is suddenly creeping further up my leg. It's made all the sexier by the fact that he's pretending to be entirely engrossed in what Pal is saying, nodding away politely while his fingers play a frisky little piano concerto on my thigh.

Well. Maybe it's the booze talking, but I'm going to get a piece of this action.

After all, Jay reckons I'm Little Miss Lusts of the Flesh, doesn't he? And I'm fairly sure I want him, right now, just as much as he wants me. So I slide my own hand underneath the pristine white tablecloth, fumble around for Jay's knee, and start playing a little piano concerto of my own.

His eyebrows lift, almost imperceptibly, and he takes advantage of a merciful pause in Pal's monologue (turning to Lucy to tell her he thinks she's had enough wine for the evening, and that she's already had a second portion of potatoes) to lean in to me and say, with a smile, 'Hey, steady on there, Charlie!'

'But . . . I thought . . .'

'Come on, babe, we have to make it through to dessert, at least. I mean, Hannah's gone to so much trouble.'

Hang on – he thinks my brief fondle was a hint that I can't wait any longer? That I want to dash away from the dinner table, abandoning my navarin half-eaten, and have a hasty knee-trembler halfway up the stairs on the way to the bedroom?

I feel my face flood with colour, at which – outrageous double standards not seeming to matter to Jay just now – he squeezes my leg all the more firmly. This time, actually, it's less of a turn on and more like he's picking out the ripest avocado in the supermarket salad section. I'm just about to mumble that I wasn't trying to cut short Hannah's carefully prepared meal when Pal turns back to us. Fresh from admonishing Lucy – who, I'm pleased to note, is simply refilling her wine glass again and knocking it back with a mutinous look on her face – he's back for more name-dropping.

'Now, I must ask you, Jay, if you've ever had the pleasure of meeting Harald Effenberg? Splendid fellow, and I wondered if you knew him from . . .'

I stop listening. Not because I'm not interested in the many virtues of Harald Effenberg – or rather, not *just* because I'm not interested in the many virtues of Harald Effenberg – but because a puzzling thing has just occurred to me.

Jay doesn't have *three* hands, does he?

I only ask because I can see that he's using his left hand for his fork, and that he's just used his right hand to pick up the nearest red wine bottle and top up first Honey's glass, then mine, and then his own.

I turn to stare at Pal, sitting the other side of me.

'Are you . . .' I realise I'm talking too loud. I lower my voice, so it's barely even a whisper. 'Have you had your hand on my leg for the last five minutes?'

But before Pal can say anything – before he can even remove his hand, come to that – there's a commotion from his other side. Lucy, who's suddenly turned a very nasty shade of green, has plonked down her wine glass, knocking her water glass over in the process.

'Who's making the room spin?' she asks, in a tone of voice that can only be described as slurry. When she follows this up with a loud hiccup, presses a napkin to her mouth, and utters the random phrase, 'Lapsang . . . parrot . . . HobNob,' I know that a) she's more drunk than I've seen her in years, and that b) if someone doesn't get her to a bathroom soon, we're really going to be in trouble.

Jay – as masterful in a crisis as I hope he's going to be in the bedroom tonight – gets to his feet, heads around the table, picks Lucy up as if she weighs roughly half of the ten-stone-two that I happen to know she actually weighs, and proceeds to carry her up the stairs to her bedroom, me and (a furious) Pal trailing in his wake.

'I *told* her she was having too much to drink!' he's

moaning from the bedroom, as Jay carefully deposits Lucy in the bathroom and I hold back her hair while she throws up barely digested lamb and peas. 'I'm so frightfully sorry about this,' Pal tells Jay, when he tactfully goes back out into the bedroom. 'I'm simply mortified.'

'Hey, don't worry about it, buddy,' I hear Jay say. 'These things happen.'

'Not to your girlfriend, they don't. Lucy's just an embarrassment.'

I don't hear Jay's reply (nor am I able to leap into the bedroom and obliterate Pal from the face of the earth with a single blow) because Lucy is retching noisily again, divesting her stomach of all of its contents and what looks like quite a lot of its lining.

'Doughnut,' she groans, incomprehensibly, from the depths of the toilet bowl. 'Cleopatra.'

I try and utter some soothing words, even though the room is getting a bit spinny for me as well, and keep holding her hair back and patting her shoulders until finally she croaks that she'd like to go to bed now, please. I call for Jay, but evidently he's disgusted enough by Pal – or scared enough of Hannah – to have headed back down to the dining room by now, because it's just Pal who puts his blond head around the bathroom door. He agrees, irritably, that he'll help get Lucy to bed, and then proceeds to haul her towards the bedroom while I fill up the tooth-mug from the sink, and dampen a flannel so that I can try to take off some of her make-up before she goes to sleep in it. I'm just going through her washbag to find her eye make-up remover when I feel a (familiar, by now) hand on my arm.

I turn round, ready to give Pal a piece of my mind, if he's lucky, and a punch in the nose, if he's not. But I'm foiled in both these plans by the fact that he's suddenly lunging at me, lips pursed like a comedy goldfish. I just have time to think, *Low sex-drive, huh?* before his goldfish lips have placed themselves on mine.

There's a brief, horrifying moment filled with suction noises and damp, wiggling tongue, and then I whack him around the side of the head with my damp flannel and – mercifully – it's all over.

'You hit me!' He steps away from me, holding his face.

'That's the least you deserve! What the hell is wrong with you, Pal? You're going out with my best friend!'

'So?'

'*So?*' I echo. Then I realise my voice has got a bit screechy, and that even though Lucy is passed out in the next room, she isn't actually deaf. '*So?*' I repeat, in a furious hiss. 'So it's OK for you to grope me under the table, when she's sitting right next to you? So it's OK for you to kiss me, when she's in the room next door?'

'Oh, well, if proximity to Lucy is your problem with this, I'm sure I could arrange to get her out of the way for a bit . . .'

'Pal, believe me, proximity to Lucy is *not* my problem with this.'

'But I really fancy you, Charlie,' he says, in a matter-of-fact way, as though this alone should be enough to make me jump on him, wild with desire. 'And I'm not saying I want a relationship, or anything. I just think we're two extremely fit, very attractive people who could bring each other a lot of sexual pleasure.'

I just stare at him. Words have failed me.

'It wouldn't even need to be a regular thing. Though I do have a fairly convenient gap in my schedule after work on Tuesdays. I don't need to get to my spinning class until seven-thirty, and I tend to be able to finish at the office by half-five—'

Feeling like I'm about to throw up myself – a state that I know is nothing whatsoever to do with my three Martinis and five (or was it six?) glasses of wine, and everything to do with what Pal has just suggested – I shove the damp flannel and tooth-mug at him and step around him towards the door.

'Put the water by the side of the bed,' I mutter, 'so she can have a drink if she wakes up feeling rubbish.'

'But Charlie—'

'And be nice to her if she's sick in the night. In fact, be a bit bloody nicer to her in general. She's worth ten billion of you. Ten *gazillion*, in fact.'

Pal regards me, his blue eyes cold now. 'Ten gazillion,' he tells me, with a bit of a sneer, 'is not a proper number.'

'Well, you're not a proper boyfriend. And if you pull this stunt again,' I add, 'I'll tell Lucy thirty seconds

410

later, and Jay thirty seconds after that, and leave them to be the ones to deal with you.'

I can hear Lucy snoring, over on the bed, as I hurry out of the bedroom. Once outside in the corridor, I lean against the wall for a moment or two, trying to stop feeling a) sick and shaky and b) the need to hose myself down with disinfectant from top to toe but especially where Pal has touched me.

But even if I could lay my hands on a hose, or several gallons of Dettol, there isn't going to be the opportunity to do anything of the sort, because Jay is heading up the stairs towards me.

'Hey! I was just coming to see if everything was all right. Is Lucy OK?'

You mean, apart from the fact she's intent on spending the rest of her life with a sleazeball who thinks she's an embarrassment and propositions her best friend for quickie sex before his spinning class on Tuesdays?

'She's OK. Well, she will be in the morning. Should we go back downstairs, to finish off dinner?'

'Oh, I think that ship has sailed. Everyone's already gone to bed.' As he reaches the top of the stairs, he leans down to place the lightest line of kisses, all the way from my ear to my collarbone. 'Which I was kind of hoping you and I could do, too,' he murmurs. 'Unless you had anything else in mind?'

'I have absolutely nothing else in mind,' I say. Which is true. Now that he's here, and kissing me like this, the memory of Pal's chilly fish-lips is receding into

411

the distance. It's pretty hard to think about anything at all, in fact, apart from the sheer bliss of Jay's touch.

He grins. 'That's what I was hoping you'd say.'

'But . . . could you give me . . . just a minute or two?' I manage to say – or rather, to gasp, as he sets off kissing the other side of my neck, even more erotically than before. 'I mean, I just need to freshen up a bit . . . after Lucy and the vomit, and all that . . .'

Remarkably, Jay doesn't seem fazed by the fact that I've just introduced the concept of vomit into this incredibly sexy encounter. He simply says he'll just pop down to the kitchen and apologise to Hannah for us all skipping dessert, and that he'll be up in a couple of minutes.

A couple of minutes . . . The moment Jay heads back down the stairs, I hurry along the corridor towards our bedroom. I need to put the awfulness of that encounter with Pal out of my mind: ignore, for the time being, my concerns about the abysmal manner in which he treats Lucy. Because right now I need to focus. I am about to go to bed with a six-foot-two, nicely muscled, smouldery-eyed, drop-dead handsome hunk of a man, who drives way too fast, and kisses way too well, and . . .

I almost trip on something that's been left outside our bedroom door. When I reach down to pick it up, I see that it's a bag from a chemist's in Ludlow.

Inside is a packet of Piriton.

Ferdy. He must have picked it up when he went in to collect Honey from the train station earlier.

Well, so much for focus. Bad enough that I was struggling to forget about Pal and Lucy. But it's really, really not ideal, when I was just getting geared up for the prospect of unleashing my inner sex kitten on Jay, to be thinking instead about the huge hug I'd like to give Ferdy. Or about the fact that I'm suddenly a bit choked up, because he went out of his way to think about me . . .

A clatter of crockery and a murmur of voices from the direction of the dining room, however, remind me that Jay is going to be finished with Hannah and back upstairs any moment. This is the return to focus that I need. I head into the bedroom and into the en suite bathroom, where I wash the vomity smell off my hands and brush any hint of minted pea off my teeth. Then it's back into the bedroom. Shoes off, dress off. Deep breath: bra off. Even deeper breath: knickers off. A hasty scrabble in my overnight bag for the bottle of Tocca's *Cleopatra* perfume that I brought for this exact occasion. A spritz all over. A hasty glance in the mirror.

Christ, no, Charlie. Shoes back on! Leg-lengthening, bum-lifting shoes back on.

I put my shoes on. I head to the bed. I sit down. Then I lie down, on my back. This feels, however, far too much like I'm waiting for Galina to come and do dreadful things to my nether regions. I roll on to my side. I attempt a come-hither face. I abandon the come-hither face. I'm just beating myself up for not taking the time to practise a come-hither face when the door opens, and Jay comes in.

He stands stock-still, staring at me, for a long moment.

'Jesus Christ,' he finally says.

Oh, dear God, what does that mean?

Is it good? Is it bad? Is there some element of necessary grooming that has slipped me by? Is my Brazilian wax too extreme? Not extreme enough? Is my spray tan too dark? Is it patchy? Are my breasts simply unrecognisable as secondary sexual characteristics, to a man accustomed to the perfectly spherical globes of Cassia Connelly? Should I have stuck with the safety net of a nice, uplifting bra after all? And if my naked top half is puzzling to him, how in God's name is he going to feel when he works his way down to my bottom half?

But just as I'm about to get to my feet, apologise profusely, and offer to take the next train home, a very, very sexy smile spreads slowly across Jay's face.

'Perfect,' he says, as he starts unbuttoning his shirt with one hand, and uses the other hand to close the bedroom door firmly behind him.

Chapter Eighteen

There are quite a few places I'd rather be at nine o'clock on a Saturday morning than a racing circuit, somewhere in the middle of nowhere, Shrops. In bed, for example. In bed with Jay, for another example. I'm sure I hardly need to tell you that last night was so unutterably heavenly and amazing that it brought a whole new attraction to the very concept of bed, which – to me, anyway – was hitherto nothing more than a place to watch TV, eat biscuits and sleep. Hence the fact I'd rather be back there right now, instead of out here at the side of a race track, sipping lukewarm tea from a Thermos flask, nibbling a bacon sandwich, and wishing a) that I could actually snarf down an entire bacon sandwich; b) then snarf down another one; and c) that I'd put practicality above glamour, and worn something more comfortable than a pair of Dad's vintage five-inch wedge espadrilles. Maggie tried these on the other day and couldn't stop oohing and aahing about how comfortable they are, but an inexperienced heel-wearer like me is already starting to suffer in them. They're hurting the balls of my feet and going unpleasantly soggy at the toes.

But the good news – though not for Dad's vintage espadrilles, I guess – is that at least it's raining.

Nobody else but me, obviously, thinks this is good news. But then I'm sure nobody else woke up in a cold sweat at four o'clock this morning and dashed to the bathroom for a clandestine half-hour of lunges and squats, just in case the dawn should bring bright sunshine, warm breezes, and the consequent need to put on the dreaded bikini. And, of course, my bathroom exploits didn't end there. With Jay safely a-slumber, I took the time to launch a full-scale tweezer assault on the tiny stubbly hairs that have already started to peek through above, beneath and between my eyebrows, followed by a second, even more intensive tweezer assault on the tiny stubbly hairs that have already started to peek through in other places, too. Then, with looming bikini threats still in mind, I dug out my tube of Bliss's Fat Girl Slim and spent a good fifteen minutes massaging great dollops of it into my hips, thighs and bottom.

By the time I'd done all this, it was almost half-past five, and I was conscious of the fact that the light peeking through the curtains might wake Jay up any minute. So I slapped on a bit of tinted moisturiser and gel blusher, zhuzzed my hair up by sticking in a couple of Velcro rollers for a few minutes, and then crept back to bed to arrange myself as prettily as possible against the sheets, in the hope that when he did wake up, he'd continue operating under the delusion that I'm naturally gorgeous (hah!) first thing in the morning (double hah!).

It's my four o'clock exertions that have made me

a bit tired right now. Well, that and the fact that I didn't actually get to sleep until close to three in the first place. Not that I'm complaining, of course – I mean, if there's a better way to stay up until three than being taken to mind-blowing pinnacles of ecstasy by a man whose sexual technique is only surpassed by his stamina and enthusiasm, then I don't know about it.

And they were mind-blowing, of course. The pinnacles, that is.

What I mean is that they were *almost* mind-blowing. And would probably have been one hundred per cent mind-blowing if I hadn't had that niggling worry about Lucy lodged at the back of my mind . . . And if I hadn't kept thinking about Ferdy, picking up that Piriton for me and leaving it outside the bedroom . . . And, let's be honest, if I hadn't been expending quite a lot of concentration and effort – concentration and effort that might have been better spent enjoying Jay's expert caresses – worrying that my body was already displaying the unattractive effects of too much lamb navarin and potato Lyonnaise. Worrying that at any moment, Jay might encounter some brand-new lump, bump, or stray patch of potato-induced cellulite that might make him swiftly reassess his earlier 'Perfect'. Worrying that, in comparison with his own casual perfection (smooth, tanned skin; beautifully defined shoulder and chest muscles; a real-life six-pack) he might finally notice that I'm not in the same league of Beautiful People he's accustomed to bedding.

Waiting, I suppose you could say, for the other shoe to drop.

Still, despite all this, sex with Jay really was pretty great. It's just that, given my lack of sleep, and my four o'clock attempts to work off that lamb and potato Lyonnaise through a rigorous round of squats and lunges (not to mention several dozen step-ups on the side of the bath), I could probably have done without the fact that he woke up all eager for an encore at six. So I'm just a bit . . . well, knackered, is all. And a tiny bit sore. And I think I might have pulled a muscle in my hamstring. Though whether from the four a.m. bathroom work-out or from my Olympian work-out, at many different angles, with Jay, I couldn't possibly say.

Jay, though – who, like I've said, turns out to have the stamina of an ox – is looking none the worse for his own exertions. But then, he's a hell of a lot more experienced at certain kinds of exertions than I am. And, of course, he's in his absolute element out here on the race-track, surrounded by cars. And I do mean surrounded. He drove me here in yesterday's cream Jaguar, and Groundsman Pete and some hired chum had already brought over three other cars from Oxley Manor's converted stables. I'm not an expert on all the names, so we'll just call them a red one, a bigger red one, and a cute little blue one that I think is some kind of MG. In addition to these four cars, of course, there's also Ferdy's green Jag Roadster that he drove himself and Honey in this morning, and a souped-up black BMW that Jay lent to Pal for the short drive to the track. (Pal came alone, because Lucy – unsurprisingly – is too hungover to get out of bed this morning. *Dying*, she texted me, about half an hour ago, followed by a second text saying, *Just had hideous flashback. Did Jay really carry me to bed last night and did I really throw up in front of him???* When I replied in the affirmative, she texted back, *OK. Flashback confirmed. Dying a bit more quickly now.*)

'OK, there, gorgeous?'

Jay is coming over from where he's been peering into the BMW's engine alongside Pal. As for Pal, he's studiously ignored me so far this morning, a fact for which I'm eternally grateful. I'm less grateful for the fact that Ferdy appears to be ignoring me too. He barely even muttered good morning on the driveway this morning, hasn't yet managed to look me directly in the eye, and now he's busying himself tinkering with his car's engine. I'm not quite sure what the problem is, especially seeing as everything was so much better between us yesterday. Maybe he's annoyed that I haven't thanked him for the thoughtful gift of the Piriton. Or maybe it's more to do with Jay: the pair of them have been circling each other like wary rhino since we all arrived at the track this morning, holding polite-but-barbed conversations about everything from the prevailing weather conditions to – I'm not exaggerating – the best condiment to serve on a bacon sandwich.

On the basis of our thawed relations yesterday,

however, I'd go and ask Ferdy if everything is OK, if it weren't for the presence of Honey. She's latched herself on to me this morning, pulling a bit of an all-girls-together act and being far less morose than she was last night. She's actually linked an arm through mine as we've stood around near the race-track's prefab clubhouse, watching the guys tinker with their cars, and keeps letting out little squeaks of terror every time one of them gets behind a wheel and starts up an engine, or slams a bonnet, or – again, I'm not exaggerating – adjusts a wing mirror.

'Fine,' I tell Jay now, keen to show that I'm interested in his greatest passion in life, and that I'm just as lusty and zesty and up for anything out here as I was in the bedroom. 'Great, in fact!'

'Not me,' Honey breathes. 'I just find all this fast-car stuff absolutely *terrifying*! You boys are all so *brave*!'

'Or stupid, more like,' Jay says. 'But, hey, I'm all about equal opportunities stupidity. Don't you girls want to have a drive, too?'

Honey squeals and cowers behind her croissant, and I'm just trying to work out a way of saying no that will still make me sound lusty and zesty and up for anything when Jay reaches out his hand and takes mine.

'You can't say no,' he says, 'you do realise?'

'Oh, I wasn't about to! Well, if I *was*, it's only because I—'

'Not when I'm giving you this little beauty to drive.' He's leading me away from Honey and over to the

420

blue MG that's parked right next to Ferdy's Jag. 'Do you like her?'

'It . . . I mean, she's lovely.'

'She's yours.'

'She's . . . *sorry?*'

'She's yours.' He laughs at my startled expression. 'To keep, Charlie. To do with, in fact, whatever you wish. I mean, obviously it'd be nice if you actually drove her. But if you just want to park her outside your flat and use her to push up property prices, that's fine by me too.'

I stare at him. Over on the grass verge, I can see Honey staring at him. To my right, I can see Pal staring at him. And to my left, I can see – OK, I can feel – Ferdy practically busting a gut with the effort of not staring at him.

'Jay . . .'

'*I couldn't possibly* is not an acceptable answer,' he tells me.

'But I . . .'

'Don't know how to thank me? Charlie sweetheart, it's only a little MG. I've got two more exactly like it in my working garage down in Kent. There's no need for thanks. Though if you really, really insist,' he adds, putting both arms down on top of my shoulders, and pulling me towards him, 'I can probably think of one or two ways you could thank me . . .'

There's a sudden loud bang from my left, as Ferdy slams his car bonnet shut with more force than is probably strictly necessary.

Jay grins, and holds the MG's door open for me. 'Go on. Hop in, Charlie, see how you feel behind the wheel. Then you can have a little spin round the track, if you fancy. At your own pace. I won't even be offended if you want to stick to a safe speed limit.'

I can hardly say no, can I? Not when I want to show Jay that I'm lusty and zesty and up for anything.

'OK!' I smile back at Jay. 'I'll give her a . . . a whirl.'

'Excellent!' He sees me safely into the car, then spends a moment or two going over the basic controls before shutting the door behind me and heading over to finish troubleshooting Pal's BMW engine.

I'm too astonished by the sudden gift to do much except sit here with my mouth open, which is why I'm glad when my mobile suddenly rings inside my jeans pocket. I grab at it and answer it before checking who it is that's calling.

'Hello?'

'Unnnggghhhhhh.'

It's Lucy. Oh, *God*, it's Lucy.

I still haven't worked out what I'm going to say to her about Pal, yet. If, indeed, I'm going to say anything at all. I mean, I know I should. If you find out that your best friend's boyfriend is a cheaty, sleazy scumbag, then you're pretty much *required* to tell her.

I'm just not sure if it's the same requirement – if, in fact, it's advisable at all – when the newest target of your best friend's boyfriend's cheaty, sleazy, scumbaggy ways is you.

But thank God for all that booze Lucy put away last night, because I think it's perfectly permissible for me to stall a little while longer while she's under the influence of such a rotten hangover. Even if I do pluck up the courage to tell her the truth about Pal, it will almost certainly be less disastrously received if she's not suffering from a headache and a churny stomach at the same time.

'Hey, Luce . . . how are you feeling?'

'Like the Hangover Fairy came in the night, cleaned my mouth out with sandpaper and stuffed my entire head with cotton wool.' She emits another groan. 'I'm so sorry, Charlie. I'm so sorry about all this.'

'*You're* sorry?'

'Of course. I ruined dinner. I made an idiot of myself.'

'You did no such thing!'

'Pal said it was all seriously embarrassing.'

'Pal's a . . . Pal's wrong.'

'Charlie, your boyfriend had to carry me upstairs before I vomited all over his dining-room table! Which is another thing I'm sorry about, by the way.' She emits a third groan. 'It can't have made for the most romantic of evenings for you and Jay.'

'It was fine, Luce, I promise you.'

'So . . . you *did* have a romantic evening, after all?' Lucy has perked up by a good fifteen per cent; I can practically hear, in her voice, that she's shuffled herself upwards a bit on her pillows. 'Charlie! Did you do it? Did you have sex with him?'

'I . . .' Despite the fact that Ferdy has gone over to speak to Honey and isn't standing right next to his car any more, I wind my window up. 'Yes. I did.'

'Oh, my *God*. And how was it? Was it incredible?'

'Yes. It was incredible.' I shove my sun-visor down, to block out the fact that Honey has just wound her arms around Ferdy and is kissing him as if he's about to go off to war, rather than do a couple of circuits round a race-track. 'Well, *he* was incredible. And he seemed to have a great time, which is the main thing.'

'And you? Didn't you have a good time?'

'Oh, yes, absolutely! Yes!' I realise that I'm inadvertently repeating my main phrase from last night. 'Everything was just . . . just brilliant. I mean, it was quite hard work at times, obviously. Quite . . . er . . . challenging.'

'Challenging?'

'Well, Jay's obviously very athletic . . .'

'You say that like it's a bad thing.'

'No, not at all! It's just that, obviously, when that athleticism translates into the bedroom . . .'

Lucy giggles. 'Oh, now, that can't *possibly* be a bad thing!'

'Right. It's not. It's a great thing. Of course it is. And I'm sure when I get a bit more . . . you know . . .'

'Limber?'

'Exactly! And put in a few more hours on the training front . . . what I mean is, you can't be expected to run a marathon, can you, if all you've done up to that point is a jog around the block?' I break off, because Ferdy has stopped being mauled by Honey and is walking back to his car. 'Look, can I come and find you later, Luce, when we're back at the house? I've got to do some driving now.'

'*Driving?* But I thought you were just going to watch—'

I hang up, guiltily, slip my phone back into my pocket and wind down my window, so I can have a chance to speak to Ferdy before he gets into his car.

'Hey!' I say, and then, when he doesn't hear, I repeat it. 'Hey!'

He glances over his shoulder, gives a brief nod, and then gets into his car and shuts the door without actually saying anything.

I'm almost as stunned as I was five minutes ago, when Jay gave me this car.

Except along with the stunned feeling, there's a pissed-off feeling as well. I gesture at him to wind down his window and – clearly feeling he can't actually ignore this direct request, the way he's just ignored my *Heys* – he complies.

'Yes?' he asks, once his window is rolled down.

I blink at him, not sure what he means.

'Did you want some help with your car, or something?' he asks, by way of clarification.

'No . . . I was just trying to say . . . well, hey. That's all.'

'Right. Well, hey to you, too.'

And he rolls his window up again, busying himself

with some controls on the dashboard, the way he's been busying himself with his engine all morning.

'Ferdy!' I flap my hand in a window-rolling gesture again, and – just as I'm about to hoot my horn to get his attention – he glances back at me. With an expression of extreme weariness, he rolls his own window back down. 'Is there some kind of a problem?'

'Problem?'

'Between you and me.'

'There's no problem.'

'Good.' I don't know what to do with my irritation now that he's flat-out denied there's an issue. I take a deep breath. 'It's just that you seem annoyed about something?'

'I'm not annoyed, Charlie.'

'OK. Well, that's . . .'

'I'm . . . unimpressed.'

I gaze at him. 'Unimpressed?'

'That's right.'

'But why . . . ?'

Oh. It's the car, isn't it? It's the fact that I accepted the car from Jay, when – as Ferdy clearly thinks – I should have turned it down.

'Look,' I say, with a smile, 'I know it's a bit full-on to give someone a car when you've only been dating them a couple of weeks. But I could hardly . . .'

'It's not the car, Charlie. I've got no problem with Jay giving you a car.' Ferdy fiddles with his dashboard again for a moment, not looking at me. 'Though, I mean, if he wanted to make it clear just how little anyone else can compete with him around here, he might as well have handed round his latest bank statement. I think we'd all have got the message loud and clear that way, too.'

'He wasn't . . . I don't think he was trying to show everyone that they can't compete with him.'

'OK. Maybe not everyone. Maybe just me.'

He says this in such a low mutter that I can't be completely sure he's actually said it.

And before I can ask him – before I can also demand of him what, if it's not the car, he's so unimpressed about – Jay calls over to me, from where he's about to get into his own Jaguar.

'Hey, Charlie! Why don't you have a bit of a practice lap? Then you can get safely out of the way when we all come thundering round.'

'Sure!' I call back. Because when the alternative is sitting here having Ferdy disapprove of me through his open window, I'm perfectly happy to shoot off in my super-duper sports car, no matter how fast it goes.

I wind up my own window, studiously ignoring Ferdy myself now, then strap on my seatbelt, turn the key in the ignition and start up the engine. It gives a low hum, quite unlike the tinny choking sound my old Fiat used to make. I slide the gearstick into first gear, and press my foot, gently, on the accelerator.

Of course, the thing about five-inch-wedge espadrilles is that they're even less appropriate as a driving shoe than they are for standing around in the rain. Factor in the fact that they've gone hopelessly soggy and you may as well have Sellotaped a couple of bars of wet soap to each foot.

My right foot, precariously perched five inches above the accelerator, slips sideways out of its espadrille and lands on the brake. Startled as the car jolts to a juddering halt, I instinctively try to get my foot back on to the accelerator again. I succeed. Only this time, flustered by all the slippery-slidey action, I don't put it down quite so gently. The car lurches forward, and even though my right foot scrambles for the brake again, it doesn't quite make it until a split second after the car has lurched smack into Honey.

I shriek. Oh, no, hang on, that's Honey shrieking. Her mouth is a perfect O as she gazes at me through the windscreen. I'm fairly sure my mouth is a perfect O as I gaze back at her. I just have time to think, *Oh, thank God, she's still standing*, when the same thought seems to occur to her. With a second, even louder shriek, she falls to the ground, suddenly invisible behind my bonnet.

'Oh, my God . . .'

Nausea rising in my gullet, I scramble out of the car. Next to me, Ferdy is doing the same, but quick enough to get to Honey first. When I get round to the front of my car, I see that she's clutching her head, even though I'm quite sure that's not where I hit her.

'She tried to kill me!' she gasps.

'It was an accident . . .'

'There are no accidents! She tried to kill me, Ferdy! Did you see? Did you see?'

'Honey, calm down.' Ferdy, compared to the two of us, is unruffled. 'Tell me what hurts.'

'*Everything!*' Her face has crumpled, and huge, accusatory tears are already pouring down her doll-like cheeks.

'Can you walk?' I'm stricken with visions of operating theatres and wheelchairs. Of me, pledging myself to another invalid for the rest of my life, trying to atone for my terrible driving error by pushing an increasingly aged and bad-tempered Honey round Sainsbury's and giving her bed-baths. 'Please tell me you can walk?'

'Of course she can walk,' Ferdy says. 'You barely bumped her.'

'*Barely bumped?* I went down like a skittle.' The full realisation of this trauma seems to hit Honey and she starts to sob louder than ever. 'She's lucky my brains aren't splattered all over the front of her car!'

'Honey, come on.' Ferdy is looking embarrassed, now, rather than merely concerned. 'Charlie's mum was killed by a car, you know.'

'*That's* what you're concerned about? Charlie's post-traumatic stress? Rather than the fact that she tried to kill me?'

'I really, really wasn't trying to kill you . . .'

'Everything OK here?' It's Jay, coming over to help. 'Ouch,' he says, cheerily, to Honey, reaching down, grasping a hand, and pulling her to her feet. 'That'll be a nasty bruise on your backside tomorrow morning.'

Honey looks so distressed at this cavalier attitude to her health and welfare (not to mention to her backside) that she doesn't seem to realise, for a moment or two, that she's standing unaided, with no sign of anything broken, fractured or dislocated. When she does notice this, she lets out a little gasp and swoons, rather prettily, into Ferdy's arms.

'Maybe I'd better take her back to the house,' he says, after a moment of rather embarrassed silence. 'Let her have a bit of a lie-down.'

'Or maybe you should take her to a doctor.' I'm still racked with guilt, and cursing the moment I ever put on these blasted wedges. 'Just in case . . .'

'Honestly, you barely touched her.' Ferdy doesn't meet my eye. He's carrying Honey round to the passenger side of his car, where Jay is waiting to open the door for her. 'She'll be fine.'

'Ask Hannah to bring her up a cup of hot, sweet tea, or something,' Jay suggests. 'And how about you?' he adds, shutting the door behind Honey and then coming round the car towards me. 'You OK, babe? That must have been a bit of a shock.'

'Yes . . . but honestly, Jay, I wasn't trying to kill her! My foot slipped . . .'

'Yeah, I should have told you it's a bad idea to drive in heels . . . but then, I can't get enough of you in heels.' He grins, and gives me a kiss. 'Look, why don't you have a bit of a sit-down and another bacon sandwich?' he suggests, leading me away from the ill-fated MG and back towards the clubhouse. 'Watch me and Pal have a go round the track. Take your mind off it.'

'Yes, OK. Another bacon sandwich . . .'

'Exactly.' Jay plants a kiss on my lips. 'Sit this one out. And, hey, I'll hop in the MG with you later, if you like. Get you straight back on the horse. OK?'

I agree that this is OK (demonstrating that I'm lusty and zesty, etc, etc, even though I'd happily never get behind the wheel of any car again after what's just happened) and plaster a cheery grin on my face as I wave Jay off towards his Jag.

Well, it was nice of Ferdy to be so openly forgiving of me. But if he was unimpressed by me before I rolled my car into his girlfriend, Christ only knows what he's really thinking of me now.

Ferdy is so late getting back to the track, after dropping Honey back at the house, that it means a proper bout of motor sport can't really begin until almost eleven. And I have to admit, it's not the *most* exciting morning I've ever had, watching Jay, Pal and Ferdy race around a track (Jay, invariably and remorselessly, winning) while I fight the boredom by (foolishly) chain-eating bacon sandwiches and playing various scenarios in my head for the best way to tell Lucy about Pal's dastardly behaviour. I eventually decide that it might come out best if I've treated her to a spa weekend, or something, and I'm so resolved on this, ultimately, that when we finally head back to the house, in time for afternoon tea at three-thirty, I head straight up to Lucy's bedroom (making sure Pal is safely downstairs) to ask her what weekend she might be free for a short break in the near future.

She's not in her room, though. Which is hopefully a sign that the hangover has finally worn off and that she's downstairs waiting for tea. I pop along to my room for a hasty freshen-up (squeezing in a quick set of lunges at the same time, in a fruitless attempt to undo the worst of the damage caused by those sandwiches) and then head back down the stairs for tea, and to find Lucy, wherever she may be.

At the bottom of the stairs I freeze, in abject horror.

Through the picturesque leaded windows of the Great Hall, I can see out on to the driveway. Jay is still out there, giving instructions to Groundsman Pete, and Ferdy is leaning against his Jaguar and chatting, rather uncomfortably, to Pal. And all of them are turning, suddenly, to look at the mud-spattered Land Rover that is just pulling up beside them. A Land Rover with an extremely surprising figure behind its wheel.

Diana.

'Oh, that's Mrs Forbes-Wilkinson, from the Old Vicarage in the next village, isn't it?' Hannah has appeared in the Great Hall, bearing a plate of mini-scones and another of jam tarts towards the sitting room, where tea has presumably been set up. 'Nobody told me she was coming for tea! Though as we're two down already, I don't suppose it really matters.'

'Two down?' I manage to ask.

'The fluffy blonde and the boozy brunette. That

nice Ferdy chap gave them both a lift to the station after he brought the blonde back here from the track. In hysterics, she was. Apparently someone had tried to kill her, or something . . .'

'It was an accident! And Lucy's *gone*? Are you sure?' But I don't, I realise, have time to stand here quizzing Hannah on the comings and goings of the weekend's guests. Far, far more important right now is the fact that Diana – *Diana* – is climbing out of her Land Rover and heading, beaming, towards Jay.

I dart around Hannah, almost knocking the scones out of her hand in the process, and head for the driveway myself.

'And here she is!' Diana declares, as soon as she sees me scurrying towards her. 'Charlie darling! Robyn mentioned that you were coming here with Jay for the weekend . . .' A swift kiss on either cheek, not to mention the fact that she's calling me *Charlie* rather than her usual *Charlotte*, suggest that she's in charm-offensive mode for some reason. '. . . so seeing as I'm only just along in the next village, I knew I had to find time to pop by!'

I get it now. This is revenge, on behalf of Robyn, for me daring to date Jay. Diana is here to do some damage. As much damage as she possibly can.

Not that she looks like it just at the moment, beaming beatifically at me like this. And, of course, it's perfectly reasonable for anyone to assume that she *did* just happen to be at her country house for the weekend. She's in full *Country Living* mode, after all:

quilted waterproof gilet, needlecord jodhpurs, Hunter Wellington boots, her bouffy hair covered by a suede outback-style hat.

'And I haven't seen Jay in absolutely ages,' she's continuing. 'Years, in fact! So I thought I really *had to* drop round and say hello. Now that he's practically *family*, I mean!'

I don't know much about the geological structure of Shropshire, but I'm fairly sure there isn't, unfortunately, too much chance of a huge hole opening up in Jay's driveway and swallowing me in one merciful gulp.

Thank God, though, Jay doesn't react to Diana's words like she's expecting him to. He just laughs, good-naturedly, and slips an arm around my waist.

'I'll have to set you to work on Charlie, then, Diana,' he says. 'Convincing her that I'm a suitable stepson-in-law!'

Crazy though this obviously sounds (I mean, he's joking, right? Or just trying to be charming?) it obviously hits a raw nerve in Diana. Just for a moment, her beatific smile wavers.

'Anyway, now that you're here,' Jay is saying, 'you must stay for some tea. Isn't that right, Charlie?'

I open my mouth (to say, *Jesus, no, for the love of all that is holy, no*) but before I can even get started, Diana has heartily agreed and is already heading towards the house, cleverly ensuring that Jay has to go with her by starting up a volley of questions about his father and stepmother, and asking when they'll next be at the house, and saying how lovely it was to see them at the Jefferies' thirtieth anniversary party last August . . . I'm forced to follow, in mute panic, though I do manage to find my voice when I realise that Ferdy has left the driveway too and is coming into the house behind me.

'Oh! Ferdy . . . Hannah said you'd taken Lucy and Honey to the train station earlier . . .'

'Yeah, that's right. They were aiming for the twelve-ten train back to town.'

'Lucy didn't say she was leaving.' I blink at him. 'Or that she'd left. Was she feeling that awful?'

'Don't know. You'd have to ask her.'

'I will . . . oh, God, Ferdy, I didn't ask – is Honey OK? I mean, she does know that I really wasn't trying to kill her, doesn't she?'

'Yeah. No. Maybe.' He shrugs, staring at his feet. 'She's not the happiest camper at the moment. With you or with me.'

'I'm so sorry.' I'm torn between the need to apologise to Ferdy for causing him trouble and the need to get into that sitting room as fast as possible before Diana can wreak any of that damage she's intent on. 'If it would help, I'll call her . . .'

'Christ, no.' Ferdy looks alarmed. 'At least, not until she's got over us splitting up.'

'You've . . . *split up*?'

How has any of this happened? Admittedly Ferdy was gone from the race track for a fairly long time this morning, but to fit in an unscheduled trip to the station *and* a break-up in that time is quite some achievement. Mind you, since breakfast this morning, I've managed to fit in: being given an MG; a quarrel with Ferdy; a minor car accident; the disappearance of my best friend; and the unwanted appearance of my evil stepmother. I suppose I shouldn't be surprised by anything any more.

'Because I hit her with my car? Because I *accidentally*,' I hasten to add, 'hit her with my car? That's why you split up? Ferdy, I don't know what to—'

'Look, it's not your problem, OK? Besides –' he nods towards the sitting room '– haven't you got bigger things to worry about right now?'

He's right. And let's be honest, from the look on Ferdy's face – closed down; pissed off; *unimpressed*, even – he's not about to stand around here and bear his soul about this sudden break-up. Certainly not to me, anyway. So I head for the sitting room, making the mistake of getting to the door at exactly the same time as Pal, who icily stands back to let me through first.

'After you.'

'Thanks,' I say, just as icily, before adding, in a low voice, 'Lucy hasn't texted or called you, has she, to say why she packed up and left?'

'Oh, I'm sure it's something to do with her silly pirates.' He snorts. 'An urgent order of plastic doubloons for a fancy-dress party in Ashby-de-la-Zouch, lost in transit on the M6, no doubt.'

'Well, is that what she actually *said* it was?' I don't

have the patience for Pal's superiority right now. 'An urgent order problem with YoHoHo? Or are you just speculating?'

'Goodness, what a marvellous spread!' Diana's voice suddenly cuts in, before Pal can reply. She's settling herself down on one of the sofas by the bay window, casting an eye over the coffee table in front of her, which is laden down with plates of Hannah's home baking and a large and rather beautiful traditional silver tea urn, complete with little gas flame to keep our tea nice and hot. 'Scones, sandwiches, cakes, tarts . . . well, that's Charlie sorted, what about the rest of us?'

As her laughter peals out, I know that the damage-wreaking has begun.

I abandon Pal and head, swiftly, for the sofas myself.

'I mean, I'm sure you've noticed Charlie's appetite by now, Jay,' Diana is saying, as I reach them. 'Hearty, to say the least!'

'Exactly.' Jay pulls me down on to the seat beside him, and gives me a smacker of a kiss. 'It's one of the things I love most about her. Especially after all these years of going out with girls who threw a wobbly at the mere sight of a biscuit!'

'Ah, well, you certainly won't catch Charlie throwing a wobbly at the sight of a biscuit,' Diana says, gamely having another go. 'Oh, yes, do come and join us, boys,' she adds, as Pal (who clearly isn't sure, yet, whether Diana is Someone To Be Cultivated or not) and Ferdy (who's looking as if he might make a break for the train station himself at any moment) head our way and sit down in the free spaces – Pal on the other side of Jay, and Ferdy, poor soul, next to Diana. 'I'll be mother, shall I?'

'That'd make a nice change,' I mutter, under my breath, as Diana starts to fill cups from the silver urn.

'It's just so wonderful to be back at Oxley again,' she's continuing, simultaneously managing to hand out cups of tea and gaze, wistfully, out of the window. 'The gardens are looking absolutely glorious, Jay. Reminds me of all those wonderful barbecues your father used to host out there.'

'He didn't do that many barbecues.' Jay helps himself to a couple of dainty sandwiches. 'One or two, is all I remember.'

'Oh, no, there were more than that! And pool parties, too . . . in fact, I have a distinct memory of Robyn, aged nineteen or twenty, sitting in this very garden in one of her itsy-bitsy bikinis . . .' She pauses, for a moment, to make sure everyone at the tea-table is envisaging the glorious equation of Robyn + itsy-bitsy bikini; even Pal, who's never even met her (though I'm quite sure he's the one doing most of the envisaging). 'You used to get into the most spectacular water-fights with her, Jay, don't you remember?'

'I think that was only the once. At my twenty-fifth birthday pool party, if I recall.' Jay pops two whole sandwiches into his mouth with one hand, and reaches for my hand with the other.

I can see Diana's eyes flare wide with fury. She's

come out swinging, that's for sure, but – so far, at least – none of her punches has even landed, let alone proved to be the knock-out blow she's obviously hoping for.

'Well,' she says, after a moment, 'I remember it as clearly as if it were yesterday. The two of you, both so bronzed and beautiful, chasing each other around the pool . . . I hope you young people have managed a dip since you got here?' she adds, gazing pleasantly round at all of us. 'Charlie? I'm sure you hardly needed an excuse to pop on an itsy-bitsy bikini of your own!'

'Not yet. But we're hoping the weather brightens up this evening, aren't we, Charlie?' Jay says.

'Absolutely,' I say, crossing my fingers behind my back. 'Fingers crossed.'

'Gosh, then you'd better steer clear of the clotted cream, Charlie,' Diana warns, reaching across the table to physically remove the plate of scones, complete with little ceramic pots of jam and cream, from my reach, as if I was about to stuff my cheeks with the lot of them, like a hamster on the run from an Overeaters Anonymous meeting. 'We don't want you busting out of your bikini!'

'Oh, I think I'd cope,' says Jay, giving my hand a little squeeze.

I could kiss him, I really could. Diana's snidey insults seem to slide off him, like water off a duck's back. This may just be because he's so supremely at ease with himself, and the entire world around him,

439

that he can't quite envisage the idea anyone would make nasty comments about someone the way Diana is doing. Or it maybe – could it be? – because he just isn't understanding the nature of the barbs. After all, he's got no idea I used to be fat. So unless Diana starts to refer, less opaquely, to my former size (which is surely quite difficult to do, unless she plans to start opening conversations with *Back in the good old days, when Charlie was a heifer* . . .), Jay is going to remain immune to her comments about me.

'Well, we all know *you'd* cope, Jay!' Diana gives one of her little peals of laughter. 'It's these other chaps I'm worried about! I don't think I've had the pleasure of meeting either of you,' she says to Ferdy and Pal. 'Are you friends of Jay's?'

'Pal's going out with Charlie's best friend,' Jay informs her, hastily (you can't blame him for being hasty, really, when trying to distance himself from Pal). 'Lucy. You must know her, Diana?'

'Oh, yes, Lucy. Lovely girl. I've always been very fond of her,' says Diana, who refused to let Lucy through her front door for the best part of ten years, and who banned me from attending Lucy's sixteenth birthday party in order that I should stay home and launder Gaby and Robyn's mattress covers instead.

'And Ferdy . . . well, he's an old friend of Charlie's,' Jay says, levelling his usual challenging gaze across the table at Ferdy, who has just put a jam tart into his mouth, and so isn't able to answer. 'Aren't you, mate?'

440

'Well, how nice!' Diana bestows one of her smiles on Ferdy. 'Do you know Charlie from school? University? I can't imagine she had too long to make friends at university, though,' she adds, with the briefest of glances in Jay's direction, 'seeing as she dropped out after barely two terms!'

'I don't know her through university,' Ferdy says, filling the awkward silence that might otherwise have followed Diana's casual trashing of my academic reputation. 'My dad is . . . an old friend of hers. And Elroy's.'

'Is your father a doctor? Some kind of physical therapist? A carer of some kind? Oh, what am I saying?' She smiles across the tea-table at me. 'Of course he isn't a carer! Elroy didn't need a carer, did he, Charlie? Not when you were there full-time to do the job.'

This time there really is an awkward silence.

Because, from the look on Jay's face, I can see that one of Diana's punches – finally – has found its target.

'You were your dad's carer?' There's a slight frown lodging itself between his eyebrows. 'You never told me that, Charlie.'

Look, I know I should be proud of what I did for Dad all those years. I know there's no shame – far from it – in being a carer to a sick person, especially when that person is your father. And I *am* proud. I really, really am.

But obviously I haven't yet got around to mentioning any of this to Jay. And for someone like him, whose everyday existence is so glittering, so glamorous, so filled with parties and champagne and racing cars and Olympic-standard sex marathons . . . well, I just don't know how he'll feel about me if he knows that all I was, up until three months ago, was an invalid's Girl Friday.

'Oh, yes, and she was marvellous at it!' There's a glitter of triumph in Diana's eyes. 'Gritty as they come, that's our Charlie! All those years, doing nothing but cooking and cleaning and spoon-feeding and bum-wiping . . .'

I shoot her a look that must be so unintentionally venomous that she actually stops talking for a moment.

'Well, I can only hope,' I hear myself say, 'that you have someone to take care of you, Diana. If you're ever struck down with a debilitating disease, that is.'

'Oh, I'm sure I'll manage. I have two extremely loving daughters, after all.'

I'm about to add that her *extremely loving daughters* weren't extremely loving – in fact, barely qualified as daughters – when their father was stricken with illness, so that I wouldn't go counting her chickens if I were her, when Jay interrupts.

'God, but that must have been so awful for you, Charlie.' His frown is deepening. 'I mean, wasn't there someone you could have hired to do all that for you?'

'He was my dad.'

'Sure, but . . .' He takes his hand off mine, and passes it over his face for a moment. He's wearing, quite suddenly, that little-boy-lost expression again, the one he had when he was talking about his mother. 'Taking care of an invalid . . . I just can't believe you did something so hard core.'

Diana's smile is widening. She's sensed the blood in the water and, like all good beasts of prey, is moving in for the kill.

'Oh, well, a lot of things have changed about Charlie since her father died. Honestly, sometimes I hardly even recognise her!'

I don't know what this latest game is, exactly, seeing as all her previous attempts to make mention of my former fatness have fallen on deaf ears.

'In fact, that reminds me! I was having a little clear-out of some old magazines at The Vicarage, Charlie, and you'll never believe what I found . . .' Diana is leaning down to rifle inside the Longchamp bag at her feet. 'Now, where did I put it?'

'Put what?' I ask.

'Well, it was in *Tatler*, two or three months ago. A picture of you and your sisters at your father's memorial! Oh, yes! Here it is!'

She slides her hand out of her bag, clasping within it a half-sheet of torn-out magazine, on which is that photo of me, Gaby and Robyn at Dad's memorial party.

That bad photo. That unflattering photo. That photo in which I am shiny and frizzy-haired after hours of waitress duty, and – more to the point – flabby and frumpy in my too-tight wrap dress, clutching a tray of lemon drizzle cakes as if I'm about to scoff the lot.

Christ only knows how it ever ended up in an issue of *Tatler*. A photo-desk error, perhaps, or a picture editor with a sadistic sense of humour.

But how it happened doesn't matter. How it happened doesn't change the fact that Diana is wielding it, now, the way a medieval king might wield a battle-axe, ready to deal the last, lethal blow to his sworn enemy.

I can't let Jay see this photo. If he sees it, he'll never look at me in the same way again.

And not only that, but isn't there a good chance he'll recognise me as the girl who dislocated his shoulder?

The world seems to go into slow motion. I watch Diana's hand extending with the magazine clipping, and Jay's hand lifting to take it. I get halfway out of my chair, wondering if there's any way I can intercept it, wondering what I can possibly do with it even if I *do* intercept it . . .

Then Ferdy's hand reaches forward, too. I think, because it's holding his teacup, that he's only reaching forward to refill it from the silver urn.

And maybe that's all he's actually intending to do.

What actually happens, though, is that somehow – I don't see how – his teacup collides with Diana's hand, knocking the clipping out of it. As it drifts towards the tea-table, his left hand comes out to catch it. But Ferdy is obviously feeling more than usually clumsy today, because instead of simply catching it and handing it over to Jay, he fumbles it for a moment.

Fumbles it, in fact, right into the gas ring at the bottom of the silver urn.

'God, I'm so sorry,' he says. 'What an idiot. I'm really sorry about this!'

He's so busy apologising that it doesn't seem to occur to him to pull the picture back out of the flame. It's already alight at one corner and burning up fast.

'Blow it out!' Diana gasps, grabbing at Ferdy's hand, which – in his confusion? – he's still using to hold the clipping firmly in the flame. 'Blow it out, for fuck's sake!'

'Yes, sorry, of course.'

And he does blow it out, now, but it's too late. There's only the smallest scrap of photograph left – the bottom right-hand corner, where, I suspect, all you can see is the edge of Robyn's black minidress, and a hint of the slender thigh it was exposing.

All evidence of Fat Charlie has been safely burned away.

'Oh, dear. Again, I'm really sorry.' Ferdy turns to Diana. 'I don't suppose you happen to have a copy, by any chance?'

She shoots him a look that could ignite a fire pretty much all on its own. 'No,' she spits. 'Not unless I track down another copy of a three-month-old *Tatler*.'

'Ah. That really is a shame.' He shakes his head in sorrowful fashion, then reaches for the plate of jam tarts beside the tea urn and proffers it, politely, to Diana. 'Tart?' he asks.

Diana doesn't want a tart. In fact, now that she's

been thoroughly thwarted in her attempts to inflict damage, she doesn't seem to want very much of anything any more. As soon as she's finished the dregs of her tea, and chewed her way, furiously, through the remains of her smoked salmon sandwich, she announces that she'd better be getting home.

'Charlie?' She smiles at me, in a frozen fashion, as she gets to her feet. 'Will you see me out to my car?'

I open my mouth to say no, when quite suddenly it occurs to me that I don't need to say no. I can say yes. After all, do I really still need to be so scared of being alone with Diana? All her attempts to humiliate me just now have come to nothing, and if there were ever an occasion when I could lord it over her, for once, instead of the other way around, it's this one. I'm here at Oxley Manor with Jay, for Christ's sake. I'm not a scared little fat girl any more.

I give Diana a dazzling smile in return as I get up and lead the way to the front door. We're only just out in the Great Hall, away from the eyes of witnesses, when I feel a hand grab my wrist from behind. I turn around and find Diana's eyes fixed on me, blazing as if they're laser-guided nuclear missiles and I'm their unlucky target.

'Just what the fuck,' she hisses, 'do you think you're playing at? How *dare* you do this to me?'

'Diana, I'm not doing anything *to* you.' Carefully but deliberately, I extricate my wrist from her grip. 'This isn't about you. I'm doing stuff *for* myself.'

'All those years,' she spits, as though I haven't

spoken at all, 'all those years I looked after you, took you in when nobody else would have you, when your imbecilic father didn't want to know and when your slut of a mother was too stupid to look both ways when she was—'

'Seriously,' I say, in a low voice that's so filled with quiet fury it takes me by surprise, 'you do not want to talk about my mother, Diana. That way or any other way. Not now, and not ever.'

Her face contorts and she makes a move to grab my wrist again, only to be thwarted when I stick my hands, resolutely, into the pockets of my jeans. And we just stand here, staring at each other, for a long moment. The only sounds are the occasional creak of an old wooden panel, and – from somewhere upstairs – the low hum of a Hoover.

'You'll regret this,' she says, when she eventually manages to speak. 'I promise you, Charlotte Glass, you'll regret what you've done.'

I could reply that I haven't 'done' anything – except for finally decide to get a life and stand up for myself, that is – but I don't want to dignify this with a response. Besides, you don't want to get sucked into a back-and-forth with Diana for any longer than is avoidable. I don't need to have experienced this type of confrontation very often to know, instinctively, that you don't antagonise the woman with the mad, starey eyes any more than you absolutely have to.

I take a long, slow breath. 'Well, it was very nice

to see you, Diana. Have a safe drive back to The Vicarage.'

Her jaw falls open, slackly, for just a moment.

Then she gathers herself, closes her mouth, and practically crowbars the corners upwards into a Diana Special of a smile. She doesn't say another word, but brushes smartly past me on her way towards the front door and the driveway.

There's something about the set of her shoulders that tells me this: she may know she's lost the battle, but she has no intention – absolutely no intention – of losing the war.

But I can't let that worry me right now. I'm just desperate to get Ferdy on his own and thank him for his heroic efforts on the evidence-destruction front (even though I have a nasty suspicion that I wouldn't be able to do this without bursting into tears and covering him with kisses). But when I go back into the sitting room, Ferdy is getting up from the tea-table to announce that actually, he thinks he'd probably better be heading home as well. He mutters a couple of things about work, and a staff member off sick at the new branch of Chill, but I can't help thinking he's really heading back to town to see Honey, and to try to smooth things over with her. He offers to give Pal a lift back so he can 'get home to Lucy', which obviously Pal is forced to accept, given that the alternative is a) looking, openly, like a very, very bad and uncaring boyfriend, and b) staying here with me and Jay like some kind of third wheel. Pal stamps off upstairs to pack his things, and twenty minutes later Jay and I are waving goodbye to the pair of them on the driveway, as Ferdy – not waving back – swings his great-uncle's Jaguar round in a huge turning circle and heads off for the main road.

Which means that it's just me and Jay. Alone.

'Well,' I say, 'I'm really sorry about my stepmother making an unannounced—'

But Jay quite literally stops my mouth with a kiss. It's an extremely long kiss, and a kiss of many phases, because around halfway through it he suddenly picks me up, carries me towards the house, continues carrying me up the stairs, takes me into the bedroom, sets me down on the bed, and starts removing clothing, both his and mine.

And if there's something a little different about the ninety-minute sex marathon that follows; if there's something oddly intense and stressed about him in comparison with yesterday's confident virtuosity; if it seems, at times, less like he's making sweet love to a naked and (extremely) willing woman and more like he's trying to get something icky off the sole of his shoe . . . well, I'm probably imagining it. It's been a seriously weird couple of days, after all.

PART THREE

Chapter Nineteen

Not that I want to be churlish, but I do kind of wish Jay had thought a little bit about the practicalities of car-ownership before he bestowed such an incredible and generous gift on me. I realise, as I head out of my flat to walk to King's Road on Monday morning, that a zealous traffic warden is about to give me a fifty-quid ticket for parking in a residents only bay. My attempts to tell him that I *am* a resident, followed by my entreaties to his good nature, fall predictably flat (I need an official resident's permit, for one thing; he's not got a good nature, for another) so in the end I'm forced to take the car with me for the day, where it'll probably cost me almost as much in parking as a fifty-quid parking ticket would.

Still, I can't deny that it's pretty good fun driving the MG on this bright, warm morning. All right, I'm a bit nervous every time my foot touches the accelerator (even though I'm in flats today), but with the roof down and the breeze in my hair, I've almost forgotten about the practicalities of car-ownership by the time I pull up in a space right outside both the store and Skin Deep, where I'm due for the second of my course of (six) agonising cellulite treatments at 9 a.m. I had considered cancelling, because – for all my anticipatory anxiety – it's not like Jay seemed to notice any orange-peel patches on my thighs or anything, but then I remembered all the calorific food I'd packed away over the course of this past weekend. Honestly, if I didn't know better, I'd almost suspect that Hannah the housekeeper was working hand-in-glove with Galina, the former determined to multiply the size of my derrière, and the latter grimly resolved to shrink it.

I've just got time to give Lucy another try, though. It was too late to call her when I got back from Shropshire last night, and her phone was off – probably because she was on the Tube – when I tried her just before I left home earlier.

Her phone is *still* off, however. So I leave a quick message, made even quicker by the fact that I can see Galina emerging from the salon and bustling out on to the street to come and greet me. Her crimson mouth is half-open in astonishment.

'You are given car?'

'Yes.'

'Is from new boyfriend?'

'Well, I suppose you could call him that now, yes.'

'Is wonderful!' There's a hint of a proud tear in her eye. 'I am remembering when you are first coming to me, Sharlee. Back then you are just pretty girl with bad eyebrow, lumpy-bumpy cellulite and too much hair in private places.'

The traffic warden (they're circling like vultures this morning) who's already lurking nearby actually stops issuing a ticket to the Mini behind in order to stare at me. He looks thrilled and appalled in equal measure.

'But now,' Galina carries on, affectionately smoothing a lock of hair behind my ear, 'you are not hairy. You have good eyebrow. We are slowly but surely dealing with lumpy-bumpy cellulite. You are girlfriend of rich man. You are given car. And soon no doubt more.'

'Oh, God, no, Galina. I couldn't honestly handle more cars.'

'I am meaning more *gifts*. I am meaning beautiful jewellery, exotic holiday, maybe even penthouse flat . . .'

'Galina! Who on earth do you think I am?' Actually, the name *Robyn* springs to mind. I feel as appalled as the traffic warden looks. 'Do you think I'm sleeping with Jay just because he's rich?'

'You are sleeping with him?'

'Yes.'

'And he is rich?'

'Yes, but . . .'

'Then what is problem?' She shrugs. 'We are only calling spade a spade.'

'But there isn't any spade! I'm sleeping with Jay because . . . look, I'm just here for my appointment,' I tell her, noticing the traffic warden staring at me again.

'To get rid of lumpy-bumpy cellulite?'

'For God's sake, Galina . . . look, can we just go inside and get started?'

Looking offended, she stamps back into the salon, leaving me to insert practically every coin I have into the ticket machine. You'd think this would pay for parking from now until Doomsday, but I still only manage to get a ticket to last me until half-ten this morning. I stick it in the windscreen, then with my head down to avoid the traffic warden's fixed gaze, scurry into the salon after Galina.

Once behind the curtain in the treatment room, I take off my trousers and knickers, pop on a by-now-familiar pair of paper knickers, and then lie down on the treatment table. Too late, I remember that I've forgotten to take two Anadin with breakfast, a vow I made to myself after the first time I had this treatment done last week.

Galina peers down at my thighs and lets out a low tutting noise.

'All right, all right, I had to eat an awful lot of extremely delicious food this weekend . . .'

'Is not fat that is problem. Well, is not fat that is *only* problem. Am not noticing this last time.'

'You are not noticing what last time?'

'Stretchmark. Now that cellulite is improving, stretchmark is much more visible.'

I crane my neck, to try to see the offending sight. 'I didn't even know I had stretchmarks!'

'Is fine. We can solve. I am just ordering new laser machine for treating stretchmark. Will be here in few days. You like I book you in?'

The thought of Galina arming herself with a laser

machine, let alone aiming it at any part of my body, is so alarming that I'm actually lost for words for a moment. 'Well,' I croak, when I can speak, 'isn't it something that might be improved by the course of cellulite treatments?'

She lets out a scornful snort. 'Cellulite and stretch-mark is two different thing. You are not going doctor and ask him to cure stomach ache and broken leg with same treatment?'

'No, of course not, but . . .'

'Migraine and urinary tract infection?'

'No, but . . .'

'Athlete foot and chronic constipation?'

'But I just don't know if I can afford . . .'

'Afford?' she echoes. 'Sharlee, you have boyfriend now. Rich, attractive man. If you are wanting to hang on to him you cannot be affording to look anything less than perfect.'

This specific word – *perfect* – suddenly strikes me with such a tidal wave of panic that I barely even notice she's started to dig her knuckles into my thighs and bottom, kneading the flesh with such intensity that my eyes are already watering.

I mean, *perfect* is how Jay described me when he saw me naked on Friday night. And perfection – the kind of perfection you can only achieve after hours of exercise, agony in the salon, and eye-watering expense at the hairdresser – feels a pretty daunting state to maintain.

Not that I'm 100 per cent sure I'm managing to

maintain it, even thus far. Already I'm getting the distinct impression that Jay, after the dizzy heights of Friday night, might be thinking I'm slightly less perfect than he boldly claimed. It's hard to pinpoint exactly why I think this. The slightly stressy way we had sex on Saturday afternoon, perhaps (and most of the day on Sunday; Jay might have been oddly stressed, but he obviously wasn't about to let that interfere with his productivity). The subdued atmosphere in the car last night when he (sweetly, to save me from having to endure the motorway) drove me home in the MG. And if it's hard to pinpoint the things that are making me think Jay is just a smidgen disillusioned with me, it's even harder to pinpoint the source of his disillusionment. He didn't, thank God, see that God-awful photograph of Fat Charlie, so it can't be anything to do with that. I don't even think it can be anything to do with the sex, seeing as he remained extremely vocal about his satisfaction with the process, and seeing as how he practically refused to let me out of bed for a full twenty-four hours from Saturday to Sunday. So I'm left with the niggling concern that it's something to do with me being, up close, somewhat short of the perfection he's accustomed to. Which is exactly what panicked me into the additional exercise, salon agonies and expensive hair appointments in the first place.

Right now, the prospect of having to maintain this standard – for weeks? Months? The rest of my life? – just to 'hang on' to Jay, is way too daunting to think about.

'Keeping up appearance for man like this,' Galina is continuing, as she pummels me with her closed fists, 'is full-time job. No, is even more than this,' she corrects herself, before I can point out that I already have a full-time job (or, at least, that I'm hoping to, if I can ever get off her treatment table for long enough to get my business off the ground). 'Is *vocation*.'

'Er, I think when people talk about vocations, they usually mean things like teaching, or the priesthood . . .'

'And is getting harder,' she interrupts, 'when you are getting older. Right now you are having it easy. You are thirty-two, thirty-three, is not so difficult to . . .'

'I'm twenty-eight!'

She stops kneading my left buttock. 'Is not possible.'

'It is! I'm twenty-eight, Galina!' I crane to look at her again, horrified. 'Do I really look five years older than I actually am?'

She studies my face, intently. 'You are having fine lines around eyes. Frown line between eyebrows. You are not having enough fat in face, perhaps.'

'But when I have enough fat in my face, I have far too much on my body!'

'Is ironic,' she agrees.

'Well, isn't there something we can do? Apart from just saying it's ironic? Should I be thinking about Botox, or something?'

'I am not offering Botox.'

'OK, but maybe you could recommend a place that does offer Botox, and . . .'

'Botox is horrible. Botox is looking artificial. Botox is looking as if try too hard.'

'And a full-body wax, spray tan, weekly threading appointments, a permanent mani-pedi and eyelash extensions *aren't* trying too hard?'

'I am not offering Botox,' she repeats, as if I haven't spoken at all. 'But am offering very nice collagen-boosting facial. Course of six is only price of five. And for you, Sharlee, I offer extra twenty per cent discount.'

'OK, fine.' I give up. Sod my looming cash-flow crisis. After all, maybe the reason for Jay's disillusionment is entirely down to the fact that – who knew? – I don't have enough collagen in my face. I've spent so long stressing about my body that I never even stopped to think about whether my face was up to scratch too. 'I'd better have the collagen facial, Galina. As soon as you can fit me in, OK?'

'Will find time later in week.' She returns to the strenuous business of kneading my left buttock. 'And you can be first client to be trying new laser machine for stretchmark. Will be very good for you, Sharlee. You will not regret.'

Maggie O'Day, who gets to the store only ten minutes late for our scheduled meeting at eleven o'clock, lets out a little whoop of excitement when she trips through the door in her gloriously impractical sandals.

'Was it heaven?'

I think, for a moment, that she's asking about my

cellulite massage, but before I can inform her that no, it wasn't heaven, that in fact it was quite the opposite of heaven, and that I haven't been able to bring myself to sit down since I left Galina's salon an hour ago, she carries on.

'I told you Jay would show you a good time, didn't I? And from the look on your face, he barely let you out of the bedroom all weekend! You're absolutely glowing.'

'Ohhh . . . I think that's probably more to do with this . . . er . . . treatment I just had at the salon next door, actually.'

'Rubbish!' she hoots, handing me a large cardboard cup from the little polystyrene drinks tray she's carrying. 'You shagged each other senseless, I can tell. Well, there's not a woman in the land who would blame you, my darling. Make hay while the sun shines, and all that. Oh, I brought us doughnuts, too.' She fishes in her capacious Balenciaga tote, a bit like Mary Poppins feeling around inside her carpet bag for goldfish and hat stands, and pulls out a Krispy Kreme bag. 'I don't know about you, but I always need a second breakfast right around now.'

Actually, I'd have liked a *first* breakfast – well, one that didn't consist of a blob of no-fat yogurt anyway (I've taken a drastic executive decision to cut out the muesli from now on). My stomach lurches with hunger and desire as I watch Maggie take a doughnut out of the bag and clamp her lips around it. The sticky glaze catches the light in a way that – and I'm including

461

the Sistine Chapel, Michelangelo's David, and sunrise across the Californian desert in this – is possibly the most beautiful thing I've ever seen. The paper bag that she's still holding out with her other hand is giving off a sweet, yeasty scent that could well, for a miserable dieter, be in direct contravention of the Geneva Convention against the use of torture.

'I'm fine,' I croak, exerting every last ounce of my willpower and managing to turn away from the paper bag. 'Maybe I'll have one later.'

'Sure. It's your funeral. Well, it'll probably be more like my funeral, to be fair, if I don't kick the Krispy Kreme habit.' She slings her tote on to the floor, parks her denim-clad bottom on one of the empty packing cases, pulls a chair towards her and puts both feet on it, using her lap as a table to drop little flakes of sugar glaze on to. 'Right, then. You're off to this scary-sounding board meeting tomorrow? Do you want me to come along with you, just so I can happen to name-drop some of the A-list clients I've already got on the hook . . . Charlie?' She breaks off. 'Uh, that was the point where you were meant to shriek with excitement and ask me *which* A-list clients I've already got on the hook?'

'God, sorry, yes.' The only reason I didn't do what she was expecting, I'm ashamed to admit, is that I can't get my mind off those doughnuts. 'That sounds amazing, Maggie! Tell me who!'

'Well, I ran into Lily at Claridge's at the weekend . . . that would be Lily Cole, as I hope you're thrilled to hear . . . and she's absolutely gagging to come along as soon as Glass Slippers is up and running . . .'

'Mm, that really is fantastic news. I wonder, actually, Maggie, if you could hand me one of those Krispy Kremes after all?'

'Sure.' She slings the bag in my direction. 'And I was styling a *Vogue* shoot with the very lovely Emma Watson on Friday – she's already inherited a pair of vintage Elroy Glasses from her mum, as it happens – and she's very excited indeed about being able to get her hands on some more.'

I would answer – because that's amazing news about Emma Watson, it really is – but I've just taken a bite of doughnut, and my brain is otherwise engaged (in raptures) right now.

'Now, Emma's got a big premiere this coming Thursday night, so why don't we pick out a few pairs in her size and I can try to get them to her stylist – he's a good friend of mine, actually – and see if . . . Jesus, Charlie. That doughnut isn't Jay Broderick, you know!'

I realise, too late, that is probably *does* look a bit weird that I'm practically snogging this doughnut, bringing it close to my lips and inhaling, so I can get some of the impact of its yeasty deliciousness without having to take another sinful bite.

'Just eat the damn doughnut,' Maggie advises, polishing off the last piece of her own doughnut, and licking her fingers with relish. 'Honestly, darling, life is too short to . . . oooh, look at that poor sod, getting a ticket.'

She's pointing out of the window to her right, where – *damn* it – the appalled traffic warden is circling my MG, pressing buttons on his ticket machine as he does so.

'Shit! Hang on!' I fly out of the door, arms waving. 'Stop! I'm right here! I just need . . .' I scrabble in my jeans pocket for some pound coins I think are in there '. . . a new ticket.'

This, thank God, is enough to stop the warden before he's gone past the point of no return. He still watches me suspiciously, though, until I've actually got the new ticket in my hands and opened up the car to stick it in the windscreen. When he opens his mouth, I assume he's about to say something about me having a lucky escape, or that I'd better be more careful next time.

'Are you sure,' is what he actually says, pointing a finger at my Krispy Kreme doughnut with the accusing air of a man who knows that only two hours ago I was having my lumpy, bumpy cellulite pummelled away by Galina, 'you should be eating that?'

I'm so embarrassed that I wolf down all the rest of it on the short walk back into the store, just so that I can make the incriminating evidence of my weakness disappear for good.

'Crisis averted,' I tell Maggie.

Her eyes are big and wide. 'Gorgeous car!'

'Oh, I know. Jay . . .' I tail off, suddenly feeling awkward.

'Jay gave it to you?'

'Mmm.'

'No need to turn so red! I don't think you're a total whore, or anything! Well, not because you accepted a car anyway,' she adds, with a cheery wink. 'Besides, Jay's always been a big giver of gifts. Remember those aquamarine earrings I was wearing at his birthday party? They turned up next to the coffee pot on the breakfast table the morning after our third date. But a whole *car*, now . . .' She lets out a little whistle. 'Like I said before, he must really, *really* like you.'

'Do you think?' I've felt awkward about discussing Jay with her before, but I'm suddenly desperate. After all, I haven't had the chance, yet, to discuss anything about the weekend with Lucy. 'I mean, I know you don't exactly go around giving cars to people if you *don't* like them! But I'm just a little . . . well, it all seems a bit . . .'

'Full on?'

'Yes.'

'Sure, but that's just Jay, isn't it?'

'Is it?'

''Course! He's the most all-or-nothing guy I've ever known. I mean, while you're with him, he'll give you the most amazing ride of your life – and, yes, I do mean the double-entendre,' Maggie adds, with another of her winks, 'and you just have to let go and enjoy it while it lasts.'

'While it lasts?'

'Oh, now, you mustn't worry about that part, darling. Jay is always so incredibly civilised about break-ups, and he couldn't be nicer to his exes. Well, he has to be, doesn't he? The poor guy can hardly step out of his front door without bumping into about five of them . . . oh, God.' Maggie stops talking. She's staring at me, no longer eating her doughnut. 'You . . . don't think this is a long-term thing, do you?'

I open my mouth to say *No, are you crazy?* and quite possibly to let out a good old rip-roaring laugh, too. But neither the words nor the laugh are forthcoming.

'Charlie . . .' Concern is etched on Maggie's usually cheeky face. 'Are you *serious*? You honestly think Jay is going to stay with you? Beyond his current record of three months, that is?'

'No!' I've found the words, if not the laugh. 'Are you crazy?'

Maggie doesn't say anything for a moment. Then she takes a deep breath. 'Look, I could be wrong. I mean, I don't think I've seen him fall as hard for a girl, the way he's obviously fallen for you, in quite a while . . .'

But I can tell, from the tone of her voice and the too-bright sparkle in her eye, that she doesn't really mean this.

'It's just,' she carries on, 'that Jay's pattern . . . well, he's not all that big on reality, that's all. And the faster and harder he falls for a girl, the sooner he starts to find fault with her.'

'Fault?'

'Oh, he's never horrible about it. In fact, I'm not

even sure he knows he's doing it. But nobody can stay up on that lofty pedestal for long.'

'Pedestal,' I echo, dimly aware that I'm sounding like a parrot. And a particularly dim one at that.

'Come on, Charlie, you can't have failed to notice that he puts his women up on a pedestal? Honestly, every moment I was with him I felt like a bloody *goddess*.'

The word jabs at me, somewhere in the region of my solar plexus. I wince.

'Oh, God, Charlie, I've upset you.' Stricken, Maggie leaps down from the table and puts an arm around me. Unfortunately she bashes into my hip as she does so, which – thanks to Galina's cellulite-battering exertions earlier – makes me wince even more. 'Look, ignore me, OK? What the hell do I know? I only managed about six dates with Jay Broderick. Six dates and a crappy old pair of Tiffany earrings.'

I'm aware that she's joking about the crappiness of the earrings – either that, or she's had her personality transplanted with Robyn's, like Galina seemed to think mine had been earlier – so I give a little laugh. It's a fairly hollow-sounding one. Oddly, though, and in a doom-laden sort of way, I'm comforted by one thing: I'm not, apparently, entirely paranoid. Jay's disillusionment isn't just a figment of my imagination.

'And who knows?' she carries on. 'Probably, a year from now, I'll be eating my words! I'll be helping you choose the designer for your wedding dress, and we'll be here picking out a pair of your dad's shoes to wear for the Big Day instead of picking out a pair for Emma Watson's premiere.'

Now I'm aware that she's trying to be extra nice, so I make sure I give her a big smile, and even suggest a second doughnut for each of us. Then I deliberately get us off the topic of Jay, of pedestals, of faults and of goddesses, and back on to the important matter of tomorrow's presentation to the board of directors.

Chapter Twenty

It's Tuesday lunchtime, and I'm standing outside Elroy Glass on Bond Street. There are five minutes to go before the directors' AGM. And I don't think I've ever been so nervous in my entire life.

It's a Diana thing, rather than a rational thing. Knowing that I've got to sit facing her across a board-room table, knowing that she's got it more in for me than ever since she's found out about me and Jay, I feel like an arachnophobe who's just agreed, way beyond their better judgement, to put their hand into a box full of spiders. I'm so nervous that I can barely swallow. So nervous that this is the first morning in months that I honestly haven't woken up thinking about a cooked breakfast. So nervous that the backs of my knees, for some reason, are slick with sweat, and there's another pool of perspiration gathering in the small of my back.

The only person to whom I'd be comfortable confessing this pathetic level of terror is Lucy.

But spilling my (queasy) guts to her, unfortunately, isn't an option. After the dozen or so increasingly concerned messages I left for her yesterday, she finally texted me late last night saying that her boss had sent her on a last-minute trip to check out some new resort hotel in the Austrian Alps, and that she'll probably be there until at least the weekend.

So I'm on my own.

Well, I'm psychologically on my own. I'm not physically on my own, not since approximately ten seconds ago when a cab pulled up outside the store and Gaby emerged from inside it.

'Hel-*lo*,' is the first thing she says to me, with an unusual smile on her face. The fact that she's smiling at all is unusual. But this is a *really* rare smile for Gaby: teasing and light-hearted, if you can believe it, rather than clipped and disapproving. 'Who's been a naughty girl, then?'

'Er . . .' I look over both shoulders, to see if there might be a naughty girl – one in full St Trinian's uniform, perhaps, complete with pigtails and ink-spatters – standing behind me.

'*Please* tell me Princess Robyn knows about this?'

'About . . . ?'

'For Christ's *sake*, Charlie!' Gaby's natural impatience can't be restrained for long. 'About you and Jay Broderick! And don't deny you're seeing him, because I know it's true. Mummy wouldn't be in such an utterly disgusting mood if she hadn't seen evidence of it with her own eyes.'

'I'm not denying any . . . Diana's in a disgusting mood?' My gung-ho belligerence of the weekend has diminished, a critical notch or two, now that I'm back in London and on Diana's home turf.

'Oh, truly vile. But that's just unfortunate collateral

damage. *Far* more important is the fact that Robyn must be *fuming*!' Gaby gives an actual cackle of laughter. It's completely at odds with her chic appearance. 'She's wanted to get her claws into Jay Broderick for years. After all, the only thing our dear sister likes more than sleeping with a man for his money is sleeping with a man she actually fancies. Though still for his money, obviously.'

This whole conversation is making me extremely uncomfortable – I may have spent years longing to be able to gossip about men with my sisters, but this isn't quite how I ever envisaged it – so I just mumble something about needing to get up to the boardroom, and lead the way into the store.

By now, my heart is hammering, most unpleasantly, in my chest. Actually, I think my heart has migrated about eight inches northwards, and is currently lodged in my throat. If I wasn't nervous enough before Gaby let slip the details of Diana's mood, I certainly am now. Like I said to Olly only the other week, it wouldn't matter if the Glass Slippers project was guaranteed to make Diana a gazillionaire for the rest of her life. If she can thwart any chance of success or happiness for me, she'll do it. And now that she's in a *really vile* mood, brought about solely by yours truly . . . well, there's honestly no telling what she's going to do. Diana is boundary-less in pretty much every way, and never more so than in her lust for punishment when she feels her authority has been flouted.

When I was eleven, she made me sleep without a duvet for a whole month (in January) because she thought I'd stolen a tenner from her wallet (it was actually Robyn, who wanted the money for Rouge Noir nail varnish). For an entire six months, when I was fourteen, she made me eat all my meals outside on the back patio, because she imagined I'd signed her up for a website that kept sending porn DVDs, indiscreetly packaged, through the post (again, it was actually Robyn, who'd just started going out with a seventeen-year-old and who wanted some tricks up her sleeve to impress him). So really, is it any wonder that I'm practically sick with nerves, now, remembering the look in Diana's eyes this past Saturday, when I foolishly dared to stand up to her?

It's an odd thing, though, because as soon as Gaby and I walk into the boardroom, where everyone is already gathered, sipping coffee and making uncomfortable small talk, Diana heads our way with a huge smile on her face.

And I don't mean one of her faker-than-fake smiles, the kind that make you want to wet your pants and/or spontaneously combust. I mean, it's still a *chilly* smile, there's no doubt about that – I'm not sure Diana is capable of anything *but* a chilly smile – but it's hovering somewhere around Light Snow Forecast rather than Blizzard Coming In.

'Darling!' This is actually directed at Gaby, whom she kisses on both cheeks. But then she turns to me and kisses me on both cheeks as well. 'And Charlie!

472

Goodness me, don't you look lovely today? I love you in that shade of grey. You should wear it more often!'

I'm all poised for the inevitable follow-up. '*Because it does wonders for a sallow complexion*'? '*I think Robyn used to wear that colour a lot when it was in fashion ten years ago*'? '*It makes a nice change from all that black you usually wear when you're trying to disguise your county-sized bottom*'?

But there is no follow-up. Diana just continues to smile at me – actually, make that practically *beam* at me – while I stand there with an open mouth like a dazed goldfish.

'And what sweet earrings,' she adds, reaching up (I nearly flinch) to touch the little gold hoops – old ones of Mum's – that I'm wearing in my lobes. 'I do like a hooped earring. I picked up some lovely ones the last time I was on holiday on Capri. Then wretched BA lost my luggage on the way back and I never saw them again.'

Again, I wait for the follow-up, even though I'm less sure what it might be this time. Some way to blame me for British Airways' incompetence? A tortuous segue on to the delicious food available on the island of Capri, and how much she's sure I'd enjoy stuffing my greedy gob with it? Honestly, none of these outlandish leaps are beyond her, usually.

But not today.

OK, OK, I get it. It's a new tactic in her ongoing psychological warfare against me. She's performing the role, today, of Good Cop, while getting Alan

Kellaway – over there by the coffee table, talking at an extremely bored-looking Terry Pinkerton, while the two Jameses are simply looking tense and talking (possibly to each other?) on their phones at the board-room table itself – to play Bad Cop. He'll be the one to put the kibosh on my dreams for Glass Slippers, while Diana just looks sorrowful and keeps up appearances as the benevolent stepmother.

Well, it's a tactic that's already borne fruit. I'm feeling quite seriously unsettled as we all start to take our places at the boardroom table. I deliberately plonk myself down at a seat along one of the sides and start setting up my laptop, so Diana can't pull her ghastly trick of getting me to take the seat at the head of the table again. In fact, she herself takes the top seat, her faithful lapdog Alan at her right-hand side. Terry Pinkerton sits down in the seat next to me, muttering a rather irritable 'Morning, Miss Glass,' but quite kindly reaching to pour me some water from one of the carafes on the table.

I'm glad of the water, and gulp it down to moisten my dry throat. Matters are not helped by the fact that my laptop is proving so slow to start up this morning. It's all I need, frankly, because a quick glance at the printed Agenda sitting on the table in front of me shows that I'm Item One, due to kick off the AGM with what's been described – either because of a typo by Diana's assistant, or just because of Diana making yet another attempt to unsettle me – as *Presentation by Charlotte Glaze.*

'Good morning!' Diana beams round the table at us all – Alan Kellaway, Gaby, the two Jameses, Terry Pinkerton, and me. Especially at me. 'Welcome to our AGM.'

There's a general muttering of acknowledgement, and a hearty *Hear, Hear* from Alan Kellaway.

'Now, I'm very excited that we're kicking off the meeting with something a bit more fun than the same old boring facts and figures . . .'

'I'd rather like it if the facts and figures *were* boring, for once,' Terry Pinkerton interrupts. It's not entirely clear whether he's addressing his coffee cup or the entire table. 'All that plummeting the figures have been doing for the last nine quarters in a row may be thrilling to some, but give me a tedious old revenue increase any day.'

'Shall I start my presentation?' I blurt, into the uncomfortable silence that follows Terry's remark. I think it must be nerves that makes me do this: certainly a couple of (apparently) pleasant comments about my outfit aren't enough to whitewash twenty years of cruelty, and make me want to save Diana from any embarrassment. I'm immediately annoyed with myself, though, for letting my nerves get the better of me, because my laptop is still dozing contentedly on the table in front of me, not even deigning, yet, to ask me for my password. 'Um . . . if you could all just chat amongst yourselves for a moment . . . while I try and start up PowerPoint . . . oh, thank God!' The laptop has just powered into life. I tap in my password with one shaky hand and try to remember all the advice Maggie gave me yesterday. (Smile. Make eye contact. Don't um and ah too much. If all else fails, imagine them in their underwear.) 'So! Since we last met, work has been progressing on . . . on Glass Slippers.'

Four blank faces and Diana's beatific one gaze back at me. I select Alan Kellaway, at random, and try to imagine him in his underwear.

But this just brings back a fifteen-year-old memory of seeing him in his Y-fronts and his Argyle socks in Diana's kitchen, and I feel a fresh wave of nausea wash over me.

'Er . . .' OK, it's not an *um* or an *ah*, but it's not brilliant. I try to remember my lines, while PowerPoint slowly loads up. 'Although the ultimate plan is still to launch a new range of cheap . . . of *good-value* shoes, harking back to the seventies heyday of Elroy Glass, a new angle has come to light which I'm extremely keen to follow up. As some of you may know, the old King's Road store has for many years been an unofficial storage facility for my father's old . . . I mean, *vintage* shoes.'

Finally, PowerPoint is ready. I flick through, hastily, to slide number four, a photo of row upon row of Dad's shoes, neatly laid out on the shop floor. 'After discussion with leading fashion stylist Maggie O'Day . . .' I flick to slide number five, which was meant to be a photo I took of her yesterday looking cool and professional, but – too late, I realise I've uploaded the wrong photo – is actually the photo I took of Maggie yesterday where she suddenly pulled up her top to flash pert, bra-less breasts '. . . who absolutely is not this person!' I say, frantically stabbing at my computer keyboard.

Opposite me, James II suddenly sits up and pays more attention. To my right, Terry Pinkerton lets out a long, weary sigh.

My computer obeys, moving off the offending slide and on to a nice, safe one featuring early press clippings that I found in a box file beneath Dad's bed.

'Anyway, after discussion with *respected industry leader* Maggie O'Day, I've come to the conclusion that in order to exploit fully the great history behind Elroy Glass, the best way to launch Glass Slippers would be—'

'To use those vintage shoes!' Diana clasps her hands to her face, looking delighted. 'Charlie! What an inspired idea!'

I just stare at her.

Is she *high*, or something?

'Are you meaning to sell them? Copy them? Simply use them for publicity purposes?'

'Um, all three. I mean, I have a pair of young designers on board who have already been working on a small vintage-inspired range, to launch later in the year if things go to plan. But to sell the originals, I, er, need to get permission from . . . well, from you guys. I mean, they're company property, so obviously you all have—'

'Well! I don't know about anybody else but I have absolutely no problem giving my permission for such a brilliant idea.' Diana turns to Alan Kellaway. 'I'm sure you feel the same, Alan.'

He gives her a bit of an *are-you-high?* look himself. 'But wouldn't we need to know more about her long-term plans for growth and expansion? How she intends to fund the production of this vintage-inspired range in the future?'

'Oh, there's no need for anything as formal as that!' Diana flaps a hand at me as I fiddle with my laptop to find the correct section of PowerPoint presentation. 'I think we can all agree that, seeing as the set-up costs of the venture are likely to be minimal, there's no harm whatsoever in setting up shop and selling the vintage shoes. We can see how it's all received and then think about how we fund production of a new line in a few months' time. Now, obviously we need to get the store refurbished, preferably as cheaply as possible. Gaby, could you help your sister with that?'

'Help *Robyn*?'

'No, Gaby! Help Charlie!' Diana laughs, indulgently, as if she hasn't spent the last twenty years trying to ignore the fact that Gaby and I have twenty-three chromosomes in common.

Gaby and I stare at each other across the boardroom table. I suspect, if her open mouth and round eyes are mirrored in mine, that we've never looked more like we share those twenty-three chromosomes than we do at this moment.

'Oh, I don't want to bother Gaby with all that,' I say, because I'm hit with a sudden and terrible vision of her sweeping into the store with a team of interior decorators and making the place just as bland and sterile as the flagship store downstairs. 'I mean, I know she's incredibly busy, is all . . . and I've got plenty of help from Maggie . . .'

'Oh, well, that's fine then!' Diana doesn't seem at all put out by this. 'You'll obviously have your own feelings about the way you want the store to look. It's your baby, after all!'

'Then can we all just bloody agree on it and leave it there?' This is from Terry Pinkerton, suddenly shifting cantankerously in his chair beside me. 'I haven't come here to make chit-chat about cushion-covers and light-fixtures. All those in favour of Miss Glass reopening the old premises and selling Elroy's old stock—' he sticks up his own hand '– say aye.'

'*Aye!*' declares Diana, with gusto.

Muttered *ayes* follow from around the rest of the table: James I, James II, and finally, after a double-checking glance towards her mother, Gaby.

Alan Kellaway says nothing. He's still blinking at Diana like a dazed goldfish. As I'm pretty sure I still am, too.

'That's that, then,' Terry Pinkerton says. He turns to me with a half-smile, half-grimace. 'Good luck, my dear. I'm sure my wife will be very excited to come along to the new store as soon as it's open. Right, can we move on to item two on the agenda, please?

My item, as it happens. The threat from Selfridges and Harrods to close their Elroy Glass concessions. Now, I have quite a few questions about this, actually, Diana. Such as number one, why did my secretary practically have to threaten your secretary with physical violence to get it on today's agenda? And why the hell haven't you told us anything about this until now?'

Ordinarily I'd be thrilled to watch Diana squirm. But for one thing, I don't like to hear more bad news about the company, even if it is all Diana's fault. And for another thing, I'm far too shell-shocked to take in much of what she's saying (not to mention the fact that, in true Diana fashion, she's managing to look supercilious rather than squirmy anyway).

Did that really just happen? Did Diana agree – more to the point, encourage everyone else to agree – to let me set up Glass Slippers? After my firm and – to be fair to me – pretty reasonable conviction that she'd walk barefoot over hot coals to prevent me from doing something, anything, that might make me happy and successful?

After the fact that she told me, only three days ago, *You'll regret this. I promise you, Charlotte Glass, you'll regret what you've done.*

I mumble something about needing the loo and nip out into the stairwell. I need to catch a breath. I also need – well, actually, I *want* – to call Olly Winkleman. Hands shaking, I scrabble in my bag for my phone, and wait for him to pick up.

'Charlie!' he says, when he does so. 'Aren't you meant to be in a pretty important meeting right now?'

'I've just nipped out for a sec. Olly – you won't believe what's just happened.'

'Diana was waiting for you with a lynch mob and you've only just escaped with your life?'

'No. Much, much weirder than that.'

'She was waiting for you with a seven-headed serpent and you've only just escaped with your life?'

'Honestly, Olly, weirder even than *that*.' I lean my addled head against the cool wall. 'Scarier, too. She's just told me I have her permission to go ahead with the store. Selling Dad's shoes, I mean. Not only that, but she practically brow-beat everyone else into agreeing to it, too! I barely even got two minutes into my presentation, and they all voted yes!'

There's a moment of befuddled silence at the other end of the line.

'But I thought you said she was never going to let you do it? I thought you said that hell would freeze over before Diana let you do anything you wanted to do?'

'Then all I can say is, I hope Beelzebub has got his thermal long johns at the ready.'

'Well, this is incredible news, Charlie!' Olly sounds pleased as punch. I can just picture him, sitting in his office and beaming. 'After all your doom and fore-boding, you're actually going to get to open this store!'

'But that's not the point, Olly. Don't get me wrong, being able to open the store is fantastic. I just . . .

481

can't believe Diana's been so easy about it.' I raise my hand to my forehead, to dab away the line of clammy sweat I can suddenly feel there. 'I can't work out what her endgame is.'

'Does she need an endgame? Maybe she's just doing it to be nice . . . OK, OK,' he says, evidently realising how silly he's just sounded. 'Then maybe she's decided to keep you on-side because she wants something from you.'

'Diana's never wanted a thing from me in my life. Except that I should crawl into a hole and die, that is.'

Though it does occur to me, as I digest Olly's explanation, that there might be a very good reason indeed for Diana suddenly attempting to get me 'on-side', after so many years of neglect and cruelty. Jay. More specifically, how it might be of no small benefit to her to be nice to me, now that I'm going out with him. Failing in her attempts at the weekend to put him off me, she might simply have decided that she'd be better off biting her lip and currying favour with me instead. After all, she's obviously spent many years trying to curry favour with the Brodericks in general. Maybe she's envisaging weekend invitations to Oxley Manor. Maybe she's just envisaging a future where she can drop the phrase, 'my stepdaughter's in-laws, the Brodericks' into casual conversation.

Or maybe I'm being too generous.

You'll regret this. I promise you, Charlotte Glass, you'll regret what you've done.

'Well, I'm thrilled for you, Charlie,' Olly says, now. 'And, you know, your dad would be, too.'

Yes. Dad would be thrilled, I think. And he'd probably be telling me, right now, to get to work and enjoy myself, instead of worrying away about Diana's precise motivation, or fretting about whether her motives are good, bad, plain selfish or pure evil.

'We should go out for a nice meal and celebrate,' Olly suggests. 'With . . . with your friend Lucy too, if you think she'd like that? I mean, she probably needs a bit of a cheer-up, I'm sure.'

'Sorry?'

'Since her break-up with . . . sorry, I've forgotten his name. The rather dreadful Norwegian.'

'Pal?' Now I'm thoroughly confused. 'Olly, Lucy hasn't broken up with Pal.'

'Oh! That must have been my mistake, then.' He sounds embarrassed. 'It was just that I thought that's what she said, when I bumped into her yesterday.'

OK, now I'm starting to get a bit worried about Olly. I mean, is he hallucinating or something?

'You can't have seen her yesterday. She's in Austria.'

'Oh, no, I'm absolutely certain she isn't in Austria! We bumped into each other in the ticket hall at Clapham Junction. And we had a really nice chat. She's such a lovely girl. Well, woman, really, of course. I'd actually been thinking of asking you, Charlie, if you thought it might be OK if I asked her out for a drink sometime.' He's talking very fast. 'But now that you say she's not single after all, I wouldn't dream of such a thing.'

'Right. Absolutely.' I just spout the words without really thinking what I'm saying.

I mean, geography was never my strong point, but even I'm one hundred per cent certain that Clapham Junction isn't in Austria.

'Anyway, I'd really better be getting on, Charlie. I have a meeting of my own to get to in ten minutes . . .'

'God, yes! My meeting. I'd better get back in.'

'Well, huge congrats again, Charlie! And let me know about that celebratory meal, OK? With Lucy and . . . and Pal, too, I suppose, if they are still together. I mean, you'd be the one to know that, wouldn't you? You are her best friend, after all!'

'Yes. After all.'

I end the call, even more disconcerted now than I was five minutes ago, and slip back into the board-room for the rest of the directors' meeting.

Chapter Twenty-one

It's damp and dismal weather this evening. I've been stupid enough to come out without an umbrella, but I can't even nip to the corner shop to see if they can sell me a crappy, instantly breakable one for ten quid. I'm waiting outside Lucy's flat, and I don't want to risk missing her return from work while I'm off being fleeced for a tenner. So instead I seek pretty so-so shelter beneath the narrow strip of porch above her front doorstep, and try to keep warm with the dregs of the coffee I bought at Clapham Junction station almost an hour ago.

It's past seven when Lucy eventually appears around the corner. She's almost comically shrouded with a huge golfing umbrella (printed with a skull and crossbones; it must be a prospective piece of YoHoHo merchandise she's trying out) and so she doesn't see me until she's opening the gate that leads to her flat's short pathway.

'Oh, my God, Charlie!' She clasps one hand to her throat. 'You made me jump!'

'Sorry. I'd have called to warn you I was here, but your phone is switched off. But maybe it's just struggling to find a signal. You know, in the Austrian Alps.'

Her cheeks flame, instantly. 'How did you know I was here?'

'Olly Winkleman.'

'Oh. Bugger. Yes. But really, I mean, how did you know I was *here*?' She casts a look towards her flat. 'Not at . . . not at Pal's, that is.'

'Olly Winkleman,' I repeat. 'He told me he'd bumped into you at Clapham Junction station. And that you'd said you'd broken up with Pal. It doesn't exactly take the detective skills of Hercule Poirot to work out that you'd come back to your old flat.' Then, because I realise I'm sounding a bit edgier than I'd like, I try a smile and add, 'By the way, Olly seems pretty keen on you, Luce! He even asked if I thought you might go out for a drink with him some—'

'I don't want to talk about men right now,' she says, abruptly, and starts to fish in her handbag for her keys.

'OK, then do you want to talk about what's happened with Pal? We could open a bottle of wine, and . . .'

'No, thanks.' She runs a hand through her hair, smoothing her scruffy ponytail. It's a style she hasn't worn for months, since before she started going out with Pal. 'In fact, I'd rather you didn't come in at all, if it's all the same to you.'

I stare at her, dumbly.

What the hell is going on?

I mean, obviously over the course of twenty-four years, we've had the occasional tiff, the odd minor squabble. But neither of us has ever barred the door to the other before.

'You . . . don't want me to come in?'

'It's just that I've got quite a lot of YoHoHo stuff to be getting on with.' Lucy's face is pinched and rather grey, though the latter could just be because of the shadow cast by the black skull-and-crossbones umbrella. 'Rearranging all the boxes I brought from Pal's flat. That kind of thing. Besides, shouldn't you be getting home yourself? I'm sure you have a . . . a run to go on, or something. Or a hot date with Jay to get yourself all dolled up for.'

Her tone is so sharp, suddenly – aggressive, even – that I actually take a startled step backwards, into a small-to-medium puddle.

'Well, is there anything inaccurate about the assumption?' Lucy slots her key into the lock. 'I mean, doesn't that pretty much sum up what you do these days, Charlie? Go for runs. Get dolled up for Jay. Or for all the other men who can't seem to help falling at your feet every time you step out of the door.'

I'm still trying to get my head around how we've ended up on this topic since, as far as I knew, I was here to find out what had gone wrong between her and Pal, when she spins round to face me again, nearly taking my eye out with one of her umbrella spokes as she does so.

'In fact, Charlie, while we're having this conversation . . .'

'*Is* it a conversation?'

'. . . I think it's ridiculous how much time you spend on your appearance these days.' Her voice is shaking. 'You know, if you put half as much time into being a good friend as you do into highlighting and manicuring and *exercising* . . .'

'You're saying I'm a bad friend? Because . . . because I exercise?' For the first time in this conversation, I feel a flash of anger myself. 'So you'd rather I was still fat, is that right? I'm a better friend to you when I'm overweight?'

'That's not what I'm saying! But if you must know, then yes. Yes, maybe I *would* rather you were still fat.' Her eyes widen, for a moment, as if she's just noticed – as I have – that she's used the F-word for the first time in our two-and-a-half-decade friendship. 'Look, all I mean is . . .'

'That's OK. You've said what you mean. You preferred our relationship when I was fat and frumpy.'

'Charlie . . .'

'And now that I've finally gained a bit of confidence, you don't want—'

'You haven't gained confidence! You've gained a boyfriend. You've gained skinny eyebrows and an overpriced hairdresser. That's not the same thing.'

I want – I really, really want – to tell her that, actually, I don't even think I've gained a boyfriend; that I have the strongest suspicion that Jay's interest in me is already fatally waning; that I'd give anything to go inside with her, open that bottle of wine, and talk about it. But I don't tell her this. What I say, instead, is, 'Well, I still don't think there's any good reason for you to be jealous of me.'

'*Jealous?*' The word drips, as distasteful as sour milk, off Lucy's tongue. 'You think I'm *jealous,* because you're skinny and blonde?'

It's my turn to try to back away from the stupid thing I've just said. 'No, I don't think that. Look, I just—'

'And you haven't stopped to think for just one minute that if I *am* jealous, it might be more to do with the fact that you hooked up with my boyfriend?'

'That I . . . *sorry?*'

'It's pretty funny, really,' she continues, with a short, mirthless laugh. 'I mean, ever since I met Pal, you've barely been able to disguise your dislike of him. And then pretty much the moment you get all thin and gorgeous, you suddenly – lo and behold – change your opinion! And next thing, you're getting off with him in the bathroom of an Elizabethan country house.'

Oh, my God.

'Honey told me,' Lucy goes on, before I can say anything. She isn't quite meeting my eyes now, though whether because she's too disgusted by me or because she knows, in her heart of hearts, that there's something absurd about this accusation, I couldn't say. 'She walked in on you by accident, after dinner. She told me the next day, when she came back from the race-track. I think she was getting her revenge for you trying to . . .' for a fleeting moment, a near-real smile flickers in the direction of Lucy's face, as though she knows what she's about to say is just plain silly '. . . trying to kill her.'

I'm way too distracted to bother pointing out that hitting Honey with my car was an accident.

Because now everything is making sense: Lucy's sudden disappearance. Her refusal to answer my calls. This horrible quarrel, on her front doorstep, that's hit me so out of the blue.

And not just these things. Something else is making sense too: Ferdy's unexpected coldness towards me, that morning at the race-track. The fact that he was so unimpressed by me. Because the previous night after dinner, Honey had come scurrying from the bathroom to tell him she'd just seen me kissing my best friend's boyfriend.

Or rather – if she'd stuck around one second longer – that she'd seen my best friend's boyfriend kissing *me*, and getting a swift whack around the chops with a damp flannel for his trouble.

'That's not what happened,' I manage to say.

'Really? Because Honey may not like you very much, but that doesn't mean she can just go around making things up. And Ferdy believed her too . . .'

'Ferdy's wrong. Honey's wrong. You're wrong.'

'And that's all you've got to say?'

OK, I really don't know what's going to help Lucy here. If I tell her the whole truth – Pal's creepy groping, followed by the indecent proposal in the bathroom – then maybe I'll get myself off the hook. But it'll come at the expense of her pride and dignity, not to mention whatever (misplaced) faith she might still have in men.

'I mean, maybe now you can see why I'd rather have the old Charlie back again,' she's saying. 'Because slim, blonde, totally bloody gorgeous Charlie seems to be the kind of girl who'd make a move on the man I . . .' She stops, unable, it seems, to make a straight-faced claim that she was actually in love with Pal. '. . . I was meant to spend the rest of my life with.'

'You were never meant to spend the rest of your life with him,' I hear myself say.

'I was!' There's a catch in her voice. 'We'd have got married . . . eventually . . . and I'd have had his children. Which is all I've ever wanted, Charlie! You *knew* that.'

'But not with him, Lucy! With someone who actually deserves you!'

'He did deserve me—'

'No, he didn't. He's a pig, Luce. A pig who puts you down, and treats you badly, and only has sex with you every second Thursday and once on Saturday mornings!'

'I told you, he just doesn't have a very high sex drive!'

'Well, he had a high enough sex drive to grope me under the dinner table on Friday night, then lunge at me in the bathroom and suggest we get together for a weekly romp before his spinning class on Tuesdays!' I see Lucy's eyes widen in shock, but I'm so determined to get her to see that she's only gained her freedom by dumping Pal, and not lost the chance of a happy family, that I have to carry on ripping off the Band-Aid. '*That's* what Honey saw. Pal making a move on me, not the other way around. I didn't kiss him back, Lucy. I don't even know how you think I could do that to you!'

When I stop talking, we stand in silence, staring at each other. After a moment, I reach out a hand to try to touch Lucy's shoulder, but she pulls herself away.

'I'm all right. I'm fine.' She looks neither all right nor fine. 'I believe you.'

'Luce, the only reason I didn't tell you about it is because I didn't want you to feel—'

'Humiliated? Stupid?' A tear, one I can practically feel the heat of, is making its way out of the corner of her eye and down her cheek. 'Second best?'

'No! You shouldn't feel any of those things! Especially not because a jerk like Pal tried to cheat on you.'

'I don't feel humiliated and second best because he tried to cheat on me. I feel humiliated and second best because he tried to cheat on me with my stunner of a best friend. When I'm obviously so worthless and undesirable that he barely blinks an eye when I walk out on him.'

'You're not worthless and undesirable. Far from it.'

'Well, I've obviously done *something* wrong,' she says, bitterly. 'Not put in enough hours at the gym. Not gone blonde or bootylicious enough for his liking.'

'Lucy—'

'Oh, what does it matter anyway?' Her entire body

seems to sag, as if she's too weary to hold herself up any more, and she sits down, suddenly, on the doorstep, not seeming to care that it's turned into a slushy-looking puddle. 'You're right, Charlie. I've been completely miserable these past few months. Pal doesn't like my job, or my family, or my friends . . . except when he's liking my friends *too* much, that is . . . And living with him has been a total nightmare. Every little thing I did was wrong. I put the coffee mugs back in the cupboard facing the wrong way, and I used the wrong setting on the washing machine to wash his socks, and I got in absolutely massive trouble for asking if I could watch *Peter Andre: The Next Chapter* instead of another bloody episode of *The Killing* . . .'

'That night you came round with the wine, you mean? When I was going out to Jay's party.'

'Exactly.' Her tone is pointed. 'When you were going out to Jay's party.'

'But Luce, I said I'd stay home with you! And if you'd told me any of this stuff, I'd have—'

'You'd have what? Listened? Because I don't remember the last time you listened to me, Charlie. You're so busy perfecting yourself that you don't seem to have time for anyone else's problems any more.'

I'm speechless at the unfairness of this. Is Lucy really – *seriously* – trying to blame me for the fact that she wouldn't admit the smallest fault in her relationship with Pal? The unsatisfactory sex life; his constant, disapproving bossiness?

But then, she doesn't look in any kind of mood to be fair right now. And maybe I wouldn't be feeling too fair either, in her position.

Besides, I can't completely get away from the fact that I know I haven't exactly been that engaged with Lucy's tribulations lately. Some of the passing comments she's made about Pal, and the way he treats her . . . well, in the old days, I wouldn't have just let those slide, time after time. Not even in the interests of being Entirely Positive about her boyfriend. In the old days, I would have said something after her housewarming, when she was all dressed up like a librarian and panicking about her canapés. I would have said more when she told me he ran their relationship like a corporate HR department, with warnings and sanctions for misdemeanours like forgetting to wipe the shower down or neglecting to switch the coffee machine off. And that night of Jay's party, when she just showed up with a bottle of wine and then burst into tears all over Mum's silk kimono dress . . . well, although I really did mean my offer to stay home with her that night, I should have made sure I got hold of her the next day to see if she wanted to talk. All right, Pal 'didn't like' her talking to her friends in the evenings or over the weekend, but I can't use that as an excuse. I needed to rescue Lucy, the way she's so often rescued me in the past. But I've been – yes – far too busy perfecting myself to find the time.

'Lucy, I'm sorry. For everything I've done – well,

everything I *haven't* done. Can't we just go inside, and have a proper talk?'

'Talk about what? About the fact that I'm single again? About the fact that if I'm ever going to have a chance of getting married and having kids, I'm going to have to get out there all over again and find myself a brand-new man? Who'll forget all about me the moment he lays eyes on you?'

I could point out that, again, she's not being fair. Or I could point out that there's more – far more – to her life than yearning for marriage and kids, if she could only recognise it. But she's looking so wretched, so determined to pick at this scab until it bleeds, that I don't think it's the right time to point out either of those things. I point out nothing.

'Would you just go, Charlie, please?' There's a catch in her voice again. 'Just go home and leave me alone?'

'But you can't stay out here, sitting in a puddle . . .'

'Please. Just go.'

I can tell from the look in her eyes that she means it. So I turn and head back out into the street, leaving her sitting on the doorstep behind me.

Except that I don't. I move two houses along and lurk behind a high privet hedge, so that I can see her but she can't see me. Then, fifteen minutes later, when she's taken her head out of her hands, dragged herself to her feet, opened her front door and gone into the warmth and dryness of her flat, I stop hiding behind the privet and make my way back to Clapham Junction.

Chapter Twenty-two

It's only six days after the board of directors gave me permission to go ahead with Glass Slippers, but already the store is more than half completed.

I've been working like a demon, day and night, to get the place looking fit for purpose. I've pored over old photographs of the store in Dad's day, and tried to come up with an interior that will hint at the way it used to look while still keeping it fresh and modern. I've papered the walls with silk-damask wallpaper in a winey shade of red that (thank God) I got for a wildly discounted price because it was an off-cut of something that an interior-designer friend of Maggie's had already used to decorate a Russian oligarch's new place in Eaton Square; the floor has been carpeted, just this very afternoon, with a hard-wearing but soft-looking terracotta-coloured carpet; and where just last week the only furniture in the place was a scrawny IKEA desk, there's now an antique chaise-longue, upholstered in embroidered fabric in elegant eau-de-nil, teak shelving units that I found in an exceptionally posh salvage yard in Queen's Park, and several cracked-leather armchairs in rich chocolate-brown.

And talking of chocolate . . . I know, I *know*, I really shouldn't be shovelling these sneaky little chunks of Galaxy into my mouth right now. But I skipped breakfast this morning because there wasn't time, after my morning run, to weigh out the required blob of no-fat yogurt before having to hurry to the store to meet the carpet fitters. Actually, there wasn't even quite as much time to do my morning run as usual. I slept through the alarm by almost half an hour, which was annoying as I managed to do the same yesterday morning as well. I wish I could tell you I was struggling to wake up because of more all-night sexathons with Jay, but in fact it was simply because I was working late both nights, sweating over adjectives in my press release and labouring over a short biography of Dad, to accompany said press release, that glosses over his Mad Morocco years and tries to put what Maggie keeps calling 'a positive spin' on his last decade spent battling serious illness.

Ah – *battling serious illness*. Now, that's a way to put a positive spin on it. I'd better write that down before I forget it. It's a big improvement on *struck down with a dismal and ultimately fatal neurological disease*, which is what I came up with at two o'clock this morning. (Honestly, the whole Media and Communications aspect of this job is really not my forte.) But yes, I think *battling serious illness* could work. And Dad certainly was a battler.

Well, up until Morocco, anyway.

The thing is that, writing Dad's biog for the press release and being here in the old store so much this past week, I've been thinking about . . . OK, *dwelling on* . . . what Lucy was saying, back in the ill-fated bathroom at Oxley Manor. And, I guess, what Ferdy's dad said to me in the café, on the day of Mum's anniversary.

Look, it's not like I'm suddenly *blaming* Dad for my fucked-up childhood, or anything. Mum was the love of his life, and her death really did send him into a terrible tail-spin. He could barely take care of himself during the Mad Morocco years, so it's obviously unthinkable that he could have looked after me.

But then, the loves of people's lives die tragically every day, don't they? And not everyone who's left behind, broken and grieving, can simply throw their hands up in despair and abandon their child for the best part of ten years while they wallow in misery in the outskirts of Casablanca.

'Charlie? You're miles away.'

Oh, I forgot to say: Eloise is here at the store right now. Eloise-from-*Grazia*, that is, the stunning redheaded journalist I first met at Dad's memorial party, in this very store, almost four months ago. This is just one of the many advantages of having a fully fledged fashion hotshot like Maggie on board with Glass Slippers: she's put the word out amongst her fashionista friends and already the press interest is starting to snowball. Eloise-from-*Grazia* has come to write the first of what Maggie hopes will be many articles about the old/new store, and she's spent the past half-hour trying on various pairs of vintage shoes and waxing lyrical about how incredibly comfortable they are. I can only hope this will be the central point of her article, because I can tell I've let her down by not giving snappy soundbites about the exciting new store opening. Like I said, the whole Media and Communications aspect of this job really isn't my forte.

'Sorry, Eloise. I was just distracted.' I don't know her well enough to tell her what I was really thinking about. 'Were you asking me a question?'

'I was just asking about the heel on this sandal?' Eloise, who's looking even more intimidatingly beautiful than the first time I met her (looking, in fact, exactly like she's just stepped out of a Pre-Raphaelite painting), lifts up one foot at the end of a long, elegant, perfectly porcelain leg. The shoe she's just tried on is a fairly plain tan sandal, made remarkable on second glance by the fact that Dad designed it with a wooden heel carved to look like a Roman column. 'Do you remember what inspired your father to create this?'

'Er . . . Rome?'

'A holiday, you mean?'

'Yes. Yes, a holiday.'

'With you and your sisters?'

I'm about to let out a snort of derision and say that the only place Dad ever took me, Gaby and Robyn was Uncle Mort's house in Finchley that one day twenty-one years ago. But then I remember that Maggie has told me to talk up the family business angle, so I rack my brains for something suitable that isn't quite a fib.

'No, no . . . Dad did most of his travelling alone . . . but that's not to say he didn't spend lots of time with us girls, of course.'

'Tell me about that.' Eloise leans forward, her little Moleskine notebook in hand, her beautiful face concentrated in readiness for a decent human-interest story. 'Tell me more about those early years with your father.'

'Right . . . er, well, they were great, of course. The early years. Just . . . you know . . . great.'

'But having a genius like Elroy Glass for a father . . . I mean, that must be the source of many happy memories?'

'Oh, many. Many, many.'

Except that now, of course, I can't, for the life of me, think of one.

Damn Lucy, and the pesky notions she put into my head about Dad and all that . . . abandonment stuff. If she were taking my calls (she's still not) I'd call her up this very minute and have a go at her. I mean, here I was, all these years, perfectly happy to be half in love with Dad the way everybody else seemed to be. Never realising that those feelings were based on a fantasy. Or rather, if not a fantasy, then certainly something pretty long-gone past its sell-by date. Those Saturdays right here at the store were all very well and good, but there were a lot of Saturdays after that, too: Saturdays spent alone in my bedroom while Diana took Gaby and Robyn to ballet classes, horse-riding and friends' houses, and while Dad indulged his grief alone in Morocco.

But I can't tell Eloise about that.

On the other hand, I don't think I can lie either.

'Would you like,' I ask, perkily, getting to my feet, 'a sandwich?'

'Sandwich?' Eloise's alabaster forehead displays a solitary wrinkle. 'But I was just asking you about—'

'Because I was just thinking of popping to the café over the road and grabbing a sandwich . . . I mean, a *salad*,' I correct myself, because I've succumbed to (big, mayonnaise-laden) sandwiches every lunchtime for the past few days, and I think my brain might need retraining. 'What would you like me to get you?'

'Er, thanks, Charlie, but I actually have a work lunch . . .' Disappointed, as well she might be, by my failure to provide her with cosy family portraits for her article, Eloise is slipping off the sandal and getting to her feet. 'But I think I've got enough for my piece anyway. I . . . well, I might give Maggie a quick call some time this afternoon, see if she'd like to provide me with a couple of quotes.'

'Yes. That's a very, very good idea.' As, I think, is the idea of leaving most of this publicity stuff to Maggie from now on.

'OK! Well . . . can I just use your loo, Charlie, before I get going?'

'Sure. It's on the second floor, sharp left at the very top of the stairs.'

She's just started up the stairs towards the second floor when I hear a familiar sound on the street outside. It's the roar of an Aston Martin's engine.

Jay has just pulled up into a space outside on King's Road. He gets out and heads towards the store.

I consider, just for a moment, hurtling up the stairs past Eloise and locking myself in the second-floor bathroom until he goes away again.

This isn't because I don't want to see him. Having been too busy with work to meet since last week, I'm actually very keen to see him. It's more that I don't want him to see me.

I mean, I don't want to get all uptight about my appearance, or anything, especially not after Lucy's accusations the other day. But honestly, even if Jay weren't the kind of man to change his mind about his women the way a child changes his mind about his favourite flavour of ice cream, I wouldn't want him to see me right now! It's not just the fact that I've somehow (still not sure how) managed to put away an entire family-sized bar of Galaxy. It's also the fact that I haven't managed to keep up the exercise this past week, and that I'm wearing jeans that (thanks to this, and to the chocolate) are visibly a full size too tight around my bum. And the fact that I've neglected my salon appointments with Galina, so my eyebrows are gross, my legs are bristly, and the less said about my moustache and sideburns, the better.

Regretting, more than I thought possible, all that Galaxy (I honestly didn't mean to eat the entire bar; the bloody thing must have taken on a life of its own and jumped into my mouth, piece by delicious piece), I head for the door to greet him.

'Hi!' I pull the widest smile I possess, hoping that might detract attention from my physical flaws. 'I thought you said you were in meetings all morning.'

'We finished early.' He leans in to give me a kiss: on the cheek, and accompanied by a pat on the shoulder. I must have looked at him a bit quizzically, because he lets out a little laugh and says, 'Sorry, Charlie, I'm trying to be professional here. I thought you were in work mode. You certainly *look* as if you're in work mode.'

This has to be a veiled criticism of my haphazard appearance. Embarrassed, I try to smooth my hair. 'I was in such a hurry this morning, I barely had time to shower.'

Good one, Charlie. Make Jay think you smell, too, along with everything else.

'I mean . . .'

'Don't be silly. You look fine.'

Which is a pretty long way removed, I can't help noticing, from his usual claims that I'm some spectacular blend of Helen of Troy, Marilyn Monroe and Scarlett Johansson.

'Anyway, grab your things,' he's continuing, swinging his car keys purposefully, 'and I'll run you home for a quick wash-and-brush-up. I've got lunch reservations at Claridge's for twelve-thirty.'

'Oh, Jay, that sounds wonderful!' (Though I can't deny I'm almost as enthused about the prospect of lunch at Claridge's as I am about the prospect of spending time with him . . . OK, who am I kidding? Lunch at

Claridge's is the *really* appealing part of his proposal.) 'But I don't have time for that today. I'm just finishing up this interview, and there are delivery men coming with some mirrors some time between one and four . . .'

'So call them and get them to come closer to four. We'll only need an hour or so for lunch . . . a bit more if you want to grab a room for the afternoon . . .'

'Um, but I have lots of other things to do too.' And anyway, there's literally no way I can agree to 'grab a room' at Claridge's, not in the disgraceful physical state I've allowed myself to sink to. 'I mean, now the carpet's down, I have to go and buy a decent Hoover, and I've got to give all the paintwork a good clean from where the carpet fitters kept getting their grubby hands on it . . .'

'Charlie, for God's sake!' Jay's eyes flash real irritation for a moment, before he covers it with a smile. 'Honestly, what am I going to do with you?' he teases, grabbing me round the waist and pretending he's about to smack my bottom. Which would all be a colossal turn-on, if I didn't think he might actually, seriously, mean it. 'You need to hire people to do this kind of thing for you! You need a cleaner, for crying out loud! Look, when we get to the restaurant, I'll give my own cleaner a call, tell her to meet you back here later on with all her equipment. She's fantastic, and she'll do everything you ask. Grubby paintwork and all.'

'That's really nice of you, Jay, but honestly, there's no need.'

''Course there's a need. You have to *eat*, don't you?'

'Sure, but I was just going to grab a sand— I mean a salad, from over the road.'

'That's ridiculous!' His mouth is set in a flat line now. 'I've barely seen you for the past week, and now you'd rather faff around with a feather duster than come out and have fun with me!'

'I never said feather duster. I said Hoover . . .'

'Does it really fucking matter? You're not Mrs bloody Mop!'

He's raised his voice, which seems to have taken him by surprise as much as it has me.

Neither of us says anything more for a moment. Then he sighs, loudly, and shoves a hand through his hair.

'Look, all I'm saying, Charlie, is that you should be focussing on the fun parts of this project. Do some more interviews. Get a photo shoot in one of the magazines. And leave the dreary parts to somebody else. God knows, it's not like you haven't done enough dreary jobs before.'

'You mean . . . taking care of my dad?'

He doesn't reply, because a sudden clatter on the stairs has announced Eloise, on her way back down from the storeroom.

'Charlie? You don't happen to have a bit of lip balm on you, by any . . . *Jay?*'

She's stopped. She's staring at him. He's staring back at her.

'*El?*' he says.

'Oh, my God!' she laughs, hurries down the final couple of steps, and goes to give him a big hug, and a kiss on either cheek. 'It's been, what – three years?'

'But I thought you were studying in New York . . . oh, wait a minute.' Jay's memory seems to jolt. 'Now I come to think of it, Ben did tell me you'd moved back home a few months ago.'

'Yeah, yeah, it went in one ear and out the other.' Eloise laughs. 'I'm amazed he even bothered to mention me at all, actually. I thought all you and my brother talked about was what kind of car you're driving and what kind of girl you're shagging! Oh, shit!' She claps a hand over her mouth, and gazes at me apologetically. 'Sorry, Charlie, I didn't mean . . . you know, seeing as you two are obviously together . . .'

I haven't really taken in anything she's said, though, because I'm just trying to take in a couple of aspects of this situation. For starters, that Eloise is evidently sister to Jay's best friend Ben.

But more to the point, that Jay is still staring at her.

And not at all in the way you'd expect a bloke to stare at his best friend's little sister. But more – much more – in the way you'd expect a bloke to stare at a twenty-three-year-old Pre-Raphaelite beauty with porcelain skin, tumbling auburn hair and eyes like emeralds.

'Jesus, El, you look . . . you look great! Last time I saw you . . .' Jay seems lost for words for a moment.

506

'Have you done something different with your hair?'

'Grown it long and stopped dyeing it Goth-black, perhaps?'

'*That's* it! Last time I saw you, you were a teenage Goth!' His face breaks into a grin. It's an expression that would best be described as . . .

Devilish.

'You know,' he's carrying on, his eyes still fixed on Eloise's lovely face, that grin still hovering around his lips, 'Charlie didn't tell me she was running some kind of work experience scheme. What are you, the Saturday salesgirl or something?'

'I'm not on work *experience*, idiot.' But Eloise laughs at his joke. Even her laugh is elegant, sounding rather like a flute solo in something by Mozart. 'I am a proper grown-up now, remember?'

'How could I forget?' Jay says, lightly.

This is accompanied by such a meaningful tilt of the head – and such a flirtatious lift of one eyebrow – that I actually see a faint blush rise up Eloise's cheeks. She looks flustered, for the first time in this conversation.

'Anyway, I'm not a salesgirl at all. Saturday or otherwise.' She waves her Moleskine notebook at him, as if this proves her point – and, I think, to distract attention from her reddening skin. 'I'm a journalist actually. I work for *Grazia* magazine.'

'Well, get *you*! With your fancy job and your little notebook!'

She laughs, and he laughs, and I shift from foot to

foot, suddenly feeling extraordinarily drab and dim-watted, like I'm being lit by one of those dreary energy-saving lightbulbs while Jay and Eloise bask in glorious natural sunshine.

'Er,' I say, which isn't exactly going to brighten me up, but is my attempt to break the spell Jay seems intent on weaving round Eloise right this very minute. 'I . . . er . . . didn't know you were Ben's sister, Eloise. I mean, not that I know Ben either yet, come to think of it, but . . .'

'Hey, then I've got a fantastic idea.' Jay is still looking at Eloise, though I get the general sense he's probably reacting to something I've just said. 'Let's all have dinner on Friday night. Me, you, Ben. Charlie.'

Oh, so the *you* he was referring to there was Eloise. I was the one who was the afterthought.

I feel my wattage decrease by another few dozen volts.

'Friday?' Eloise screws up her lovely forehead. 'Oh, I don't know, Jay, I have this party to go to . . .'

'All right, all right. Little Miss Popular. How about Saturday instead? And hey, if there's a man lurking around on the scene, then bring him along as well. Ben and I can team up to interrogate him. Good Cop, Bad Cop. Find out if he's good enough for you.'

There's a nasty, rather nauseous feeling in my stomach, one that only intensifies when Eloise replies.

'God, no. I'm footloose and fancy-free ever since I came back to London.'

'A trail of broken hearts left behind you in Manhattan, I assume? Desperate men throwing themselves off buildings the entire length of Fifth Avenue?'

'Yeah, right.' Eloise pulls a face, but there's an even deeper hint of a blush on her porcelain cheekbones. 'Shit, is that the time?' she suddenly says, glancing down at her watch. 'I'm due in Maida Vale for lunch in twenty minutes!'

'Hey, I can drop you, if you like.' Jay finally turns his attention back to me. 'I mean, if you're sure you can't join me for lunch today, Charlie?'

Which is obviously a perfectly reasonable question, seeing as I've been the one refusing to leave the store and claiming I have far too much to do. It would just be less unsettling if he weren't asking the question with a slight glaze over his eyes, as if he's barely noticed I'm there even though he's looking right at me.

'Um, no. I mean, yes. I mean, I can't come for lunch . . .'

'Oh, my God, then a lift would be absolutely amazing, if you could,' Eloise tells him. 'Would you mind, Charlie?'

'Mind? Why on earth would I mind?' I laugh. Or rather, I make a kind of grim, awkward, ha-ha-ha sound that bears little relation to a laugh. If anything, it bears more relation to the noise I made last night when I accidentally whacked my foot on the corner of the bed when I hadn't got any slippers on. 'Like I say, I've got loads to be getting on with here . . .'

'And will you let Maggie know I'll be giving her a call?' Eloise is already picking up her bag and pulling on the wedge heels she abandoned, so as to avoid marking the new carpet, when she first came in this morning. Once in her shoes, she's close to six foot. Her elegantly pale legs, in her linen mini-skirt, look longer than ever. It's not an effect Jay has failed to notice either, I can tell.

'Oh, sure. I think she'll be a great deal of help, if you need to know anything about . . .'

But neither of them is paying me a huge amount of attention. Jay is making some joke about Eloise's notebook, and she's laughing again, and blushing, and there's so much electricity crackling and fizzing between them that any minute now I fully expect a power surge to blow every appliance within a five-mile radius.

I mean, Jay does suddenly remember, just before opening the door for her, that he hasn't said goodbye to me properly. So he does, to be fair to him, dart back over to me and give me a quick kiss, plus an assurance that he'll call me later.

But his mind, I can see, is already elsewhere.

And from the way he's looking at Eloise, as he opens his car door for her and shuts her safely inside before driving away, at his usual high speed, I know exactly where it is.

Chapter Twenty-three

'So! You are finally coming back.'

'Galina, it's only been a week . . .'

'Week is long time in beauty maintenance.'

'I think that's politics, actually, Galina.'

'Now I am having to work extra hard on you to get you back to scratching.'

'Back to scratch. Yes. I know that. I've been very busy, Galina.'

'You are needing pedicure. You are needing eyebrows done. You are *seriously* needing moustache done.'

'I know, I know, and I'll come back for all that tomorrow. But I don't have much time today. I have to go and visit my sister in hospital this afternoon . . .'

'Is serious?'

'Is bunion.'

'Is painful.'

'Sure, but I'm not actually here to talk about my sister's bunion removal. I've come to see if you might be able to fit me in for—'

'Stretchmark laser treatment?'

'No! God, no! For that collagen-boosting facial you were talking about the last time I was here.'

'Is emergency?'

'Oh, no, no. Of course it's not an emergency! An emergency facial sounds . . . crazy. I just wanted to try to look a little bit younger. I mean, there's no chance a collagen facial could make me look twenty-three, is there? Or anything like . . . well, like a Pre-Raphaelite masterpiece?'

'Depend if you book full course or not.'

'I see.'

'But am having to be honest with you, Sharlee. Even full course is unlikely to make you look like Pre-Raphaelite masterpiece.'

'Right.'

'Or twenty-three.'

'Thank you, Galina, you've made your point.'

'Boyfriend has met younger woman? This is why you are desperate?'

'I'm not desperate! It's just that Eloise happens to be an old friend of his, and . . .'

'Redhead girl I am seeing with you at store earlier this morning?'

'Yes.'

'Then am very sorry, Sharlee.'

'Thanks, but there's no need to say it with such a sense of doom!'

'But *is* doom. Is no way you can be competing with girl like Eloise.'

'OK, but surely . . .'

'Girl with face like angel. Girl with skin like full-cream milk.'

'All right, Galina, I get the point!'

'I am hoping for your sake that you are real tiger in bed. I am not thinking you are standing any chance otherwise.'

'Right, well, then there's absolutely no point in me being here, is there? I mean, if I'm never going to be able to compete with the Eloises of this world, what's the fucking *point* of it all? The pain, the indignity, the expense, the sheer bloody effort . . .'

'Am not saying is no point!'

'But you just said I didn't stand a chance, no matter what I did.'

'You are misunderstanding, Sharlee. Is always point to improving appearance. What about confidence? Self-esteem?'

'Honestly, Galina, I'm not sure I'm any more confident than when I started. All I am these days is more . . . paranoid.'

'Then you know what you are needing? Nice relaxing reflexology treatment. Soothing for the stress. Restoring for the mind.'

'I don't think that'll make any—'

'I am offering you full hour for price of half-hour. Is very nice treatment. You will not regret.'

'You know what, Galina, I think I might very much regret. I pretty much regret everything else I've agreed to since I walked through these doors. But fine. If you really think it'll stop me from stressing out about Jay and Eloise, I'll book a reflexology treatment for the next time I come. But for now, can you please, *please*, just do whatever you can to make me look passable?'

'Of course. Will start with eyebrows. Lie back, please, Sharlee, and pull skin taut. I am not wanting it to hurt any more than necessary.'

Four hours later, I'm heading into the Wellington Hospital in St John's Wood (which, I've been reliably informed by Maggie, is 'the *only* place to get your bunions lopped off') to visit Robyn. I'm still not quite clear how she's managed to wangle a second overnight stay, but I suspect she's just having too good a time being the centre of attention to give it up. Anyway, despite the fact that the last time she talked to me she was screaming bloody murder at me for having the temerity to date Jay, I still feel like I ought to be there for her in her hour of need. And it clearly is an hour of need, because when I texted her to let her know I was coming, she texted back a list as long as your arm of all the things she required 'to take my mind off the pain': a 2.5 kilo luxury Jo Malone Grapefruit candle, silk pyjamas from Shanghai Tang, a jar of Crème de la Mer body moisturiser and/or hand treatment (my choice), a box of Itsu takeaway sushi, a (freezer-cold) bottle of Grey Goose, a DVD box set of either *The Hills* or *Keeping Up With The Kardashians*, and a silver stiletto charm from Links on Marylebone High Street, 'to keep my spirits up and remind me that one day soon, with everyone's love, help and prayers, I may be able to walk again'.

I ignore the list. I pick up a box of Quality Street

and a copy of the latest *Grazia* from the newsagent's near the Tube, then head for the hospital.

Then I feel just a little bit guilty, and turn round to go back to the nearby flower stall, where I also pick up a bunch of slightly droopy tulips in Robyn's favourite shade of hot pink.

I'm amazed, given my paltry offerings – and given our most recent encounter – that she's as pleased to see me as she apparently is.

'Ooooh, Quality Street, *yummy!*' she squeals, from the comfort of an extremely cosy-looking hospital bed.

The room is more like a hotel suite than any of the hospital rooms I used to sit in with Dad, and she's actually brought her own bedlinen: crisp white Frette sheets that I recognise from her bedroom at home. Someone has already brought her a giant Jo Malone candle (Lime, Basil and Mandarin – knowing Robyn, she quite fancied the Grapefruit one just to make up the full citrus collection), and someone else – or, perhaps, several other people – has showered her with bouquet after glorious bouquet of fresh-cut flowers. They're filling every available vase I'm sure the hospital had to hand – calla lilies, and red roses, and at least three glorious arrangements of peonies. In the midst of it all, Robyn is sitting up, queen of all she surveys, dressed in an extremely fetching pale-pink silk peignoir and, in brave defiance of her current hardship, a six-inch-high Christian Louboutin sandal on her left foot. Her right foot is wrapped in a bandage that – and I do know I'm not a bunion-removal surgeon – looks at least four times larger than it really needs to be.

'I had the most enormous lunch, so I won't actually dig into the chocs until later,' Robyn carries on, summoning me towards her with a wave, then kissing me warmly on both cheeks, 'but you were sweet to remember that I like them, Cha-Cha.'

'Well, I know they used to be your favourite.'

'Oh, no, darling, they were never my *favourite*. Charbonnel and Walker champagne truffles were always my favourite.'

'But when you were eight or nine, I remember you loved the praline triangles . . .'

'I'm sure you're thinking of Gaby. Who, by the way, hasn't even bothered to *text* me to say she's thinking of me. I mean, what a bitch! I'm lying here, in complete and utter agony . . .'

'You seem reasonably comfortable.'

'. . . not knowing if I'll ever walk again . . .'

'Now, Robyn, there's no need to exaggerate.'

'. . . and my so-called sister can't even get off her gigantic arse to come and visit. I'm not talking about you, Charlie, by the way. You *have* got off your gigantic arse to come and visit. And I love you for doing it. You know,' she goes on, putting one hand over her heart, to show how very much she means it, 'I promise, here and now Charlie, that when you get your bunions done, I'll stay with you night and day until you're given the all-clear.'

'That's really nice of you, Robyn, but I don't actually have any bunions.'

'Well, not *yet*, you don't. But carry on wearing those shoes, Cha-Cha, and you'll be booking a slot here faster than you can say . . . well, something pretty fast. I *love* those shoes,' she says, gazing down at the Roman-column sandals on my feet with an expression of such genuine mourning that I do feel truly sorry for her for a moment. 'In fact, you look very nice altogether today, Charlie. Are you going out with Jay tonight, or something?'

'Tomorrow.' I still feel awkward discussing him with Robyn.

'Oh, God, you're not feeling funny about discussing Jay with me, are you?' Robyn asks, as if – for the first time ever – she's read my mind and understood what I'm thinking. 'Darling, don't worry about it! I wouldn't touch Jay with a ten-foot bargepole, I promise you. And I've got the most amazing new boyfriend, you wouldn't believe!'

'Oh, Robyn, I'm so glad!'

'You won't be, when you meet him. You'll be, like, literally dead with jealousy. Anatoly is *so* sweet . . . well, his bodyguard is really sweet, anyway, he's the one who has to do most of the translating between us . . . and he's *so* sexy, and *so* good in bed . . .'

'And his name is Anatoly, you say?'

'Who, the bodyguard? No, he's called Boris.'

'But you were just talking about Anatoly.'

'No, *Boris* is the one who's sexy and good in bed.

Though you mustn't say a word to Anatoly about that, of course! But really, he can't seriously think I'm supposed to actually *enjoy* having sex with him. I mean, he's so old, and bristly, and gross.'

I feel a faint stirring of despair, and am glad, for a moment, that Dad is dead and long-buried.

'Robyn, why on earth are you going out with a man you find . . . bristly and gross? When you'd rather have sex with his bodyguard instead?'

'Because Anatoly has the most amazing house in Eaton Square, of course. *Eaton Square*, Charlie! *And* he owns his own island in the Seychelles, and two private jets, and, like, literally every diamond plant in Siberia.'

'Mine.'

'Fucking hell, Charlie, don't be so unreasonable! You've already got Jay! You can't have Anatoly too!'

'No, I mean diamond *mine*. Not diamond *plant*.'

'Oh, well, does that really matter, Cha-Cha? I'm not going to go out there and dig for the bloody things. I'm only going to be wearing them.'

At this point, her phone rings. It must be Anatoly – hang on, what am I thinking? – it must be *Boris*, because Robyn goes all giggly and whispery, and sends me out of the room to go and find a vase and some water for my tulips ('Vittel rather than Highland Spring, please, darling, I find flowers are so much happier drinking French mineral water than chilly Scottish stuff') while she and Boris put both their lives at terrible risk by shamelessly flirting over the telephone.

The nurse at the nearby nurses' station has obviously had her fill of Robyn already, because she's none too pleased about having to rustle up yet another vase for modom, and positively choleric when I risk asking if there's anywhere on the hospital premises where I might find a bottle of Vittel. Still, she directs me towards the coffee shop on the second floor, and I'm just heading up there (keen not to become any kind of witness to anything that might put a Russian billionaire's nose out of joint) when the door to a nearby room opens and a man steps into my path.

He's wrestling, hot and bad-tempered, with a wheelchair that contains a patient and serene-looking woman. He's Terry Pinkerton, from the Elroy Glass board of directors.

'Miss Glass!' He recognises me at exactly the same moment as I recognise him, and – rather endearingly – doesn't bother to try to hide his bad temper with the wheelchair situation. 'Wretched bloody thing! Its nearest relative must be a supermarket trolley, it's got such a bloody mind of its own. What are you doing here? You're not bunion-afflicted too, I hope?'

'No. Visiting my sister. Who *is* bunion-afflicted.'

'Oh, dear, the poor thing,' says the patient-looking woman in the wheelchair, extending a hand. She's in her late-fifties, and rather smart and chic, in a navy twinset and cropped trousers. 'I'm Caroline. Terry's wife.'

'I'm Charlie,' I say. 'Nice to meet you.'

'Nicer if I weren't wearing this undignified thing!'

She waggles a bandage-clad foot at me. (It is, I note with interest, roughly thirty per cent the size of Robyn's bandage.) 'I've been de-bunioned today too, I'm afraid!'

'Well, I hear this is, um, the only place to do it.'

'Yes, every stiletto-loving idiot in town is knocking down the door!' Terry scowls, more annoyed than ever. 'Caroline, this is the girl I was telling you about the other evening. Elroy's daughter. The one trying to persuade bloody silly women like you to put on a pair of sensible shoes for a change.'

'Oh, that's not quite what I'm trying to do! I'm going to be selling my father's vintage shoes, at his old store on King's Road,' I tell Caroline. 'They're not exactly what you'd call sensible. But they certainly are much more comfortable than the new Elroy Glass ones. I mean, I can't guarantee you'll stay bunion-free, of course . . .'

'Nevertheless, it sounds absolutely terrific!' She smiles at me. 'I'll come straight down for a nose around, just as soon as I'm back on my feet again. I can still remember that King's Road shop from the old days, you know. The place in permanent chaos, and champagne corks popping, and your father flirting with everyone . . .'

'Yes. I remember too.'

'Well, I give you full permission to go there and spend as much as you bloody like,' Terry tells his wife, grumpily but rather fondly at the same time. 'Sensible shoes for you, and a sure-fire way to piss off Alan Kellaway for me. The stupid sod,' he informs Caroline, 'is the only one who doesn't think it's the best idea anyone's had in the bloody company for ten years.'

'Ugh, Alan Kellaway.' Caroline actually shudders. 'Horrible man. You know, I still remember him from twenty, thirty years ago, when he thought he was a bit of a Jack-the-lad. Racing around town in that ridiculous purple sports car, ordering the most expensive champagne at Annabel's. Terry still hates him,' she leans in to tell me, 'because he mistakenly thinks I once went on a date with him to—'

'I'm sorry.' I abandon my manners and interrupt her. What she just said – what I *think* she just said – is far too important for me to stand on ceremony. 'Did you say . . . that Mr Kellaway used to drive a *purple* sports car?'

'Oh, absolutely. Shiny, flashy thing. Exactly the colour of the foil wrapper on a Cadbury's Dairy Milk bar.'

'All *right*!' Terry suddenly bellows at his phone, as it rings briskly from somewhere within the depths of a trouser pocket. '*Bloody* taxi driver. We all know he's charging me an arm and a leg for sitting outside reading the paper while he waits. There's no need for him to harass me at the same time.'

'Well, we shouldn't keep him waiting any longer.' Caroline extends a hand to me again. 'Very nice to meet you. And I'm sure I'll see you again, at the shop! You know,' she adds, as Terry wrestles her wheelchair into a one-hundred-and-eighty-degree turn and starts to shove her towards the exit doors, 'I was very fond of your father, all those years ago. I'm sure he'd be terribly proud, Charlie, of everything you're doing.'

'Charlie, calm down. I can't understand a word you're saying. Now, take a deep breath and go back to the beginning. And if you could possibly do that,' Olly says, lowering his voice and making little puffing noises, as if he's heading out of his office and up a secluded nearby stairwell, for example, which I suspect is exactly what he is doing, 'without hurling around accusations of vehicular manslaughter against my boss . . . while it's still office hours, at least—'

'Not vehicular manslaughter! *Murder!* It was his car that killed my mother, Olly!' I'm still shaking so hard that I'm in danger of dropping my phone right into the cup of sugary tea I've just bought myself in the Wellington Hospital coffee shop. Two elderly ladies at the next table, one clutching two crutches and the other parked on a mobility scooter, are watching me with curious concern (possibly because of all the shaking, or possibly because I've just crammed an entire KitKat, for medicinal purposes, into my mouth in two bites). 'Mrs Terry told me!'

'Who's Mrs Terry?'

'Terry Pinkerton's wife. Caroline.'

'And she told you that Alan Kellaway knocked down your mother?'

'No, but she told me that he used to drive this flashy purple sports car. "Dairy Milk-purple", she called it. And the old lady who witnessed the accident saw a Dairy Milk-purple sports car speeding away from Mum's body! DI Wright always told me that! But they never made any headway on finding the car, because Jane Brearly – she was the only witness – was adamant it had the name of a planet on the bumper, and the police always thought there weren't any sports cars named after a planet.'

'Well, isn't that the kind of thing your racing-driver boyfriend might know about? If there were any sports cars named after a planet, I mean.'

'Oh, my God, Jay *might* know about that. In fact, he *would* know about that!' I'm shaking more than ever. 'I have to go now, Olly, I have to call Jay and ask him if there are any sports cars named after . . .'

'Charlie, wait!' Olly's voice is almost commanding, for a change, though he's still speaking very low indeed. 'Look, I think I might even be able to go one better than that.'

'What do you mean?'

'Well – and I don't want you to go getting too excited about this, Charlie – if memory serves correctly, I may have seen a photograph of a purple sports car in Alan's office.'

My mind, addled by the shock of what Caroline Pinkerton told me, and racing ten miles a minute with the extreme sugar hit from my KitKat/sweet tea combo, struggles to process what Olly's just said.

'I don't understand. How did he get the sports car into his office to take a photo of it?'

'No! The photo is in his office, not the car! It's a photo of Alan, actually, standing next to a very shiny purple sports car. The bonnet of one, I mean. It's a pretty old photo, I think, because he's got a lot more hair. I think that's partly why he keeps the picture on his shelf, to be honest with you, just to prove to the world that he wasn't bad-looking when he was younger . . . anyway, do you think it would help, at all, if I could get you the photograph? To show to Jay, that is?'

'Olly, that would be amazing . . .'

'OK, then I'll stay late tonight and try to get one of the cleaners to let me into Alan's office after everyone's left. But Charlie, I'll only do it if you promise you're not going to go off the deep end about this. The man is still my boss, you know. We can't go around hurling baseless accusations.'

'They wouldn't be baseless. But don't worry, Olly, I won't do anything of the sort. I'll just run the photo by Jay, and then take it to DI Wright . . .'

'Just one thing, Charlie. I mean, you know I'm not exactly a fan of my boss.' Olly is actually whispering into the phone now, his voice barely audible thanks to this and the fact that whatever stairwell he's in has got a serious echo going on. 'But I don't know if he's actually the kind of person who'd drive a car into a defenceless pedestrian, deliberately or otherwise, and then just drive off without stopping.'

'No, but he is! He's exactly that kind of person! He has to be!'

'Well, I admit, the whole Dairy Milk-coloured sports car thing is quite a coincidence. And I guess he must have known your mother back in those days. But if the stories I've heard about Alan back then – actually, if the stories I hear about him now – are anything to go by, I'm not sure he's capable of *killing* a woman. He's far too busy doing . . . well, other things with women to do anything like that.'

Which is when two things happen, just seconds apart from each other.

Robyn, presumably having tired of phone sex with Boris/dicing with death and disfigurement, and wanting to know where I've got to with her vase and Vittel water, starts calling me on my other line.

And I realise that it didn't have to be Alan Kellaway driving the purple sports car after all. It could have been one of those women he was busy with.

It could have been Diana.

'Dear, are you quite all right?' One of the elderly ladies reaches an arm across the aisle. She puts a papery hand on my shoulder. 'Do you want us to find your doctor for you, or something?'

'No, thank you. That's really nice. But I'm . . . I'm all right. I'm not a patient here, in fact.'

'Really? You suddenly looked to be in such terrible pain.'

Because it's slowly dawning on me that my evil stepmother, the woman who blighted my entire childhood with her arbitrary cruelties, may well have been the person who killed my mother.

'I'm fine, thank you,' I mumble, getting to my feet. 'Olly,' I say, into the phone again, 'just get me that photo, if you can. Then call me when you've done it and I'll come and meet you.'

'OK, Charlie. I'll speak to you later.'

I mumble a goodbye, slip my phone into my pocket, and then stumble away from my table and out of the café.

I'm already halfway back along the bunion ward before I remember that I've forgotten Robyn's Vittel water, and have to stumble back to buy it.

Chapter Twenty-four

Jay hasn't offered to pick me up before dinner this evening, instead suggesting that we meet at the restaurant in Aldwych where we're meeting Eloise, Ben, and Ben's wife Amanda. This is, obviously, a break from tradition for Jay, who usually insists on a formal pick-up. But I don't have time to worry about why he's not insisted on this occasion.

The worst thing about it, I'll be honest, is that it's forced me to make my own way to Aldwych rather than hitch a lift in a swanky sports car. Because I'm not used to this by now (how quickly one's standards change) I leave it far too late to order a minicab, and then have to spend ten minutes painfully tottering up and down outside my flat in Mum's crystal shoes, trying to hail a black taxi, and then a further ten minutes painfully tottering around the corner to get the Tube at Earl's Court instead.

By the time I reach the restaurant, another painful totter from Covent Garden Tube, I'm practically ready to haul myself back to the bunion unit at the Wellington Hospital and demand instant surgery without further delay. I don't care what Maggie claims about Dad's vintage shoes being more comfortable than the instruments of torture everyone is cramming their feet into these days. Clearly I'm going to have to face the fact that I'm just not cut out for high-heel wear, no matter how (relatively) comfortable. If I'm not teetering about the place in agony, I'm mowing bystanders down when my feet slip on accelerators. The world will be a better place, probably, if I restrict myself to UGG boots and comfy Converse. Which is not an ideal state of affairs for the owner of a shoe company.

I'm assuming I'll be the last there, but to my surprise, I'm second only to Jay, who is already at the table waiting. He's sipping a Coke, and there's a small wrapped package on the table beside him. He glances up as I totter towards the booth, and his smile dims merely by the faintest of wattages when he sees it's me.

Honestly, only someone like me who's recently become obsessed by wattage would even have noticed at all.

'Charlie!' He leans over from his side of the booth to give me a kiss. 'You're looking lovely. I mean, a tiny bit windswept, obviously.' He pushes some strands of my hair gently behind one ear. His touch, sweet rather than sexy, makes me almost want to burst into tears again. But I've already alarmed Olly by bursting into tears, this time yesterday night when he joined me after work, and I don't want to spoil Jay's evening with his friends by doing it to him too. 'Sorry I couldn't come and collect you, sweetheart, but I was out on a test-drive in Hertfordshire this afternoon, and it didn't make sense to come all the way back west to pick you up.'

'That's perfectly OK. Actually, Jay, talking of cars . . . oh, yes, a Martini, please,' I tell the waiter, who's suddenly hovering beside our booth. 'Extra gin. Or whatever it is that makes it really strong.'

'Very, very dry,' Jay tells him, smoothly. 'And with a twist. Unless you prefer it dirty, Charlie?'

I'm half-expecting him to follow this up with a cheeky raised eyebrow, one of his devilish grins, and maybe even a hand on my thigh beneath the table. But he doesn't lift an eyebrow or grin, devilishly or otherwise, and his hand, though it does move from where it's resting on the tabletop, simply goes to rest on top of the small parcel beside his glass instead.

'No. I . . . don't want it dirty. A twist is fine.'

The waiter slides away, leaving Jay and me alone in the booth again.

'Are you all right, Charlie?' Jay asks, before I can say anything. 'You don't look quite yourself.'

'I'm fine.' I'm scrabbling in my bag for the photo Olly gave me yesterday, after he'd purloined it from Alan Kellaway's office, after hours.

'Really? You just don't seem quite as chilled-out as normal.'

'Well, no, I'm probably not.' In fact, I'm struggling to recall when I might *ever* have been chilled-out with Jay. Certainly not during the marathon sex, or the fitful nights' slumber, or the hundred-mile-an-hour motorway journeys. Or any of the times when I've been concentrating so furiously, desperately hard on being sufficiently goddess-like to hold his interest. 'That's what I wanted to talk to you about, actually, Jay. Something has happened. Something . . . kind of serious. And I need your help.'

'*My* help?' He laughs, but there's a look of unease in his inky eyes. 'Charlie, if it's as serious as all that, you almost certainly aren't going to need my help! The only thing I'm ever known to be serious about is cars.'

'Yes! Exactly.' I find the photo, lurking between my wallet and my lip balm, and pull it out of my bag. 'This car, Jay. The purple one, in this photo. You don't happen to know what make it is, do you?'

'Let me see.' He takes the photo out of my hand and looks at it closely, beneath the hanging lamp above the table. 'Oh, yeah, I know exactly what that is. It's a Jowett Jupiter! The fifty-four, from the look of the bonnet. I'd have to get a look at more of the car to be absolutely sure of the year.'

'But you *are* absolutely sure –' I'm struggling to keep a tremor from my voice '– that it's a . . . what did you say? . . . Jowett.'

'Jupiter.'

'Named after a planet.'

'Yeah. You don't see too many of them around these days. Actually, you wouldn't even have seen many of them around in nineteen fifty-four, to be honest with you. They're not exactly well known.'

'That's why the police thought Jane Brearly had it wrong . . .'

'Sorry?'

'Nothing.'

'Are you thinking of buying one or something, Charlie? Because if you're getting interested in collecting classic cars, there are quite a few I'd point you towards before I suggested a Jowett Jupiter. They're decent enough, but if you want something with a real zing in the engine . . .'

I'm just glad that the waiter is making a return with my Martini, because I need the steadying warmth of forty-per-cent-proof alcohol right now.

'Whoah, Charlie! You might want to slow down on that Martini!' Jay smiles at me, in a kind way that reminds me, ever so slightly, of the way he smiled at me that first day we met, in the lift. 'I don't mean to be judgemental, Charlie, but knocking back nearly neat gin like it's water isn't exactly elegant!'

Elegant.

He's comparing me unfavourably – as if there's any other way I could be compared – to Eloise.

I don't know if it's the whoosh of alcohol or, more likely, the fact that I have bigger things on my mind right now, but I don't care as much as I thought I would. I'd never have thought this possible until now, but I'm not even taking it all that personally. It's just like Maggie said: Jay needs things to be shiny and new. Shiny new cars. Shiny new women. Maybe, like she warned me, reality can never live up to Jay's hype.

And Jay isn't very big on reality.

Handsome, charming and physically faultless though he is, he's not without his own fatal flaw too. Probably it was set in stone many years ago, when his mother died. But really, I was pretty much doomed, wasn't I, long before Eloise floated on to the scene? Not because of all those surface things I was stressing about: cellulite, a millimetre of stubble, a below-par performance in bed. A photograph of me looking fat and frumpy, even. But because of that tiny seed that Diana planted oh-so-cleverly in Jay's head. The mental image of me tending my dying father. I don't think there's a woman in the land, no matter how perfect in appearance, that would survive Jay's cull after that.

And now, of course, he's re-encountered Eloise. Who is just so beautiful, and refined, and elegant. Who probably doesn't have an inconveniently dead mother, or a dying father.

Who is – for now at least – Jay's brand-new vision of perfection.

'You know,' I start to slip my jacket back on and take the photo of the Jowett Jupiter from him, 'I think I . . . I might have left something on somewhere.'

'Left what on?'

'Or unlocked. Yes. That's it. I think I've left the store unlocked.'

'Oh! That's not good, Charlie.'

'No, it's not. I think I'd better . . . well, I'll just slip away, before the others get here, if you don't mind. Head back to King's Road and make sure everything's OK.'

'Well, sure, if that's what you feel you need to do.' Jay's brow is creased with polite concern, and he's reaching for his phone. 'Let me order you a taxi.'

'No, I'm fine, honestly . . .'

'Charlie, come on. It'll be much quicker and easier for you if you get a taxi.' He gives my arm a little squeeze. 'Then maybe you'll still have time to come back and join us for a drink later.'

We both know I'm not going to come back and join them for a drink later. Or actually, maybe I'm the only one who knows that. Jay, from the look of him, is already so far off in the stars thinking about Eloise that he's really not thinking about anything else at all. His natural, friendly good manners are kicking in, but if it weren't for that, I'm not even sure he'd know I was still here.

'Honestly, Jay, I'll be quicker on the Tube. But thank you. Thanks for . . . well, everything.' I lean in and give him a swift kiss on the cheek. As I do so, my handbag knocks his little parcel off the top of the table and into my lap. 'Sorry.' I hand it back to him. 'This is yours.'

'Oh, yes, it's just a little something I got for Eloise. A notebook.'

'A notebook?'

'Yeah, I was kidding around with her when I drove her up to Maida Vale, about how serious she looked with her little notebook. So I called up this writer

533

friend of mine who lives in Italy, and got him to courier me a notebook from this incredible stationer's in Rome. Best in the world, apparently. Leather-bound, acid-free paper, gold-monogrammed with Eloise's initials . . . oh, here they are!'

He's already sliding out of the booth and heading towards the door where Eloise has indeed just appeared, with a tall, good-looking man who must be her brother, Ben, and an attractive blonde woman, with incredible eyebrows, who must be Ben's wife Amanda.

Jay's face, as he greets them, is wearing a familiar expression. It's the expression he wore the night of his birthday party, when he took me up to his rooftop hideaway and gazed at me as if I was the second coming of Christ and the eighth wonder of the world rolled into one. As if nothing, before or since, could ever look so beautiful.

I slip past them towards the door, careful to put my head down, because I don't want Jay to see me and stop me and make me look as if I'm being rude.

But he doesn't stop me. He's caught up in helping Eloise off with her jacket, and none of them even notices that I'm leaving.

Outside, it's drizzling, and the totter to the Tube feels impossible. So I hail down a taxi and, when the driver asks me where I want to go, hear myself asking him to head towards Clapham.

Towards Lucy.

Then I realise that it's probably a good idea if I

call her and tell her I'm on my way. *Ask* her, more to the point, if she *minds* that I'm on my way. I'm only hoping she picks up the phone at all, when she sees it's me calling.

I hear several rings, and then just when I think she's ignoring me after all, and start to direct the driver towards home instead, she picks up.

'Charlie?'

'Luce! Look, I know you probably don't want to talk to me, still. But something's happened, and I really need you. Not something silly, like Jay dumping me – although he *has* dumped me, pretty much – but something serious. Something about Mum . . .'

'Charlie, where are you?'

'Currently, Soho. But I'm on my way to your flat in a taxi.'

'But I'm on my way to *your* flat in a taxi!'

'You're kidding?'

'No! I was just about to call you to see if you were in. I've been out for a drink with Olly . . .'

'With *Olly*? Oh, Luce, that's fantastic!'

'. . . and I had such a good time that . . . well, I just really wanted to tell you about it.'

This is such good news that it wipes away everything else, for a moment. Not just the fact that Lucy's been out on a date with Olly. Not even just the fact that she had a fantastic time. But most of all, the fact that she really wanted to tell me about it.

'Look,' she goes on, 'why don't I head south, you head west, and we'll meet in the middle?'

'Around King's Road, you mean?'

'Yes. King's Road. Oh, I know! I'll stop for a bottle of wine and we can go and talk in the store. I've been dying to see it. I came along the other day, actually, but you were inside with this scarily gorgeous girl, and I lost my nerve.'

'Eloise. Yes, I have to tell you about her. I have to tell you about an awful lot of things. If you don't mind, that is?'

'Oh, Charlie. What are best friends for?'

I redirect the driver towards King's Road and sit back in the leatherette seat, trying to stop myself from smiling.

I mean, on paper, obviously, this isn't the best of nights. I've effectively been dumped by Jay for a younger and more beautiful model, and I've just found out, beyond pretty much any reasonable doubt, that my mother probably wasn't so much accidentally killed as coldly, callously murdered by my bitch of a stepmother.

But, for some reason, I'm actually happy.

I'm so excited to be on speaking terms with Lucy again, I don't even want to talk about what I've discovered about Mum's accident, and Diana's connection to a purple car named after a planet. That can wait until tomorrow. Tonight, I'd rather pretend it's not an issue. Pretend that the accident never even happened. I'd rather just sit and listen to her tell me all about her date with Olly; enjoy the fact that we can perch on packing cases in the stockroom and talk, over a bottle of wine, the way we used to sit and talk over Capri-Sun pouches on Saturday mornings more than twenty years ago.

I'm so content, thinking about this, that I don't even notice that we've reached the King's Road or that the traffic has suddenly ground to a halt, just two blocks away from the store.

'Something nasty going on up here,' my taxi driver is saying, as we suddenly see blue flashing lights and hear wailing sirens up ahead. 'Where was it you wanted on King's Road, love? You might be better off just getting out and walking.'

Seeing as the meter has just crept past the twenty-quid mark, I can't disagree with him.

'Dear, oh, dear,' he adds, as an ambulance suddenly speeds past us, going the opposite way on the other side of the road. 'Some poor bastard could be dying in there. Smoke inhalation, third-degree burns . . . it's a fire,' he adds, by way of explanation. 'Look, you can see the smoke. Something's burning somewhere around here. Must be one of the shops on that next block.'

That next block being . . . Oh, my God.

I pull some money out of my purse, shove it through the screen at the driver, then get out of the taxi and start to walk, very, very fast, in the direction of the smoke, the sirens, and Dad's store. When I realise that I could actually go even faster if I weren't being slowed down by these *bloody* heels, I take them off and start to run.

At the next junction, my fears are horribly confirmed. It's Dad's store. Dad's store is burning down.

Smoke is pouring from the shattered windows. Fire-fighters from two separate fire-engines are dousing the place with powerful jets of water. The section of the road it's on has been closed off to traffic, but crowds of people are clustered along the strips of yellow tape: some in their pyjamas and nightgowns, who are presumably residents of the various flats above the premises along here, and others in regular clothes who are mostly on their way to pubs and bars down the better end of King's Road but who have stopped to have a look.

I cross over and stand amongst them for what feels like about five hours but is probably only about five seconds, staring slack-jawed in horror at the sight in front of me.

When someone with a firm hand grabs my elbow and pulls me round, I can barely focus on who it is for a moment. Hair scraped back in a bun . . . baggy striped pyjamas . . . slash of crimson lipstick . . .

'*Galina?*'

'Sharlee. Is catastrophe.' She gestures at the burning building. 'I am asleep in my bed above salon. I am wakened by smoke alarm. I am looking out of window and seeing your store down in flames.'

'Up in flames.'

Shock must be doing very peculiar things to my brain. At least, I presume this is the reason why, amidst all this, I've just taken the time to correct her

English. And why I can't stop wondering whether Galina stopped, on her way out of a smoke-filled building, to put on her lipstick, or whether she actually sleeps in it.

Mind you, I think she may be suffering from shock, too, because she's staring at me absolutely wild-eyed. 'I am seeing that light is on in store. I am thinking you are inside.'

'Oh, God, Galina . . .' I reach out and put a hand on her shoulder, though I'm not sure if it's to comfort her or to keep myself standing upright. 'No. I wasn't there. I'm here.'

'I am not knowing that at time! And nice man from ice-cream shop is not knowing it either!'

'Ferdy? He's here?'

'Ice-cream shop is open late. Is doing roaring trade. But fire start and he is coming running out into street. He was seeing light on also. He was thinking you are inside. So he is running in.'

He is . . . running in?

A terrible feeling of nausea washes over me. 'I just saw an ambulance.'

Galina nods again. 'Am hearing paramedicals say they are taking him to Chelsea and Westminster Hospital . . .'

Which is all I need to hear.

I don't care that my beautiful store and everything in it is slowly vanishing in clouds of smoke and high-pressure water behind me. I don't think I've ever cared less about anything in my life.

Chelsea and Westminster Hospital is only a five-minute run from here. Three minutes, if I put on a sprint.

I mean, all that bloody exercise I've endured for the past four months has got to be useful for something.

It's a cliché but it's true: hospital casualty departments aren't exactly fun places to be at ten o'clock on a Saturday night. Bruised, battered and – in some cases – profusely bleeding people are crammed into a waiting area filled with orange plastic chairs or queuing up, with varying degrees of patience, at what looks almost like a bulletproof window immediately to the right of the sliding entrance doors. Behind this window, a pair of girls who look far too young and far too bored to be doing such an important job are directing the walking wounded towards the ever-more-crowded waiting area, or – for the lucky few, with injuries deemed serious enough to escape the orange plastic chairs – behind a set of swing doors.

By the time I reach the front of the queue, my nerves are shredded and I've already bitten away four of the ten fingernails that were manicured into perfect, Jay-worthy ovals only this morning.

'Injury? Illness?' one of the bored girls asks me, from behind the window, her hand hovering over a computer mouse. A sign behind her warns that 'Anyone acting in a threatening or aggressive manner may be removed by hospital security'.

'Neither. It's not me who's injured. It's a . . . friend of mine. Ferdy Wright? He was brought in, I think, about fifteen minutes ago?'

'Name?'

'Ferdy Wright! I just said . . .' I break off as I look again at the sign behind her. 'Ferdy Wright,' I repeat, fixing a pleasant and polite smile to my face, in the hope that this will warm the girl up and she'll be quicker about helping me. 'He's thirty-two, I think . . . I don't know his exact date of birth . . . he might have smoke inhalation, or awful burns . . . I mean, he tried to save me from a fire, for fuck's sake . . .' Again, I break off, because I'm fairly sure that use of the F-word could be interpreted as threatening or aggressive, even if I'm not actually directing it at a staff member.

'If he came in less than half an hour ago, he might not be in the system yet.'

'But he might be? Could you look? Please? It's Ferdy Wright – well, Ferdinando, if you need the full version . . .'

'Funny name.' But at least she starts to click a couple of things on her computer screen.

'Yes. His mother's Italian, so . . .'

'No, I meant Wright. I mean, if you think about it, that makes him Mr Wright, doesn't it?'

I stare at her, blankly.

'Like *Mr Right*?' she snaps.

'Oh! Oh, God, yes, I suppose he is . . .'

'Yeah, anyway . . . uh . . . it looks like he was

brought in tonight, actually.' She peers more closely at her screen. 'Oh, sorry. He's gone.'

Everything starts to go very black and fuzzy. I can actually feel, as if in slow motion, my legs begin to crumple beneath me.

'Yeah, they took him straight off to St Mary's Hospital, soon as he got here. Our burns unit is pretty full tonight. They're re-directing the minor cases to St Mary's instead.'

I see, quite suddenly, why the hospital feels the need to post a warning about refraining from abusing its staff.

'So when you said you were sorry that he'd gone,' I manage to croak, 'you just meant he'd gone across town to St Mary's Paddington? Not . . . into the next world?'

'Yeah. St Mary's Paddington. Exactly. You'd better go and look for your Mr Wright there. Now can you move aside, please? You're holding up my queue.'

Just as I obey her, my phone starts to ring. I'm so glad to see it's Lucy calling that I almost burst into tears.

'Charlie?' she gasps, when I pick up. 'I've just got to the store! Are you here? It's fucking chaos . . . an Arson Investigation Unit has just arrived . . .'

'*Arson?*'

'This guy standing next to me says he used to be a fireman, and he says there's a real pong of accelerant in the air . . . Look, where are you?'

'I'm at Chelsea and Westminster Hospital.'

'*Charlie!*'

'It's all right, I came here to find Ferdy. He ran into the store because he thought I was in there. But he's OK, I think. I mean, he's been transferred to a different hospital, for minor injuries. St Mary's Paddington. I'm going to go there now.'

'OK, wait where you are, Charlie, and I'll find a taxi and come and pick you up. We'll take it on to Paddington together.'

'Oh, Luce, if you don't mind . . . oh, I'm so sorry,' I say, over my shoulder, to a woman I've just accidentally backed into.

'If you were looking where you were going,' she snaps back at me, 'you wouldn't . . . *Charlie?*'

It's Gaby.

She's waiting at the back of the queue of unfortunates, and I just have time to think how ironic it is that this is the second time in two days that I've bumped into someone I know in a hospital, when all those years I was carting Dad around various medical establishments, all by myself, I never ran into anyone who knew me, when Gaby carries on.

'Are you here for . . . for Mummy?'

'Mummy?'

'Did they call you? The hospital? I thought they'd only called me. Well, I assume they tried Robyn first, because I'm sure she's the first one on Mummy's emergency contact list, but obviously she's far too busy recuperating from her life-or-death bunion surgery to pick up her phone . . .'

'Gaby, hang on. Has something happened to your mother?'

'Obviously. Isn't that why we're both here?'

'Um, well, it's not why I'm here. There's been . . .' I take a deep breath. 'Gaby, there's awful news about the store, I'm afraid. Dad's store. There's been—'

'A fire.'

'Yes!' I stare at Gaby, who stares – rather wide-eyed – back at me. 'How did you know?'

'I didn't.' Her voice is hoarse all of a sudden. 'I mean, I didn't know it was at Dad's store. I only knew there'd been a fire. There had to have been a fire. Because Mummy's hands have been burned.'

Diana's hands have been burned?

'She told me to call Alan Kellaway. Said she thought she might need a lawyer.' Gaby's face has turned a ghostly shade of white. 'Charlie . . . what has she *done?*'

I could confirm her worst fears, by passing on what Lucy has just told me about the Arson Investigation Unit and the pong of accelerant. I could pile yet another shock on top of that by producing Olly's picture from my bag, pointing at the Cadbury-coloured Jowett Jupiter, and explaining to Gaby precisely why I've drawn the conclusion that her mother killed mine in a hit-and-run 'accident'. I could just let her wait in the queue by herself, knowing full well that the moment she encounters the eye-rolling rudeness of the girls behind the window, she's cast-iron certain to act in a threatening or aggressive manner, and quite possibly find herself ejected from the hospital by security.

But I don't do any of those things. I link my arm through hers, and wait in the queue with her. Gaby doesn't say a word. But she doesn't pull her arm away from mine. And when we finally get to the front of the queue she turns to me, to let me speak on her behalf.

Chapter Twenty-five

Ferdy's flat, on the top floor of a slightly scruffy Victorian house in Shepherd's Bush, is exactly the way I'd imagined it. By which I mean that it's mostly kitchen. As far as I can tell, there are three rooms: a bedroom (that I haven't seen into yet, because Ferdy is sleeping), a bathroom, and the room I'm in now, which estate agents would probably call a large open-plan living/dining area, but which I would call Mostly Kitchen.

And what a lovely kitchen it is, too – light streaming in through half a dozen windows and a big skylight, gleaming granite worktops, a huge eight-ring hob and an even huger fridge-freezer, which (I've already peeked) is full to bursting point with all of Ferdy's latest ice-cream experiments, and a big, square wooden table, with mismatching chairs, where Ferdy's dad and I are sitting now.

'Ferdy's really going to appreciate this,' Martin says.

He nods at the dish I'm making. Beef Stroganoff, in fact, because I remember how much Ferdy said he liked it at my disastro dinner party. And because even though it's July, it feels right for the weather: grey skies have gathered, bringing heavy showers of rain. There's a shower going on right now, as it happens, raindrops splashing down with repetitive gusto on the wide skylight. It's an incredibly soothing sound, and I hope Ferdy is hearing some of it, through the closed bedroom door, and through the veil of sleep.

'Well, he did try to save my life last night. I think making a few meals for his freezer is the least I can do.'

'For his freezer?' Martin sips his tea. He's looking remarkably calm for a man who was woken in the middle of the night with the news that his son had just been admitted to hospital with (albeit mild) smoke inhalation after running headlong into a burning building. But I guess thirty years on the Metropolitan police force prepares you pretty well for things like that. 'So you're not planning to stick around for dinner and eat it with him?'

'Well, I didn't plan *not* to . . . I just thought . . .'

'Got to get home to that new chap of yours, I expect.'

'No, no. God, no.' I feel myself redden, and try to pretend it's some kind of reaction to chopping this onion, as if these days onions have stopped making you cry and started making you blush instead.

'Nice bloke, is he? Ferdy told me you all spent a weekend in the country together. Spoke very highly of him. James, is it? Jason?'

'Jay. But . . . well, we're not really together any more.'

'Ah. Well.' Martin takes another sip of his tea. 'Sorry to hear that. But if it's any consolation to you,

547

Charlie love, Ferdy didn't speak highly of him at all. Said he was a bit of a flash git, as it happens.'

'That's . . .' I can't help smiling, because I can practically hear Ferdy's voice as Martin says this. 'Actually, that's unfair. Jay was a bit flash, but he was a nice guy.'

Still *is* a nice guy, as it happens. He called me this morning only five minutes after he found out about the fire at the store last night. And even though I'm fairly sure he was lying next to Eloise at the time (OK, I'm absolutely sure: I heard her in the background, talking on her own phone), it still doesn't change the fact that he was solicitousness itself. Wanting to know if there was anything he could do, offering to help me find new premises, giving genuine commiserations when I explained that unfortunately there isn't any point in looking for temporary new premises because all Dad's shoes were incinerated in the fire. He even promised to take me out 'for a good old sorrows-drowning booze-up, whenever you've got the time'. Which – I'm fairly certain, even if he wasn't – was his way of letting me know that our relationship is over. But that, as Maggie said, he'd like it if we could stay friends. And I'd like that too, even though I'm not sure I'm cut out to be quite as good at it as Jay obviously is. But if there's anyone who'll make it easy to do so, it'll be Jay. And given a little time, maybe I'll find myself joining the serried ranks of ex-lovers with whom, in an oddly civilised way, he maintains friendly relations. Sort of like a Bond girl, perhaps, easily replaced but – hopefully – never quite forgotten.

'Well, Ferdy was never exactly going to be the guy's biggest fan, was he?' Martin is staring rather fixedly at the tabletop, but there's a determined tone to his voice that implies he's damn well going to say whatever it is he wants to say, no matter how awkward it makes either of us. 'You know. Feeling about you the way he does. And all that.'

Again, I'm hoping my blush can be explained by the onions. Because, if anything, it's even deeper than it was before.

'Dad?'

This voice takes both of us by surprise, and we turn round to see Ferdy standing in the kitchen doorway.

He's still looking a little bit the worse for wear, mostly because of the huge purple bruise right in the middle of his forehead, sustained (he admitted to Martin, who swore me to secrecy) when he got confused by all the billowing smoke and ran headlong into one of the teak shelving units. Other than that, he's managed to get away with nothing worse than that mild smoke inhalation, for which the hospital let him go, after a few hours of observation, first thing this morning. It's miraculous, considering that Galina had me convinced he'd been burned to a crisp along with all Dad's shoes.

'You two look thick as thieves,' he adds, padding into the kitchen in his bare feet. He's pulled on a pair of jeans and a faded navy T-shirt, and his dusty-coloured hair – genuinely dusty after his brush with the flames – is sticking up at angles that would confound even the most skilled mathematician. He looks so handsome and so sweet, with that ridiculous bruise on his head, that it makes my heart hurt just to look at him.

'Oh, I was just telling Charlie the latest about her stepmother,' Martin says, rather more smoothly than I'd have given him credit for. It's not a lie – he *has* been telling me the latest about Diana – but it's not, of course, precisely what we were discussing when Ferdy came in.

'About Diana?' Ferdy's face hardens. 'Are they charging her with arson? Manslaughter? She's not going to get away with it by hiring some fancy lawyer, is she? Or claiming insanity?'

'Oh, I don't think there's a fancy lawyer in Christendom who can get Diana out of the hole she's dug for herself. But as for insanity . . . well, if she wants to spend the rest of her life in a hospital for the criminally insane, instead of in prison, I don't think anyone would bother trying to stop her.'

Martin gets to his feet, pocketing the photo of Alan Kellaway and his Jowett Jupiter as he does so. I gave the photo to him at the hospital last night, and – as he's just been telling me – he took it to the station to show one of his former colleagues first thing this morning. Only a couple of hours later, two uniformed policemen dropped round to Alan Kellaway's office to ask him a couple of questions about his ownership of a car that's linked to a twenty-year-old hit-and-run. Barely had the questions begun when Alan Kellaway (apparently) turned into a blubbing, quivering wreck and admitted that Diana had been driving his car that day, that he'd happily give evidence to that effect, and that he'd very much like it if he weren't charged with being an accessory to manslaughter and/or perverting the course of justice. He even told the officers where the car is still kept – in a locked shed on the grounds of his cottage in Cornwall. Although it hasn't been driven, or even let out on the road, in twenty years, Martin is dubious about the idea there'll still be any evidence of the 'accident' on it. Still, Alan Kellaway's evidence, plus the accompanying charge of arson, is going to get Diana into some extremely hot water.

She's under arrest at the moment, even though she's still being treated for her burned hands in hospital. Gaby, with whom I'm in text-message contact, is taking charge of the (increasing) press interest, and Robyn, as far as I can gather from the various phone conversations we've had so far today, has checked herself out of the Wellington bunion clinic and is planning to jump straight on to Anatoly's private plane to Sardinia 'until all this yucky stuff with *bloody* Mummy blows over'. It seemed (though I really didn't want to know) as if Boris the bodyguard was going too, deputised by Anatoly to be Robyn's shoulder to cry on.

'Anyway, I really need to be getting home now. Leave you two to it.' Martin gets to his feet before elaborating on what, exactly, is the 'it' he's leaving me and Ferdy to. 'Now, your mother told me to tell you she'll be over later this afternoon with one of her lasagnes.'

'Great, Dad,' Ferdy says. 'Thanks a lot.'

'And don't forget, she's got a key. So . . . well, I'm just saying that I'd put the chain on, if I were you. If you were wanting, you know, any privacy or anything . . .'

'Great, Dad,' Ferdy says, his voice heavy with sarcasm and embarrassment this time. 'Thanks a lot.'

While Ferdy sees (OK, hurries) his dad out of the flat, I get up and busy myself with the onions. If anything's going to stop me from getting flustered right now, it'll be cooking.

Not that I'm completely sure, yet, that there's anything to get flustered *about*. Even though Lucy has told me, at least half a dozen times since last night, 'But he *ran into a burning building to save you*, Charlie!' . . . well, I still can't quite believe that Ferdy likes me. After all, people save strangers' lives all the time, and it doesn't mean they're madly in love with them, so I can't seriously believe, the way Lucy seems to, that this is proof positive that he's wildly in love with me.

But then, there was that thing Martin said just now. About the fact that Ferdy was bound to dislike Jay 'feeling about you the way he does'.

But dads get things wrong all the time, don't they? They're notorious for it. If my own dad, bless him, could get the upbringing of his motherless daughter so spectacularly wrong, I think we can allow Martin Wright the occasional error in discerning the ways of his son's heart. After all, he was so obviously luke-warm about Honey that he's bound to be keen to see Ferdy settled down with someone – pretty much anyone – else.

The fact is, really, that I don't want to think about whether Ferdy likes me or not. Because I want him to like me so very, very badly – the same way I like him – that I can't even bring myself to entertain the possibility that he might. If I'm wrong (if Lucy is wrong, and Martin is wrong), I'm honestly not sure I could handle it.

'Sorry about that,' Ferdy says, coming out of the tiny hallway and back into the kitchen.

'Sorry about what?'

'Dad. You know. He talks.'

'Oh. Yes.'

'I mean, I think you've got bigger things on your mind right now than . . . well, than . . . *you* know.'

Do I know?

'Your stepmother's just been arrested for burning your store down, for Christ's sake! And for murdering your mother!'

'Well, we don't know that it was actual murder.' I leave the onions to soften and head back to the table to start cutting the beef into chunks. It strikes me that this is the most extraordinary conversation to be having while doing these mundane tasks. But I still think I'd rather have this conversation than the other conversation. Because it didn't sound as though Ferdy was about to say that his dad was right, and that, smoke inhalation and bruises permitting, what he'd really like to do right now is throw me on to the kitchen table and make blissful love to me. 'Um, where was I? . . . Oh, yes . . . we don't know whether or not Diana actually planned to do it, or whether she just happened to be driving along that evening and saw Mum crossing the road, and couldn't help herself.'

Ferdy stares at me, running a hand through his hair. It sends a small cloud of dust skywards. 'That's incredibly forgiving.'

'I didn't say I was planning on forgiving her. I'm just saying that could have been the way it happened.'

Or maybe this is just what I'm telling myself so that I'll be able to take the same line when I talk more to Gaby and Robyn about it. Because I think it'll be better for all three of us if we don't have to circle anxiously round each other, all of us knowing that their mother killed mine. Bad enough that she did it at all. But how are we ever going to navigate these waters if we think she did it with malice afore-thought? It's the same way that I'm trying not to dwell on the fact that – quite obviously, now – the only reason Diana was suddenly so enthusiastic about my setting up Glass Slippers was because she planned to torch the place; to let me get within a hair's breadth of succeeding at something and then destroy it, and in an all-too apt reprisal for the burning of the Fat Charlie picture she'd wanted to show Jay. I knew I couldn't trust her apparent goodwill at the directors' meeting the other day. Her apocalyptic assurance that *you'll regret what you've done* was always, with a woman like Diana, bound to be made true.

'Besides,' I carry on, 'in some ways, she's done me a bit of a favour. Burning down the store, I mean, with all Dad's shoes in it. Obviously it's dreadful that they've all gone up in smoke.'

(Dreadful, by the way, is a very mild description compared with the phrases Maggie was using, when I called her to tell her about the fire this morning. Her horrified reaction, more the sort of thing most people would reserve for things like – oh, I don't know – the end of days or something, made me realise that I'm probably not all that cut out for a career in high fashion after all. I mean, those vintage shoes were all that was left of my own father, and even I could only think, after the brush with losing Ferdy, that shoes don't matter anywhere near as much as people. Whereas Maggie, bless her, seems firmly convinced of the opposite.)

'Perhaps, though,' I carry on, 'this is an opportunity to let the whole shoe thing go. No one could say that I didn't give Dad's legacy a chance. But maybe I could be doing something more *me*.'

'Now, hold on just one minute.' Ferdy is wearing a mock-serious expression. 'Are you saying you'd like to return to your old job as head of Research and Development at Chill?'

'Well, I was thinking of something food-related, as it happens,' I say, shyly. 'I mean, Lucy did mention, once, that she'd like me to work as a party caterer alongside her party-supply company. So maybe if I sold my shares and invested some money in her – in *us* – she could start offering a catering option to her London customers. I'd love that. And I think I could be pretty good at it.'

'You'd be great at it. It's much more you than the shoe thing. But I still think you're being pretty generous to Diana!'

'Oh, don't get me wrong. I'm not *feeling* very generous towards her.' The odd thing, now that I think about it, is that I'm not feeling anything towards Diana. The only thing I'm quite sure I'm *not* feeling is frightened. Which, after twenty-odd years of living, to a greater or lesser degree, under Diana's reign of terror, is too much of a relief to put into words. 'I just want her to realise that she didn't destroy me when she destroyed the store. That she didn't destroy me when she killed Mum. Besides, I can't help thinking – actually, I can't help hoping – that she's been eaten up with guilt all these years. That would be a suitable punishment for what she's done.'

'You think a woman like that felt *guilty*?'

'Well, it might explain why she was so vile to me when I was just a child. Why she couldn't stand having me in her home. And why she looked so freaked out when she first saw me after I lost weight. Because I look more like Mum than I used to.'

'She had a Banquo's ghost moment, you mean? Well, I suppose I shouldn't be surprised you're not actually spitting teeth and baying for her blood,' Ferdy goes on, before I can reply. 'You're a nice person, Charlie.' He turns to open the fridge-freezer and starts rooting around for something. 'One of the nicest people I know,' he adds, in a rather muffled voice, and sending out little puffs of warm breath in the icy air that comes out of the freezer.

This favourable (and extremely unexpected) comment on my personality reminds me of the last time Ferdy commented, not anything like so favourably, on my personality, and before I can stop myself, I'm suddenly blurting, 'I didn't kiss Pal, you know.'

'Sorry?'

'Pal. I know what Honey saw. Or rather, I know what Honey *thought* she saw. But I wasn't kissing Pal. He was kissing me. And I was hitting him with a damp flannel.'

Ferdy stops rooting in the freezer for a moment and glances over his shoulder to look at me. 'Damp flannel?'

'It was the only thing I had to hand. But I've explained it all to Lucy now, and she—'

'It's OK, Charlie. You don't have to explain anything to me. The more I thought about it, the more I knew Honey had to have got something wrong. And she wasn't exactly your biggest fan. Especially after you tried to kill her with your driving.'

'Ferdy, I honestly didn't try to kill her!'

'I'm kidding! Anyway –' he turns, quite suddenly, back to the freezer '– Honey wasn't your biggest fan long before that. Seeing as she had this obsession with . . . well, with the ridiculous idea that you were wildly in love with me.'

His words hang in the air for a moment, while I try to work out the best way to reply to them.

Before I've done this, however, I hear myself say, 'Ridiculous?'

'Exactly!' Ferdy laughs. It's slightly too loud a laugh, and with an extra ring from the fact that he's directed it into the freezer compartment. 'Honey always admitted the reason she could never maintain a long-term relationship was because she got paranoid about that kind of stuff. But I don't think even *she* has ever been that paranoid before. I mean, thinking you were chasing after me, when you're going out with a guy like Jay Broderick! Rich, good-looking, successful, charming . . .'

'Sounds like *you* might want to go out with Jay Broderick!' I say, lightly.

'Very funny.'

'He's all yours,' I add, 'if you want him. You'll have to compete with his brand-new girlfriend, of course. And most of the other women in Britain. But seeing as I'm not with him any more, there's at least one less girl to stand in your way.'

Ferdy stops rooting in the freezer. His back is still turned.

'You're not with Jay any more?'

'No.'

He still isn't looking at me. 'I'm . . . sorry to hear that.'

'Don't be. It was fun while it lasted.' If you take the definition of *fun*, that is, to be *exhilarating at times, nerve-racking at others, and ultimately just plain exhausting*. 'And at least I got a vintage MG out of it . . . OK, now *I'm* kidding,' I add, hastily, as Ferdy finally turns to look at me, his eyebrows raised in mild shock. 'I'm giving the car back, obviously. Though knowing Jay, he won't accept it.'

'Oh, I don't know. Seeing as I still think he gave it to you partly to make me jealous – which it did, by the way – he might feel it's served its purpose and be happy for you to return it. Scratchy Umbrella?'

'*Sorry?*'

'Scratchy Umbrella?' He holds up the carton of ice cream that he's been rooting for. Sure enough, the words *Scratchy Umbrella* are written on it in large black letters. 'It's a new ice cream I'm trialling. I mean, it's another new version of *stracciatella*, obviously, but I always liked the way you got the name wrong, so when I was—'

'No, I didn't mean . . .' Touched (and delighted) though I am that he's been creating an ice cream based on a silly mistake that I make with the name, this isn't what I was trying to get him to repeat. 'You just said that . . . that Jay giving me the car made you jealous.'

'Yes.'

'Do you mean that you were jealous because you liked the car?'

'No.'

'Do you mean that you were jealous because . . . you like me?'

He puts the ice-cream container down on the worktop, opens a nearby drawer for a scoop, opens a cupboard for some bowls, and opens another drawer for some spoons.

Then he says, 'I like you so, so much, Charlie, that I keep accidentally putting crushed walnuts in the raspberry sorbet.'

This is so far and away the nicest thing I've ever had anyone say to me that I don't even care that I can't make any sense of it.

'What I mean,' he continues, turning slightly pink, 'is that I'm currently working on a banana-and-walnut ice cream and on a raspberry sorbet, and because all I can do is think about you all the time, I keep muddling up the two different batches. And I don't know if you've ever eaten raspberry sorbet with crushed walnuts in, but it's really not a terribly pleasant experience. Which is ironic, because it's a really, really pleasant experience thinking about you. In a weird, tortured kind of a way, that is.'

OK, that last sentence was a bit less nice.

'Thinking about me is weird and tortured?'

'Well, obviously. I mean, that's why Honey was so crazy. Because I know you're not interested in me,

Charlie. You didn't reply to any of the emails I sent you while you were away, and you only wrote one brusque line letting me know you were going. And then when you came back, you were—'

'Hang on. What emails you sent me?'

'The emails. Stupid stuff, really, just wittering on about ice cream.'

'I didn't get a single email about ice cream. I didn't get a single email about anything. Are you sure you were sending them to the right address?'

'To the email address you sent me that one line from. You told me it was a new AOL address you were going to be using while you were in America. CharlieG1985, or something. I assumed that was the year you were born.'

'I was born in 1983.' (But does Ferdy *really* think I'm almost twenty-seven instead of almost twenty-nine? If so, it's curtains for the booking I made for Galina's collagen facial!) 'And I didn't set up an AOL account, Ferdy, much less email you from one.'

'But then who . . .' He stops. 'Oh, God,' he groans. 'Honey was born in 1985.'

'Ah.'

'And Honey had access to my email, because when she was helping me refurbish the new store, she was always using my iPad for one reason or another.'

'And you think she must have seen the email I sent telling you I was going away, deleted it and then set up CharlieG1985 at AOL to send you a fake email from? So that I wouldn't get any emails you sent me?'

Ferdy is looking more embarrassed than I've ever seen him. 'I did tell you she wasn't a fan of yours.'

'You didn't tell me she was plain psychotic!' Though obviously I'd worked that one out for myself a while ago. 'Jesus, Ferdy, what were you doing, going out with a girl like that?'

'I don't know . . . she was just so bloody *persistent*, and every time I ever tried to slow things down, she'd suddenly have some crisis she was terribly upset about . . . and anyway, you'd buggered off to America, Charlie, without so much as a by-your-leave, as far as I knew.'

'But you never said anything *before* I went to America.'

Ferdy shoots me an incredulous look. 'What, you mean I didn't turn up on the doorstep with three dozen red roses and sweep you off to the bedroom when you were frazzled to the end of your tether with the stress of caring for your dying father? Anyway, I did try to ask you to lunch that day of your dad's memorial, but you seemed keen to keep it as a friends-only thing instead. Inviting me to dinner with Lucy and Pal, and all that.'

'I'd just sat on a Sachertorte,' I say, helplessly. 'I didn't know what I was doing.'

'And when you came back from America, I was just really pissed off with you for ignoring me for four months. And then you were going on about queues of men, and strings of suitors . . . and anyway, you looked so *different*.' He uses the ice-cream scoop, now, to gesture vaguely at me, from head to toe. 'Blonde, and tanned, and gorgeous . . .'

'You thought I was gorgeous? I thought you found me repulsive!'

'Charlie, why on earth would I have found you repulsive? I'm not *blind*! I was just a bit intimidated, because you never used to look like that. And if I'm being completely honest . . . well, I kind of missed the way you looked before. I really liked it.'

'You fancied *Fat Charlie*?'

'I never knew any Fat Charlie. All I knew was Pretty Charlie. Sexy Charlie. Charlie-with-the-beautiful-smile.'

Right now, I'm Charlie-with-the-goldfish-mouth-and-the-startled-eyebrows.

'Don't get me wrong: it's not that I *don't* like the new hair, and the great clothes, and the jaw-droppingly awesome body.' Ferdy stops talking for a moment, swallows rather hard, and then carries on again. 'But I'd like it a lot more if you looked happy. If I didn't worry that you're too busy fretting about the way you look to have any fun. If you'd just sit with me at the table and have a taste of my new Scratchy Umbrella ice cream and tell me what you think about it.'

The smile that I know is spreading across my face right now is so huge and bright that I can actually feel it lighting me up from the inside. As if I'm bathed in natural sunshine, today, instead of standing under one of those energy-saving lighbulbs.

'Trouble is,' I hear myself say, 'that if you really do like the . . .' what did he call it? . . . 'jaw-droppingly awesome body, you're going to have to stop tempting me with offers of ice cream.'

'Hmmm. That's quite the dilemma. Do you think there's any way we could find some kind of happy medium? A little less of the jaw-dropping awesomeness, but a soupçon more of the ice cream?' He looks mortified all of a sudden, his own smile vanishing from his face. 'Oh, God, Charlie, not that I'm telling you what you should be doing with your own body! That's totally up to you! I mean, you're not standing here telling me what I should be doing with my body . . .'

'True. But actually,' I say, taking a deep breath, 'there are one or two things I could think of. That you could do with your body, that is.'

'Hey, I know. I know I'm no Jay Broderick. I know I'm not Mr Six-Pack Adonis. There are a million ways I can't compete with him, and that's just one of them.'

Which just proves, once and for all, that I should never, *ever* try being flirtatious. Here I was, just trying to hint that Ferdy should take a big step towards me, take my hands in his and kiss me, and somehow I've got him thinking I'm expecting him to hit the gym and whittle away his hint-of-a-paunch before I'll so much as deign to look at him.

'Ohhh . . . *I* get it,' he says, clearly reading the expression on my face. 'You weren't saying I'm not Mr Six-Pack Adonis.'

'I wasn't.'

'You were saying you fancy me.'

'I was. I am. I mean, I do.'

And *that's* when he takes a big step towards me, takes my hands in his and kisses me.

Well, OK, he only takes my right hand. Because he's still holding the ice-cream scoop in his left.

But the kiss is none the worse for that. The kiss, in fact, is perfect.

Perfect despite the fact that he's holding an ice-cream scoop, and that we're surrounded by a distinct aroma of singeing onion, and that his hair is still leaking dust, and that I'm still in the clothes I wore to dinner last night, which anyway are looking a little bit tight on me thanks to the fact that I seem to be inexorably creeping from an exhausting size ten (twelve around the bum) to – hopefully – a more manageable twelve (fourteen, God willing, around the bum), and that I haven't had the chance to do my hair or put on any make-up or tweeze my eyebrows . . .

'Hey.' Ferdy stops kissing me and gazes down for a moment. He's wearing a huge smile on his lovely soft lips, but a slightly puzzled frown on his forehead. 'Am I going mad, Charlie, or didn't you used to be taller than this?'

'In heels, yes.' I glance at my bare feet, grubby and slightly battered from the evening's pounding of pavements and sitting around in hospital waiting rooms. 'I dropped Mum's crystal shoes somewhere last night.'

'Charlie! I'm sorry. Weren't they her special shoes?'

'In a way.'

But the thing is, I can't honestly remember an occasion when I ever saw Mum wearing them. In fact, what I mostly remember, now that I've thought about it, is Mum getting them out of the wardrobe before her dinner parties, admiring them in their silvery tissue for a couple of moments, and then putting them away and deciding to go barefoot instead.

'Do you want me to help you go and look for them?' Ferdy asks. 'Retrace your steps . . .'

I shake my head. 'It's fine. Thanks, though, Ferdy. Besides,' I add, as I reach up on tiptoes so we can get on with some more of that heavenly kissing, 'when all is said and done, it was only a pair of shoes after all.'